Betta Greenaway

Leanna Greenaway

FAIRY SOAP

To dear Caroline
with love from us both
xxx 2020

FAIRY SOAP
Spellbound's Seduction

(For Grown Ups Only)

By
LEANNA GREENAWAY & BELETA GREENAWAY

Printed in the United States of America

First Printing, 2020

ISBN-13: 978-1-949003-56-7 print edition
ISBN-13: 978-1-949003-57-4 ebook edition

Waterside Productions
2055 Oxford Ave
Cardiff, CA 92007
www.waterside.com

For Anna Mckenna

A clever, talented lady and a true friend.
We thank you from the bottom of our hearts for
all your hard work in editing this book
and for helping to make our dream come true.

Beleta & Leanna

AUTHOR'S NOTE

How many girls get to write a book with their mother? I'm guessing not many. During the last 20 years I've been blessed with a successful writing career but what many people don't realise, is that my lovely mother, Beleta Greenaway, was the first to inspire me to put pen to paper and above all, she taught me to write fiction. I've always had a skill for expressing myself through writing, but she was correct when she said that writing a novel is an entirely different matter. The first time I saw the brilliance of her creativity was when I was at school and I couldn't sit my exams because I had just had an appendectomy. Unusually, I was allowed to complete the essays for English Literature at home and then submit them to the examination board for marking. It was at this time I realised just how ingenious she was. She turned my average D grade paper into a fictional masterpiece! Of course, I received an A, or rather she did, and we still laugh about it now - how the only O'level I managed to achieve in school was in fact hers! However, for years I felt terribly guilty about the whole thing so in my thirties, I retook the exam and thankfully passed it with flying colours, this time, all on my own.

Some years ago, I penned an amusing short story about a mischievous little fairy called Spellbound. I emailed it to mother and she immediately fired it back to me with suggestions and corrections, before re-composing the piece so that I could see how it should look. I took on board what she had said, adding another chapter, this time copying her style. Once again, I mailed it to her for approval but when she returned it, she had inserted more content and introduced new characters.

This back and forth writing went on for an entire year and before long, we had written twenty chapters. It was at this point I started to daydream about it being published and so we knuckled down and poured over every word. Mother naughtily added 'fairy swearing' and sexy scenario's, which I was unsure about and then, horror of horrors, she suggested I write the sex scenes for Spellbound! Having the great British reserve, it took some time to drop the embarrassment and get into the swing of it. Later we toyed with the idea of whether to leave out the swearing and sex, as our existing publishers and readers might be shocked! On asking friends, relatives and volunteer readers whether it should stay or go, they all unanimously said, *"Keep it in!"* It was such good fun; I don't think either of us has ever laughed so much in our lives! Along the way, I became educated in the art of imaginative fiction, with the added joy of being able to write with my darling mother. When we read it back now, neither of us know just who wrote what, as the different threads of the story all eventually merged into one voice. Since then, although each of us have other published works to our credit, Fairy Soap has become the most treasured novel we have ever had the pleasure of creating. We really hope you will like the book and it will take you on a journey of discovery and imagination.

I've had the happiest times of my life writing Fairy Soap with you mum.
Thank you so much. With love
Leanna

TABLE OF CONTENTS

CHAPTER 1
A RECIPE FOR DISASTER

Spellbound hurtled into Broomsticks Cottage. She was seriously out of breath, but she had to get upstairs and it had to be quick. Three Hoppy meals, a McCricket sandwich and a Snadderfly salad with extra mayo had left her stomach in a very delicate state. With only one thing on her mind, she barged through the old oak door, almost knocking it off its hinges, then clattered up the stairs two at a time, swinging the bathroom door closed with a resounding bang.

"SPELLBOUND!" Leticia shrieked, "Spellbound! You are infuriating! Will you please try and be a little more restrained, you frightened the very life out of me, child!"

Leticia Zamforia was a Fairy Witch and entirely up to date with the latest Alchemist, glitter gold PC, which she used daily. She was under a punishing contract to write three romantic novels a year for Spells and Swoon. Her best techniques for producing her books were a lit pink candle, lavender incense and complete silence. She also had a stash of fairy porn to help her add some passion to the stories when her inspiration was low. They had arrived in a plain brown envelope from the famous Anne Winters catalogue. Leticia had prayed no one would guess the contents of the paper parcel, especially as they had thrown in a free vibrator, the jumbo-sized Afro Boy. She had cast a spell and made it invisible, just in case Spellbound had stumbled upon it unwittingly. Oh, the chances she took, she inwardly scolded herself. Her daughter's noisy intrusion had entirely disrupted her thought process, causing the worst writer's block she had experienced for months.

"SPELLBOUND! GET DOWN THESE STAIRS NOW!" she shrieked.

"You'll have to wait a minute, Mamma. I'm on the tootle-hole, nature is calling."

Leticia tapped her foot impatiently. "Don't forget to wash your hands!"

"Won't be long, Mamma," she called sweetly.

At the bottom of the stairs, Leticia was furious, her hands on her generous hips, her wings flickering in a sinister fashion, backwards and forwards. Spellbound realised she was in trouble but her rebellious nature shone through with a demure little smile. She hesitated three steps before the bottom, kicking the stair rod with an outstretched toe.

"What have you been eating, Spellbound?" Leticia said with an interrogative look.

"Nothing much, Mamma," she replied with a pained expression.

"Don't try and patronise me my girl and wipe that sickly smile off your face this instant. Oh, just look at you, your bladderbart father all over again," she lamented, looking deeply into her daughter's eyes. "Now you know I am psychic, Spellbound. I've been telling Fairies' fortunes for more years than I can remember, so give me some credit for knowing when my daughter leaves a perfectly good plate of newt's legs for…wait, it's coming…the vision is appearing …" Leticia closed her eyes and bent her head back, concentrating very hard. "Oh, futtle-shucks Spellbound, there's so much of it, I can't even make it out! It was only yesterday you were at that new place, Costa Packet Diner in town and you gobbled up two waspy whoppers, and a beetle burger! You are aware of the effect that high-fat food has on your figure and now your innards are aching. I also object to you spending your pocket coinage on food, especially when I prepare perfectly delicious meals here at home." Spellbound winced. She was always being found out. Having a psychic mother was no fun.

"Oh, but am I surprised?" Leticia said, droning on and on, shaking her wand in an authoritative manner. "Nooo ... maybe I should have called you gutso at birth!"

But then, in answer to Spellbound's prayers, there was a loud rapping on the door. Leticia turned and glared at her daughter, "I'll be back young fae; don't you dare move!"

The Duchess of Sparkleshire stood at the door, smiling broadly and bearing a basket full to the brim with cherries. The prestigious label of 'Horrids' was emblazoned on the lid. Leticia smoothed down her long dark hair and greeted her with a smile. For now, she had forgotten about her daughter's greedy nature, as she welcomed her newest and most significant friend. The two Fairies immediately launched into the local gossip whilst Spellbound breathed a deep sigh of relief and tiptoed back up the stairs unnoticed. Her bedroom was a typical teenager's haven; the fuchsia pink walls were plastered with pictures of her favourite pop stars, Wesley Presley and the famous Fairy boy band, Wrong Direction, which Leticia said, sang like a bunch of comatose caterwaulers. Then there were her 'everloving' nineties idols, Lionel Witchy and Take Twat, who Leticia tolerated. Spellbound was not particularly tidy. Her shoes were strewn on the floor; her bed looked like an explosion and gossamer dresses littered the bottom of her wardrobe. Leticia despaired, but Spellbound would happily step over the mess, without a care.

The young Fairy furtively closed the door and then pressed her little ear against it to make sure her mother and the Duchess were still chatting. At last, when she heard them both saying goodbye, she skulked downstairs, biting her bottom lip nervously. Leticia may have put off the interrogation for the moment but Spellbound knew that it was far from forgotten. As she approached the door, she was amazed to find her mother fluttering around the kitchen cupboards, singing merrily to herself.

"Hello, sweet Fairy child," she sang joyously.

"Hello Mamma," Spellbound replied apprehensively. "Erm, you sound happy?" She squirmed uneasily and started to twist a length of her thick, red hair behind her ear.

"Oh, I am, Spellbound, I am!" Leticia exclaimed. "The Duchess kindly came to inform me that Zingo has been called off tomorrow, so I took the opportunity of inviting her and Eddie over for supper instead. She holds such a prominent position in the forest and is on all the community projects. She's also invited us both to her place, Sparkleshire Hall. I've never seen it, but it's rumoured to be stunning. They've even got two Pixie pools and a sauna, not to mention the three dragonflies in the faerodrome ..." she babbled on excitedly.

"Now, Spellbound, I will want you to wear something special and put a bow in your pretty hair. You really will have to make a good impression. Everyone knows that Edward Elf is sweet on you and of course, it's natural! You're such a beautiful little thing, when you make an effort. Apparently, he speaks about you constantly, and now his mother, *the* one and only Duchess of Sparkleshire, is just dying to meet you!"

"Oh great," fumed Spellbound under her breath. She promised herself that if Eddie tried any funny business, she would definitely zap him in his mushrooms with her birch twig wand and if need be, she would have no compulsion in doing so in front of the noble Duchess herself!

Spellbound was seated at the table, glaring at Eddie. In her mother's eyes, this was a scene of pure, domestic bliss: Mamma to her left, Eddie to her right and the Duchess directly opposite her. Everyone in Bluebell Forest was aware that the Duke and Duchess of Sparkleshire were the most highly respected couple in the Britannic Realm and so it was her mother's mission to constantly encourage her to date Eddie. He was the sole heir to a massive fortune and Leticia wanted nothing more than to shove her only child into the limelight so she too could have elite status.

"So, Spellbound," the Duchess said, endeavouring to make conversation. "Your mother tells me that you would like to be a Tooth Fairy someday, how wonderfully exciting!"

Spellbound slowly lifted her eyes from her plate and smiled politely while trying to digest an overcooked cricket's leg.

"Oh, yes!" interrupted Leticia. "She has always talked of it – for years now. The head of Molars Inc. will be sure to employ her once they catch a glimpse of my special young fae." She smiled proudly at her daughter. "You see Esmee," she said, reaching out to touch the Duchess's hand. "You don't mind me calling you Esmee, do you dear? It's just that I have a feeling you and I are to become firm friends," she winked ever so slightly. "Maybe even family some-day," she tittered under her breath, pausing at the thought. "Molars Incorporated only employ the slimmest and most stylish of Fairies and my little Spellbound, well … she'll have no trouble squeezing through the cracks of any window, will you darling?" she said, turn-ing affectionately to her daughter. "She has the perfect image and that is so important these days, don't you think Esmee?"

"And have you applied for the position yet?" the Duchess enquired in a kindly manner. Spellbound opened her mouth to speak.

"Oh yes she has, haven't you, dear?" said Leticia, butting in before her daughter could say a word. "We filled out all the forms last week and handed them in at reception only yesterday. It won't be long now before we hear from them."

"Oh Mamma," Spellbound interrupted in a tired tone. She took her napkin from her lap and placed it on the table. She was really getting tired of all this Tooth Fairy twaddle. "You know I never wanted to be a blewdey Tooth Fairy in the first place! I mean, from the time I was a faebe in hankies, you have gone on and … on and … on and …"

"SPELLBOUND, darling!" Leticia said, smiling nervously. "We have guests, dear!" Spellbound took another bite of the cricket, screwing up her little face as she swallowed.

"I'm just not sure I want to be launched into the human realm, only to get lost under some mammoth pillow, never to be seen again or crawling through teeny cracks and getting covered in dust. No, I'd much rather open a potion store in town or be a nurse like

Papa's sister, Aunty Histamine, she works in the hysterical rectum unit, which sounds fascinating or…" she said pausing for moment, "I could help the elderly." Leticia's eyes darted from side to side in embarrassment.

"Now, now, dear," she said, a little irritated. "I've told you before, no daughter of mine is degrading herself by wiping the bottoms of ancient Pixies. You will be leaving yourself open to all manner of bugs and infections, which, dearest, you could even bring home to Mamma. Never, Spellbound … do you hear me? Never, never, darling!" Leticia was fast becoming red in the face as she turned to the Duchess. "I do apologise," she said, trying to calm her temper. "Teenagers, eh! They think they know it all!"

Eddie sat captivated, looking adoringly at Spellbound.

"I think you would make a super Tooth Fairy, Spelly, and if you like, I could always accompany you on ya first mission." His periwinkle blue eyes glazed over as he ran his fingers through his tousled blonde hair, hoping she would notice him. "I could hold all of those little toofy pegs for you!" he said with a nervous giggle. "In fact, I would follow you to the ends of the Britannic realm if you would let me," he lisped, staring dreamily at her little rosebud mouth, as if in a trance.

"Listen, cloth ears," Spellbound cut in haughtily, "if I do have to be a Tooth Fairy, I'm sure that I'll be quite capable of holding my own toofy pegs thank you. Besides, you'd be sure to mess the whole thing up. It's as clear as day that you don't possess a single brain cell!"

Eddie didn't seem at all phased by Spellbound's rudeness; he just grinned at her in a gormless fashion and shrugged his shoulders.

"Every word she ever says to him remains indelibly on his mind," the Duchess said quietly to Leticia. "He's got such a crush on her; the Duke and I really don't know what to do with him!" Spellbound glared over at Eddie and then rolled her eyes dramatically. Just for a second, she wished that she were a million miles away from this drippy Elf.

"Awww, but I think they make such a perfect couple?" Leticia twittered back to the Duchess. Eddie continued to sport a sickly grin and leaned in to whisper in Spellbound's ear.

"Spelly, will ya walk out with me tomorrow? We could have a picnic and maybe a kissy or two."

"Stop being such a pathetic grunt-futtock, Eddie, or I swear I will go to my room!" she said, with a mouth full of food. Leticia's pained expression turned to horror.

"Spellbound, language child and refrain from speaking with your mouth full!" She chastised under her breath. "That is no way to speak to our guests!" She gave an uneasy laugh, rising quickly to her feet. "Anyone for a slice of twinkle pudding and custard? Eddie, surely you will have some; you must have a huge, Elfy appetite?" she chuckled, trying to hide her embarrassment.

"Yes, I do have an appetite but mainly for your daughter!" He swung back in his chair, his laughing eyes delighting in Spellbound's furious face. Leticia groaned under her breath and went off to the kitchen to get the pudding plates, the Duchess hastily following her.

Spellbound's eyes remained transfixed on the pink paper napkin that she was systematically shredding to pieces under the table. She knew that Eddie was enjoying every single minute of this and she was hell bent on not making eye contact with him. In complete silence, she reached out and deftly took another napkin and began folding, creasing it one way and then another, before pleating it again. Slowly she opened out some ears and began shaping the head. Bit by bit, the napkin finally turned into the shape of a cat, a trick her father had shown her when she was little. Eddie gazed in admiration at her attempts at origami. As the two mothers returned to the room with the dessert, Spellbound immediately snatched the napkin and hid it in her lap. Anything that reminded her Mamma of her father would put her in the sourest mood for weeks! Leticia started to serve out the pudding and stopped when she noticed Eddie crouching down, peering beneath the tablecloth. The Duchess had also noticed her son's absence from the table and peered over at her host, smiling weakly. They both shrugged and looked at Spellbound for an explanation. Fidgeting slightly, Eddie bent even further down, adjusting his bottom as he went.

"What *are* you doing down there, Edward?" said the Duchess stiffly. "Have you dropped something?" He shuffled and bumped his head slightly as he tried to emerge from under the cloth.

"I'm just looking at Spelly's little, pink pussy under the table Ma," he replied nonchalantly. Leticia, having taken a sip of tea, half-choked and showered the hot liquid over the tablecloth. Eddie glanced upwards and saw everyone's shocked, frozen expressions, not to mention his mother pouring the custard all over the teapot! The Duchess's face blushed a furious crimson.

"Edward, when I get you home, I will see to it that your father kicks your Elfin arse right into next week!" She stood up and cuffed him hard around his ear. "I'm so sorry, Leticia, what must you think of us!" Spellbound collapsed into peals of laughter, holding her stomach as the tears ran down her face, while Leticia buried her head in her hands and sighed.

"Spellbound, get to your room and stay there until I say you can come down," she said sternly. Spellbound got up from the table and made her way to the staircase, still laughing loudly. The Duchess rose to her feet and walloped her son again across the head before frogmarching him to the door, "HOME THIS INSTANT…RIGHT NOW…AND MOVE IT!"

Chapter 2
A Fairy Happy Birthday

As the sun began to rise over Broomstick Cottage, Leticia was busily preparing for the day ahead. Today was Spellbound's eighteenth birthday and tonight she would be coming out into society and attending her very first birthday ball. It was a tradition that once a fae child reached the age of ten and eight, a ball would be held in their honour. The occasion was a grand event, celebrated at Lord and Lady Wizard's Grand Forest Hall. It was possible that almost every Pixie, Fairy and Elf in the realm would arrive, usually laden with gifts. In events such as these, no invitations were sent out as there was no need, every magical creature in the realm was welcome to attend. The more guests who arrived, the higher the status given to the Fairy. Leticia raced through the cottage, whizzing in and out of rooms with armfuls of sequins, glitter and lace. She quickly but carefully arranged them on the old wooden table, hunting frantically in her belt for her wand. Sitting quietly nearby, Spellbound watched in awe as Leticia filled the table with all items necessary for her spell: eleven silver pins; a full-size human bodkin; four limpet shells and six blue tit feathers, which the birds had devotedly given to Leticia that morning. Closing her eyes in intense concentration, she zapped the wand over her head. Momentarily the cottage fell into an eerie silence and taking a deep breath she chanted in Elvish:

Oh wand so great, and magic so fine,
Make this ball gown look divine!

Sparks of magic flew from the tip of the staff, showering orbs of light which began dancing around the room in every direction. Spellbound clapped her hands together with delight; she was always wide-eyed and amazed whenever Leticia conducted a spell. She wished that she possessed the same talent and would be as powerful as her mother someday. Everyone told her that she would follow in Leticia's footsteps but so far, that hadn't happened. She cast her mind back to her sixteenth birthday, when her powers were unbound and she received her first wand. Leticia had stood by, proudly watching with an excited look on her face. It was a special moment in every Fairy mother's life. At this age, a child was considered ready to learn the dynamics of magic and so attended the spell craft academy five mornings a week. At the gates of the college on Spellbound's first day, a little tear glinted in Leticia's eye as she waved goodbye to her daughter. By the end of the week, it was a very different story. It seemed that every other pupil in attendance was casting spells successfully but no matter how hard she tried, Spellbound failed at every attempt. Her teacher, Miss Whiplash, had set a straightforward task for her to focus on taking three white daisies and turning them red.

"Now concentrate," she said, as she cracked her whip three inches from Spellbound's ear. "Think red in your mind … the power of the mind … think hard, you foolish student." Spellbound hated her teacher. She was tall and wrinkly and smelled of old mothballs. She thought nothing of punishing a pupil by turning them into a stick insect for a few hours.

"CONCENTRATE, SPELLBOUND," she bellowed, and so, biting her bottom lip, Spellbound zapped the daisies with a bolt of fire and they burnt to a crisp! It didn't get much better from that day on. Leticia returned the wand to the maker calling it an 'old warped baton', but even the replacement rod failed to cast the perfect spell. Leticia had been so distraught. How could her daughter, the offspring of the ever so magnificent, Leticia Zamforia, be cursed with such inferior powers? She immediately blamed Spellbound's inabilities on the genes inherited from her 'spaddywacking father' and proceeded to spend at least four hours a day wand-training the child herself. Within two years Spellbound had managed to master the odd bit of magic but was still a long way behind.

The air in the cottage became icy and soon a huge gust of wind entered and began circling the room, as Leticia's spell began to work. Her wand started to crackle and spin, while puffs of green smoke began to emerge before their eyes. Like a tornado, it whirled and swirled around the items on the table, until finally, it stopped, leaving behind the most glorious sight. Spellbound coughed and wafted the air a little with her hand as she walked over to the table. There before her was the most incredible gown she had seen in her life. Dewdrops of pearls fell romantically from the silken lavender skirt and silver glitter encrusted the heart-shaped bodice. She gazed over at her mother, open-mouthed. Leticia's critical eye scrutinised her divine creation and then she smiled in secret satisfaction.

"Oh, Mamma," gasped Spellbound, "that is so SIC... Oh my gawd, it's awesome!"

"Well, my dear, you are only ten and eight once in your life and with this being your very first ball you have to look sensational. We can't have you over-shadowed, can we? Now pay attention, dear," she said, scooping the gown up into her arms. "Twirl the dress this way and it turns silvery pink, then twirl back and it's iridescent turquoise. You will be a cascade of captivating colour, my dear child."

Spellbound ran into Leticia's arms and the two Fairies embraced. "Thank you, Ma," she said, "you're the best, you really are!"

Leticia patted her on the head and smiled affectionately. "Ah, sweet child. You are so much like your Mamma. Now run along to the store and fetch me an ounce of hogweed. I need it for something very special."

....

Leticia viewed herself in the cheval mirror. Her ample bosom spilt over the top of her most exquisite blue chiffon ball gown. It was a little tighter since she had last worn it. She turned around to view the back of the dress and gazed at the reflection of her plump derriere.

"Good grief this will never do," she said in irritation. "My daughter's eighteenth birthday and look at the sight! I'm just like an oversized butterball!" She sidled up to the mirror again, this time peering closely at her face. Tiny lines had started to emerge around her eyes and spider trails encircled her mouth.

"Ummm, dare I do it?" she pondered. "No, I mustn't, it's against all of the rules. I'm not old enough for one thing." She peered again, this time with more scrutiny. "Oh fookin' hell, I'm doing it!" and without another thought, she went over to the large oak dresser and reached into the secret compartment to retrieve a magical potion. She gazed at the pink glass bottle, inlaid with gold, and remembered what her Grandmamma had said: "Only use this for a special occasion and don't forget to add the fresh hogweed."

"Well," she muttered again, "it's my daughter's birthday ball and I shall be mixing with the whole of the Fairy kingdom, and anyway, my magic is great enough to be able to reproduce this potion in the future, I'm sure of it, it can't be that hard!" She carefully added a pinch of chopped hogweed to the liquid, giving it a good shake and after unscrewing the lid, she gulped down the contents greedily. A strange fizzy feeling started to permeate her body and then suddenly, her wings wilted, and she fainted.

....

The ballroom was a flurry of activity. Fairies of all shapes and sizes had gathered, some had even come from the more distant realms, dressed in dazzling gowns, looking their best. A sixty-piece band was on the stage playing some lively, joyful tunes and Lord and Lady Wizard, known and respected elite socialites of the forest, were greeting everyone who had arrived. There was an air of anticipation amongst the crowd. Spellbound was often talked about but few of the guests had ever seen her. Leticia's reputation with spellcraft was

widely known in every realm, as was her beauty, esp
raven black hair, incredible violet eyes and porcel?

Eddie was dressed in his finest brocade dc
his blond hair gelled immaculately back into a ᴗ_
Smiling a toothy grin, he felt very stylish indeed, although onᴄ
ear had become somewhat swollen and red from the bashing his
mother had given him after the paper napkin incident the evening
before. Many of the younger female Fairies tried to catch his eye;
he was, after all, going to be a Duke one day. His mother, the Fairy
Duchess of Sparkleshire, stood by his side, resplendent in deep
purple, wearing the famed Tregora Diamonds clasped around
her neck. By her side was her husband, the Duke of Sparkleshire,
a tall, striking Elf who was a good head and shoulders above the
rest. Eddie's gaze frantically scanned the huge golden ballroom in
search of Spellbound and after what seemed an age, the room fell
silent as the resplendent Major Domo, attired in pale blue satin
and a matching tricorn hat, adjusted his wig carefully to make his
announcement.

"My Lords, Fae folk, Pixies and Elves. May I introduce our
Guests of Honour, Spellbound Elspeth Zamforia, and her mother,
the respected Leticia Elva Zamforia!"

"I still don't get it, Mamma," Spellbound said out of the corner
of her mouth as both Fairies awaited side by side. "This morning
when we embraced, I nearly drowned in your boobie's and now
they've just miraculously disappeared! Where the fook have they
gone?"

"Shush, dear child," Leticia seethed, as she coloured slightly
whilst surveying the crowds, "this is your big moment. I promise
I will tell you all later."

"Another thing, Ma," Spellbound persisted, "your hips are suddenly miniature, and your face looks a whole lot younger. It's like
you just went and got a full-blown makeover!"

"Spellbound," Leticia said through gritted teeth, fanning herself madly as she tried to change the subject, "I don't know what you
mean, now focus on your entrance, come, come!"

The band started to play the Happy Birthday song and all the guests began to clap and cheer. Spellbound was standing at the top of the grand staircase with Leticia at her side, her beautiful gown glistening under the lights. She was the complete picture of perfection with her long red hair carefully entwined with freesias, orchids, cowslips and a perfect floral wreath that sat neatly on the top of her head. Her dress was the colour of a rainbow making her green eyes shine. Everyone gasped in astonishment as the Zamforian Fairies stood side by side, for all to see. Leticia had decided that following her magically aided facelift, breast reconstruction and painless liposuction, she would abandon the blue chiffon dress as it was now far too big and instead, opted for a cascading, silver sheath. Both Fairies looked towards one another and Leticia squeezed her daughter's arm reassuringly before they descended the staircase together.

Eddie eyed Spellbound at the top of the stairs and gasped. "What a sight! What a Fairy!" he muttered under his breath.

Spellbound tried very hard to recall the advice Leticia had given her before they had left the cottage. "When you enter the ballroom, my dear," she had insisted, "just look up and don't stop smiling. You must collect your skirts elegantly and always look up, never down, do you hear? When the music begins, take the stairs in time to the rhythm and don't stand gawping; be as sophisticated as your Mamma. Remember, you are Spellbound Zamforia, daughter of Leticia Zamforia. Fae folk will travel miles and miles to get a glimpse of you. Spellbound was so absorbed by her mother's instructions that she hardly noticed the five hundred or so Fairies, Pixies and Elves below her.

"Keep your back straight at all times, Spellbound, and remember dear, SMILE ..." Gracefully, Spellbound gathered her skirts up, exposing two little golden slippers. Very steadily she tiptoed down, one step at a time, trying to keep up with her mother. Mamma was right, there must be a trillion people here, she thought nervously, as she continued to glide down the marbled flight of stairs.

In the midst and splendour of the occasion and the gasps of admiration, a tiny fragment of lace hung like a demon from the bottom of Spellbound's silken skirts. Leticia cordially began waving and smiling as she descended the staircase, oblivious to everything, other than savouring the moment. With the next move forward, the lace continued to graze the jewel-encrusted metal and was now directly suspended over the buckle. At that moment she lost her balance. With arms outstretched, she plummeted downwards, to loud cries of horror from the guests, her wings fluttering madly. Eddie rushed forward, colliding with a footman at the bottom of the staircase. Leticia watched in dismay, as her daughter made the most significant entrance of her life.

"Well isn't that typical!" she spat under her breath, "just like her futtle-shuck of a father, always making an exhibition of herself!" Spellbound tumbled down the last five steps, before landing in Eddie's arms.

"I knew you would fall for me eventually, Spelly," he said triumphantly as he caught her. The guests cried out with cheers of "Hurray!" and "Well saved, Eddie!"

Under her breath, Spellbound hissed at Eddie, "Foooweeee ... You sure do need to use some Minty Mouf wash, elf boy, your breath smells like a turdwart fly!"

....

Leticia took another small sip of Gin Fiz. She was enjoying a gossip with Lady Wizard. "Word in the Wood claims that Edward is wonderful husband material and worth quite a tidy sum when he inherits. I have great hopes for them both." She clasped her hands in delight and then waved gaily to Esmee across the room. The ball was in full swing and the throng were all happily dancing, drinking and chatting. Oh, how good it was to be young and thin again. Her neat little figure was perched high on the chair and her gaze dropped admiringly to her small, firm breasts. She gazed down and smiled at her feet. Been a while since I saw you from this angle, she thought gaily. If only this miracle could last. Still, as long as she impressed the masses this evening, tomorrow she could go back to her old self. She would stay in the cottage for a few weeks so as not to draw any attention to herself and if anyone should comment on her appearance, she would simply explain that she had gained a few ounces.

"Well, hello there, and who is this enchanting creature?" said a deep voice next to her.

Looking up, Leticia espied a tall, Elf standing at the table, his handsome face smiling down at her.

"And who is this?" she said, turning her slim little body to face him. "Have we met?" She held out her dainty hand to greet him. "How fairy nice to meet you."

"The pleasure is most definitely all mine," he replied, as he gently planted a kiss in the palm of her hand. "My name's Philip Macavity, founder of Molars Incorporated," he said in a low, sexy drawl, "and you must be the ever so beautiful Leticia Zamforia." He stared deeply into her half-closed, violet eyes. "My goodness, they said you were a beauty but pray tell me, am I hallucinating?"

"You are too kind, Philip," Leticia tittered.

"Would you do me the honour of having the next dance with me?" She looked into his eyes, and saw the perfect opening to secure her daughter a job as a Tooth Fairy.

"I'd be delighted!" she twinkled up at him. The ballroom cleared as Leticia and Philip stepped onto the crystal, sprung dance floor.

Spellbound looked over frantically at her mother who was dancing with a stranger. "What's going on?" she mouthed silently, but Leticia just raised her eyebrows knowingly in her daughter's direction and gave a minuscule wink. As the music came to an end, she did a perfect pirouette towards Philip.

"Oh, I haven't had so much fun in years!"

"Me neither," Philip added, as they made their way back to the table.

"We must do it again sometime, perhaps a little candlelit supper for two," she said, demurely, and then with no further ado, she planted a small kiss on his cheek.

"Madam, you are enchanting," he whispered as he kissed her hand again.

❧ ❧ ❧

The birthday ball had begun to wind down. The guests were still chatting and laughing loudly, but most were definitely feeling the effects of too much food and drink. Spellbound was relaxing on a huge purple flower with her Fairy friends Pumpkin, Daffy and Taffeta. She had expertly managed to duck and weave around Eddie for most of the evening, although on the four or five occasions she did catch sight of him, he was secretly blowing onto the palm of his hand and smelling his breath quizzically. This made her feel a little ashamed; after all, he had caught her with such skilled precision at the bottom of the grand staircase and his breath really didn't smell at all. Maybe next time he cornered her, she would apologise, but for now, she was happy being the belle of the ball. Finally, she was growing up and although she had made one hell of an entrance, only one other thing could have made the evening more perfect and that would have been to have her beloved Papa share her special day. Her mood suddenly changed from being contented to feeling slightly sombre, but the sound of her mother's voice snapped her out of it in an instant.

"Spellbound darling, do come over here, I have some exciting news child." Spellbound lifted herself off the cushion and flitted over to Leticia and Philip Macavity, who were sitting happily at a nasturtium leaf table drinking more Gin Fiz. Leticia turned to Philip and patted his hand conspiratorially.

"Mr Macavity here has agreed to give you an interview as a trainee Tooth Fairy, dear. You're to go next week. Isn't that wonderful, darling? Aren't you pleased?"

"Oh, blewdy hell," Spellbound muttered miserably under her breath. "That's just great that is, fookin' great!"

CHAPTER 3
THE BLING THING

Leticia Zamforia was a strict but doting parent. She had single-handedly raised her daughter for the past three years and it hadn't been easy, to say the least.

She was seated in her humble parlour, sipping nettle tea and gazing out of the window. The skies were overcast, and the wind had started to whip up, causing the windows of the cottage to rattle. She feared a storm might be approaching. Resting back in her chair, and taking another mouthful of tea, she began to cast her mind back to a time when Spellbound was much younger and to some of the dilemmas she had faced.

"Aww, Mamma, why not? Why can't I have my belly button pierced? Every Fairy in the forest has hers done. Am I to be the only one who is different? It's not fair Mamma, really it isn't!"

"I've told you before, Spellbound, and I will tell you again," Leticia had said sternly, "if the great Goddess above wanted you to have a diamante in your navel, you would have been born with one. Now go! I am trying to compose a raunchy sex scene for my latest book. The publishers have specifically asked me to step up the tempo. And as it's been a while since I've had rumpy, I must really concentrate, child!" She returned to her writing and began silently mouthing something erotic.

"What's rumpy like, Mamma? ... does it hurt? Pumpkin said something about an oo'gasm. What's an oo'gasm like? ... did you have an oo'gasm with Papa in the olden days?"

Leticia peered over the top of her tiny, designer, crystal spectacles and drummed her perfectly polished sugar pink nails on the desktop.

"Enough! Spellbound ... you are infuriating me!"

"I should be able to know about these things by now," she said defiantly. "Pumpkin said that she heard her parents moaning and groaning in the next room and the bed was creaking. It went creak ... creak ... and then very fast ... creak, creak, creak! She said they were screwing. What's screwing, Mamma?"

"SPELLBOUND! Do you want to be grounded?"

Spellbound hung her head and prodded the chair repeatedly with her red satin ballet pump. "So… can I have my belly button pierced then? ... can I? … oh, pleeease?"

Leticia decided to ignore her daughter's whining and carried on. Maybe the fae would whoosh off somewhere and leave her in peace if she pretended not to hear.

Spellbound had sauntered slowly over to the desk where Leticia was working and peered over her shoulder to read the unfolding story. Sticking her fingers down her throat and rolling her eyes dramatically, she groaned.

"OH, MY GAWD, Mamma!!! UGH ... that SUCKS! yuk ...! I can't believe he sticks THAT in her pee-pee hole!" She turned on her heel and stomped upstairs to her bedroom. As she slammed the door with a resounding crash, Leticia heard her muttering. "Drat Mamma and her silly Spells and Swoon book. It's all lies anyway, none of it is real. I'M GONNA LEAVE HOME AND LOOK FOR MY PAPA!" she hollered, this time making sure her Mamma could hear. Leticia shook her head, let out a deflated sigh and continued to type busily.

Still reminiscing, she remembered how Spellbound had sneakily tiptoed into her bedchamber and had taken her prized wand out of the cupboard from above the bed. It was made of apple-wood and had a petite little amethyst crystal glued firmly to the tip. Spellbound must have made up some kind of rhyme because she heard a sudden, explosive crash and a yellow, murky fog had started to drift down the staircase. The cloudy mass was so thick that Spellbound was choking and coughing on the fumes.

"WHAT THE FOOK WAS THAT, SPELLBOUND?" Leticia yelled up the stairs.

"GET DOWN HERE RIGHT NOW, CHILD! You are really getting out of hand. I just don't know what I am going to do with you!"

Spellbound skulked down the stairs two at a time, glowering under her absurdly long eyelashes.

"Have you quite finished banging and clattering about? The noises you are making resemble that of a Troll, not that of the dainty little Fairy you should be growing into, after all of my efforts." Leticia took one look at her daughter and stepped backwards, placing her hand on her throat. "Oh just blewdy look at you!" she said under her breath. "What in heaven's name have you done to yourself?"

Spellbound sauntered over to the cheval mirror in the corner of the room and stood back aghast when she viewed her reflection. Her hair was stiff and stuck out in all directions, her face was as black as soot and a glittering emerald sat perfectly in the middle of her nose. She immediately began tugging at the jewel to try and remove it from her face and, when it wouldn't budge, the tears streamed down her cheeks.

"I just wanted my belly button piercing," she whimpered, half defiant, half snivelling. "I thought I'd borrow your wand and try to magic one up for myself. I'm the only one in my group who hasn't had it done. Everyone else is in crop tops with slashed jeans and what do I have, Mamma, eh! … what do I have?" She finally broke out in a dramatic wail, "I HAVE GLITTERY FROCKS AND A NAKED BELLY BUTTON … ARGH HA!!!"

It was getting late and Leticia had just about had enough of Spellbound's histrionics for one day. She had a deadline to get her latest book into the editor or she would be in breach of contract. It wasn't often that she gave in to her daughter's demands, but this was so important, and she really did have to crack on. If Spellbound had what she wanted, just this once, she might get the chance to finish.

"Okay, Spellbound," she said quietly.

Spellbound was still playing the drama queen, sobbing dramatically into a tea towel. She blew her nose loudly, fixing her tear-drenched eyes firmly on her Mother.

"Well, well, my girl, it might be an idea to send you to Fada Drama College, you would make a perfect actress. I think you get that skill from your bladderbart father! Now stop this ear-splitting racket. You have just about given me the worst headache since I gave birth to you!"

Spellbound's theatrical climax ebbed away and she started to twiddle with the emerald, still clearly stuck fast to her nose. Leticia winced and walked over to her, waving her dainty fingers ever so slightly in the air.

"I'll cast a spell, just this once for you to have the navel nonsense, *if*, and *only if* you promise to behave and let me get on with this wretched book. I'll whiz you up a pair of slashed jeans and a ... what was it?" Her mind started to wonder, "Oh yes, a crap top. But be warned, Spellbound," she continued with a steely expression, "this is just for tonight, do you hear? Just for tonight. I don't want any fae of mine parading the streets looking like a scarlet harlot, what *would* the neighbours say! Now then," she said, rummaging around in the pocket of her green velvet gown for her wand, "have you any preference as to the belly bling's colour?"

Not wanting her mother to change her mind, she answered very sheepishly, in a high-pitched squeak.

"Um, err," she snivelled, "red would be quite good, Mamma."

"Red it is then."

"And ummm..." she hesitated, before hiccupping loudly, "... A ruby ... um ... A real one if poss Mamma ... with teeny diamonds around the edge, please."

Leticia scratched her head with her wand for a second, searching her brain for the correct incantation and then stood to face her daughter.

"Good grief, child," she said, looking her, "all that weeping and wailing has turned your eyes bright red. You look like something out of a Goblin horror movie! I suppose I will have to fix that too." She gently touched Spellbound's shoulders with the tip of her wand before reciting her spell.

"Make a red-hot top that's cropped,
Let the emerald from her nose be dropped.
Wipe the tears from her face,
And make sure the navel gem's in place.
Finish off with jeans of red,
And wipe that soot from off her head!"

The usual whirls and swirls of colour encircled the room, as they always did when Leticia made her magic. Before Spellbound knew what had hit her, a strange, fizzy feeling erupted throughout her body and her appearance started to change. She quickly ran to the mirror again.

The first thing she looked at was her nose. The emerald had gone. Then, glancing down, she saw a pair of the sexiest little red shredded jeans, which sat snugly on her narrow hips. A good-sized sparkly ruby and diamond cluster was neatly ensconced in her navel and, casting her eyes upwards again, she noticed the fantastic deep red crop top that just about covered her chest. To finish it off, Leticia had added a few extra touches. Spellbound saw to her delight that she was wearing black suede booties, with killer heels and she had a tiny tattoo of a unicorn on her lower back. Her glossy copper-toned hair was now streaked with blonde and had been scraped back and piled up into a sexy, high ponytail.

"WHAT THE FOOK, MAMMA!" Spellbound said in awe, "How do you do it? You are the most incredible Mamma in the whole Fairy kingdom and …OH MY GAWD …you even got my wings of emerald to match my eyes! Oh, Mamma, I love you, I REALLY love you!"

"Now, now, less of the grovelling dear," "Leticia said, smiling. She was pleasantly surprised to see how successful her spell had turned out. She was indeed a stickler for Fairy tradition and liked nothing more than to see Spellbound in gowns with twinkles and tiny sequins, but she had to admit, any teenager in Fairyland would have to go a long way to match this amazing getup. Perhaps she should have been a fashion designer instead of an author, she mused dreamily.

"Right, now go out and have some fun," she said, with a slight smile on her perfect lips, "and remember, the belly bling is just for tonight and tonight only. Off you go and make sure you're back by nine!"

Spellbound needed no further encouragement; with a flutter of Fairy dust and a cheery goodbye, she was gone.

Leticia sat up and placed her empty cup on the small wooden table beside her. It had been a struggle over the last three years, raising Spellbound without any support. Teenage Fairies were renowned for being difficult and hard to handle but even though she was strict with her daughter, she wasn't a complete control freak, she did let her off the lead from time to time. The fact that Spellbound was now ten and eight meant she was reaching maturity and could even be wed at this age if she wished, with or without her mother's permission. Unthinkable!

She started to muse again, recalling the time when she had been ten and eight and married to that grunt-futtuck, Marco Zamforia. She silently scolded herself, feeling foolish that she had not been more savvy.

Every god-damned female Fairy in the wood had tried to snare him and a few Elves too! But oh no, she had to make a point of completely captivating him, ensuring that no one else had a chance with him. She bit her bottom lip, feeling ashamed for a moment about the powerful spell she had cast on him. Not only that but she had gone one step further and had programmed him to love her for life! That was one hell of a big spell, she mused bitterly. It had taken her the best part of a month to prepare and implement and the fact that he was engaged to the *'ever so awful'* Tinky Bonk at the time, only made the challenge more thrilling. Of course, his wealth and his Lotus 3 Convertible had clinched it for her too; it matched the colour of her eyes and because Marco clearly adored his young and beautiful wife, he would often change the hues of the car to blend with her clothing. She sniffed disdainfully and flicked her long raven locks over her shoulder. He should have known better than to try and hoodwink her, she seethed.

Marco Zamforia was a handsome Elf and although he held a certain amount of magical power, he was no match for Leticia. Her abilities were ten times more forceful than his and she delighted in reminding him of that. The only time she was not in control was when they made love, as he was very talented in that particular area. She sighed as she remembered how he would look intensely into her eyes. They were magical, a most unusual shade of green, just like Spellbound's, and he had this cute little dimple in the middle of his chin and his nose was a tiny bit … With a jolt, she pulled herself up short. Okay, so he was more than competent in bed, but he'd had enough blewdy practice, hadn't he? The bastard!

Leticia had a knack for reading minds, some even called her an empath. Not only did she read Spellbound's on a regular basis, but she would often tap into Marco's thoughts too. Unfortunately, having a male brain, it did tend to be somewhat dull at times. He would frequently excite himself over the state of the Fairy Financial Times and ponder for hours over which dragon would win the annual Great Air Race. Then, of course, he would do the usual Elf thing whereby extremely racy thoughts would enter his mind every three minutes or so, which frankly made Leticia's eyes water! The good part was that she was always at the centre of his fantasy, so this made her feel secure in the fact that he would never stray. But when all was said and done, on that fatal day she, the 'great' Leticia Zamforia had failed to read his mind. Oh yes, where were her extrasensory powers then, huh?

"Don't you dare think of that no-good bladderbart," she berated herself sternly. Her heart ached. Even after three years, the pain was as acute as ever. The only way she could deal with the grief and heartache was to stay as mad as hell at him.

She glanced across to the corner of the room. Clifford Eyesaurus was loyal to the hilt and had served her for all her growing years. He was her eyes, her ears and most of all, an essential ally to have around if she ever needed to know what her daughter was up to. He was one of the selected few in Fairyland who knew of the spell she had cast on Marco.

Like many times before, she began to wonder just how her husband was coping in his 'faraway' place and decided to unveil her trusty friend to get some answers.

On the rustic table in the corner of the kitchen sat a large crystal ball, covered in a sumptuous swathe of purple velvet. Leticia carefully removed the cloth and with a perfectly manicured nail, tapped lightly on the glass.

"Clifford," she whispered. "Clifford dear … do wake up." The glass ball lay dormant with only a faint sound of snoring emanating from its depths. "Clifford!" she said again, this time a little louder. It's no good, she thought, this just won't do. She picked up a silver spoon from the table and began banging loudly on the glass, her wings flapping in annoyance. "Blewdy wake-up Clifford!" she shouted. A single eye appeared in the transparency of the ball.

"Ah … so … you are in there then, she spat sarcastically. Clifford's huge hazel eye blinked a couple of times and began looking around.

"Milady," he said, slightly startled, "I do apologise, I was just taking a nap."

"This is no time for napping," she sighed loudly, "I need you. I must know if the gruntfuttock is still suffering! Do come along and take a peek for me; put my mind at ease."

"Milady, is it absolutely necessary for you to keep spying on your husband? I'm sure little has changed since yesterday."

"Oh Clifford, you know I can't read minds at such a great distance. You're the only one who can show me. Come, come dear and give me a vision in the ball."

Clifford Eyesaurus had been cursed some three hundred years ago by Leticia's ancestor, the evil Bella'Donna. She was renowned for being the most powerful Fairy sorceress in the kingdom and had tried relentlessly to snare the stunningly handsome Warlock, but at the time, Clifford's only interests were his magic and sorcery. Finding nothing remotely attractive about her, he had rejected her advances, so with venom and unrequited love in her black heart, she cast a dark curse on him which could never be broken. She gave him immortality and encapsulated him inside her crystal ball. He served the wicked sorceress for many years, until she finally met her demise during a battle between two warring towns. As Bella'Donna was the only one who could reverse the hex, upon her death, he resigned himself to his glass prison and to the realisation that he would never again be a great Warlock. He would spend an eternity trapped inside the ball and be handed down throughout the generations of Bella'Donna's family line. Leticia's mother had gifted the ball to her when she left the realm some years before and this had caused Spellbound no end of trouble! She disliked Clifford intensely. He had a habit of alerting Leticia whenever she became a bit too rebellious. Once, she had refused to speak to him for six months when he had revealed her plans to get a tattoo which resulted in her being grounded, with no wand privileges for two months. For Spellbound, her only consolation was that Clifford was imprisoned inside the crystal ball and that somehow made the situation more bearable.

As the glass turned from clear to smoky green, Clifford let out a sigh. It was evident he was searching for his mistress's answers. Leticia stared into the ball intensely and after a few minutes of watching, the swirling reflections started to unfold before her eyes and the image of her husband appeared. Her heart jumped erratically, as it always did when she saw him. He was walking up and down a long stretch of beach, raking his fingers through his thick auburn hair. He was all alone and clearly depressed.

"Yes," said Clifford, "he's still despondent, just as you wished it, although why you still need to have this kind of sadistic satisfaction, Milady, I will never know! It's also very childish to leave those rude and blasphemous messages to him, scrawled in the sand where he walks every day!"

"Yes! And they will stay there until I decide to remove them and whatever you say Clifford, I need to do this because it makes *me* feel better." Leticia moved closer to the ball, squinting a little in order to see more clearly. "Marco was the complete and utter love of my life and he wronged me. No one wrongs me, do you hear! That senseless twattafock crossed the most powerful Fairy in all the land. He deserves his punishment and trust me; I will not be completely happy until I have made him feel as wretched as me!"

Clifford let out a little groan. "I do understand Leticia and one cannot blame you for banishing him to some faraway land, but don't you think you've taken it a little too far? It's been three years now!" Clifford's ball began to clear until only his eye was visible again.

"He shall remain in limbo until the day that I die," she hissed. "I am the only Fairy who can reverse the spell and I shall never free him, do you hear me ... not ever!"

"Well, that may be true," Clifford spoke gently "Spellbound is young and skittish at the moment but she's a bright and clever young fae and although her powers are somewhat erratic, should she ever discover exactly what did happen to her father, I'm sure she would endeavour to bring him back herself. She does have your magical genes, after all!"

Leticia sniffed defiantly, turning slightly pink. "Well, she will never find out! As far as she is concerned, her father abandoned us and he's never coming back. And, lordy, lord, Clifford," she continued in a raised voice, "if she ever did find out, I would know exactly who told her. For your sake, I wouldn't breathe a word. NOT A WORD, do you hear? Or I'll banish you to Bella'Donna and her Fairy hell pit!"

"I wish you would banish me from this ball Milady and do us all a favour," Clifford said in a deflated tone. Leticia's mood softened for a moment as she sensed her friend's unhappiness.

"You know I have tried Clifford," Leticia said, calming down from her angry outburst. "I don't have any idea which potions and herbs Bella'Donna used, and I would need that kind of information to break the hex. Believe me Clifford, if I could free you, I would do it in a heartbeat but until I can figure that out, you'll just have to stay there, I am sorry, really I am".

Clifford secretly worshipped the ground his mistress walked upon and in truth was more than a little bit in love with her. Her figure was womanly and deliciously curvy, her milky skin, iridescent. In fact, she looked just like an older version of Snow White. He had seen her grow from a faebe to a child who would tap his glass mischievously when her Mamma wasn't looking. Over the years, she had become the most stunning of all Fairies and ever since then, his heart had almost burst with the longing and love he felt for her. Being an unusually gallant and genteel Warlock, he had to frequently shake off the shameless emotions that began to surface whenever she peered through the glass in her cleavage-spilling gowns. He would silently curse himself at his lack of self-control but thankfully, she only saw him as a faithful servant and knew nothing of his secret passion for her. If he could just get out of this glass prison, he would show her what a *real* Warlock was and make her forget Marco Zamforia once and for all!

CHAPTER 4
MOLARS INC.

It was Spellbound's interview day at Molars Incorporated, and as she sat in the large marbled reception area, she glanced around curiously at the other applicants, wondering if they were as apprehensive as she was. To her right was a little blonde freckled Fairy, nervously chewing on a fingernail which had already been bitten down to the quick. She smiled shyly at Spellbound, who politely nodded back, before looking to her left. Seated a few feet away was a voluptuous, pale blue creature, with two, long, forehead antennae, her massive boobs spilling over the tight bodice of a shocking, lime green tunic frock; Spellbound knew her from the Fairy club scene as Norma Snokkers, and she really did live up to her name. She was flicking idly through a copy of "Ofay" magazine. On the cover was a striking photo of Wesley Presley, with his jet-black hair greased back into a high quiff. Spellbound strained her neck to get a better look at her idol. Norma Snokkers sniffed disdainfully and shook the magazine, glaring daggers at her for being so nosy. Spellbound raised her eyebrows haughtily, the way that Leticia always did and settled back into the overstuffed chair.

Her thoughts returned to a few days before, when Mamma was frantically racing around Broomsticks Cottage, trying to magic up an appropriate outfit for Spellbound's interview. She had point-blank refused three of the garments she had invoked until Leticia gave in and settled on a pale blue silk blouse, black slacks, topped with a sparkly belt and spike-heeled boots. The whole creation was very *a la mode* and Spellbound loved it. She hadn't taken the trendy ensemble off for two days, just in case her mother changed her mind and spelled it away. She had even remarked that she might like to borrow Spellbound's new outfit later, as she was going to a 'Bad Taste Party'. "Fookin' great!" Spellbound fumed again. Why she didn't just act her age, after all, she was ancient at thirty-nine years old! Looking around the rather grand marbled reception, Spellbound saw a large portrait of Philip Macavity, the CEO of Molars Inc. He was famous for being the only Fairy in the history of Molars to ever bring back a gold tooth from the human realms. No one was ever quite sure how a human child ended up with a gold tooth in its mouth - perhaps its father had been a dentist! But nevertheless, it was now proudly displayed in a secure walnut cabinet, with a shining plaque beneath it, inscribed with the words:

We get the tooth, the whole tooth, and nothing but the tooth.

"Miss Zamforia, please," said a slender blonde Fairy, with a rather snooty voice. Spellbound stood up quickly.

"This way." She ushered her towards two large double doors.

Spellbound nervously followed the Fairy who was dressed in a no-nonsense, navy pencil skirt and pristine white starched blouse. She was guided into a plush office, where Philip Macavity was seated behind a sumptuous abalone desk. On the table were a collection of spell-phones, an orange High Pad, a bright red laptop and one photograph of a rather dashing younger Elf, who was probably his son, she thought. She hadn't taken much notice of Philip Macavity at her party a week before and now, as she observed him, she found him to be quite distinguished for an old Elf, with huge brown eyes and thick dark hair, with two white flashes at each temple. As they eyed each other, Spellbound quickly got the measure of him: he was as shrewd as they come.

"Miss Spellbound ... aah ... do come in and take a seat. We met briefly at your birthday bash if I remember correctly." He gestured to her to take a seat directly opposite him. "My word, you certainly are a carbon copy of your glamorous mother, and how is that lovely Fairy? Be sure to pass on my felicitations and remind her we never did go out for that candlelit supper I was promised." He frowned, tapping his silver pen erratically on the highly polished desktop. Spellbound smiled nervously.

Placing the tips of his fingers gently together, he continued in a more business-like manner.

"Anyway, you may not know this, Spellbound, but teeth are seriously big business here in Fairyland." Her gaze drifted over him as she tried to look interested. "Every tooth that is collected from a human child is precious, and once it's brought back to the fae realms, it is ground down to make things such as cement, to build our houses, fairy expensive talcum powder and of course, the finest bone china. I myself, have the very rare sixty-piece Toofy Pegs dinner service. There were only two ever made in all the realms. Ours was displayed on the Fairy Ant-eeks Toadshow last year. Your father, Marco out-bid me for the other set and was fortunate enough to acquire the six extra soup tureens too…with matching ladles," he mused enviously.

Yeah right, how exciting is that? She thought to herself. So, what Fairy doesn't know that dinner plates and talcum powder come from human teeth? Did this guy think she was dense? And of course, she knew all about the Toofy Pegs dinner set and six extra tureens. Her father had said he bought them for her and her alone, as an investment for when she was older, she sniffed proudly. Leticia had been outraged and had scolded Marco for spoiling her, splashing his cash out like that and wasting his fortune, as if he had coinage to burn. She remembered how he barked out, "Leticia ... mind your own fookin' business. What I do with my wealth is MY business, so shut it!" Her mother had glared daggers at him and for a second, her hand had hovered over the wand in her pinafore pocket menacingly, but then she'd giggled and purred like a little Dodibell, kissing him on the tip of his aquiline nose. Her mother loved strong Elfmen and her father was nobody's fool; he knew exactly how to handle her, that was for sure.

With a start, she realised that Macavity had cleared his throat to get her attention.

"I think I might like to offer you this job," he said flatly. "I'll give you a trial period of one month. We'll call it work experience for now and see how you get along." Spellbound forced a smile. She was half hoping that by simply attending this interview, it would be enough to cease her mother's nagging, especially if she didn't get the job.

"Every Fairy starts their missions with a work colleague, Spellbound," he continued, lighting a large purple cheroot, then rudely blowing a cloud of pungent smoke towards her. "I think I might partner you with my loyal and long-standing employee, Mike Hunt." He pushed a button on his desk and within a nano second a male Fairy appeared with a flourish. He was at least six millimetres taller than her, with a tanned, fit, muscular body, gold hoop earrings and a whiter than white smile. His dark brown hair was immaculately groomed with Slugga-Slug gel, and a tiny diamond was fixed to his front tooth so that there was a great dazzle every time he smiled. Spellbound glanced over at him and it didn't take her long to realise that Mike Hunt was right up his own hairy, Fairy arse. He may have the face and body of an Adonis, but the compact mirror tucked neatly into the back pocket of his sexy tight-fitting jeans just didn't appeal. He also spoke with an annoying lisp and could not pronounce his r's correctly. Spellbound's mouth gaped open when he said that he was a "vewy pwoud Faiwy" and that he "impwessed" people with "having such a wesponsible caweer wepwesenting The Molar Tooth, Wemoving Company". The most hilarious part was that after each sentence, he also had the habit of saying, "Blinding! Hey, hey!" Spellbound stifled a giggle.

"No-one who works for Molars Inc. is expected to work alone, Miss Spellbound," said Philip Macavity in a low drawl. "Your job will be to accompany Master Hunt here, four nights a week and liaise with the local 'spider intelligence web-work'. Do you have any idea how that operates?" he added.

SPIDERS, thought Spellbound. Oh, twattershack! She wasn't the greatest lover of spiders. No one had told her that she would have to work with a team of sinister, creepy crawlies. She gulped and shook her head.

"Ah, well, I will enlighten you, my dear," Philip Macavity said, as he swung the swivel chair around and crossed his large feet on the desk. "We're in constant contact with an extensive network of Widder spiders in the human realms. Their role is to keep an eye on the state of the children's teeth and inform us when a tooth is loose and about to drop out." They lurk in the deepest, darkest corners of the children's bedrooms, sometimes hanging on the ceilings above, although we do try to dissuade them from doing that, as they often lose their lives to those evil adult humans who pulverise them. Not to mention the spray deterrents they use; which I do hope you'll never have the misfortune of experiencing. One squirt of that lethal liquid and it's goodnight to both spiders and Fairies alike!" He glanced at her. Spellbound gulped again. Her mother had said nothing about it being like a fookin' assault course!

"You will meet many spiders en-route, Spellbound," he continued, "so always be sure to be polite as they are venomous, especially the females and try not to get caught in their cobwebs. You could be there for days ... nay ... weeks, if you are not careful." Philip could see the look of horror on Spellbound's face. "Rest assured dear, spiders don't usually devour Fairies!" He paused and then remarked quietly, "apart from once! There was a young fae called Daisy Dildo, yes, she was a little unfortunate. Anyway ... we gave her a nice Fairy funeral, what was left of her ... at our expense, of course," he added quickly before moving on. "You will enter the bedrooms after dark, through the spiders' entrance holes and for the first week your job will be to keep watch while Mike here removes the teeth from under the children's pillows. He will then slip a silver coin in its place. As you might know, human coinage is extremely weighty, so you won't be expected to do any heavy lifting.

You see, dear, we employ the male Fairies around here purely for their strength and stamina."

Mike grinned and flexed his muscles proudly, giving Spellbound a cheeky wink.

"Looking at you, I'd say that you are ideal for this role. As you may have heard, I am very particular in employing only the finest Fairies from the most elite families." He then became slightly lechy, adding, "Please do remind your mother about our little candlelit supper!"

Mike Hunt was checking himself out again in the mirror, preening his hair and moulding it with some more of that strangely smelling slug gel. "What do you think of me 'air colour, Spelly?" he said, tweaking the little spikes with the tips of his fingers. "It's all me own ya know, not dyed or nuffink. I got it styled today at the 'air dwessers. Blinding innit …? Hey, hey!"

Sod your fookin' hair, she thought sulkily. She was going to have a very short life if those pesky spiders got hold of her. Surely her mother didn't know about the monster-sized creepy crawlies. She knew how she hated them. She really wished her father was here. He would never let her go anywhere near evil Widders, let alone have her venture into the human realms.

Later that evening, she was seated in the Intelligence Room reading the work rosters, trying to sort out exactly where they were heading tonight. She looked at her Fairy Tumex watch. "We have to go at 7 p.m. according to this," she said, "which means we have five minutes." Mike turned his attention away from his appearance and looked at his own massive silver and gold watch. "I make it fwee minutes on me twendy, top of the wange, Wolex wistwatch. Blinding! Hey, hey!"

Both of them were called on the internal sound system, into the Molars main hangar. Waiting for them was a rusty coloured, brown bat, which kept on yawning. Spellbound had never ridden a bat before and was extremely apprehensive as everyone knew their eyesight was awful. "Why bats?" she gulped, as they mounted the creature.

"Cos bats work better at night. They use their wadar to get about, didn't you know that?" said Mike, "and they hang awound for us at the end … hey hey, blinding!"

He sat up front and punched the postcode into the Batnav system and within a mouse's squeak they were flying like the wind through the trees, dodging other bats, also with Fairy fliers onboard.

"Tuck yer wings in, Spelly, we got dwatted wing dwag and it's dwaining me power."

Spellbound attempted to fold her silver wings into the back of her very tight trousers but wasn't having much luck. Thankfully, after a few minutes of struggling, she managed to fix them neatly into the sparkling belt her mother had magicked up, making the speed of the bat much faster.

"That's better; we're making good headway now, Spelly," he said shouting over the noise of the wind. "Blinding … hey, hey!"

It wasn't long before Spellbound could make out the human world fast approaching. A strange odour drifted into her nostrils, like rotten eggs and mould; it had a cheesy kind of stench that she couldn't quite make out.

"Very sowwy 'bout the smell, Spell, must be the cuwwy I had before I left. I'll shake the bat awound a bit to get wid of the pong!"

The poor bat began to gag due to the pungent stench and weaved and heaved, swinging its passengers one way and then the other. Spellbound slid, lost total hold of the saddle and fell straight off the back of the bat and into the darkness. As she tumbled through the air, she instinctively tried to flap her wings, but they were fixed firmly into her sparkly belt. Worst of all, she had forgotten her wand!

"Fookin'… twutting … ahhhhhhh!" she screamed as she spiralled downwards. She plummeted through some very prickly holly bushes before finally bouncing off a plastic bottle lying on its side, into a small pool of a sticky amber liquid.

Meanwhile, Mike was unaware of Spellbound's plight. He was pleased with the new bat's performance because they were actually ahead of schedule. Steering the bat towards his destination, he found the aerial hole, which according to the Widder spiders, was the best point of entry. He brought the bat to a screeching halt and looked around furtively.

"Where's the fwiggin' Faiwy gone?"

Spellbound managed to stand up. Sticky goo covered her body and the tall grass stuck like glue to her thighs. Thinking quickly, she began rolling around and around in the grass, then grabbing a giant dock leaf, she wiped the gloop from her eyes and her sight returned to normal. It was then she spied the bold red label on the bottle she'd bounced off.

"Oh, for fook's sake, self-tanning lotion! That must be the same as 'Elf tan' back home. If this were the case, she would have a change of colour in less than four hours. Glancing around, Spellbound found herself in a garden next to a large sun recliner. Unfastening her sticky wings from the twinkle belt she wondered if she would ever fly again! In the distance, there was a swish and a splatter of water which then hit her with full force. It was freezing cold, and with a gasp it knocked her backwards. The water jet was spinning quickly around, showering the entire lawn. Why didn't these stupid humans just order rain like at home? Running towards the spray, she stood where it was less forceful and started to rinse the lotion off, letting the droplets of water bring her wings back to their former glory. Well, at least she could fly again now. How she wished she was at home in her bedroom, all safe and sound, texting her friends on her new spell phone.

Mike decided to re-trace his journey and fly at a low level. Fortunately, the Batnav was very accurate and kept on the same course.

It was not long before he saw a long trail of orange lotion. On closer inspection, he made out a bedraggled moth-like creature in a sparkly belt, looking rather sorry for herself.

"Spell, is that you? You pwat! What are you fwiggin' doing down there? You ain't a pwetty sight now, are you?"

Spellbound scowled at him furiously as she clambered back on the bat.

"I fell off because ... you, git face, farted a stench that could kill a dragonfly and whilst we're at it, have you shit yourself you fooking cretin?" she snapped irritably. "Also, if you think I'm gonna tie my wings up again, you can think on. Are you sure you've got a bat license?"

Mike had the grace to look guilty and offered her a weak smile.

"Sowwy, Spell, I pwomise. No more bweaking wind and I will go a bit slower now."

At last they managed to get to the aerial hole where they could enter the appropriate house. As Spellbound held on to the flex, she noticed her hands were becoming much darker compared to the white cable.

"I'm bright bleedin' orange!" she screeched at the top of her voice.

" Do be quiet, Spell and can you stop fwiggin' swearing? I'm sure you've got Tuwwets syndwome. Now shush or you'll wake up the kid."

He pushed her forcefully through the hole into the bedroom and Spellbound spiralled into the room just below the ceiling. This was awesome, she thought, spotting a colossal plasma screened TV, it was a hundred times bigger than anything in fairyland!

"This kid has a Neon Nintendo 12!" she shouted excitedly down to Mike. "I've heard of these, they're similar to the Buzzbox 120!"

"Blimey Spell!" Mike replied in a loud whisper. "Keep the wacket down, I've gotta concentwate on finding the tooth!" As he was deeply engrossed in searching for the elusive molar, his cute little backside stuck out from under the pillow. Somehow Spellbound summoned all of her will power not to give it a massive kick!

Curiously, she flitted over to Mike and observed the face of an angelic-looking female child. This was one hell of a big kid; what on earth did they feed them on? She tried not to be fearful of the giant infant, but her heart was beating very rapidly. After all, this was her first glimpse of a human being. She fluttered in for a closer look, hovering over the beautiful child's face, who was about six years of age. Her hair was spread over the pillow in a golden fan. Spellbound was fascinated with the child's eyelashes that were so long, they resembled butterfly legs.

Suddenly, a little dewdrop of water, which must have been trapped inside her wings, plopped onto the girl's face with a splash. She awoke with a start, her blue eyes opening in panic and then she quickly switched her bed side light on.

Spellbound placed her hands firmly over her ears to drown out the loud screaming of the child. Within seconds the mother appeared, to soothe and comfort her.

Making a mad dash Spellbound hid behind the curtains. Mike had managed to find the tooth, placing it in a little velvet bag attached to the waist band of his trousers and was struggling to push the large silver coin under the child's pillow. "Sod it, no time for this, let's get outta here ... pwonto!"

He spotted Spellbound and grabbed her roughly by the arm, dragging her back through the aerial hole quickly. He pushed her clumsily onto the back of the bat and they leapt into the air with a loud whoosh!

Faintly they could hear the distraught mother trying hard to calm down her daughter.

"Look, dear, I may as well tell you now," they heard her say, "there really are no such things as Fairies, especially not little orange ones!"

Chapter 5
Gone! Gone! Gone!

Two weeks had passed and Spellbound was seated at the kitchen table on one of her rare evenings off, her mother was busy preparing their supper. Apart from the initial hiccup of falling into the self-tan lotion and turning bright orange for three whole days, she had settled down well, and her supervisors seemed to be satisfied with her progress. Leticia was fussing around in the larder, complaining because she had run out of bee-balm and sweet clover, it was clear she was becoming crankier by the minute.

Spellbound's mind drifted back to her father, his absence seemed to dominate her thoughts more and more these days.

"Mamma, can I ask you a question?"

"Yes, yes, dear, what is it?"

"Why do you always call Papa a bastard and a grunt-futtock?" In the past Leticia's mood would become explosive at the mere mention of her father's name. Lately, she was becoming increasingly worried about his whereabouts, she knew without a doubt, he would never have missed her birthday ball. She had to get some answers.

"I have no wish to discuss your father, Spellbound," Leticia bit out, turning away from the food cupboard and walking towards the cauldron by the hearth. The fire was burning fiercely, which was welcome, as winter had set in with a vengeance.

"Look, I think I have a right to know why you hate him so much and …"

"Quiet, Spellbound!"

Clifford's eye appeared hazily in the ball, as he had been roused by Leticia's sharp response. "All that you need to know is that your father is a complete spaddywacker. Anyway, it is of no concern; he's away somewhere in the Austrial realm on business, I have told you this already." Leticia's tone was terse and Spellbound sensed her anger would boil over at any minute.

"I'm sorry Mamma but I am having trouble believing that. For one, I know he would never abandon us and secondly, I'm not so sure he is in the Austrial realm at all because if he were, he would call me like he always used to when he was away on business. No, I don't believe it. I have a funny feeling in the tips of my wings." Spellbound stood up and started pacing the room. "He would never miss my ten and eight birthday, not ever! Something bad has happened to him, I just know it."

"Can we PLEASE change the subject. I've told you over and over again and I WILL NOT tell you again."

"Look, I know he's obviously done something to upset you Mamma," Spellbound persisted.

"ENOUGH, I TELL YOU!" Leticia roared.

"Wherever he is, I think he'll come back and say sorry for whatever it is that made you call him a bastard, I really do." She pushed her point relentlessly, "You must have some idea where he is … have you?"

"I don't know, now please stop all of this!"

"We can always ask Clifford … he will know exactly where he is," Spellbound bravely suggested as she walked towards the ball.

"Leave Clifford out of this," Leticia spat.

"Why? I've seen you looking at his visions in the ball. I'm sure if you worked together, you could locate him, if not for you, for me, at least! Or if you want, I could try and find him and bring him back, if you'll let me that is. Oh, Mamma, I miss him so much and I'm so worried."

"Trust me, Spellbound," Leticia interrupted through pursed lips, "your father will not be coming back. He has gone, so get rid of this silly, childish fantasy. He has gone, do you hear me? Gone, gone, gone! He is never coming back. Never ever, coming back, do you hear?"

The air turned icy cold in the room as Spellbound fell silent. She glanced at Clifford and saw his huge hazel eye snap shut. She wandered quietly back to the armchair and drew her knees up defensively, clasping her arms around her legs. No ... something was definitely not right. Clifford knew something, she could tell!

"So, have you heard from him at all these past three years? I mean, has he been in contact, has he even asked after me?" Spellbound's voice became exasperated and raised an octave. "I get it that you two might have fallen out but I know he loved me. I don't understand why he would just disown me like this! You must have had some contact with him, Mamma. I've even tried calling his spell phone but the message just keeps saying that the phone's no longer in service!"

"SPELLBOUND, WILL YOU SHUT UP!" That was it, Leticia finally snapped. "Go to your room NOW," she said, pointing her wooden spoon at the staircase, "and don't come down until supper. I am sick to death of your constant droning. Just go!"

In one slow movement, Spellbound got to her feet and smoothed her hands down her green dress. She walked towards the old, oak door and glanced over her shoulder, shooting her mother a look that would kill a beetle. Her eyes were filled with angry tears.

"You'd better be careful, Mamma, very careful or I might not love you anymore," she wept pitifully as she threw the door open and flew away into the night sky.

Leticia dropped into the chair by the hearth and held her head in her hands despairingly. She started to cry heart-rending sobs, something she hadn't done since that fatal night. Why, oh why, were teenagers such hard work? Spellbound was as stubborn as her father when she wanted something; she was really wearing her down with this cross-examination. What a mess it all was.

"Milady," Clifford said respectfully, "I fear this day was bound to come sooner or later. She is no longer a child you can boss around.

41

Spellbound is changing and maturing and by the sound of it, she will not back down. Be careful you don't lose her."

"I know, I know, Clifford," she sniffed and dabbed her watery eyes with the edge of her snow-white pinafore.

"It is very natural for her to be curious about him, Leticia. They were so close and loved each other very much. She has a right to know where he is."

Suddenly Leticia's voice hardened again, "If that turd bag had been the good and proper husband and father that he should have been, then none of this would have happened. It is his fault. All of this is HIS FOOKIN' FAULT … NOT MINE!!"

Spellbound was sitting at a bright red mushroom table with a group of her friends in the McFlys Diner, drinking Zimpto out of a jumbo-sized glass. As she swirled the straw around the purple liquid, she noticed that Pumpkin was all dewy-eyed.

"What's up with you Pump, you look miles away?" Pumpkin continued to look dreamily into space.

"Oooh, Spelly! … I think I'm in lust for the first time in my life."

"Who with?" they all chorused together, giving Pumpkin their complete attention.

"Drillian Macavity, y' know, your boss's son. Oh, my gawd, he's lush and so snatched, not to mention the big fat wallet he carries around in his pocket."

Daffy looked at her friend in amazement, "Yeah, I've heard about him. Doesn't he manage the Northern branch of Molars Inc. in Toncaster for his Pa?" Pumpkin turned to face Daffy and nodded.

"Oh my goodness, oh hell!" Taffeta started waving her napkin around in an excited fashion. "They say he's one of the richest Elves there is, nearly as well coined as ya Pa, Spelly, and they say he can have any fairy gal in the realm that he wants … just with a click of his fingers, Fairies just go all limp and fall at his feet."

"Well, I had my first experience with him last night behind the Rainbow Club," Pumpkin confided quietly under her breath with a snigger. "I shouldn't have had all those fookin' poppy chasers. After downing nine shots, we had rumpy-pumpy," she added dreamily. "Twas my first time so my wings flopped a bit, but when it was all over, he smacked me on the arse and said he'd see me around sometime. He sauntered off without so much as a kiss on the cheek and started chatting to some other Fairy gal."

"Well, what did he say to this other Fairy?" Spellbound asked, aghast.

"Dunno, not quite sure," Pumpkin replied, scratching her chin, "sumink about being ready to rock and roll in twenty minutes. I guess he wanted to go dancing, but still, it was great while it lasted!"

Spellbound frowned and leant over to touch her friends arm sympathetically. "He sounds such an un-cool, big-headed git. Don't you be mooning over him, Pump … stay well away from him in future."

"I don't know if I can, Spelly, he's got such a huge todger!" All the other Fairies, apart from Spellbound, dissolved into fits of laughter.

She worried about her friends. Everyone knew that rumpy-pumpy was readily enjoyed in Fairyland, without the social stigma upheld in the human realm. For the Fae folks, a night of passion was just like enjoying a nice meal or a blueberry ice-cream. No one got pregnant unless they wanted to, and there was no such thing as venereal diseases. Spellbound accepted the way it was in Fairyland but she had a completely different attitude to everyone else and didn't have the need for such antics. Her mother had told her that somewhere, hidden within the genetic make-up of their female family line, a little 'Victorian' gene, which belonged to Aunt Hester's side, had made its way into their DNA. She would not perform the rumpy-pumpy act until she was in love and married. Although they never judged the other Fairies for doing what they did. This mother and daughter didn't share the same views.

"Oh, oh … talk of the devil," Pumpkin gasped, "look who's over there. Ooh heck, he's coming over RIGHT NOW … am I blushing?" She started fanning her face feverishly.

All four Fairies stared open-mouthed at the hunky Elf approaching them. He was tall, ripped, and drop-dead gorgeous. His thick brown hair was longer than usual and his big brown eyes scanned the group of Fairies lasciviously.

"Hi Pumpkin," he said, making direct eye contact. The slight smirk that touched his lips and the sexy twinkle in his eyes told her in no uncertain terms that he would like to repeat the activities of last night.

"How ya doing, sweet cheeks?" he drawled, touching her face with the tips of his fingers, before turning away from her and fixing his attention on the rest of the group. "Well are you going to introduce me to your friends here?"

Pumpkin blushed and looked at him adoringly, "Yes, of course, Drill." She cleared her throat nervously, "This is Daffodil, or Daffy as we call her, and her sister Taffeta, or Taffy, and of course, you might know Spellbound, she's just started working for ya Pa as a trainee Tooth Fairy."

Her friends stared and nodded adoringly in his direction.

"This Elfin guy is so hot he even gives Eddie a run for his money," Daffy whispered to her sister. Drillian picked up Taffeta's hand and gently opened her palm and kissed it romantically, before repeating the gesture with Daffy.

Spellbound very slowly and firmly sat on one hand. He wasn't going to fookin' well kiss her, that was for sure. What a big head! He glanced briefly at Spellbound who totally ignored him and was looking down intently at her spell phone.

He turned his attention back to Pumpkin. "So, what are you doing tonight, baby doll?" he grinned down at her, showing off his perfectly white, dazzling teeth.

Pumpkin once again blushed the colour of crimson and replied, "N..n..nothing really, Drill."

"Well how would you like to go bowling at Ziggies?" he said, with a sly wink.

"That's sic, yeah, oooh yeah, so cool!"

Spellbound tutted and rolled her eyes. Her friend seriously needed a reality check. This was so unbecoming, falling all over some guy, like some kinda … her thoughts were distracted as she turned and saw that all three of her Fairy friends were gazing rapturously at Drillian and drooling like idiots!

"Anyway, my little rampant butterfly, get your pretty little ass ready and I'll see you there in an hour… and if the rest of you want to tag along, that's fine by me. We'll hit a nightclub and have some real fun." He flashed a sexy smile and turned on his heel. Daffy's mouth was still hanging open and Pumpkin and Taffeta sighed dreamily.

"Just look at the bleedin' sight of you all!" Spellbound spat in disgust. They chose to ignore her.

Pumpkin, in a daze got up to leave. "I gotta go and find something sensational to wear!" In less than a nano-second, she had whooshed off in a cloud of pink smoke.

"Well, waddaya think of him Spell?" Taffeta leant over. "What a hottie! They say he likes group rumpy as well, the more Fairies, the merrier. Perhaps we ought to take him up on his offer!"

"Well, he won't be having me. I've only just met him, and I can't stand the smarmy git," she said screwing up her face in disgust.

"Just as well then, Spelly," Taffeta replied, "all the more for us!" They began falling about in fits of raucous laughter.

Leticia's mood had softened somewhat by the time Spellbound returned home. She had even asked if her daughter was feeling all right, had tutted sympathetically about the black Widder spiders and promised that she would do a protection spell so they didn't bite her. At first, Spellbound was very solemn and decided not to broach the subject of her father again, not tonight anyway. Falling out with her mother made her feel utterly miserable so it was a relief to find her in good spirits.

Now that her daughter was ten and eight, Leticia suggested doing something she had never done before and brought out her Tarot cards from the jewelled pentagram box, to give Spellbound her very first reading.

She knew this was her mother's way of apologising for shouting at her earlier and although they were renowned for having a fiery relationship, she couldn't stay angry at her for long. Spellbound's mood lifted, and in and instant she became excited and captivated, while she watched the colourful cards being laid out. They were literally alive, and the pictures kept changing like a TV screen.

"Umm!" Leticia sighed deeply and then paused. She laid another card on top of the one in the center and then looked directly over her tiny designer glasses. "Oh, I say, I say! I see an Elf here who's going to fall completely and madly in love with you, Spellbound." She glanced back down at the cards. "It's a stormy ride and full of emotion."

"What's he like, Ma, and who is he? It's not fookin' Eddie the Elf is it?"

"Shush child … I'm concentrating." Leticia peered even closer at the cards.

"You know, I was sure that Edward was the one for you child but alas, it seems that he is in for some stiff competition! This Elf is going to be a match for you, and it appears that you will be as much in love with him, as he is with you!"

Leticia fell silent for a moment and squinted as she rearranged the cards.

"Is he handsome, Mamma?" Spellbound giggled.

"He's utterly fetching but he also looks like trouble with a capital T!" She scrutinised the cards even more. "He's into the rumpy-pumpy and the jiggy-jiggy thing … in a big way!" she gulped. "Mmm … perhaps I should weave some more magic to protect you, darling."

Spellbound's face lit up and her mother looked at her affectionately, gently leaning over to push a lock of hair away from her daughter's bright eyes.

"My sweet fae is so young and naïve. Mamma is going to have to teach you all of the tricks of the trade," she cooed.

Leticia wondered if the Elf in the Tarot cards was part of Spellbound's Karma. She was a Zamforia Fairy after all and couldn't be enticed into being intimate with anyone who she didn't love. She paused and gazed into space. She had interfered with Marco's Karma, she thought, shuddering slightly as she wondered what her punishment would be. She quickly brushed the thoughts aside, focusing her attention once again on her young fae.

"Anyway ... we will cross the bridges as we come to them. Mamma is very clever about love wisdom, Spellbound, and I will teach you all you need to know, so don't fret and, lordy lord, you better learn quickly, child. This Elf will do ANYTHING to get you!"

CHAPTER 6
LETICIA REMEMBERS

Leticia poured herself a drink of freshly squeezed cranberries and settled down in front of her new book. Her publisher, Spells and Swoon, had explicitly asked her to put together the next bestseller, and as she had nosed fifty or so top writers out to win the job, she really had to get it right. Her agent even had plans to televise it as a mini-drama in the spring of next year. She was so excited and could barely contain herself!

This time, she had been given carte blanche on the storyline and so after much deliberation and hours of pondering over the plot, decided to base the book on her own life story. After all, it was always better to write about familiar topics. With this in mind, she had chosen Marco to be the male protagonist. Usually, she would angrily cast him out of her mind and draw on all her strength to resist thinking about their happier times. However, this book was so important for her career and she felt that writing it may help her to heal and overcome the effects of the emotional roller-coaster she'd experienced over the last few years. No, she would have to think up pseudo names to protect everyone's identity and get on with it.

Leticia started to think back to the first time she had set eyes on him at the Fairy ball. He was twenty and she had just turned ten and seven, but from the very beginning, the sexual chemistry was undeniable. It was common knowledge that he was engaged to a stunning Fairy called Tinky Bonk and their marriage was to be the most glamorous event in the Fairies' social calendar for the following year. Tinky was beautiful, in a painted sort of way and always wore the shortest 'ruffled' skirts, showing off her tanned, shapely legs.

Her hair was as silver as spun cobwebs and her wings resembled those of a dragonfly. It was safe to say that she was not popular, by any account, and was renowned for her acid, sarcastic tongue and spiteful nature. Throughout her years in spell school, she had slept her way through most of the Elves, Pixies and Fairies, but then again, that was nothing new. Fairyland's laid-back attitude towards rumpy-pumpy had always repulsed Leticia but no one else seemed to care. Only once you were married, were you expected to be monogamous; until that time, it was a free for all! She was definitely in the minority and even teased about her Victorian principles, but she couldn't help the way she was made and as far as she was concerned, she would only give herself to someone she loved.

Her mind drifted back to when she was watching the elite couple dancing to a dreamy waltz; Marco was laughing at something Tinky had whispered in his ear; his hand slowly caressing her back as they moved to the rhythm of the music. It was apparent for all to see that they were already lovers.

Leticia had heard of him, of course, who hadn't? He was as good looking as the grapevine had reported: thick auburn hair, green eyes and taller than most other Elfmen. His presence filled the room and it seemed that everyone was enchanted by him.

She had spotted his Lotus 2000 automobile as he came up the drive earlier. It was the only one of its kind in all the realms. He could change its colour at any time and tonight it was bright red. Suddenly her hand was grabbed, and her cousin Lennox whirled her onto the dance floor.

"Hi Tish, you look all lost and alone. Come on, let's do the trog-stomp gal!"

She laughed and was swept along with her cousin's enthusiasm. He was an excellent dancer with a terrific sense of rhythm. After a while, the music drifted to a stop and the compere announced that the next dance was to be an 'excuse me'. Lennox winked.

"I'm going to ask the gorgeous Tinky for a dance, okay?" Leticia shrugged good-naturedly and started to walk off the dance floor. Tinky was handed over to Lennox and just as Leticia was about to reach her seat, Marco Zamforia approached her for the exchange. Her heart skipped a beat and her knees went weak; for a second, she thought she might melt away. No other Elf had affected her like this and for the first time in her life, she felt terribly gauche. Before she knew it, she was in his arms, staring into those incredible green eyes. He gave her a sexy smile, his pearly white teeth dazzling the young fae. He was the first to speak.

"My name's Marco Zamforia, and you are?"

Get a grip, she remonstrated with herself as he tightened his arm around her waist, pulling her closer. She cleared her throat slightly and smiled at him, her violet eyes misting over.

"Leticia," she answered with a whisper, and as the waltz started to play, it seemed natural that they should move in perfect time with the music.

"Well I must say, you're a very quiet Fairy," he said with a glint of humour in his voice. "Are you enjoying the ball?"

"Yes," she replied demurely.

"I don't think we have met before, have we?" He smiled down at her, and this time, his eyes focused on her pink, rosebud mouth. "Which part of the realm do you live in?"

"Br..Br.Broomsticks Cottage," she stuttered. "It's on the outer perimeters of the forest and ... er ... no ... we haven't met before." She cleared her throat a little.

"Well, trust me," he said, his hand pressing down firmly onto the soft skin at the base of her wings, "if we had, I would have remembered."

"I hear you are to be married soon to Tinky Bonk," she said, trying to make conversation. He continued to look deeply into her eyes, his gaze not faltering for a second.

"Yes, we hope to set a date for some time next year." Leticia smiled and nodded before he negotiated a swift move around another couple. All too soon the dance was over and as the music came to an end, Tinky strolled over to them, her wings twitching menacingly. She had been watching her in Marco's arms, her silvery-blue, cat-like eyes glinting with jealousy.

"Leticia, how nice to see you again," she purred. "How's your mother, Elspeth and her toy boy, what's his name ... Brod Twit?" Leticia had to control her temper. It had taken some time for the rumours of her mother's affair to die down. Brod was ten years younger and had swept her Mamma well and truly off her pretty, Fairy feet. She had fallen madly in love with the young Elf and planned to start a new life with him in another realm. Leticia had flatly refused to go with them and so it was finally agreed that she would stay behind, under her cousin Larissa's watchful eye.

"They are married now and live in the Americus Realm." Leticia spat out icily.

"Ah, so that's where they ended up after the scandal then," said Tinky smugly. "So, your parents divorced ... and your Pa, what happened to him?"

Leticia flushed. Was this any of her goddamn business? She fumed. Through gritted teeth, she answered, "He is also married and lives in the Austrial Realm with his new wife."

Tinky laughed scornfully as she clung on to Marco's arm.

"Jeez ... what a dysfunctional family you have! I'm surprised you don't need Fairy therapy or a shrink to sort you all out."

"Shush, Tinky." Marco looked embarrassed. Leticia picked up her swishing lavender skirts and spinning around, she marched off the dance floor with as much dignity as she could muster. If she had had her wand with her, she seethed, that fookin' Fairy would be a heap of fox shit on Marco Zamforia's shoe. Fook the pair of them!

Later that night, she sat up in bed going over the events in the ballroom. Tinky Bonk was so obnoxious; she'd better keep out of her way in the future. Her magic was far more potent when she was angry. Marco was welcome to her. She punched the soft feathered pillows with her fists and tried to settle down to sleep. Tomorrow, she had agreed to read palms at a Fairy Fete for the charity PFD, (Protection for Dragonflies), so she needed her rest.

The next day was scorching hot and Leticia was taking a well-earned break from her palmistry readings. Her psychic gifts were already well known, and the Fairies were queuing around the block to see her. She took her wand and magicked fresh, perfumed air into the dome-shaped tent. Her gown was slightly dishevelled, so with another flick of her wand, she changed it into a stunning turquoise creation. She heard the flap of the tent open.

"Tea break time, please come back later!" she called out over her shoulder.

Marco took no notice of her instruction as he moved towards her.

"I'm sorry, Leticia. I didn't mean to disturb you, but I had to see you to say sorry for Tinky's behaviour last night. I don't know what came over her. I did try to get her to come and apologise to you in person, but she wasn't having any of it."

For a moment, Leticia was speechless as she gazed at him. He continued more earnestly.

"I could see you were very upset and embarrassed."

"No worry," she said, smiling through gritted teeth, "I am quite able to look after myself. Yes, I was angry, spitting wagtail feathers actually, for a second, I had to stop myself from turning your precious soon-to-be bride into a beetle … or worse. All water under the bridge now," she shrugged nonchalantly."

"Please let me take you to lunch Leticia, as an apology, and let's forget the whole sorry incident."

"No, no," she answered stiffly. "There is really no need. We don't want to upset your fiancée any further now, do we? Please don't worry, as I said it is all forgotten." She gave him a polite little smile and turned to her small table, sitting down. "I have another two hours of palm readings to do, so I must really ask you to leave."

Marco hesitated, not used to being dismissed by anyone, he cleared his throat. "I hear on the jungle drums you are very good at psychic matters. Would you read my palms?"

"What, now?" Leticia sounded surprised.

"Yes, please."

As he sat in the chair opposite, he held his open hands towards her, and she lifted them in hers. They were strong and masculine, and he had a very long lifeline.

His heart line was true and faithful, it was clear to her that he would never cheat. She had no chance of snaring him then from the dratted Tinky Bonk. The only way that could ever happen, would be if she were to magically remove the obnoxious Fairy, once and for all.

She cleared her head. No, she would never resort to such unethical means. Then she smiled to herself, but oh, what fun it would be to wipe the self-satisfied grin off Tinky's face.

Concentrating on his palms again, she told him of events in his past, as he gazed at her in astonishment. "You are one very incredible Fairy, Leticia, all that knowledge and from one so young." Smiling secretly at the compliment she went on to tell him about the present; his business plans and investments.

"Wow, what can I say. You're brilliant! Now for my future, Leticia, what's in my future?"

She stood up. "Sorry, you must go, Marco. My pre-arranged appointments are waiting. I'm doing this for charity today, so I must crack on."

"Well, perhaps I can come another time for my future … may I?"

"Perhaps," she shrugged mysteriously.

He flicked open his wallet and dropped a considerable bundle of banknotes on the silken tablecloth. "Please put that towards whichever charity you are supporting today."

As he left, she whistled through her teeth, counting the cash. Hell's fire, the Elf was not only sex on legs; he was stonking rich as well! She picked up a stray Tarot card and began fanning herself feverishly.

The heatwave continued and so Leticia and a group of her friends decided to visit the river in Bluebell Forest. It was fast-flowing and very cold, just what she needed. Her pals had hitched a lift on the back of her Magpie, Stanley. She had mended his broken wing the year before and taught him to speak. In return, she would just call his name and he would be there for her in an instant. The banks were covered with other Fairies, sunning themselves and enjoying the coolness of the river. Leticia dropped her floaty sarong to the ground and dived like a blade into the sparkling waters.

"Absolute bliss," she breathed, lying on her back. Suddenly, there was a noise above the trees and a smart, ebony Swirleybird hovered over the grassy bank. It landed with a flourish and out stepped Marco and Tinky, already dressed in their suits, ready for a swim.

"Oh fookin' hell, not her again!" Leticia spat out under her breath. Her head bobbed above the waterline as she spied Marco on the bank. He was in the tiniest white bathing trunks, showing off his elf-hood very nicely. His tan was picture-perfect, his hair was impeccable, and his body was faultless. She groaned and looked up to the sky, "Drat him and his putrid fiancée!"

Tinky was in a bright, scarlet, polka dot bikini, showing off her tanned curves to perfection. Leticia doggy paddled for a while, enjoying the coolness of the crystal water, her black hair swirling all around her.

"Come on, Tish, over here!" Caitlyn, her best friend, was waving on the other side of the river. "We've got some very potent, poppy punch!"

Leticia started to swim actively against the current, passing Tinky on the way, who hissed, "If I were you, I'd stay in the water, lardy-bum. You wouldn't want anyone looking at a butterball like you … surely!"

"Fook that Fairy… always when I haven't got me friggin' wand!" she steamed angrily. Pulling herself up on the bank she spat out to Caitlyn, "I'll swing for that Tinky Bonk, I will, I swear it! Does my arse look fat in this bikini? Come on now, be honest, Cait!"

Caitlyn soothed, "Of course not, dearest. You know you have a perfect hourglass figure and please, dearest, try not to keep cussing so much."

Leticia frowned. Caitlyn had the most beautifully, refined voice and was the most genteel of Fairies in the Brittanic Realm and if she said her arse wasn't big, then it wasn't! After arranging her towel, she took a big swig of the poppy punch, still fuming. Lying back, she closed her eyes, letting the sun warm her curvy little body. She and Caitlyn drifted into a light sleep until she felt droplets of water being dribbled over her bare tummy. She opened one eye and saw Marco smiling down at her mischievously.

"Hi Leticia, are you enjoying the sun?"

She sat up like a jackrabbit and Caitlyn giggled girlishly.

"Um ... yes, thank you," she replied, looking frantically around for Tinky.

"Tinky has gone to get champagne and fickleberries from the tent. Would you like some?"

Leticia shook her head, trying not to look at the bulge in his trunks. Suddenly, he flopped down next to her, drawing the attention of all the other Fairies. Leticia felt very uncomfortable, especially as she could see Tinky stomping towards them, laden with delicious delights.

"Did you make lots of money for the charity the other day?" he enquired pleasantly.

"Er ... I did, yes ... especially with what you donated, thank you for that."

"Good ... good ... and will you be doing any other charity events soon?"

"Not until the Primrose Ball at the end of the month."

Tinky was now within six feet of them and was clearly enraged. "Marco, I could really do with some help with this lot," she glared at him.

"Sorry Tink," he said, rising to his feet. "Here, give me the bottle." He glanced at Leticia and Caitlyn. "Sure, you two won't join us?" They both shook their heads in unison. "Well, see you at the

Primrose Ball then … bye for now!" His gaze lingered a little longer on Leticia and for a moment, their eyes locked.

"Wow, what an absolute hunk," Caitlyn breathed, as they walked away. "It's true what they say about him, isn't it? He really is drop-dead gorgeous! Don't you fancy him just a little bit, Tish, he's certainly got his eyes on you?"

Leticia pulled a face. "Nah … not a bit! And he's as near as god-damn married anyway, so what's the point!"

Three weeks had gone by since Leticia had last seen Marco and tonight was the night of the Primrose Ball. It wasn't all work, she thought, only the first two hours, and then she could relax and have some fun. She was determined not to let Tinky Bonk get the better of her and had her powerful Moldavite and yew wand secured in a secret pocket in the folds of her stunning magenta and gold gown.

She had worked all week on the spell for her dress, which she knew would go unmatched for its stylish elegance. The material had come from the Americus realm. Her mother had sent it a few months ago and the fabric had never been seen in Bluebell Forest. As she moved, it subtly changed colour and she was over the moon with the flattering results.

On entering the ballroom, she spied Caitlyn and waved gaily to her. Looking at her Tumex watch, she pointed to it and mouthed, "See you in two hours."

As usual, there was a queue of eager Fairies and Elves waiting to see her. She was becoming increasingly well known for her psychic powers and was booked up for private readings well into the following year. This kept the wolf from the door and made her very self-sufficient. In fact, she was getting a nice little stash of cash together. If this good run continued, she might even be able to move out of Broomsticks Cottage into something a little more comfortable and possibly pay her dear mother a visit.

After a gruelling two hours of work, she was quite thirsty and headed for the drinks table. Caitlyn was waiting there with a tumbler of her favourite tipple.

"I really need this," she smiled at her friend, downing the drink in one go.

"Wow, be careful, dearest, you don't want to get squiffy too soon."

Leticia smiled and helped herself to another tumbler and drank half the contents.

"I've just seen that awful Tinky Bonk," she hissed to her friend. "I need some blewdy Dutch courage if I have to eyeball her again."

"Don't let her upset you, darling, she's just not worth it. Relax and let your hair down a little, you deserve it."

The silver bombshell was eyeing Leticia's dress, and with a sense of satisfaction, Leticia knew she was envious of the beautiful creation. Marco waved a greeting before being pulled away to join a group of friends. Within seconds Caitlyn and Leticia were surrounded by young Fairy and Elf suitors and spent the next hour on the dance floor enjoying all of the attention.

Leticia really needed another drink; she was still so thirsty. Dodging the throng, she managed to guzzle down a colossal glass of iced luminous, green fairy-aide and then tucked herself away in a quiet corner behind a huge fern plant, to ease her aching feet. She smiled as she saw Caitlyn doing the thrust with a hunky Elf, she'd had a crush on for weeks.

"So, there you are." It was Marco, smiling down at her, looking striking in a black and crimson doublet.

"Oh, hello there. Enjoying yourself?" She said coolly.

"You certainly are the belle of the ball in that wonderful gown, aren't you, Leticia? Do you fancy a dance with me?"

She shook her head and her long black hair tumbled over the low bodice of her dress.

"Feet are killing me, so sorry, no and besides, we don't want to go and get Tinky in a bad mood again!"

"Tinky's gone home. I'm afraid she got a bit tipsy. I had my chauffeur take her back. So," he held out his hand, "do we dance or not?"

Before she could answer, he pulled her forcefully out of the chair and onto the dance floor. Her heart leapt. Just what was his game, Elf handling her in this way?

"Marco … you'll have every tongue wagging in the place. Why are you dancing with me when you are engaged to be wed?"

He pulled her a little nearer. "Umm … that's what I keep asking myself," he said in a low husky voice. "You captivate me, I guess … your perfume is amazing."

She was just about to respond when there was a commotion at the far end of the ballroom. Tinky was back, worse for wear, swaying like a tree in a storm. She careered over to them, screaming at the top of her voice.

"Get your fookin' hands off my fiancée, lard ass!" The dancing throng stopped, and all eyes turned on them in a hushed silence. The band stopped playing and the guests circled around the trio.

"Tinky, will you shut up," Marco barked at her. "You've had far too much to drink, now apologise to Leticia this minute!" Without any warning, she lunged at Leticia, just missing her face.

"You're a bloated cheap tart, just like your prozzie Ma!"

Leticia straightened her back and became as cold as ice. Caitlin rushed to her side in a flash.

"Dearest, come away from them, they are both trouble makers. Please don't get mad, they're just not worth it, now come."

Tinky continued to sway, slurring her words belligerently. "Yeah, yer just like ya Ma. Any Elf will do. You can't get one of your own, so you decide to go ahead and steal my guy. Why don't you prey on someone else? Trolls would be more your style? That's if they would want a blubber ball like you."

A white mist had descended over Leticia and she began chanting in Elvish under her breath. She slowly took out her wand and pointed it at the jealous Fairy. Tinky's goading fell silent, as gasps of horror came from the crowd.

An icy wind blew Leticia's hair behind her as she circled the wand high into the air, taking Tinky with it. She tumbled her three times then sent her spinning around and around the ballroom ceiling. Plumes of red, green and yellow smoke crackled and lit up the vast room.

Suddenly Tinky Bonk was changed theatrically into a huge, brown slug, which landed with a squelch at Zamforia's feet.

"Your fiancée will need a little help to get home; be sure to scrape her up carefully now. The spell will wear off at noon tomorrow," she spat out unemotionally. "My patience is running thin with the pair of you, so stay out of my way from now or you'll be next."

There was a hushed silence and a pathway opened up hastily, as Leticia walked out of the ballroom with her head held high.

As the door slammed shut in her little cottage, Leticia ran upstairs and threw herself on the bed. She cried for an hour, which turned her eyes red and made them smart like hell. She wished her Mamma and Papa were here to kiss her better. Once the tears had subsided, she started to reflect on the recent events and anger began to surge through her Fairy veins. She was ten and eight next week, when her powers would truly come into their own.

"At least that jumped up Fairy will never come near me again," she said aloud with a vengeance. "As a further punishment for Tinky Bonk, I'm going to have Marco Zamforia for myself. When I'm ten and eight, I can spell for whatever I like, and I want him and his wealth ... and oh, I *shall* have him and you, Tinky Bonk, you can rot in Fairy hell!"

A good night's sleep had not calmed her down and she woke the following morning still seething with anger. She set about searching her cottage for every spell book she could find. In the dark and spooky attic, she came across some ancient grimoires on Fairy magic, that had been handed down throughout the family. After blowing the dust off them, she studied them intently for a few hours, until her questions were answered. She emailed her cousin Larissa, for advice. Leticia had been her apprentice for as long as she could remember which was lucky because Larissa was phenomenal with her spellcraft. She had cautioned her about using magic to influence another's mind and told her emphatically that it was highly unethical, but Leticia didn't take any notice.

Marco tried to get in touch with her many times in the ten days that followed, but she ignored him, staying at home, feverishly gleaning as much information as she could from the grimoires. This was going to be the most significant spell she had ever concocted in her young life, so she had to get it right. On one of the days, he had knocked on her door for so long that she had had to resort to using her wand to cast a powerful force field of protection around the cottage, so that he couldn't enter.

Tomorrow was her eighteenth birthday and traditionally, every single person in the realm was welcome to attend her party. She wondered if Marco would come along. Larissa had helped plan the event and with powerful magic and oodles of coinage thrown in, it was certainly going to be an impressive event. Her parents and their spouses had already transported themselves in for the party and she was quietly excited. Her silver gossamer gown was her mother's gift and the tanzanite tiara, necklace and earrings were presents from Aunt Hester. She twirled in front of the cheval mirror and knew she had never looked more beautiful.

As was tradition, her birthday ball was to be held at Lord and Lady Wizard's Grand Forest Hall. The ballroom was outside, in a small forest glade, surrounded by multi-coloured mushrooms, along with three grand marquees, each themed with exotic, speciality dishes from various realms. These huge tents were cleverly lit with thousands of glow worms and fireflies and already they were packed to the brim with Fairy guests. Leticia's parents reunited just for the party and were delighted at the considerable number of guests who had decided to put in an appearance. The orchestra was in full swing and many couples were already dancing. The whole event was stunning, all thanks to her cousin.

With her Mamma on one side and her Papa on the other, Leticia greeted each of the guests and thanked them for attending. As she looked up, Marco came striding towards them. Her heart double flipped as he gave a neat little bow and kissed her open palm. His striking green eyes gazed at her in amazement, but he managed to maintain a sense of calmness, enough to politely chat with her parents for a while.

Caitlyn drew her into a small alcove. "Wow, you look stunning, Tish ... what a gown! What a party! There are hundreds of Fairies here. They must have heard about you zapping Tinky Bonk the way that you did," she giggled. "I noticed she hasn't turned up here tonight, dearest. Bet she wouldn't dare show her face. Oops! Here comes prince charming: the one and only Marco Zamforia. I'm off, see you later, dearest." Leticia turned to meet him, and he smiled unsure of himself.

"You're always running away from me," he scolded playfully, with a grin. She frowned and he held his hands up in mock horror. "Promise you won't zap me with your wand now!" She smiled half-heartedly as he took her hand and led her to the ballroom.

"Your fiancée isn't going to turn up here and spoil my party, is she?" He coughed, slightly embarrassed.

"Um, no, she won't be doing that, so relax. I seem to spend my life apologising for her."

"You would do better to get rid of her, she's a social embarrass-ment." Leticia tossed her head.

"She is a little hot-headed," he replied, "but I think she may settle down now, after you ...um ... changed her into a slug!"

Leticia sniffed irritably; he still thought he was going to wed the stupid Fairy. She must be red hot in bed to have this kind of devo-tion because she had nothing in between her ears! She would show Tinky Bonk! She was more determined than ever to marry Marco

Zamforia and have his love, status and coinage. Throughout the evening he never left her side and they danced until the early hours before he sped her home in his Lotus 2000.

The next morning, after her parents had decided to take a stroll into town, she gathered everything together for the spell. The table was laden with various herbs, potions and crystals. Her mother had brought her a selection of the most sumptuous fruits from Americus, which was now tastefully arranged on a golden platter. Three leather-bound Grimoires lay open on the table and the steaming water in the cauldron was almost at boiling point. Leticia collected all the ingredients and threw them into the cauldron while singing in a long-forgotten Fairy Elvish tongue. Her sweet voice rang out as the room disappeared and a magical portal opened.

Witches rising from the East,
I summon you now to this magical feast.
Witches from the North give power,
Awaken the spell in this sorcerous hour.
Witches from the South bring light,
Quench my desire, burning bright.
Witches from the West I need,
You take my offerings and do this deed:
Make Marco Zamforia, love only me,
From now and for eternity.

The four male Elf Witches she had summoned stepped out of the portal and approached her and then encircled her, spinning her around and around until she was dizzy. She felt her body fizz and crackle and then she passed out.

Opening her eyes, she saw she was neatly tucked up in bed. Her parents leaning over her, most concerned.

"Ah, at last, she is awake. What a fright you gave us, child. We thought you were dead. Have you been visiting the outer astral, dear?"

Leticia smiled weakly and nodded, "Something like that, mother."

"Oh, you nearly gave me a heart attack!" Her father said with a twinkle in his eyes.

Two hours later she had fully recovered and with the protection spell neutralised, Marco Zamforia's furious, loud knocking could be heard at her door. This time, she opened it tentatively and wondered if the magic had worked. Without invitation, he marched into her modest abode and gazed longingly down at her.

"Leticia, I have been such a fool. I have told Tinky that it's you I love and that the wedding is off. How could I not have realised this before? I must have been blind. Please, say you could love me too, sweetest fae." He dropped down on one knee. "Can you ever love me, Leticia?"

"Ye gods!" she said to herself. That was one powerful spell and it had undoubtedly worked big style!

"Marco, please get up. I don't like to see you on your knees."

"I will stay here forever until you say you will marry me."

Leticia giggled. "In that case, I have no other option but to accept."

He stumbled to his feet and took her into his arms. As their lips met for the very first time, her mind reeled. He was so sexy, and he was going to be her husband. Very soon she would be Leticia Elva Zamforia.

Their stunning house was finished at last. It sat in splendid isolation on an island in the middle of Bluebell Forest. The vast lands had belonged to the Zamforian clan for countless generations and Marco insisted that his new wife have the best of everything. He had built the house for her as a token of his devotion. They had been married for twelve wonderful years and their daughter was soon to be thirteen. Spellbound was a beauty and her features were a true testament to her father. She had inherited his red, auburn hair, albeit hers was three shades lighter than his, both had identical green eyes and the same sense of humour. Marco lavished his wealth and love on his only child. Leticia often felt guilty at the way she had snared him. He was a powerful Elf and the richest in all the realms, but he could not hold a wand to her magic, and she had used hers unashamedly to get him. He was the love of her life and she wanted no other but him.

Tinky Bonk had fled the shame of that eventful evening by moving to the northern end of the wood and no-one had seen her for years. It was rumoured that she had feared Leticia's magic so much that she would never show her face in public circles again.

Tonight, many guests were expected at their house-warming event. The bowers and gardens were a delight and the caterers from Horrids had provided the finest foods and wines. Spellbound was allowed to have four of her closest friends for a sleepover; they were zipping around the grounds hysterically and enjoying themselves. Leticia had magicked larger wings for them all and they were having great fun experimenting with them.

Life was so wonderful, Leticia mused. Marco stood behind her and held her in his arms as he nuzzled hot kisses into her neck. She still felt heady with excitement at his touch and turned to kiss him.

"You look stunning tonight, darling … so … so very beautiful," he whispered. She peeped up at him and laughed at his compliments. Spellbound swooped over to them and she and her friends all yelled,

"Yuk, they're kissing, how uncool is that?!"

Zamforia gave her one last kiss. "Sweetheart, our guests are arriving. Shall we...?" He held his hand out and they strolled towards the entrance.

The party had been an enormous success and when it was over, Leticia went to stand on the balcony for some fresh air. Spellbound and her friends had been in bed for some time now and at last, they had all gone to sleep, their wands exhausted and depleted of power. The noise had been horrendous and it took a stern talking-to from

Marco to calm them all down. He had such a way with children, she smiled.

Whilst he was away dealing with the last of the caterers, Leticia decided to explore the grounds of her new home. For more speed, she used her wings to get to the large glittering pond, where she stayed for ten minutes or so, before she went in search of her husband. Marco was nowhere to be seen. She frowned and continued to look for him.

She swooped into a part of the acreage she had not seen before and saw the most beautiful building. It was a domed, Grecian-style structure, made of pale pink alabaster and marble, with gold embellishments. Two female angel statues guarded either side of the door. Inscribed above the arch were the words, *'Dedicated to the love of my life'*. She gulped back the tears and stared mistily at his message. He must have built this secretly for her. Pushing the door open silently she gazed in amazement at the hundreds of lit candles. The rooms were elegantly furnished and bathed in a soft glowing light, a romantic and passionate boudoir of devotion.

From a room somewhere further inside, she heard voices and she walked towards another door, which was half-open. In the centre of the aquamarine room was a large hot tub with bubbling crystal water. A bottle of crystal rose champagne was open and beside it, two glasses half-filled.

Then with a shock, she saw Marco and Tinky Bonk in the water, kissing passionately. His long legs were entwined around hers and both his hands were on her naked breasts. In horror, she realised they were having sex and Tinky was moaning into his neck, her arms encircled around his bare waist. Marco was whispering passionately, "Darling, dearest heart … you are my life, how could I ever survive without you?"

Leticia blinked hard; she was rooted to the spot. Surely, she was seeing things. Maybe someone had spiked her drink and she was hallucinating! She watched in horror as they writhed and clung to each other as they reached their climax together.

With a frozen face, she turned on her heels and flew to the top of a tall tree. She sat there in total shock, the tears streaming down her face. It was apparent her spell on him had weakened or been broken somehow, she sobbed. All along, his heart still belonged to Tinky Bonk. He must have asked her to the party. That's the only way she could have got here: at his invitation. And then a terrible coldness engulfed her, and she felt her heart turn to ice. She stood on the tallest limb of the tree, the strong gusts of wind blowing her hair into a mass of black, tangled knots. Her heart was now thumping hard in her chest as she began to summon the darkest magic she could muster. Reaching for her wand, she pointed it in the direction of the pink pagoda and screamed like a banshee.

"Dark Witches of East and Witches of North,
Take this foul Fairy and speed her forth,
Dark Witches of South and Witches of West,
Take this foul Elf with whom she's obsessed.
Banish his strumpet to rank smelling caves,
And make of his fate the wet sand and waves."

The sky became a deep swirling grey, which instantly blocked out the moon. A fork of lightning raced across the sky and four sinister figures from the Underworld rose from the ground and began circling the embracing couple like a tornado. A few seconds later, they were gone. Leticia went back to the empty pagoda, and with a final wave of her wand, she magically sealed the door shut: no one would ever enter the wretched place again. She turned back to the house, where her daughter and her friends were still sleeping, completely unaware of what had just happened.

Leticia leaned back onto the pillows and put her pen down. She closed her eyes wearily. Her mind drifted to Spellbound. She had been inconsolable after her father's disappearance. Every day she had cried and ranted about his return until Leticia couldn't stand it anymore. In a fit of desperation, she performed a well-being spell on her, to calm her daughter's emotions. Gradually over the last three years, the spell's potency had diminished, allowing her to re-adjust and become normal again.

Lifting a lock of her silky black hair away from her eyes, Leticia sighed bitterly and thought of Marco on his desert island in the middle of the ocean. At least there was food and water there, she grimaced. She had provided him with that, not that he'd deserved it.

She hardly spared a thought for Tinky Bonk, who had been sent away to dwell in deep dark caves, where unseen and unheard-of creatures lurked.

A few days after Marco's banishment, the beautiful house they had built together was made invisible and inaccessible. His coinage had disappeared with him, as well as all the luxuries he had pro-vided for them as a family. Even her powerful spell casting could not have retained the Zamforian wealth, which had been handed down over the centuries as his birth right.

She and Spellbound returned to Broomsticks Cottage and set-tled into a modest lifestyle. The only possession they were allowed to keep was the Toofy Pegs dinner set, as this had been a gift for Spellbound. She had the option to sell it when she reached one and twenty and it would probably make her wealthy beyond belief, but Leticia wouldn't have a penny from the fortune.

Afterwards, the gossip had been rife, and Leticia had to think quickly in order to avoid a scandal. She announced to everyone that her husband was away in the Austrial realm for a few years on business. Eyebrows were raised and no-one had really believed her story, especially as she and Spellbound were living so modestly back at the cottage. They whispered that Marco had run off with some-one else and that Leticia was too proud to admit it. They dared not ask her outright as she might become angry and inflict her ruthless magic on them.

Once she had finished the book, she knew it would be a bestseller for Spells and Swoon, and if she could make some money from selling her story, then all the better for her and Spellbound. She had to be careful to hide the true identity of all the characters in the story and to make up a happy ending to please the readers. No one would ever know.

She still loved Marco, and would always love him, she mused bitterly. She had well and truly inherited Aunt Hester's blasted genes, which meant that she would never be able to find happiness with another partner.

She thumped her pillow despondently and lay down into the bergamot scented sheets. She must sleep now, and somehow, she must try to put it all behind her once and for all.

CHAPTER 7
YOU'RE IT!

The evening was warm and sunny and Spellbound was ensconced inside the wing hangar at Molars Inc with Mike Hunt, awaiting her next tooth mission. Oh, how she would love to be sitting outside right now, hanging out with all her friends down at the lake.

This job was fast becoming a pain and she still hadn't got over her fear of the dreaded Widder spiders. They were very unpredictable and one of them had cornered her only yesterday. She had zapped it with her wand, and thankfully, it had shrunk down to the size of her little fingernail. The trouble was there were so many of them and they were constantly breeding. The baby Widders had no manners and would bite just for the hell of it. Fortunately, because of her mother's protection spell, she had escaped this. You had to have eyes up yer bleedin' arse and that was for sure, she thought miserably.

All this danger for no pay, well not until she had completed a three-month probation period. No money could change hands until you had passed the final test. Leticia was unsympathetic and had said that she must persevere and just get on with it, adding that she had no fear of the dear little spiders; instead, she had an affinity with them and kept a huge one called Hairy Mary in the biscuit tin as a pet. This, of course, made sure Spellbound never got any biscuits.

She sighed and thought a bit of extra pocket coin would come in really handy right now, especially as she had her eye on a new top of the range Spell Phone 11.

If only her father were here, there would be no need to worry about finances. Her heart sank. She missed him so much; sometimes thinking her soul would burst with the pain she was experiencing and lately, the deep-down longings were getting worse by the day. Little did she know that her mother's well-being spell, which had been cast three years earlier, was diminishing by the minute.

"Cheer up," Mike said with a cheesy grin. "It's okay, honest it is, sometimes you have to kiss a pond full of fwogs before you find yer pwince! Blinding ... hey, hey!"

"I don't want any frogs and no princes, thank you very much."

"Awwww, just thought with ya being all down and sulky, that some Pixie had gone and broke ya heart!"

Spellbound shook herself out of the black mood that was about to engulf her. "Trust me, I have no Pixie about to break my heart. As far as I am concerned, they're all dung beetles and I don't want anything to do with them, they're all grunt futtocks."

"Oooh ... that is pwetty harsh, Spelly. What about Eddie? He likes you, why don't you give him a go? He's vewy good looking, blinding hey hey!"

"Eddie is a twut," she said finally. "Just like all the rest of them and I have no intention of having a relationship with anyone ... EVER!"

Just then, raised voices echoed throughout the hangar and Mike and Spellbound turned around to hear what the commotion was all about.

"What do you mean you can't arrange the meeting with Incisors Limited?" a familiar voice demanded. "You know damn well I intend to take over the company in the autumn. Get me the MD on the phone right now or I shall demote you, girly!"

Spellbound looked through the open door and saw Drillian Macavity taking giant strides towards the hangar, followed by fifteen or so Fairies and Elves. His PA, a striking female with an ample chest and platinum blonde hair, was running at his heels.

"What could I do, Drill?" she shrieked. "He said he doesn't want to see you. I can't make him see you if he doesn't want to!"

Drillian stopped dead in his tracks and glared down at her.

"My PAs in the past have always been capable of getting me exactly what I want, Miss Copper-Penny, so how it is that you never seem to be able to manage the simplest of tasks?" He paused for breath and then sniped cruelly, "It's a pity you are not as efficient at work as you are in my bedroom! I demand that you get him on the phone, right now, and I don't want any more of your pathetic excuses."

"HE'S NOT IN THE OFFICE, DRILL," she cried.

"WELL, WHERE THE HELL IS HE THEN?"

"He's on a train," she said between sobs. "The Horny-Mental Express, going somewhere on holiday!"

"Well buy the fookin' train, then!" he spat out furiously. "Just get me that meeting and get it NOW!"

"I tell you what, Mr high and mighty," she wailed, the tears streaming down her cheeks, "arrange your own meetings from now on! I am done with you and your impossible orders, not to mention your insatiable rumpy drive. Go and find some other shmuck to do your dirty work. And don't come banging on my door for any more nookie, okay? Because that's off-limits now, FOREVER!"

She threw down her planner and ripped off her name badge. She was so upset, her wings refused to work, and they flapped limply behind her in total disarray. With a stifled cry, she turned on her heel and ran out of the hangar.

"Oh, great!" Drillian said, pushing a hand through his thick dark brown hair. "What now?" He glanced around at the other members of the group who were all looking at their feet in embarrassed silence. None of them could do the job, he thought irritably, they were all hopeless and pitiable. He cast his eyes around the reception and then in the direction of the hangar. At that moment, he saw Spellbound sitting open-mouthed on the back of her bat.

"Hey, you ... Fairy girl!" he shouted, pointing at Spellbound. She looked behind her and then back at Drillian before finally pointing her tiny manicured finger to her chest and mouthing the words, "Who ... me?"

"Yes, yes, you," he replied impatiently. "Get down from that dratted bat and come here. Let me take a look at you." Spellbound gulped and looked towards Mike, who was wondering what Drillian was going to do next.

"Better do as he says, Spelly," he warned under his breath, "Don't wanna piss off the big boss man now, do you?"

Spellbound slid clumsily down the colossal bat and quickly made her way towards Drillian. He stood a good centimetre taller than her, making her feel a little intimidated. He walked around her in a circle, eyeing her from top to toe and then a cynical smile touched his lips. "You have the exact ingredients that I need," he said, with his arms folded. "But tell me, you look a little familiar, have we met before? I seem to remember you from somewhere, now where was it?" He scratched his designer stubble thoughtfully and turned to face her. "Have we had rumpy-pumpy somewhere?" Spellbound glared at him furiously and hissed.

"WITH YOU! ... you must be joking!" she said, stifling a sarcastic laugh. "I wouldn't give you a second look buddy boy! If I remember rightly, you were cavorting with my friend Pumpkin. She introduced us only a few days ago; you obviously have a huge ego and a bad memory."

Surprisingly, he ignored her sarcastic comments. "Of course, I recall it now, how could I have forgotten? You deliberately sat on your hand, didn't you?" He raised his eyes to the heavens and laughed deeply. "You're not quite like all the others, are you?" he chided. "Well, well, never mind that now. I need a new PA ... pronto and ... you're it, so go home, get out of those jeans, make yourself look presentable and be back here in an hour."

He turned to leave but then stopped suddenly and glanced over his shoulder. "Oh, and what did you say your name was? I'll need to have you badged up and cleared for security?" She glared at him.

Pompous git, he couldn't even remember her name. She gave him a steely look.

"My name is Miss Zamforia," she said in her snootiest voice. Drillian whistled through his teeth and turned back to face her.

"What, *the* Zamforian daughter? And your mother, of course, is the Fairy, psychic sorceress that everyone talks about, isn't she? Don't make her angry and stay well out of her way, that's what the local gossips say. Great ... we only want the best employees for Molars Inc. and we like the finest, pedigree families. You'll be a real feather in our Elfin bonnets."

He held her gaze for a moment and then gave her a sexy wink before striding out of the hangar towards his offices, his adoring entourage following at his heels. Spellbound watched his departure, for once, totally speechless!

Mike nudged her, "Better do as he says Spell. At least you'll get a fantastic wage stwaight away and your vewy own top of the wange Damselfly. Blinding, hey, hey!"

She suddenly felt a little tingle of excitement in her tummy as she realized with relief that there were *no more spiders*! It might not be so bad, she thought, to be earning some real cash for a change and of course, her Mamma would be over the moon to hear she had got promoted. She'd be on the spell phone to all her Fairy cronies, who would praise her glowingly. And of course, there was another upside. She wouldn't have to tell Leticia where she was all of the time. Yeah, she was really going to enjoy this adventure. But just let that big-headed twaddle-fart try any funny business and she would zap that ever so famous todger of his into a gnat's knob, as quick as a flash. Boss or no boss!

Spellbound whizzed into Broomsticks in a gust of wind. Leticia's eyebrows disappeared into her thick fringe.

"Spellbound! You frightened me to death, what's the hurry, child?"

"Mamma ... you are going to be so pleased with me, really you are," she said, all out of breath. I have just got a new job as ... wait for it ... Drillian Macavity's PA!" She started jumping up out down in total excitement. "I have to be back at base in," she peered closely at her Tumex watch, "gawd, in thirty minutes!" Leticia fluttered to her feet.

"WHAT!" she screeched.

Spellbound was halfway up the stairs. "He says I must wear something more appropriate. Ditch the jeans and all that!"

Her mother raced up the stairs after her and before Spellbound could get through the bedroom door, she had flicked her wand and changed Spellbound's outfit into a formal, cream pencil skirt and matching blouse. Leticia began fanning herself with the back of her hand.

"Now, sit down, just for a second and tell me all about it."

Quickly, Spellbound related the whole story and Leticia clasped her hands together delightedly.

"Do you realize you have just got one of the most desirable jobs in this realm? You clever, clever fae! You're so like your Mamma; you really are darling. I can't wait to tell the girls at the Fairy Fraternity, they'll be so envious! Now, dear," she lowered her voice to a dramatic whisper as she leant forward, "just one thing. I have heard through the grapevine of Drillian Macavity's reputation, so be very careful. He's more dangerous than any of those Widder spiders you've encountered. He rumpy-pumps anything that's not nailed down."

Spellbound was hunting around for her favourite silver hair clip.

"Don't worry, Mamma, I'm not interested in him anyway. He's a big-headed pulluck, with far too much dosh for his own good. If he were the only living Elf in the whole of the realm, I wouldn't consider him."

Leticia breathed a sigh of relief. The last thing she wanted was her daughter being a notch on that Elf man's bedpost. There were too many others on it already!

Spellbound's office was somewhat superior in comparison to all the others in the company; but then when you were the PA to the boss's son, you wouldn't expect anything less. She had sped back to Molars Inc. to seek out Drillian, but one of his entourage had said he was in a meeting and showed her to her new desk.

"I'm sure he'll call you when he needs you," the slim little Fairy had said to her. As she sat there waiting, she wondered if she should file her nails or something, but Drillian might not approve. No, she would just stay here and twiddle her thumbs and await his instruction.

As if he had read her thoughts, his voice came out of the speaker-phone, in front of her.

"Can you come in here, please?" he said. "Pronto!"

Darting towards his office door, she went straight in without knocking. She screeched to a halt as she saw the scene in front of her and blushed a furious crimson.

There, sprawled on the large mahogany desk, lay a half-naked, blonde-haired fairy, looking all flushed and dreamy-eyed while Drillian, who had obviously been giving the Fairy an excellent seeing to, was quickly adjusting his attire.

"Pop off and find Delilah a cigarette, would you girly, and make sure it's a Camel; that's the only brand she likes," he drawled lazily.

Delilah smiled sweetly at Spellbound and mouthed a snooty thank you, as she adjusted the strap on her Hairmarni top. Spellbound was gobsmacked. Find a fookin' cigarette? So, this is what her job would entail. Mopping up, after he had had his wicked way with all these stupid Fairies. What a creep, what a shit 'ed, what a grunt-futtock, she fumed silently.

"Oh, and empty this bin would you, on the way out." He paused for a second, looking confused. "Sorry, what did you say your first name was again?" Spellbound walked over to retrieve the bin and as she bent down to pick it up, he trailed his fingers down her back.

"Excuse me!" she shouted, "get yer grubby hands off me! I'm not one of your floozy Fairies that'll drop at yer feet, Macavity!"

"Drill," he spoke quietly. "Call me Drill." Spellbound tossed her head in the air and looked up at him disdainfully.

"I shall empty your bin and I will find a cigarette for your … friend here, but listen carefully, I will not be Elf handled, do you hear? If you so much as lay another finger on me, I swear I'll wear your mushrooms for earrings. Got it?"

Delilah stifled a giggle, whilst Drillian looked askance at Spellbound. What a little spitfire and so cute with it, he thought, a real little firefly if ever he saw one. He'd never met a Fairy who wasn't interested in him before. Totally unique, utterly brilliant, how very refreshing, he mused! Mmm, it would be nice to have a challenge to see how long it would take him to bed her. Spellbound stomped out with the bin under her arm and handed it to one of the office juniors.

"Anyone smoke Camels here?" she asked irritably, as her eyes scanned the room. A trendy Elf man who was in charge of admin, took one out of his jacket pocket and handed it to her with a cheesy smile.

"Wanna light, gorgeous?" he said, and raised one eyebrow lasciviously.

"No, it's not for me dick head, it's for Macavity's latest conquest!" He nodded his head and then laughed heartily.

"You'll get used to him and his ways … he's not a bad boss really."

Taking the cigarette from him, she held it well away from her, crinkling her nose in disgust.

Back in the office, it was handed over to Drillian who passed it to Delilah.

"Thank you … umm … what did you say your first name was?"

She glared at him before she spoke. "I've just told you. You can call me Miss Zamforia, my first name needn't bother you. Now, what are my duties because I am ready to get started?"

He lifted Delilah to her feet and gave her backside a little slap.

"Off you go butterfly. I'll call you later." She gave him a goofy smile as she disappeared around the door, taking her nauseating cigarette with her.

Spellbound stood silently in front of Drillian's desk, her wings as stiff and pert as her facial expression, one hand on each hip.

"What's with the look?" Drillian said, with half a smile.

"You wouldn't wanna know," she replied snootily.

"Nah, come on," he said mischievously. "If you've got a beef with me, you might like to tell me now, rather than later."

"These silly Fairies, they must be so stupid to fawn over an Elf in such a way." She lifted her chin and proceeded to look down her nose at him.

"Well, all Fairies enjoy a bit of slap and tickle. Don't tell me you haven't had your moments?"

"We are not here to discuss my rumpy drive".

"I bet you have all the Elves and Pixies chasing after you, being so attractive and all!"

"Of course, but I have no intention of indulging in any kind of slap and tickle, as you so crudely put it ... not till I'm married anyway." She was becoming bored with the third degree and turned her head to glance curiously around his office.

Drillian leaned back in his chair and placed his hands behind his head.

"How very intriguing," he said with a glint in his eye. "I can't say I have ever met anyone who wasn't into the carnal pleasures before wedlock." Spellbound looked at him scornfully.

"Okay, so this job you forced me into, what would you like me to do?" she snapped.

"Well, I'd like you to tell me why you are so averse to a little bit of hanky spanky?" he replied in an amused manner. Spellbound counted to ten in her head, trying desperately to control her temper.

"Is this really appropriate, asking me all these personal questions on my first day? "

"Yeah, it is!" he said lazily. "Like I said, I'm intrigued!"

"Well, not that is it any of your business but I, like my mother, possess my Aunt Hester's genes," she said arrogantly. "The family line always waits until true love comes, before giving themselves freely so now you know. Could you please tell me my duties so that I can get on with my job and forget all this stupid sex talk?"

He lifted his black eyebrows and smiled a dazzling smile, "So, tell me, I am curious ... who is this Hester?" Spellbound was getting more frustrated by the minute but paused for a moment and collected her thoughts. He was after all to be her boss.

"Hester is a great aunt of mine and has a Victorian outlook on life. 'No rumpy-pumpy before marriage' is her motto, just like her grandmother and the one before her. We can't change our genetic makeup, and so we're just not interested, it's as simple as that, so please, no more pestering or I'll scream ... leave me alone and go and have your hanky-spanky sessions with one of your Fairy fans. Got it?"

"And have you ever been in love?" he persisted stubbornly, looking deeply into her incredible green eyes.

"WHY are you constantly asking me these personal questions?" Sighing, he admitted defeat, as he walked over to her.

"You may have heard of my Northern branch in Toncaster? We'll be going away for approximately six days. We are already booked in at The Glitteritz. I have a whole floor at my disposal, at all times. You'll have your own suite of rooms and," he stopped suddenly, "I've just remembered your name ... it's Spellbound!" he smiled as if he was rather pleased with himself. "We're leaving tomorrow so ..."

"TOMORROW?" she shrieked with surprise. "I must go tell Mamma and I need to get her to zap me some clothes as well," she babbled quietly to herself.

"By all means, ask your Mamma but don't worry about clothes. The hotel has an excellent shopping mall and I have your store cards ready; just charge whatever you need to the company."

Spellbound gulped. Fookin' hell, she thought. What a job! She nodded, swiftly turned and disappeared in a flurry of silver stars. She couldn't believe how her life was about to change!

CHAPTER 8
MOONFLOWER

Spellbound slept in the darkness, tucked up safely under gossamer layers of lavender-scented covers. It had taken her some time to drift off, as she just couldn't get her beloved father out of her thoughts. His absence in her life had begun to seriously affect her, and the sharp pangs of grief she felt every time she thought of him, were becoming unbearable. Her only welcome distraction was the thought of travelling to Toncaster the following morning.

She was dozing in and out of restless sleep when suddenly, she became aware that she was rising towards the ceiling of her bedchamber. She was a little frightened, not knowing whether she was asleep, awake or levitating but the feeling was so pleasant, that she surrendered herself to it and floated into soft weightlessness.

As Spellbound continued to soar, she glanced down at her slumbering body in the bed. Then in a split second, she was ricocheted outside of the cottage, whizzing in and out through the trees in the forest, darting and flitting so much quicker than she could ordinarily fly. The night breeze was on her face, but at the same time, she knew instinctively that she was still tucked up in bed. "This must be what they call astral travel," she gasped and was not allowed in the fae realms, until one was much older. Spellbound spiralled higher and faster, as if some form of magical power was controlling her every movement. Her heart was beating faster than a bee's wings. Without warning, she was rocketed into space and then her astral body was plunged into a pink, Fairy paradise, surrounded by rosy candy floss clouds and lime green shooting stars.

Stopping abruptly, she gazed down at her arms and discovered she still had no physical body. All she could see was the transparent form of her fae self, encircled in a golden light.

"Oh, fookin' hell!" she swore silently. "Where am I? Have I died and gone to heaven?" As if someone was reading her mind, a gentle, musical voice answered her.

"Ah, Spellbound! You've finally arrived dear. And I can safely say that you are not dead."

Spellbound whipped around to see where the voice was coming from but there was no one there.

"Who's there? Where are you?"

Before her eyes, a glorious vision began to unfold. Tiny sparkles of silver orbs appeared in a flurry of purple light and within the image, were glittering beams of gold that raced upwards in a mystical whirlwind. A stunning Fairy Goddess appeared before her. Her hair was the colour of wheat, with eyes of sparkling blue and her sweet rosebud mouth was smiling tenderly. To complete this wondrous vision, a pair of magnificent wings started to appear from behind the female being. They were like nothing Spellbound had ever seen before, huge feathered extensions that oscillated translucent light, changing colour every few seconds.

"Wow!" said Spellbound, completely taken aback. "Who are you? And more to the point, why am I here?" The Fairy being smiled again and turned to face her.

"I am Moonflower," her voice tinkled, "and in your realms, I suppose I would be referred to as your Godmother." Spellbound looked on in awe. "I have been assigned to you since the moment of your birth as your spirit guardian, always watching, always protecting."

Leticia had told her that there were such things as Fairy Godmothers, but many folks thought that they were just a myth. These legendary entities were known to be above any other and their magic was so incredible that no Fairy, Witch, Wizard or Warlock could influence the power they had. Spellbound fidgeted nervously.

"I have summoned you here, Spellbound, for a very special reason. We are all concerned about your safety." Spellbound was only half-listening, as she was captivated by her surroundings and still in disbelief as to what was taking place.

"You are presently entering into a very negative phase. We call it the 'yearning', dear."

"The yearning?" Spellbound repeated anxiously. "What is it and why do I have it?"

"We have noticed that you have been missing your father very much and it is getting worse each day." Spellbound nodded.

"Yes, I miss Papa terribly," she whispered, forlornly.

"Three years ago, when he went away, your mother cast a power-ful spell on you dear, to stop you from missing him. We don't fully understand why she did it but alas, the magic is wearing off and it is not possible to repeat such a mind-altering spell. If your yearning starts to get out of control, the Feathered Ones of this realm fear that your magic will vanish."

"VANISH!" she half shrieked. Suddenly Spellbound began to realize the seriousness of her Godmother's words. It was common knowledge that if a Fairy lost her powers, then her wings would disappear and her fae form would fast turn into a golden hare. She gulped again, she didn't want to end up eating fookin' grass all her life and being bonked senseless by them humpy, rumpy bunnies. And if that happened, she would have to learn to box when it was the full moon and then she'd be called a fookin' mad March hare ... and have endless baby leverets. Her thoughts started to race out of control.

Spellbound finally gathered her senses and cleared her throat.

Moonflower sighed and smiled compassionately at her charge, changing her tone to one of kind authority.

"Spellbound, it's imperative that you find your father. It is so important that you should focus on nothing else. We here in the

Spirit realm can usually locate those who are missing but we feel his whereabouts is somehow cloaked in magic."

"I knew something was wrong," Spellbound said desperately. "I had a really big fight with Mamma about it recently, but she wouldn't listen to me. Why would he be hidden, and who would hide him? I don't understand!"

"That, we don't know," Moonflower replied, "but if your yearning progresses further, you will be transformed into a hare and once that happens, there is nothing we can do about it. Your mission now is to find him and quickly!"

"I have no idea where to start looking and my magic isn't that great either if you haven't already noticed! Last week I tried to cast a spell to find my flute and everything went terribly wrong. It ended up in a field full of fox shit! The ritual didn't work and before I knew it, I had burnt out yet another wand and …"

Spellbound was silenced. In her hands, Moonflower held a glowing, tiny white orb. Gently, she let go of the sparkling ball of light and it slowly levitated towards Spellbound, dropping into her outstretched hands.

"Go to Clifford Eyesaurus. He is the key. You need to give him what he wants. He knows exactly where your father is, so use this magical orb to get him his heart's desire. We hope that in turn, he will tell you where your Papa is!"

Moonflower's image slowly disappeared and suddenly Spellbound was seated bolt upright in bed. "What a fookin' dream that was!" she said out loud, rubbing her eyes in disbelief. She moved her body sideways to lie back down and just as she did, she felt a small round bulge in the bedsheets. Uncovering it, she saw the orb, still as bright and luminous as ever. Carefully, she placed it in the drawer of her nightstand and without another thought, she determinedly slipped out of bed and went down the big oak stairs, into the kitchen. There on the rustic table sat Clifford's glass ball, covered in the usual piece of purple cloth. She sped over to him and removed the fabric.

"Clifford, wake up, wake up! I need to talk to you NOW," she whispered loudly.

Clifford's eye appeared suddenly, after being jolted out of his sleep. He blinked several times and then glanced upwards when he saw Spellbound's nose pressed hard on to the glass.

"It's the middle of the night!" he said. "Go back to bed, child; can't you see I am trying to sleep."

"Never mind that now," she replied impatiently. "You know where my Papa is and I am not going anywhere until you tell me EXACTLY what you did with him."

"What I did with him?" he spat out irritably. "Now listen here, Spellbound, I have had no truck with your father. His whereabouts are nothing to do with me whatsoever. Go to bed and leave me in peace before you wake up your mother."

"I was summoned to my Godmother tonight, Clifford, and she told me that you DO know where my Papa is, she said you were the key. Now tell me before I throw you and your glass fookin' ball into the lily pond!"

Clifford's eye squinted. "Your Godmother, eh?" he said quietly. "Don't be silly Spellbound, you were probably dreaming. It's impossible to be summoned by a Godmother, it's a known fact that they never visit the earthly realms."

"Well, I beg to differ Clifford. I was summoned to travel to *her* in the astral. She is called Moonflower and said I was in danger of going into something called the yearning and if I didn't find my Papa, my Fairy magic would disappear and I could turn into a fookin' golden hare - and if I do, Clifford, it will be YOUR fault entirely!" Spellbound's fury turned into desperation and just as Clifford was going to answer, Leticia came storming down the stairs in a fit of rage, her white satin nightgown billowing around her.

"What is all the blewdy commotion about? And why the hell are you talking to Clifford at three in the morning, Spellbound? You know Clifford is out of bounds after 7 p.m. Get back to bed this instant and stop stomping around the house in the dead of night." In a flurry, Leticia threw the purple velvet cloth back over Clifford.

"Goodnight, Clifford dear, I am so sorry Spellbound has disturbed you."

"But Mamma …"

"Now, Spellbound, I have a heavy day of writing tomorrow and my deadline is Friday. If I don't get this blewdy book finished, we will all be done, done, done! And I will have to keep spelling for our food and as you know very well … spell food doesn't fill you up! Now get to bed and do as I say. RIGHT NOW!"

It was no good, thought Spellbound. There was no talking to her when she was in one of her moods. She would just have to try to speak to Clifford tomorrow before she left for Toncaster and in the meantime, she would think about how she could make the silly one-eyed Cyclops spill the beans.

Once her daughter was out of sight, Leticia looked around cautiously and removed the cloth from Clifford.

"What was all that about?" she whispered. "Why in heavens name was she down here half screaming at you, Clifford?"

"You really don't want to know!" he replied in a defeated manner. "You had seriously better watch your back, Leticia. The Feathered Ones are on to you. I believe your clever daughter went astral travelling tonight, summoned apparently by her Godmother who happens to be called Moonflower. She informed her that I am the one who knows where her father is and I fear she will not relent until someone tells her the truth!"

"Oh, fookin' lordy lord, Clifford. Lordy, fookin' lord!! Not the Feathered Ones! What are we to do?" Leticia was raking her dainty hands through her mass of untamed, dark curls. "I can't believe that she has met her Godmother; no one gets to meet their Godmother!" Leticia was frantic. "I have never ever in my life met mine and Spellbound is so young. How can one so young meet her Godmother, Clifford … how?" Clifford was just about to respond when she continued with her babbling.

"Maybe Spellbound is to be as powerful as me someday," she said. "Maybe even more so! Well, listen here, you must not breathe a word to her, is that clear Clifford? Not a word! If she ever finds out, I shall know it was you who told her and …"

"But Leticia …"

"No, I mean it, Clifford. This will all blow over, you'll see." She bent over to retrieve the velvet cloth.

"There's one more crucial thing, Milady."

"Not another word, Clifford. No excuses!"

"But Leticia …!"

It was too late. She had covered him up and was fluttering back up the stairs. Somehow, he had to tell her about the yearning and the danger Spellbound was in, but how? Oh, what a mess she had got them all into, he thought despairingly.

CHAPTER 9
TONCASTER

Spellbound was secretly excited; she had never been in a Swirlybird before. As they started their journey to Toncaster, the vehicle rose high above the trees, she could actually see the roof of Broomsticks Cottage. Leticia, who was slightly concerned that her daughter would be staying away for six whole days with a sexy rogue like Drillian, had flown over to him before they left, to give him harsh words of warning.

Drillian was lazily snoozing in the Swirlybird outside of the cottage, while Spellbound collected together the last of her bits and pieces. He half-heartedly shouted down to Leticia that they would be arriving in Toncaster within the hour. She flitted up to the Swirlybird gracefully, wand in hand, and eyed him sternly.

"You will take care of my fae now, won't you?" she said with an acid smile. "Remember she is a Zamforian Fairy so no blewdy shenanigans." She waved her wand in a slightly menacing way.

Drillian looked up through his half-closed eyelids and nonchalantly nodded his head. He wondered if the rumours about Leticia Zamforia were real and if she could really turn Fairies into slugs. He decided it was all gossip.

Spellbound was gazing out of the window. With all the fuss her mother had been making about the trip, she hadn't been able to get Clifford to one side to question him. It would just have to wait until she got back and hopefully, the nagging pain in her heart would subside a little. Spellbound was still lost in her yearning when Drillian interrupted her thoughts.

"So, have you ever had a crush on anyone Spellbound?" he said flashing her a sexy smile. For a second, she thought she had never seen such perfect white teeth. But then, being the son of the owner of Molars Inc, didn't that come with the territory?

"No Pixies or Elves tickled your fancy?" He chuckled a little. "Or is it Gnomes and Trolls you're into?"

Spellbound sighed as she gave him a withering look. She really didn't want to share any of her secrets with this idiot.

"Here we friggin' go again. You've certainly got a one-track mind, boring, boring, boring!"

"Aww, come on, Spellbound," he said in a low drawl, "spill the beans, I'm your boss now and I should really know a bit more about you."

"That's my private life and it has nothing at all to do with my work. You wouldn't want me asking about your love life now, would you?"

"Ask away, sweet Fairy. Anything you like. I don't mind."

"Everyone knows about your fooking love life. It's the constant gossip of Bluebell Forest. I even know how big your todger is, as does everybody else! Now what do you want me to do when we get to Toncaster and what will my duties be?"

He sighed and shrugged his shoulders irritably before replying.

"Make sure my life runs like clockwork. Handle the female Fairies and whatever you do, don't get their times and dates mixed up. Be charming to my clients and see to their every need; the usual PA stuff. You'll soon pick it up."

Suddenly he stretched over and grabbed her hand and within a flash, pulled her swiftly onto his lap.

"Now, how about a nice little kiss? We've got nearly an hour to kill until we reach our destination."

Spellbound looked into his brown eyes, which had suddenly become very dreamy. For a second, she was drawn into their depths. Did this Elf have some sort of magic charm? She mentally shook herself and without warning, boxed him hard around his ears, making them ring like a chamber of church bells.

"Are you thick … I mean … are you really, really fookin' thick? I've made it very clear that I am not in the slightest bit interested in you and whether you believe it or not, you don't do a thing to turn me on. I'll tell you this, Mr snog everyone's face-off. When we get to Toncaster I will be flying the fastest bee out of there and you can get yourself another PA to mess around with!" He was genuinely shocked and looked at her in total amazement.

"Okay …okay, I give in. You win Fairy; from here on in, I'll behave myself. I've got the message. It's a first for me but hey ho, I'll live." He rubbed his sore head and felt his left ear begin to swell.

She glared at him sullenly as she slid back into her seat.

"But don't go buzzing off on some bee, Spellbound," he said a little more humbly. "It's a good job at Molars, with fantastic pay and as much as I hate to say, it's kinda nice having you around."

Spellbound glared at him again.

"Can't we at least be friends?" He held his hand out and she reluctantly placed her small hand in his. "Friends?"

She nodded warily and then deliberately looked out of the window, remaining silent for the rest of the journey.

The hotel was fantastic, just like an ice palace. The colours were themed in pale peach and lime green and there were fabulously attired major-domos, stationed on every floor. With a click of a finger, they were known to give the best service around. Drillian and Spellbound sped to the top of the hotel in a crystal lift, illuminated with the newest whizz-wave lighting. As they walked along the vast, softly lit corridor, Drillian stopped at his door.

"Well, this is me. You have to tap your door three times for it to open," he said, pointing to the door opposite his. He handed her a small laptop. "Give the fairies a call for tonight, just four will do, and tell them to meet me in the sauna on the fifth floor. You'll find their names in the file marked *Totty*."

Spellbound looked around her impressive room, she'd never been somewhere so luxurious. The bed was a four-poster, with white satin coverlets and lace drapes. She peered through an open door into the bathroom and saw a sunken bath, already full to the brim, with sweet-smelling aromas rising from the steam. There was a huge plasma screen TV and soft cream rugs beneath her feet. This job certainly had some wonderful perks, she cooed with pleasure and then undressed and sank down into the perfumed bubble bath. Bliss, utter bliss!

All the commotion the night before, as well as the trip this morning, must have completely exhausted her because her soak in the hot, fragrant bath, made her fall asleep instantly. She was drifting in and out of peaceful slumber when she was rudely awakened by a loud ringing object, which was dancing over her nose and saying, *"Please answer your spell phone."* She grabbed it quickly and saw Drillian's name on the screen. Swiping it right, she suddenly realised that she was face timing with him.

"Oh, jeez, are you in the tub?" he said, grinning from ear to ear. She quickly sunk further down into the water, relieved that the mass of bubbles was protecting her modesty.

"Yeah, yeah, very funny!" she said sarcastically. "What do you want?"

"Have you been in touch with the girlies yet?"

"I've nearly finished rounding them up," she lied convincingly.

"Okay well, tell them 8.30 p.m. and not a minute before. I'll be busy with the maid until then. So, are you gonna get out of the bath then?"

Spellbound rolled her eyes and silently mouthed to him, *"Fook off,"* as she ended the call. Reluctantly, she hopped out of the bath, wrapped a rose-scented towel around her body and raced to the computer, her wings limp and dripping water everywhere. She would try to spell the puddles away later with her new wand. She clicked on the file, *Totty* and a hundred or more names were organised into alphabetical columns. She quickly looked through the list and left a message for Barbie Beaver, Sally Slapper and Lexa Kimbo. With only one more Totty to arrange, she scanned the list and saw a transgender Elf called, Walter Surprise and wondered whether she should give him a call. "Yeah why not? That'll give the boss man a big shock!" she chuckled to herself. They all confirmed that they would come to the hotel, so she sat back in her chair and breathed a sigh of relief.

Sometime later she was just about to snuggle down to sleep when her spell-phone hovered in front of her face again.

"Spellbound, could you go into my room and get my robe, body rub and a large tube of lube? Bring them up to the sauna with the Frisky Whisky, you'll find that in the drinks cabinet." "It's my own brand," he added arrogantly. "I can't stand anything but the best." Once again, the phone went dead.

Five minutes later, she was outside the sauna doors with everything he'd requested. She braced herself before going in, quite prepared to shut her eyes quickly if necessary. He was standing in the middle of the pool, like a Greek god, waist-high in lavender-scented bubbles, three naked Fairies draping themselves all over him. Suddenly a head bobbed up from under the water. Walter Surprise glanced across at Spellbound and winked before taking a deep breath and ducking down again.

Spellbound, having never witnessed passion first-hand, placed the robe, lube, body rub and whisky on an ornate table and tried to slip out unnoticed.

"Filthy grunt-funking pullock!" She hissed under her breath.

"Thanks, Spellbound. You can have the rest of the night off."

"Pervy git," she snorted in disgust.

"I heard that!" he retorted.

She had been given instructions to arrive promptly at 9 a.m. the next day and wait outside his room. At the exact time, the door flew open and the three Fairies trailed out. Drillian smacked each one of them on the botty but Walter was nowhere to be seen.

Spellbound was propped up against the wall in the corridor, examining her nails nonchalantly, a smirk on her face. When everyone was out of earshot, Drillian stormed over to her side.

"I should fire you for that!" he expostulated. "Why did you send a fookin' Elf to the sauna. I thought he was a *she!* The totties didn't stop laughing all night long and I couldn't get him to leave!"

"Well, to be fair he was on your totty list, how was I to know you didn't swing both ways?"

"Don't ever call him again, do you hear? He was completely over the top and wouldn't take no for an answer. I had to pay him off and then call security to get rid of him!"

"Okay … okay, calm down it was just crossed wires, I'll strike him off the list right away. Look, I'm starving so let's go and eat." Throwing her tote bag over her shoulder, she sauntered down the hall, suppressing her laughter as she went.

Over breakfast, Drillian took a deep breath and his face softened as he attempted to engage her in conversation.

"Anyway, do you like your room, is everything okay?" She nodded absently and bit delicately into a turdy burger.

"Yeah, fantastic thanks. Talk about being spoilt; the room's a dream."

He placed his napkin on his lap and smiled. "And did you sleep okay?" he asked kindly. Not looking up, Spellbound nodded again and proceeded to spread a thin layer of celandine butter on her toasty.

"I bet *you* didn't get much sleep though. Really Drill, talk about a male, bleedin' slut …" she teased humorously.

Drillian choked on his Fairy flakes and without having time to finish her sentence, she had to get up and smack him firmly between his shoulder blades. When he finally got his breath back, he was steaming with rage.

"Spellbound, I've had about enough of this. Just remember you are my employee and have some respect. From now on, how I conduct my life is none of your business. Do I make myself clear?"

"Conduct your life! I'd heard about you and your shenanigans," she sighed, "but I never thought for one minute to believe them." She stuffed the last of the turdy burger into her mouth and wiped the corners of her lips daintily on her napkin. "You seriously need to go and get some rumpy-pumpy counselling. They say Carmella Cackle Juice is a brilliant therapist!"

He stood up angrily and threw his napkin on the table.

"For your information, I don't need any shrink poking around in my head. You really are the most inflexible and difficult female I have ever come across, you're impossible! Maybe it was a big mistake hiring you!"

As he turned to walk away, she glanced up frostily. "Your choice stud … who cares a gnat's fart anyway!" Leaning over she picked up his untouched toasty and shoved it into her mouth.

The rest of the week passed very quickly, with Spellbound rushing about, responding to Drillian's every command. Each night he had another succession of Fairies in and out of his suite, and the more she saw, the more she realised that males, whichever form they appeared in, were definitely off the agenda. On three occasions, he had tried hard to win her over by taking her for a nice meal and then suggesting that she cancel his female entertainment for the night and join him instead. Spellbound had given him a pitiful look and told him in no uncertain terms to go fook himself.

Leticia had been on the spell phone every day, checking to see if she was okay and to be honest, by the fourth day Spellbound was beginning to miss her. The only consolation was that while Drillian was busy with his Fairies and his meetings, she got to trawl around endless boutiques and buy some of the most fantastic clothes, without ever having to look at the price. One dress appealed to her so much that she bought it in six different colours.

As she showed up for work that evening, Drillian's eyes nearly popped clear out of his head when he observed his sexy little PA in a pale saffron, low cut mini dress, edged with real gold thread and wearing matching killer-heeled shoes. She seriously had to ditch the twinkly frocks, she thought to herself. When dressed to kill, she felt so empowered. This was the only way forward for her and deep down as much as she disliked the smarmy, sex-crazed boss man, she was secretly pleased that she had got his attention.

The journey home proved to be long and tedious. Drillian spent the entire time on the phone with a clingy Fairy who wouldn't take no for an answer. He was fast becoming impatient and in no uncertain terms told her not to call again. When he finally did get off the phone, he was in a sour mood. "Why didn't you make it clear to her that it was just a one-off?" Spellbound glared at him from across the cream leather interior of the Swirlybird.

"You know damn well I hate that sort of pressure from Fairies," he went on. "And being my PA, it is your job to see to it that I don't get hangers-on."

It was true. Spellbound's job was to make sure that no one got hold of Drillian's personal number and stupidly, she had left his private business cards lying around while she went down to breakfast that morning. The loved-up Fairy must have sneakily picked one up on the way out of his bedroom.

"Oh, Drillian, maybe you shouldn't be such a lothario," Spellbound said yawning.

She stretched her arms above her head and then rubbed her nose a few times, something she always did when tired or bored.

"You are paid to make sure that ALL my needs are met," he said irritably.

"Ha! Not all, Drill, just remember that"

Drillian eyed her curiously. Was she seriously trying her best to remind him yet again that she wasn't the least bit interested in him? It was only a matter of time, he mused, as he turned away and rested his head on the window, falling asleep for the rest of the journey.

CHAPTER 10
SPARKLESHIRE HALL

Eddie was extremely excited. It had been three long weeks since he had seen Spellbound at Broomsticks Cottage and tonight, his mother the Duchess was returning the compliment. She had invited Leticia and Spellbound for supper. Spellbound had been so busy with her toofy job at Molars Inc. that she had found it easy to avoid him, but tonight there would be absolutely no way she could dodge him. He planned on setting the scene and having her all to himself!

As he stood in front of the full-length mirror in his luxury, oak-beamed bedroom, he admired his appearance. Turning to the left, he stuck out his chest and squirted some 'Minty Mouf' spray to the back of his throat, and then he carefully ran his fingers through the thick mass of golden curls which framed his handsome face. Eddie gave himself a winning grin and blew a kiss at the mirror. Then, with great care and concentration and 'come to bed' eyes, he proceeded to snog the back of his hand with ardour, whilst keeping one eye firmly fixed on his reflection.

"Mmm, you're definitely the biz, Eddie!" he said out loud. "Spelly is gonna be blown away tonight, man, blown away!"

"Edward," the Duchess shouted. "Edward, come down, dear. Our guests are expected in less than ten minutes and your father would like a word with you before they arrive."

Eddie stopped snogging his hand and grimaced. "Choofin' ell," he whispered. "Talk about bad timing."

"Edward dear, get yourself down here, NOW PLEASE!"

"COMING MOTHER," he yelled back sweetly, leaping onto the swirling walnut bannister, and sliding down to the bottom of the staircase in a flourish.

"Oh, I wish you wouldn't do that, Edward. The cleaners do complain so when you put your dirty feet all over the woodwork, dear, and it makes the seat of your trousers shiny."

"Sorry," Eddie said with a twinkle in his eye. "Just being an Elfboy an' all!"

"Mmm, well, off you go into the parlour. Your Papa is waiting, and I must say, dear," she said in a proud voice, "you look positively dashing tonight. Have you made an extra effort because the lovely Miss Spellbound is joining us?" She affectionately patted his shoulder. "Oh, and one more thing, please be polite tonight. We don't want a repeat performance of what we had at Broomsticks Cottage, now, do we? Spellbound is to inherit a huge fortune when she's older and already owns the Toofy Pegs dinner set. You won't find a finer nor richer Fairy in all the realms. Her Mamma and I would really like you two to get together. So, no leering, dear." Eddie nodded while his mother lifted a stray hair away from his eyes. "and remember, it is common knowledge that she has her Aunt Hester's genes and will not be wooed with lewdness." Eddie had the grace to look a little ashamed but then scooted off down the long corridor which led to the parlour. He glanced back over his shoulder and chuckled.

"I'll be good Ma," he laughed.

Inside the parlour, the Duke of Sparkleshire stood with his hands behind his back, rocking backwards and forwards on his heels, facing the huge gold and silver fireplace. His presence was astounding. His neatly trimmed beard showed off regal features and his mop of golden hair was still as thick as it was when he had been Eddie's age.

"Pops!" said Eddie, as he sprinted into the parlour, slightly out of breath. "You wanna see me?"

The Duke turned around to face his son. His expression was serious, and his eyes showed a little apprehension, not something Eddie was used to seeing in his father.

"Son, I think it might be time to have that Elf to Elf talk. Have you ever heard of the 'birds and the fleas'?"

Eddie cast his mind back to the sweet-as-a-buttercup Fairy he had happily entertained the night before. Mmm, she was a real little corker, he thought to himself, but seeing his father's anxious expression, he just couldn't miss this for the world.

"No Pops, can't say I have", he replied innocently.

"Hellooooo, hellooooo," trilled Leticia. "How wonderful to be invited. Come along, Spellbound, and wipe your little feet, dear, on the fairy expensive mat." She smiled nervously. This was her first visit to Sparkleshire Hall and she really wanted to make a good impression.

"Esmee, dear," she enthused, as the Duchess greeted her with open arms. "I must say, Esmee, you look the picture of perfection."

"And you too, dear," came the reply. "Utterly sensational. I love your gown, Leticia, where did you get it? Or did you zap it up like the clever Fairy witch you are … ha-ha!" she joked.

Leticia handed Esmee a hand-wrapped box of Blake Magic chocolates from Elfredges. They tittered over the naughty treat like Fairies do!

Spellbound looked spectacular in a raspberry lace mini dress, with spaghetti shoulder straps. Her shoes were cute ruby and diamante pumps with killer heels in crystal. Leticia had tried to insist that she wear a gown for the occasion, but Spellbound, who had started to choose her own fashion, would not be persuaded. In the end, and after an afternoon of quarrelling, Leticia had given in and was quite shocked when she saw her beautiful daughter descend the staircase at Broomsticks Cottage, looking well-groomed and all grown up.

The Duchess escorted the two Fairies into the drawing-room and as Leticia looked around in wonderment at the sumptuous tapestried drapes and hand-carved furniture, Eddie sidled up to Spellbound from behind.

"Hi, Spelly," he whispered, so as not to let the adults hear.

"My word, you look the bizz tonight! I'm surprised your Ma let you dress like that ... jeez and just look at the bling; must have cost her a small fortune. Coo, Spell, I'm having all sorts of thoughts now, think I might be in love!" He giggled.

Spellbound turned around and shot him a look. "What is it with you, Eddie?" she asked in a half-whisper. "Can't you think of anything other than slushy stuff and romance? You really are start-ing to make me feel sick with all this mooning around. It's not cool, Eddie, really it's not!"

Eddie sported a cheesy grin then cast his eyes over to the corner of the room where his mother and Leticia were now seated.

"Oh, don't they make a sweet couple, Leticia dear?" said the Duchess as she smiled a sickly smile in the youngsters' direction.

"They certainly do, Esmee," Leticia replied. "I know they are young and getting used to one another, but I have high hopes, Esmee, high hopes!"

"I agree, dear, give them time and I am sure Spellbound will come to see that they are a perfect match. There couldn't be a finer Fairy for him, especially as her father is the great Marco Zamforia; and speaking of whom, when is your notable husband returning, dear? I'm dying to meet him."

Leticia coughed slightly and quickly changed the subject. "Was Eddie a good baby Elf, Esmee, did he cry much when he was in hankies?"

"Not a bit, dear, no, he was the perfect child. Look, I'll show you." The Duchess pulled a large book from under the side table and began to show her pictures of Eddie as a young Elf.

"Oh Spellbound, do come over and take a look at these won-derful pictures of Edward," Leticia called. Spellbound raced over to her mother's side - anything to get away from the dratted Elf and his mushy comments. As the Duchess turned the pages, images of Eddie with his little pointy ears and naked, Elfin body, lying on a fluffy rug made Spellbound choke with laughter.

"Haha," she gasped, "look at his winky dinky!" Tears streamed down her face as she laughed even harder. Leticia and the Duchess couldn't help but join in with Spellbound's infectious giggling until Eddie stormed across the room and glared at the trio.

"Really, you are seriously embarrassing me!" he screeched. "Whatcha doing showing everyone pictures of me Elfhood?"

"I beg your pardon, but your other guests have arrived Duchess," said the butler in a snooty voice as he entered the drawing-room.

"Oh, please excuse me, Leticia," Esmee said, as she got up from the chair and walked into the grand hall.

Leticia stopped laughing and looked at Spellbound, intrigued.

"Other guests?" she mouthed silently. "I wonder who they can be?"

She strained her neck to see if she could take a peek through the door, but the butler stood directly in the way and just smiled in her direction.

Eddie was somewhat red in the face, obviously still put out that his Elfin pictures had been the butt of their jokes.

"Would you like to follow me through to the dining hall?" the butler said to the two Zamforian fairies. "Dinner is about to be served."

The dining hall was a vision. A large, majestic table, which could seat forty guests, dominated the centre of the grand baronial room. The chairs were gold and upholstered in royal blue damask, with silver threads that were woven into a subtle pinstripe. Six candelabras, all lit with flashing ice blue flames, were placed an exact distance apart. Abalone handled knives and forks were positioned with precision and before each setting, was a silver goblet, embossed with an image of the Duke and Duchess.

"Please do come in and take a seat," Spellbound heard the Duchess say. "And I must introduce you to the Zamforian fairies. This is Leticia Zamforia and her daughter Spellbound Elspeth."

Spellbound and Leticia turned around in unison to face Philip and Drillian Macavity. Spellbound's eyes met Drillian's in surprise, as he casually strolled over to her. He confidently lifted her hand to his lips and gave it a warm kiss.

Just out of earshot, he whispered, "Nice to actually be allowed to kiss these hands for a change, Spell." She looked up at the ceiling and sighed and Leticia began to giggle nervously. Fookin' Philip Macavity! How was she going to get out of this little scenario, she wondered?

"It is quite all right, Duchess, you don't have to introduce us," said Drillian in a low husky voice. "Spellbound and I are already acquainted, aren't we, Spell?" He lifted his head from the kiss and smiled at her. "She kindly agreed to join the company as my new PA last week," he said, turning his attention back to his hostess. "She is doing remarkably well, considering." Once again, he looked intensely at Spellbound. "We've just returned from a week-long business trip in Toncaster, have we not?"

"Oh, that is wonderful, just wonderful," the Duchess gushed, clasping her hands together, "and what a fine assistant I am sure she will make. You didn't tell me about that, Leticia," she said, turning to her friend. "You must be so delighted for Spellbound to have such an important job. We were all thrilled that she had become a Tooth Fairy but to now be the PA to the boss's son is indeed a wonderful promotion!"

Eddie was standing in the doorway with his father. No one had told him Spellbound was personally working for Drillian Macavity! He grumbled to himself. Everyone knew he was a rumpy-pump maniac and could 'do' any Fairy he wanted!

Throughout dinner, Leticia observed Drillian closely. He was sitting opposite Spellbound at the dinner table, gazing at her intently the whole time. Oh, lordy lord, this Elf is a handful, she mused, wondering if he was the one, she had seen in the Tarot cards.

Philip was trying very hard to make polite conversation with her, but her thoughts were firmly fixed elsewhere. How was she going to protect her daughter's innocence from such a rake? If Spellbound couldn't handle him, she was going to have to do some severe spellcasting on her behalf; but then again, she breathed deeply to calm herself, she did have Aunt Hester's genes. Her daughter was still so young and naive. She might look all full-grown and mature with her long legs and fabulous dress sense, but she was still her faeby!

Leticia continued to watch Drillian as he expertly engaged Spellbound in conversation and fortunately, her daughter looked calm and even a little bored. Secretly she was pleased. Perhaps she could handle him; maybe she was a chip off the old block after all!

Eddie was red-faced and furious. His plans had been thwarted. He coughed and interrupted the hum of conversation. "Hey, Spelly, why don't ya come to the Fairy flicks with me tomorrow and we could go dancing afterwards?"

She looked up from her frogs' legs. "Thanks, but no thanks ... I've been away a week and I need to spend some time with my Mamma," she said, tossing her glossy red hair over her shoulder. Eddie looked downwards in disappointment.

Leticia was trying to listen to the conversation, but Philip Macavity was demanding her attention.

"Dearest Leticia, you look absolutely divine. It seems an age since we last met. When are we going to get together for that quiet, intimate little dinner you promised?"

Leticia was frantically searching for a reply when Drillian clipped in quietly, "Father, please don't embarrass Madam Zamforia in such a way and don't forget you are a married Elfman. Mother would be very hurt if you had dinner with someone else, who is married too, in case you had forgotten. I just can't believe you sometimes!"

Leticia breathed a little sigh of relief as Phillip started to hurriedly shovel food into his mouth, looking rather embarrassed. For a moment she could relax, she was off the hook.

Not to be thwarted, Eddie looked up from his plate. He could seize this opportunity to engage in adult conversation. He sat up boldly in his chair and addressed the older Macavity.

"If you don't mind me mentioning it, sir," he said bravely, "I didn't see Mrs Macavity at Spellbound's birthday ball, and she's not here tonight. I do hope everything is alright with her?"

The Duchess went a little red in the face, and the Duke scrambled on the ground to retrieve the fork that he had dropped. Leticia gazed at Eddie in astonishment. They all turned to look at Philip, who was calmly finishing another mouthful of food.

"My wife is in the best of health, thank you very much for asking. But she does have a rather pressing duty to fulfil regarding her own family. Some years ago, her mother had a very unfortunate meeting with a cat, which left her wings in terrible shape, not to mention her state of mind. Regrettably, she now cares for her full time, as she is the only Fairy her mother now recognizes. It means that she cannot always be at my side at social functions such as these but rest assured, I always arrange to take her some of the wonderful food that is served - like these frogs' legs, absolutely delicious, Duchess," he said, expertly changing the subject. He raised his wine glass in her direction.

"Why thank you, Mr Macavity, the cook will be very proud when she hears of your compliments and I'm sure she will prepare a Froggie bag for Mrs Macavity later. Please send her all our love and good wishes, and please do forgive my son his blunt curiosity," she said, somewhat embarrassed.

Drillian decided to focus his attention on Leticia. Perhaps if he got her on his side, he would stand a better chance to win over the lovely Spellbound.

" Madam Zamforia, I hear you perform fantastic magic. Have you inherited this great gift from an ancestor perhaps?"

Leticia's violet eyes flicked icily over his face as she gave him one of her polite little smiles. She should be courteous to him as he was Spellbound's employer, after all.

"Yes, from my cousin Larissa. She was my guardian and mentor until I was ten and seven. She taught me all I know and in turn, I shall pass that knowledge onto Spellbound." She looked towards her daughter and smiled.

"And does the great Marco Zamforia have magic powers as well?"

Leticia swallowed very delicately and took a quick sip of her pink champagne. All eyes were turned in her direction. "He does, indeed ... but he has a very different kind of magic to me."

Drillian gave her the full benefit of a dazzling smile, as he asked nonchalantly, "When is he to return home? You must miss him."

"I miss him terribly," Spellbound cut in. Leticia took in a sharp breath, refusing to be shown up.

"Sometime in the Autumn, I think he said he would be returning. He has been very busy these last few years in the Austrial realm, making sure his vast fortune stays intact."

Spellbound knew that Leticia had been backed into a corner and was lying through her teeth. "I've heard he's one of the wealthiest Elves in the forest," Drillian continued. "What I don't understand, and please don't think me rude but why would you live in such a humble cottage, when he has so much wealth?"

Leticia gave him a black look, as all eyes rested on her.

"That is a very interesting question," the Duchess said kindly. "I never even thought of that, perhaps Leticia will explain for you?" She sensed that the entire party was awaiting an explanation, so she chose her words carefully.

"When my husband leaves this realm for any great length of time, by the laws of his ancestry, his fortune *must* go with him. That is his birth right and it cannot be changed. When he returns, the beautiful house he built for us will be made visible again and we will dwell there once more." She moved her food around her plate. "We quite like it though at Broomsticks Cottage, don't we dear?" she said to Spellbound. "It was my home as I was growing up and well, it seems nice to snuggle down there, for now, anyhow."

The Duchess nodded. At last, some of the mystery surrounding Marco had been explained. The Duke joined in the questioning. "They say the house was magnificent, Leticia, and set in vast grounds, is that so?"

Leticia nodded to the Duke and smiled dreamily as she placed her cutlery down.

"Yes, a beautiful house; we even had a crystal stream running through the lounge. Marco spared no expense. He is always so generous."

Drillian was confused, "Pardon my curiosity, Madam, but business or no business, why has he been away for so long?"

She sighed, her eyes turning to ice as she looked at him in irritation. He was as sharp as a knife and this scenario was becoming increasingly uncomfortable.

"Marco's absence has been a strain, to say the least, but he is determined to succeed in all things pertaining to wealth, business and privilege. So, one must just shrug one's shoulders and accept it. I knew all this before we were to be wed. After all," she lied convincingly, "he will be home soon enough, and we can get back to full family life."

The Duchess tittered and stretched her hand over to Leticia.

"You are so courageous, my dear, and so strong to be on your own for so long; it must be agony for you and of course Spellbound too. When Marco returns, the Duke and I will throw a huge ball in his honour, won't we, dearest?"

The Duke nodded, "It would be a great privilege to do that for you, Leticia, and I can't wait to meet Marco again. We used to play Bugbee together when we were at college. He is a fine upstanding Elf with great dignity."

Leticia thought of Marco wrapped around Tinky Bonk in the sauna and tried her best to hide a scowl. "Yeah, some fine upstanding bladderbart, my foot!" she thought.

Eddie was looking utterly miserable as the dinner party came to an end. Spellbound hadn't looked over at him once during dinner. As the evening wound down, everyone began making their way to the door and words of thanks were exchanged by the older members of the party.

"Spellbound," Drillian said, as he separated her from the other guests. "We've got to head off to Toncaster again tomorrow. I've got an important meeting with Incisors Ltd in the afternoon. I'll be collecting you early so can you be ready?" Spellbound wasn't impressed. She really had to finish her conversation with Clifford. Every time she tried to talk to him, Leticia would psyche in and distract her.

"Do I have to be there?" she sighed flatly. "There's something important I really have to do and ..."

He interrupted swiftly, "Yes, I need you to take recordings of the whole meeting and keep an eye on the stock market, this deal is way too important to screw up, it will bring in at least another 30 million." He gave her a dazzling smile, "And if this comes off, I'll be giving you a hefty raise and the latest Digisoft High Pad. Tell your mother, we'll be back the following day!" Spellbound nodded, the extra money would be great and a Digisoft was every Fairy's dream.

Later when she was on her own and there were no distractions, her thoughts drifted to her father, the feelings of sadness overwhelming her, leaving a leaden feeling in her heart. She was terrified of going into the yearning and needed to speak to Clifford urgently, as she felt her time was beginning to run out.

Spellbound was finally in bed and Leticia was seated in the kitchen, feeling very disturbed. She was exhausted at having to pretend about Marco's disappearance to the Duchess and their guests. Her daughter had been sullen on the way home and unusually quiet. Where would it all end, she thought, as she pulled herself wearily out of the chair. She walked towards Clifford's ball and removed the purple cloth.

"At last, Milady; I have wanted to speak to you for days about something extremely important."

She sighed, why was everyone so demanding? "Fire away, Clifford, and make it quick. I'm shattered."

"When Spellbound was summoned to the astral realm by her Godmother, Moonflower, she was told that you had cast a powerful spell on her three years ago to stop her from missing her father. The spell is wearing off very quickly and now she is well into the yearning phase and you know what happens when a Fairy is in yearning!"

Leticia's eyes darted around the room in a blind panic. Slowly, her skin changed to pale alabaster and for a moment she felt she was going to faint. She clapped her hand over her mouth. "Yearning phase? Surely not! Not the yearning!" Clifford blinked a couple of times and then continued.

"If Marco doesn't return, Milady, Spellbound will lose her wings and be transmuted into a golden hare and if that does happen, there won't be a thing you can do about it, even with your powerful magic."

Leticia slumped into the chair opposite the ball and started to cry. This was just turning out to be an awful day. What was she to do? How could she fix this mess? She lifted her head, revealing two very swollen and puffy eyes.

"How long has Spellbound got before the change?"

Clifford's eye rolled dramatically, "That I do not know; all I do know is that the Feathered Ones are not happy, they know that Marco's whereabouts have been cloaked ... something must be done soon to get him back or your daughter will be hopping off, sooner than you think!"

She dropped her head into her hands. Everything was coming back to bite her; Leticia thought despairingly.

"Clifford, dear," she snivelled. "Look into the future. Tell me how long I've got to keep my Spellbound from turning into a hare. If I were to cast a spell to get him back, that could take months, and that's if I can even do it! You know and I know that I banished him for life. I would need a hundred wands and a thousand potions to sort this muddle out."

Clifford clucked like a mother, hen, "Well dear, that's what you get for being so reckless and impetuous. You will need to wait while I concentrate."

A full ten minutes passed while Clifford's ball clouded over in a mass of magenta mist. Leticia paced up and down, wringing her hands in desperation.

Suddenly the ball cleared, and Clifford's hazel eye became visible again.

"Well," she screeched impatiently, "what did you see?"

"You have three months, maybe a little less. Spellbound is fine for the present but you're going to have to speed forth and bring Marco back as soon as you can!"

Later that night, Leticia was seated in bed with four powerful grimoires in front of her. She scanned the pages carefully. Each book told the same story: to reverse a spell such as this would take sixteen full weeks of daily ritual to return a banished soul - and that would be one month too late. My beautiful daughter is to become a golden hare and it's entirely my fault, she cried desperately.

Downstairs, Clifford mulled over the events of the night. Seeing Leticia so upset had really unnerved him. How he would just love to embrace that perfect Fairy and sweep her up into his Warlock arms. Since the day she was born, he had watched over her, and as she developed into a grown-up fae, he fell more deeply in love. One thing was for sure, he thought to himself: if and when Marco did return, there would be no re-kindling of passion between the couple. The proud Zamforian Elf would never forgive his wife for banishing him to some far-off realm.

CHAPTER 11
THE INHERITANCE

Over the past few days, Leticia had thwarted any chances Spellbound might have to speak to Clifford, keeping a beady eye on her. As much as she trusted Clifford, she had an uneasy feeling that he might just reveal her secret. He hadn't hidden his disapproval and she could tell that he was battling with his conscience. More than anything, she didn't want her daughter discovering that it was she who had banished her father. Any more bad news might tip her over the edge and the thought of her daughter transmuting prematurely into a hare was just too much to take in. Once Marco was back, Spellbound would be cured of the yearning and then it didn't matter.

The anti-banishment spell was well underway, and she was more than confident it would be finished in time. Larissa spent an entire evening at the cottage giving her some magical tips, along with a welcome confidence boost and for now, things were looking up. However, if Marco were to return, she'd have to look stunning! She would need to change her appearance, and quickly. The last time that grunt-futtock had seen her, she was as trim as a blade of grass and even though she hated him with a vengeance, she wasn't going to let him see her with these wobbly sized hips!

Leticia gathered together the ingredients for Larisa's hippo-suction potion and had added a spoonful of Mugwort, so the effects of the spell would never diminish. She leant over the steaming cauldron, gazing into its depths, while sniffing the heady aromas wafting up from the bubbles. Oooh, if this works, I could sell the elixir far and wide and make a fookin' fortune!

Taking a tiny blue glass bottle, she submerged it into the magical liquid, filling the flume all the way to the top. She studied the contents with avid interest. Holding her nose, she downed it in one fell swoop. The familiar fizzy feeling engulfed her body and very slowly, her shape began to change. The tiny lines around her mouth and eyes melted away and her breasts instantly lifted into the most perfect cleavage, spilling above her pale pink night shift. Her rounded hips were transformed into a slim yet voluptuous curve and as she turned to look behind her, she noticed that her derriere was pert once more. With one last glance in the mirror, she grinned at herself and winked.

"That'll do nicely!"

Suddenly, the musical doorbell chimed and she flitted over to open the large oak door. A smartly dressed gnome in uniform grinned and saluted her respectfully.

"Recorded delivery, please sign here."

She took the long, cream, vellum envelope from him and stared hard at the red seal on the back. With a flick of her wand, her signature was done. She closed the door and opened the letter; it looked very formal and more important than her usual Pixie post. Seating herself comfortably, she unfolded the two embossed sheets of paper.

Dear Madam Zamforia,
We wish to inform you that you have been left a legacy.
Please come to our offices at your earliest convenience for further instruction.
Yours Sincerely,
Peri and Manson
(Solicitors)

Her eyes scanned the pages excitedly. "A legacy, but from whom?" She just couldn't think, her head was spinning. She had not done any money spells lately, so this must be for real.

As she was ushered into the offices of Peri and Manson, her heart skipped a beat in anticipation. A plump, bearded gnome led her to a purple swivel chair and peered at her over his silver spectacles. When they were both seated, he cleared his throat and proceeded to read the document in front of him.

"Madam Zamforia, some years ago you did a Tarot reading for a gentleman Elf called Wilfred Pickle-Nickle. You advised him to start a new business and to move to the Zeeland realm to make his fortune. Well, he followed your instructions to the letter and became very wealthy indeed! Sadly, he passed away a month ago, but as a thank you, for your wisdom and insight, he has left you a sizable sum."

He wrote down a figure with rather a lot of noughts on the end and passed it across to her. She gasped with utter astonishment.

"As it is such a huge amount, Madam Zamforia, we will, of course, help and advise you how best to invest." Leticia sat back in a daze. She was rich beyond belief! Once Marco came back, he was sure to divorce her for banishing him for the past three years, but at least this way she would be made for life and not have to work anymore. She could even open her own publishing company, she thought with excitement.

Spellbound's Fairy spell-phone danced in front of her nose to let her know she had a call. As she held it to her pointy little ear, she heard her mother's animated voice on the other end.

"Darling, sweet, sweet fae child! You must come home this instant dear … take a break! I could magic you back here, but I know it will make you tired afterwards. We have struck it rich dearest and we will never have to worry about money again. We are going to buy a new house, so hop on the Swirlybird contraption and get yourself back to the cottage immediately: we're going shopping!"

Spellbound was seated opposite Drillian at the luncheon table, picking daintily at a fruit fly salad.

"What are you talking about, Mamma? Have you gone mad? I can't just hop on the Swirlybird and …"

"Hop on it, RIGHT NOW," Leticia demanded excitedly, "I'm clearly not mad, dear, the most astonishing thing has happened. I've been left a huge legacy. Come and help Mamma spend it!"

Spellbound screamed in delight as Leticia flapped around on the spot with the phone in her hand.

Spellbound turned to Drillian enthusiastically. "I gotta take some time off and go home. You won't mind, will you, Drill?" Flashing him an enchanting smile, she fluttered down from the high stool. Her turquoise wings had stiffened in excitement and were turning bright shades of orange.

She looked a vision, thought Drillian, with her long red hair tumbling around her face and her eyes flashing and dancing like sprites on a lily pond. He couldn't ever recall seeing that sweet, rosebud mouth smile so wide before. She really was something only an Elf could dream about. He gathered his thoughts quickly and for a second, froze. His jaw tightened and a knot began to form in his stomach. Spellbound was waiting for him to say something. Finally, he ran his fingers through his dark brown hair and met her gaze.

"What's all the fuss about; won't you tell me?" he asked.

Spellbound began hovering two inches from the ground, something she always did when she couldn't contain herself.

"Mamma has just received a tremendous inheritance from an old client and we're going to buy a new home as soon as possible, can you believe it? Oh, this is so exciting, Drill! I always hated that cottage, all dark and drab. Now we can live in the lap of luxury, just like when my Papa was here."

Her face changed a little at the mention of her father and the light in her eyes suddenly faded. Drillian had come to the conclusion that Spellbound was indeed showing signs of the yearning. The vacant expression on her face didn't last long though, and before he could say another word, she began to speedily collect her personal belongings together.

He looked down to inspect his fingernails, suddenly feeling annoyed.

"How long were you thinking of being away, Spellbound?"

She thought of the first thing that came into her head.

"A month? I dunno, haven't had time to think. Guess I'll be as long as it takes," she chirruped.

"A month, that's a little steep, isn't it? Hmm … I'm not sure about that." He continued to look down at his nails, feeling deeply frustrated. Spellbound stopped dead in her tracks and turned her sweet little figure to face him.

"Take it or leave it, Drill, I couldn't care a fig. In fact, I don't really need to work at all now, do I?"

Drillian was immediately on his back foot.

"Okay, two weeks. That's all you're getting and then I want you back here with me, doing the job I pay you very well to do. Enjoy your spending spree and …"

Spellbound didn't wait for him to finish. She was heading out of the restaurant and towards the door in a shower of silver stars.

"I'll miss you Spelly …" he whispered under his breath, but she was already gone.

Drillian sank down into the richly upholstered chair in his office. Why did he feel so dejected? Maybe he would get the laptop out and look at his *Totty* list, he thought. That would be a welcome distraction. His eyes scanned down the Fairy register but he was unable to summon his usual enthusiasm. He could call Passionflower. She was very bendy, especially in the sauna … his thoughts drifted. Then there was Maybelle, she really knew how to mushroom bounce. He sighed. Just lately he had lost interest in them all. Why was that he wondered despondently? Then like a bolt of lightning, it struck him. That was it! For the first time in his twenty years, he was feeling an emotion he had never felt before. He had a crush … he had a huge crush on a stroppy little cute-assed Fairy, called Spellbound!

Leticia and Spellbound had found the perfect house. Fingleberry Manor was situated in a large clearing, in the very heart of Bluebell Forest. Nearby was a vast lake with over fifty pale, blue Swannikins gliding on its mirrored surface. The surrounding trees were an unusual shade of lilac and pink and little furry Dodibells, in every colour, swung from branch to branch, singing in tinkle-tones. On the moving in day, one of the kitten-like creatures landed on Spellbound's arm and cuddled into her, sucking its furry thumb cutely. Spellbound stroked its little pointed ears as it trilled contentedly.

"Ahh … Mamma, isn't she adorable? She has such soft spotty fur and beautiful, turquoise eyes!"

"Divine, absolutely divine dear," Leticia replied. "I always wanted one as a child but was never allowed and now we are over-run by them. Don't bring them into the house though darling, they disappear like magic into all of the cracks and crevices and breed like mad, especially the yellow ones; plus, they sing all night long and keep you awake. They also have a nasty habit of getting into the bedclothes. If you're sensitive, believe me, dear, you'll get the itch bug. No doubt soon, we will have to get the little wooden wheelbarrows out to collect them all and put them further afield."

They flitted over the rolling lawns and back towards the house. It was an exceptional, pale granite building which had two large pillars at its entrance. Inside there were over thirty large rooms, which the previous owners had modernised. There was a swimming pool and a fly zone at the back for Swirly-birds, and a spell room in the basement which Leticia immediately claimed for her own. She had given Spellbound her own wing and was told that she could entertain as many friends as she wanted. She even had her own top-of-the-range, bright red and white spotted Ladybuggy, a maid and her own rather snooty personal butler, called Biff Wellington.

Leticia had also been very kind and affectionate and allowed her to choose all of her own furniture and drapes. She wondered why her Mother had suddenly stopped dominating her and had given her all this freedom, after years of being so exacting and strict. There was a real change which she liked and they seemed more like friends since she had inherited all of this wealth. Nearly everything was perfect. She had her freedom, a fantastic job, her own house and a kinder, thinner, more glamorous Mamma. The only thing missing was her Papa.

Spellbound had toyed with the idea of telling her mother about Moonflower and her father's disappearance, but something she didn't entirely trust was keeping her silent. As much as she adored her, she had a feeling her mother was behind it all! Soon she would get Clifford on his own and make him spill the beans. Until then, she would just revel in their newfound wealth.

CHAPTER 12
A BROKEN BALL

Drillian was riding around the forest on the most magnificent male dragonfly, feeling thoroughly despondent. It had been a whole week since Spellbound had whizzed off at the speed of light to spend some of her mother's inheritance. This silly cock-assed Fairy had filled his thoughts every single minute of each day, and he just couldn't get a thing done. Luckily, he had enough Elf power to keep his father's business ticking over nicely. Still, the second he tried to make a conscious decision or put a deal together, the delightful little winged nut job, would invade his thoughts yet again. This was extremely out of character. Sure, he was renowned for having a string of fae gals at his beck and call but never, not ever, had he had any kind of feelings for them. These days, it was Spellbound that consumed his every thought. He lamented that unless he got to savour her sweet kisses soon, he would never be happy again.

As he drew the dragonfly to a steady hover, he pondered the Victorian gene story and decided it was nothing but a myth. He also reckoned that one night of passion with Spellbound would put a stop to all of this nonsense and then he would lose interest, as he did with all the Fairies. The only reason he had this fascination with her was that she was out of reach.

"Well, Drill," he said, under his breath. "You are just gonna have to try a bit harder, dude. Turn on the charm like never before and make her yours for the night."

In the distance he saw Spellbound's palatial new home, set back in an avenue of tall Cyprus trees. As he flew closer, he espied her sitting by the edge of the lake, dipping her toes into the cool, translucent water. She was dressed in the cutest, cut-off denim jeans and a white strapless, floaty blouse.

On approaching, he could hear her crying bitterly, her slender body shuddering, as tears ran down her face. "Oh, crap," he said in a whisper. This wasn't at all what he had expected. Leaping down from the dragonfly, he walked towards her tentatively.

She looked up in surprise, before trying to quickly wipe her eyes dry. The last thing she wanted was for this berk to see her in this state.

"What d'ya want, Drill?" she said with a hiccup. "I'm not coming back to work, so just do one and get lost," she snivelled. "Just go!"

"Hey you, what's wrong and why the tears?" he said, gently. The sympathy in his voice made Spellbound feel even worse; covering her face with her hands, she tried to compose herself.

"None of your business, Drill. Just leave me be ... please."

"Hey, I'm not leaving until you tell me what on earth is wrong with you!" He strode over and squatted down in front of her, lifting a curling lock of her red hair behind one of her little pointy ears.

Drillian could feel hot tears pricking his own eyes. This Fairy's pain was contagious, he thought. Why the hell do I want to cry like a faeby when she does? She was fookin' right about one thing, he did need some therapy, but it wasn't for his rumpy drive and that was for sure!

"Listen, Spell," he said softly, "I haven't got a magic bone in my Elfin body but if I could wave a wand of any sort and remove all this crap from your life, I would. Just tell me what it is that's making you cry like this, and somehow, I'll try and fix it. I promise I will."

"I doubt you're gonna be this nice to me when I turn into a mad March hare!"

"A what?"

"A hare!"

"Did you say a hare?"

"Yeah!"

"Damn, you *are* in the yearning phase, then," he said, looking horrified. "I kinda half guessed you might be. Some Pixie boy really did get to you, huh?" He looked down at the grass, feeling wholly defeated.

"It's not a Pixie!" her voice quivered.

Drillian lifted her trembling chin with his forefinger and continued, "I don't understand!" She tugged hard on a blade of grass and sighed unhappily.

"It's my Pa," she said. "I thought he'd just left us, well, that was what Mamma had said, you know, business in the Austrial realm and all that. But it seems that isn't the case because the Feathered Ones can't even find him either and ..."

"*The Feathered Ones?*" he gasped. "How do you know this?"

"I know because I visited my Godmother, Moonflower, on the astral plane and she told me."

Drillian raised both eyebrows. "Wow, you got to meet your Godmother. That's jammy, what did she say to you?"

"Just that! No one up there can trace his whereabouts and because I'm missing him so much, if I don't find him soon, I'm gonna go into the yearning and turn into a hare! Bringing him back is the only way I get out of this awful situation!"

"I can get the Spider Web Intelligence on to it straight away," he said optimistically. "We have a whole network on every single realm ..."

"It's no use Drill, really," she interrupted. "The Feathered Ones suspect that some dark magic is cloaking him. Moonflower told me that I had to go and see Clifford. He's our Warlock trapped inside a glass ball and that he'd tell me the whereabouts of my Pa."

"And ... did you go and see him? Did you ask him?"

"I can't get near him," she spat out, in total frustration. "Mamma is watching my every move. Something fishy is going on, Drill, and I need to figure it out."

Spellbound continued to wipe her eyes. Taking her wand, she flicked it twice to produce a snowy white tissue. Drillian, glanced over at the house and began chuckling.

"Er … no time like the present! By the looks of it, your dearest Mamma has just left the building, basket on her arm and ready to shop till she drops. Come on, step to it. We probably don't have long!"

Spellbound glanced across at the house and quickly stood up. Leticia was summoning Stanley, before flitting daintily onto his back. Within a nano-second, they were airborne and out of sight.

Spellbound and Drillian sped into the house. Inside the grand hallway, they turned left and entered the beautiful library, its bookshelves lined with fantastic fairy-tales from centuries passed, along with a selection of Leticia's own raunchy Spells and Swoon books. There in the corner of the room was Clifford's ball, this time covered with a piece of the most beautiful shimmering muslin. Spellbound ordered Drillian to wait while she raced upstairs to collect the magical Orb from her night stand. Once back in the library, she uncovered Clifford, who was waiting, wide awake.

"Spellbound my dear," he said a little shaken. "Ah, I see you have brought a guest!"

"Never mind the small talk, Clifford; it's time to rock and roll. Now get to it: what have you done with my Papa?"

Drillian stood back and watched speechlessly. The atmosphere in the room was electric.

"I really don't know what you mean," Clifford lied, "and I would like it if you showed some respect, young fae. Your rudeness is quite hurtful, you know!"

"Dude, just tell her how to get her Pa back, or I'll see to it that you never look out of that fook-eyed ball again!"

Spellbound turned to him in astonishment. "I can handle this Drill. If you must be here, at least be quiet. I am quite capable of fighting my own battles, thank you!"

Drillian didn't take a blind bit of notice and walked over to Clifford.

"Listen, mate," he said, glaring at Clifford's eye. "You tell her NOW where he is, do you hear? We are running out of time and I am losing patience!"

"I am not breathing a word," said Clifford. "It is not my place to divulge the details of her father's whereabouts. Ask your mother if you really want to know, she holds all the secrets, this generation has got to be the most complicated and dysfunctional I have ever served. I am tired of it all!"

Spellbound took the Orb from behind her back and held it in front of Clifford.

"I know what you want, Clifford," she said quietly. "I know your heart's desire. I can feel it through the power of this orb. You want your freedom, don't you?" Clifford gulped as he looked at the small, round, shining ball of light, sitting in the centre of the Fairy's hand.

"You have a magical moon Orb, Spellbound. Pray, tell me, where did you get it from? How did you come by such a thing? There are only two in the entire universe!"

"Moonflower gave it to me, and she said you would know exactly what to do with it. Spellbound was enjoying the moment, tossing the Orb from one hand to the other. "I have a certain amount of power over you now," she taunted.

Clifford's voice began to shake. "Spellbound, I'll say it again. You have the one and only thing in the entire universe that can release me from this godforsaken ball! You have to do it for me. You have to use that Orb to free me!"

"Nah … I think I'll hang on to it for now," she replied cockily, making Clifford plead even more.

"You have no idea what you have there, do you?" he said in a pained manner. "That Orb can reverse any curse or hex instantly. It's the most powerful, magical thing that has ever existed in this land, now …"

"I've about had enough of this," Drillian said. "If you know where her Pa is, tell her, before I do something I'll regret!" Drillian surprised himself. He was filled with fiery anger and had become very protective of the young fae.

119

"Drill, will you just shut it for a sec please," Spellbound whispered behind her hand. "I am trying to blackmail the snoop! If I'd known you were gonna play big brother, I'd have left you outside on your winged thing!"

Clifford looked at her, disbelieving; this tiny Fairy held his entire future in her hands and with such ruthlessness. What could he do? His loyalty and love for Leticia went beyond bounds, but to be freed from this glass ball; to walk in nature once more; to enjoy food again; practise his magic and open his own school of sorcery, there was no contest. His thoughts started to race away with him again. He might actually be able to have Leticia by his side and take her for his wife. For hundreds of years he had been entrapped, following Bella'Donna's curse and now, today, this very day, he could be free to live out his life as he should. He sighed and spoke very quietly.

"Okay, Spellbound … you win. Release me from this ball and I will show you where your father is."

"Oh, no, Clifford! I wanna know everything first. You don't think I am THAT stupid to set you free before you give me the answers. You are going nowhere until I have *all* the facts."

"Okay," he sighed, defeated. "It will take me a moment. When the ball clouds over, look closely into the mist."

Spellbound and Drillian both took a step closer and peered into the swirling fog. At first, they could see nothing at all but then slowly the visions began to emerge. There before their eyes was the fateful scene. A beautiful silver-haired fairy was wrapped like a silken ribbon around her beloved father in a hot tub. They were kissing passionately, completely absorbed in each other.

"Ouch!" said Drill. "Is that your Pa Spell? Not good that … nope, doesn't look good."

"WHO THE HELL IS THAT?" Spellbound screeched.

"That, my dear, is Tinky Bonk, your father's ex-fiancée, and the reason why your mother banished him away to a deserted island, some three years ago. Your father was engaged and supposedly, very much in love with Tinky before he met your mother. Sadly, Leticia walked in on them having romantic relations in your parents' new home and was utterly heartbroken. She then became so outraged and banished them both to lands as far apart as possible, for the rest of their sorry lives."

"Banished? I can't believe it," Spellbound cried. "Papa cheated on my Mamma? No ... not my Papa! He would never do such a thing, no, no, no ... it can't be true, the ball is lying Clifford."

Spellbound started to shudder and she could feel herself becoming faint. Drillian was there like a shot and affectionately put his arm around her shoulders to support her.

"The ball never lies," said Clifford softly. "What you see is exactly what happened. Your mother was inconsolable; she loved him so much, you see."

"I just cannot get my head around why Papa would cheat on her! They had the happiest of marriages. He adored her!" Spellbound wailed pitifully.

"Do not blame your father Spellbound," Clifford continued. "There is something else you should know. When your mother was a young and reckless teen, it was no secret that she and Tinky were sworn enemies. Over a short time, your mother fell in love with Marco and made a fateful decision. She spent an entire month casting a spell to make him fall madly in love with her and leave Tinky, thus interfering with their Karma."

Spellbound stood transfixed, her heart beating so loudly she thought everyone could hear it. She glanced up at Drillian with total disbelief in her eyes. He looked at his feet, feeling as though he was intruding on something very personal. Clifford knew that he was betraying his beloved Leticia but carried on.

"She used all the magic she could muster and then finally programmed him to love her for life. Something must have gone wrong with the spell as Tinky and your father ended up together that night. Sometime after the banishment, your mother did feel pangs of guilt for using her magic in this way, and she quickly reversed the love spell, so at least he is free of that enchantment now. As he walks the lonely stretch of beach where he has been banished, he no longer has thoughts of love for her. What your mother did was terribly wrong, Spellbound, but in all fairness, she has put things right, after a fashion."

"So, what you are telling me Clifford, is Papa never really loved Mamma in the first place; that she used enchantment to get him and Tinky Bonk was his true love the whole time?"

"It would seem so, child," Clifford replied in a soft voice. "It would seem so."

Spellbound started to sob uncontrollably. All of her dreams and aspirations had just crumbled around her. As much as Clifford had his issues with this young, wild Fairy, he hated to see her so disturbed and was concerned she might go into the yearning before he had the chance to escape from the glass ball.

"Your father truly loves you though, Spellbound, as does your mother," he added kindly. This made her cry even harder.

"It's okay, Spell," Drillian said quietly. "Don't cry." He lifted her chin and gazed sadly into her drenched eyes. Just how much could one Fairy take, he wondered? Why did life have to be so rotten for such a lovely little thing as this? Here I go again, every time I'm around this chick, I go all GOOEY! I must get a grip, he told himself firmly. Then, without even thinking, he lowered his head, kissed her tear-stained cheek and waited for the slap!

Leticia placed her basket on the hall table and smiled smugly. She had bargained ruthlessly with the jeweller for the triple-stranded emerald necklace and earrings and had got the best price ever. Of course, she could have afforded to have paid the full price for the gemstones, but once a thrifty Fairy always a thrifty Fairy, she told herself.

The much-needed shopping spree had temporarily taken her mind off the need to release Spellbound from the yearning. She had been working on her spells feverishly to ensure that Marco returned in good time but summoning the dark forces of the

Underworld for a second time was dangerous and out of the question. She had to break this hex the conventional way. Larissa had said it would be a close shave and nearly impossible, but Leticia had always achieved fantastic results with everything magical she had undertaken in the past, and so she felt confident that this would be successful too. It had to be. After all, she couldn't have her only child turning into a mad March hare!

She made her way over to the ball to see if Clifford could predict whether she was on target or not. She removed the muslin cover with a flourish and stepped back in amazement to see the familiar ball smashed clean in half.

"OOOOOH! Fookin' lordy lord. Ohhh!!!!! Lordy Lordy … fookin' LORD!"

Leticia began wringing her hands frantically, her eyes darting around the table in a frenzy. "What's happened … what's happened to the ball?" she shrieked, "Clifford, oh my word, Clifford, Clifford, where are you?"

"I am right behind you, Milady," said a sexy, deep baritone. She spun around in a flurry of Fairy dust and found herself face to face with a stunningly handsome stranger.

"Who the hell are you?" she screeched like a harridan.

He smiled a dazzling white smile, his hazel eyes crinkling at the edges mischievously. His eyelashes were longer than she'd ever seen on anyone and his hair was a thick glossy black.

"Clifford Eyesaurus, Milady, at your disposal." He bowed ever so slightly, and his purple velvet cloak billowed to show a long, lean athletic body and broad chest.

Leticia gulped. "Clifford? But it can't be," she said in a small whisper. For a moment, she stood in complete silence, her mouth slightly open. She glanced quickly again at the broken ball and then back at him. He approached her and knelt at her feet, kissing the hem of her gown.

Not taking any notice of his gesture, Leticia gawped at him in total disbelief. "I…I…I don't understand," she stuttered, still suffering from the shock. "How did you get out of the ball?"

He led her to her favourite chair, sat her down, and knelt at her feet, his hands cupping hers as he surveyed her beauty. To finally touch the object of his affections was better than he could ever have imagined. He gazed up into her eyes and lost himself in the vision of her creamy white skin and delicate frame; her perfume drifted over him, igniting his senses.

Pulling himself back with a jolt, he stood up and replied earnestly, "Leticia, when Spellbound met Moonflower, she was given a Moon Orb."

"A Moon Orb? I've only heard of them, never seen one."

"Moonflower told her to bring it to me and grant me my heart's desire, but alas," he said more seriously, "in return I had to tell her everything about her father and how you had spelled for his love, only to banish him once you discovered his infidelity."

Leticia looked dazed and bewildered; for a moment, she thought she might faint.

"You have to pardon me, Leticia, I dared not refuse. It was a direct order from the Feathered Ones, and it has brought me my freedom."

"What exactly does my daughter know and what did she see?"

"She knows the truth, my dear. And she has seen all that she had to see. There are no secrets between you now."

Leticia dropped her head into her hands, in despair. "No … no … this can't be so. What will she think of me? I am so ashamed!"

Clifford took Leticia's hand and pulled her to her feet. He put his arms around her and looked deeply into her beautiful, violet eyes.

"Let us not talk of shame, Milady, not now," he said, as he gently held her head against his shoulder. "I have looked after and cared for you since you were a little child. I have watched you grow and blossom into the magnificent Fairy that you are today. We have shared so much together, and no one knows you as well as I do, would you not agree?"

He caressed her face tenderly and she nodded as tears ran down her cheeks. In an impressive flash, he magicked up a snow-white handkerchief and wiped them away.

"He was never mine, was he, Clifford? I should have been wiser and not so free with my wand, spells and potions."

"You were but a hot-headed child, dearest, and all is not lost, you do have Spellbound."

She pulled herself away, her body visibly trembling like an Aspen leaf. "Where is she now?"

"She is with Drillian, and before you say anything else, I think he is somewhat sweet on her. You have meddled before but this time, you must promise me you won't interfere with her Karma, as you did with your husband. I know you have your heart set on her being with Edward, but now you must let fate decide. Promise me?" Leticia nodded wearily and pulled away to return to her chair.

"My life is ruined, Clifford. I have this wealth, all of these possessions but no happiness. And I get what you're saying about Spellbound and her fate but what good is that if I can't stop the yearning from happening. She will turn into a hare if I don't get that spell right. And to top it all off, I have to bring back the very person who lights up my soul and breaks my heart, all in an instant!" She quivered, her nose a little red from all the crying.

"You told me once that your magic was as powerful as mine, Clifford, can you help me? Do you think that you could bring back Marco so I can put this sorry mess behind us?"

Clifford stood before her, feeling empty because she was no longer in his arms.

"Spellbound has the magical Moon Orb, which can reverse all spells and curses," he replied. "We must speak to her soon and show her how to use it so that *she* can bring him back."

Suddenly a heavy weight lifted from her shoulders; of course, the Orb would solve all of the problems. It wouldn't be long now and Spellbound would be released from the yearning.

Seeing her father canoodling with Tinky Bonk had upset Spellbound so much that she felt she would never recover. It had also been a shock to see Clifford crash out of the glass ball in a flurry of electricity, which nearly knocked both her and Drillian clean off their feet.

Over dinner that evening, Leticia tried hard to justify her actions all of those years ago but Spellbound was clearly traumatised and sat in stunned silence, not listening. Clifford thought it best to remain silent but he was secretly worried about Spellbound.

"Darling, you have to understand that Mamma was young and foolish and of course very smitten with your Papa. We all do things that we regret, don't we dear. You're not going to hold this against your Mamma, are you?" Spellbound glanced up, her eyes drifting coldly over her mother. Leticia licked her lips nervously, "That awful Fairy, Tinky Bonk would constantly try and upset me dear. She called your Grandmamma all sorts of unfortunate names and didn't care who was listening. I know I was wrong but I would challenge any Fairy not to have done the same thing, given that they had my powers and all!" Her eyes were searching for her daughter's forgiveness, but none came. Biff Wellington entered the room and removed the full plates. Spellbound took the opportunity to quietly excuse herself, leaving Leticia and Clifford alone at the table.

"It's no use Clifford," Leticia sighed in a deflated tone. "She's never going to forgive me, oh, what have I done!"

"Give her time Milady, she will come around. Tomorrow I will speak with her about the Orb and we'll free her from the yearning before long.

Throwing herself on the bed, Spellbound continued to cry her heart out. She could not stop this infernal weeping. It was draining the life out of her and her eyes were swollen beyond recognition. She slowly walked into the tootle room, adjacent to her bedchamber and began running the hot water into a large round, crystal tub.

Sinking into the water, she closed her eyes, but the images she had seen in Clifford's ball kept jumping into her thoughts. No …

Papa would never do such a thing and MAMMA, I mean, what was she thinking! no… no…I can no longer bear this, I wish I was dead, she thought, with a breaking heart.

She started to cream her little body with expensive Fairy gel and then suddenly let out a huge scream.

"Ahhhhhhhhhh!!!!!! Ahhhhhhhhhh! Ahhhhhhh!! No!!!!!!!!! No!!!! No!!!!!!!!!!!"

Leticia and Clifford heard the screams from the dining hall and tore up the stairs in a whirlwind, throwing open the door of Spellbound's bathroom. She was standing in the middle of a puddle examining a tail on her bottom. She continued to scream and wail at forty decibels, when a long golden ear, plopped out of her head.

"Mamma, I've grown a hare's tail and look, I've got another ear! Mamma, make it go away … make it go away now, I can't bear it!" she screeched hysterically. As she spoke, golden hairs sprouted from her arms and legs and her nose was already beginning to change shape.

Leticia swooned and fell into Clifford's arms. As he patted her cheek repeatedly, the blood drained from her face.

"Oh, lordy lord, Clifford, it's started, do something, please!" she gasped weakly.

"Now everyone be calm, Spellbound, stop this wailing instantly, and Leticia, sit down before you fall down. Let me think." Leticia was wringing her hands in consternation when Spellbound continued to bawl at the top of her voice, as another ear appeared.

Clifford wrapped a sheet around Spellbound to conserve her modesty and went back to Leticia.

"Right, we have to work quickly, we need the Orb immediately. Where is it, Spellbound?"

Leticia pulled herself together, running over to her child and glaring into her hysterical face. "The Orb, where is it, darling?"

Shaking uncontrollably, she pointed to the top drawer of the night-stand and Leticia quickly retrieved it and passed it to Clifford.

"We must all do this together," he said. "Spellbound, stop caterwauling and come here and put your finger on the globe. You too, Leticia; your magic will enhance the spell, we have but a few seconds."

All three stood in a circle, as Clifford held out the Orb, which oscillated and throbbed, changing colour constantly.

He spoke tersely, "When the it is pink and only pink, say this in unison:

Three forces together,
Three forces we be,
Magical orb of strength and power,
Set Spellbound, Marco and Tinky free."

It left their fingers and whizzed around the bathroom, growing larger and larger and then exploded with a blinding light, before zooming back into the open drawer. Spellbound's legs collapsed from underneath her and Clifford caught her before she dropped to the floor. Leticia was swaying, with not a hint of colour in her face. She drew a deep breath and walked across the room to her daughter's side. The tail and ears had disappeared, and her skin was free of hairs. She was in an exhausted sleep, surrounded by an eerie, green and white neon light.

Gently, Clifford carried Spellbound to the adjacent bedchamber and laid her on the bed, pulling the covers up to her chin.

"Your daughter will sleep in enchantment for three full days Leticia and must NOT be disturbed. When she does awake, Spellbound will be renewed, happy and free of the yearning, so fret no more, my dear."

Leticia clung to him as he wrapped his arms around her quivering body.

"You must sleep too, Leticia. The spell was powerful, and I can see it has drained all your strength. We won't know when Marco and Tinky will come back, probably after Spellbound's recovery, but for now ... rest. The ordeal is over."

He gazed into her beautiful, violet eyes and snapped his fingers once. Her eyes closed immediately, and she fell into a deep slumber.

He lifted her into his arms and carried her to her own room. His lips touching hers softly.

Clifford dared not rest and stayed by Leticia's bedside, watching her sleep. He would guard her until she had her full faculties again. He knew Spellbound would be protected by the Orb's shield but the last thing he wanted was for some dark force to take possession of Leticia when she was unconscious and vulnerable. He breathed a huge sigh of relief that this whole sorry episode was almost at an end. He gazed down at the sleeping sorceress; her hair tumbled all around her heart-shaped face, her skin the colour of cream alabaster. He longed to capture and keep her heart. Marco Zamforia was now free to wed Tinky, and he would make sure Leticia would stay safely by his side forever.

CHAPTER 13
FENELLA PHLEGM

About eight miles south of Bluebell Forest, there was a dank, dark wooded area, hidden away, surrounded by a filthy swamp. Very few would dare to go anywhere near it because it was renowned for its sinister energy. The ghosts of evil and depraved Witches, corrupt and banished Wizards, as well as the souls of malevolent Warlocks who had fallen in battle, were said to haunt the deep hollows. Those who practised the dark arts would gather there to cast their evil deeds. Hardly any birds or animals occupied the area as the air was fetid and stank of rotting flesh and vegetation.

The only reason that any Fairy or Elf would venture into this part of the realm would be to get hold of the most fantastic Sillyphilly mushrooms, that when eaten, would produce a powerful hallucinogenic effect of astral travel. Trolls and Ogres frequented the outer perimeters and if bribed with enough of their favourite tipple, poppy punch, could be persuaded to go into the depths of the hollows to gather them.

Drillian was getting desperate. He simply couldn't function anymore. For the last three days, Spellbound had continued to bombard his thoughts. He had not seen her since the crystal ball had exploded and Clifford had leapt out into the room. He'd never seen anything quite like it!

Leticia had been polite when he had called at the house and asked to speak with Spellbound but she was resolute that her young fae could not be disturbed. Clifford explained that Spellbound was recovering from the yearning spell and would not be around for a week or so.

Every time Drillian so much as tried to focus on his business empire, she would pop into his head. Before he knew it, he'd be fantasising about gently sweeping her up into his arms and taking her across to his king-sized passion pouffe to indulge in the sweetest nookie of his life.

His sexual appetite was more than quite Elfy, but lately, no other Fairy had tempted him. He was moping around with a knot in his guts with no interest in food or socialising. This must stop, he berated himself. He just had to get back to normal. In a last ditched attempt, he decided to act on Spellbound's advice and call on Carmella Cacklejuice, the local Fairy shrink. She was well known for her wisdom and sound advice in such matters of the heart. Her therapy sessions were said to be phenomenal and she specialised in impotency and Fairy frantic sex, a technique she had learned during her numerous visits to the Asiatic realms in her youth. It was rumoured that she could make an oo'gasm last half an hour! After two sessions with Drillian, she deduced that he was seriously obsessed, probably just 'in lust' and needed to get a grip. She also agreed that if he could simply take Spellbound to his bedchamber and have a steamy, rumpy-pumpy session, his notice-able fascination with her would probably be cured in an instant. Drillian had always had everything he'd wanted in life. As an only son, his every need and whim were met by his doting parents. Not to have the one thing he desired the most, sent him into a frenzy, so he had to take drastic action and fast. He was behaving like a love-sick teenager. After hours of agonising over the situation, he told Carmella that he had decided to seek out a potion or spell that would deliver his dream come true: one night of passion with the young fae. The only problem was that Witches and Warlocks had certain moral ethics about influencing another's mind with magic. It wasn't going to be easy finding a spell that would circum-vent Aunt Hester's Victorian genes for any period of time. No, this would call for one hell of a ritual. Carmella scratched her chin in deep thought.

"There is always Fenella Phlegm," she said, with a slightly worried look. "She's one of the more powerful Fairy Witches and dwells in the darker regions of this realm. She was banished there for having rumpy with a grasshopper some ten years ago. Rumour has it that if you pay her enough, she can magic anything up."

"How do you know of such a Witch?" Drillian asked with curiosity.

Carmella turned to him and gave him a mysterious smile. "There have been times when I have resorted to her magic for myself and my more difficult clients. But perhaps you need to be extra careful, Drillian. After all, Spellbound's mother is the most powerful Fairy in the forest and her father, Marco Zamforia would hang you up by the heels if he ever found out … you better watch your step! You might find yourself turned into some kind of slimy insect …" she trailed off with a frown.

Drillian was aware that he was on dangerous ground, but he wasn't to be deterred. He shrugged his shoulders and resolutely declared, "Sod it, I want her!" And when he wanted something, he always got it.

"To Fenella Phlegm, I shall go!"

The verdant beauty of the forest had long since disappeared. The trees were bare and putrid smelling mists hung around the rotting foliage. Drillian carefully picked his way along the overgrown path towards a gnarled stump that resembled the face of a demon. He glanced down at the map Carmella had given him. It had cost him a week's wages to get it, but he was determined in his quest for Spellbound. Today he had decided not to bring his Swirly-bird or Dragonfly for fear of being heard or spotted by the locals. His reputation was too important and if he were seen, tongues would definitely start wagging and gossip would spread like wildfire.

A clearing came into view and up ahead was an old, rickety cottage, with peeling plaster and a wonky chimney. The filthy windows were covered in sinister insects and strange noises could be heard from inside. It had a menacing, disturbing feel about it, definitely a place where one wouldn't enter unless they were desperate, which of course he was! As he stood in front of the old, wooden door, the ivy that clung to the walls of the cottage began winding itself slowly around his ankles. He pulled his dirk from his belt and slashed at the vine. A piercing screech came from behind the door and it was evident that someone was pulling across a rusting bolt. With a deafening creak, the door slowly opened to reveal a wizened Fairy creature. Her salt and pepper hair was long and matted. Disturbingly, there was a nest of the dreaded Widder spiders crawling around on her greasy fringe and when she eyed him cautiously, he could see the signs of blindness in one of her opalescent eyeballs.

"What do ya want, pretty boy?" she wheezed, revealing her stumpy, discoloured teeth. Her breath stank and he stepped back a few paces in alarm. Her ragged black and magenta wings twitched from side to side in a sinister fashion. She stepped nearer to him, and the tip of one of them stroked his face, as she cackled. "So ... you are the sexpot of Bluebell Forest. I've watched you a few times in my ball when I've needed a little stimulation." She grinned lecherously, "You're better than any porno movie. Can't say as I remember your name though!"

"My name is Drillian Macavity and I have come to ask your assistance in a matter," he said, speaking with more courage than he felt. This Fairy was hideous.

Fenella cackled again, the lines on her face becoming more prominent. She took another step forward to get a better look at the handsome Elf standing in her doorway. He was dressed in light, stonewash, denim jeans and Fleabok trainers. He ran his fingers nervously through the sides of his hair to reveal his two perfectly formed, pointy ears. He wasn't so sure that he liked being scrutinised in such a way but felt it best not to comment, under the circumstances.

"Aye, you're a fine-looking specimen, that you are, and I can see why you have the Fairy fan club," she leered, stroking a gnarled stinking finger over his lips. Drillian pushed her hand away and stifled a wretch. "What is it that you want from a poor old Witch such as me … perhaps some scintillating sex?" She screeched with laughter, her bony frame shuddering in mirth as she turned back into the cottage, leaving the way clear for him to enter.

"Let me see … ah yes, I remember you now. Son of Philip Macavity and heir to Molars Incorporated. In trouble, are we?"

"It is not that, the business is doing very well, thank you. No, it is about another matter that I wish to see you," he hesitated for a moment, "a more personal matter!" Fenella prodded the open fire with a large log, whilst Drillian observed her closely. He could tell that in her youth, she might have been quite a beauty but now all that remained was a skeletal caricature of a century-old Witch.

"You had better tell me whatever it is you have come to say," she said, still stoking the flames. A giant bobbly toad suddenly leapt out from nowhere and landed on his trouser leg. He swiped it off, but it immediately jumped back on his designer boot.

"Don't mind Tiptoe, sir… she means you no harm."

"I need a spell to enchant a Fairy and make her mine for the night," he said quickly, feeling slightly embarrassed about having to divulge such intimate information to this old crone.

Fenella spat a considerable ball of mustard phlegm into the fire and it sizzled on a lump of coal. Drillian winced and tried again to remove the toad, which was stuck like glue to his other foot. He doubted whether he would ever wear the boots again.

"A handsome Elf like you needs a spell to enchant a Fairy? Surely not! You surprise me, laddy!"

"This is no ordinary fairy, Madam. She has Victorian genes, inherited from some obscure Aunt. She will only surrender to an Elf if she is in love, and as she is not in love with me, I can't have her; therefore, I want her all the more," he sighed in exasperation.

Fenella turned and stared at him. Then she spat again into the fire and wiped her filthy hand over her mouth. She walked over to the dusty, grey table and sat down on one of the rickety chairs. Closing her eyes, she fell silent, and then her head dropped forward on to her chest. Drillian was shocked and wondered if she had died suddenly but with a jolt, she threw her head upwards and opened her eyes.

"So … you need a love spell for the elusive, Miss Zamforia then! Yes, I know of whom you speak," she said, with a worried frown on her face.

"But only for one night. I don't want her permanently, you see. I just need to bed her so that I can get this obsession out of my mind," Drillian said earnestly.

"Umm … I don't know, Elf man. Her mother is, after all, Leticia Zamforia; even I am frightened to death of her. If she were to find out it was me who cast the spell, I would be dead meat and that is for sure. Perhaps this time I will have to say no to you. It's really not worth my while, you see." Fenella, stood up again and kicked another log into the fire. "Spellbound is a Zamforian Fairy; her father is revered, and Leticia also has the powerful Warlock, Eyesaurus, as her devoted guardian. I psychically saw him emerge from his glass prison recently. If I angered any of them, I would be finished!" Fenella frowned and shook her head. A large Widder spider ran over her weather-beaten cheek and she gently lifted it back into her hair. Drillian shrugged arrogantly. "Surely this gossip about Madam Zamforia is just stupid supposition?"

"No … you are mistaken. You must take care, too, if you cross her. She has great powers and guards her only child with a vengeance. It is far too risky, you must leave. Go now!" She moved past him towards the door.

"Fenella," he said, desperately, "I will be more than generous. I will give you five hundred fettials as payment."

Fenella paused and brushed another of the larger spiders from her eyes. That was a serious amount of coinage, she thought to herself. She turned to face him again. "For two thousand ginnagonds I might consider it," she growled, her eyes glinting with greed. "Just the one night you said?"

Drillian sucked in his breath and tried not to look shocked at the amount. Yes, he was rich, but this was six months' wages! "A thousand and no more," he bit out aggressively.

She hobbled back to the fire, spitting once more into the flames.

"I'll bid you good day then, sir."

In a defeated manner, he reached into his breeches and took out a black, cloth purse, bulging with shiny golden coins. He tossed it angrily onto the table. "Here, you win," he snarled. "I'll give you half now and the other half when I collect whatever it is you make for me. My only concern is that I don't want this spell to last. Just one day and one night, that's all I want. No more do you hear?" Fenella's eyes lit up. She clawed the purse towards her and shoved it into the bodice of her filthy dress.

"The deal is done then, Macavity," she cackled softly, pushing him out of the cottage, "Be back here for your potion after the cock crows twice!" she cried.

"What cock?" he asked, a little confused.

"In two days … you stupid fool!" she shouted and slammed the door behind him.

Chapter 14
Spellbound's Seduction

"Spellbound dearest, please get down from the sweep fan. You'll bring the whole ceiling down in a minute and that will never do. You have been spinning around and around for over an hour now and frankly, dear, you are doing your Mamma's head in!"

Ever since Spellbound had awoken from her three-day rest and the yearning had finally dissipated, she'd been out of control. She was stupidly happy and zapping anything and everything at the drop of a cap. Every time someone spoke, she guffawed loudly, and Clifford and Leticia had had to cast a 'volume reducing' spell on her, for half an hour a day, just to get some peace. Leticia was so relieved, as Spellbound had lost all traces of the depression and had miraculously forgiven her for all her wrong doings.

"I'm so happy, Mamma," she shouted from the top of the ceiling. "All that crappy sadness has left me, and I have so much energy. I am on top of the mountains, on top of the ..."

The spell phone began to jingle in front of her nose and with a swift twirl in the air she let go of the sweep fan and fluttered down to the ground.

"Heeeelllllllllloooooooooooooooo," she sang happily, "this is the one and only, Miss Spellbound Zamforia at your service, may I ask who the devil is calling?"

Spellbound was giggling uncontrollably, as Leticia raised her eyebrows and gave Clifford a withering look.

"Spell, it's Drill here," a deep sexy voice drawled. "Have you been on the poppyade?

"HAHA … no, I'm not drunk, silly willy, I am just remarkably happy, that's all. I have good news, Drill, in fact, I have the bestest news ever," she said, pausing for a second and awaiting his response.

"And what would that be?" he asked, feigning interest.

"I am completely free of the yearning," she said excitedly, "and somehow, all that sadness has been replaced with sheer and utter happiness. I am *so, so, so, so, so, so, so, HAPPY … hehehehehehehe HAHAHA!!!!!!!!!!!!!!*"

"Mmmmm," he responded. "Well, I am delighted that you are feeling better but I need your Fairy, happy backside over here at my place, pronto. We have some serious invoicing to catch up with and as you have had quite a lot of time off work lately, I suggest you tell your folks that you're not going to be back until tomorrow morning. I had the maid make up the west wing for you, so bring an overnight bag. My guess is that we are going to be at it well into the night." Drillian slapped a hand to his mouth. Crap! Did I really say that? he thought. "At the invoicing, that is," he amended quickly.

"HAHA, glad you went and put that last sentence right, Drilly boy, 'cause you know I would never be at it with you, not in a zillion years." She continued to laugh hysterically.

"MAMMA, MAMMA," she bellowed, causing Drillian to hold the spell phone away from his ear, "THE ALMIGHTY, FOOKIN', TOOFY PEG MAN NEEDS ME TO WORK … UGH … WORST LUCK, EH? MAMMA, CAN YOU HEAR ME, I HAVE TO GO … I'VE BEEN SUMMONED … MAMMA!"

"Spellbound dear, stop shouting like a foghorn, I am right behind you! Yes, I heard you, who wouldn't?"

"Oh, good, Mamma. Hey, I'll be gone until tomorrow morning. Is that okay, Mamma? Do you need me for anything? Y'know, you only have to say the word and I will tell the smarmy spaddywacking git to fook off! We could have a girly day instead Mamma, and play Wesley Presley records till the small hours or perhaps you, Clifford and me could have a Karaoke party, I could sing to you and play the Fairy flute … what d'ya think?"

"No, no, that's fine, perhaps another time, you get yourself off, now," Leticia said in total exasperation. "And thank the fookin' hell for that phone call," she muttered under her breath. "A whole twenty-four hours of peace and quiet … I can barely contain myself. Just let me go and lie down in a darkened room!"

Drillian sent his fine Sparrow Hawk, Jock Strap, the fastest bird in the forest to collect Spellbound. She had decided to make herself look ever so sweet today and was wearing a short lavender swirly skirt and matching top. She had waved her wand over her hair that morning and added champagne coloured highlights to the red tresses, which tumbled romantically around her heart-shaped face. Her wings were changing shades by the minute. Each time she got a rush of happiness, they went a pearly pink and when her mood settled down a bit, they changed back to lilac and bright orange.

The Sparrow Hawk sped in and out of the trees as Spellbound gaily waved down to everyone on the ground, who looked up in amazement at the sparkling spectacle. With her wand now fixed firmly in her right hand, she was zapping and pinging magic all around her, sending a cascading array of silver Fairy dust about the wood. She changed the Sparrow Hawk's plumage to bright yellow with a luminous plume of green on its head and gave him a little golden crown and a blazing, red saddle just for good measure. Spellbound's magic had never worked this well. Leticia figured that because she was now free of the yearning, she had channelled something within her which was making her more powerful by the second.

Drillian was pacing up and down outside of Cumalot Castle, waiting for the crazy Fairy to arrive. He knew that she was getting nearer when he heard the distant sound of whooshing and whirring, followed by raucous laughter. Jock, the Sparrow Hawk looked positively petrified when he pulled up outside the grand entrance. Spellbound showered his face with a million kisses and tickled him under his wings. If this were to become the norm, he fumed, he would give in his notice and bogger back off to Snotland.

"WOWEEEE … Drill," she shouted as she leapt off the back of the bird, changing him back to his former plumage.

"I didn't know you lived in a castle!" she said excitedly. "What a place, what a wonderful place!" she exclaimed. "Not as big as Papa's pad or Fingleberry Manor, but hey ho, I'm no snob. I don't mind slumming it for one night. You don't have ghosts, do you?" She chortled hysterically and slapped him on the back. "If you do, I'm gone!" Drillian lurched forward, nearly losing his balance. He'd never been with a Fairy that was richer than him, nor had he been with one this excitable and unpredictable!

Spellbound glided towards the immense golden doors, where two footmen stood to attention, one at each side. In true Fairy fashion, she did a sweeping curtsey and held her hand to her breast before speaking in her most genteel voice.

"Why thank you, kind sirrahs!" she said, as one of the footmen stood aside and ushered her into the grand entrance. In two seconds flat, both servants were turned into giant green bunny rabbits chewing over-sized carrots. Drillian looked up to the heavens and tutted as he followed her inside.

Spellbound stopped abruptly in the grand hall and gazed in awe at her surroundings. She had always had a passion for history and loved anything to do with the past. It was as if she had stepped back in time. She paused to take in the opulence of the spiral staircase before her, and the imposing pictures of the family's ancestors which covered the walls. Her giddy mood subsided as she began investigating each of the portraits and then she lifted her arms and fluttered upwards.

"WOW, what a hottie" she said, as she looked closely at a painting of a handsome Elf. He resembled Drillian a little, but his hair was darker and he had a deep, sensitive look in his sparkling blue eyes. "Is everyone here from the Macavity clan then?" she shouted down with genuine interest.

"Yep, every single one of them," he replied. "Cumalot Castle has been in the family for generations! That dude you are looking at there is one of my great, great, ancient Uncles called Maximus Macavity. He owned all the lands around here back in the 18th century. The historical documents say that he was half Warlock, half Elf. I think the painting of his mother is somewhere around here ... Er Spell, you are going change my doormen back to their original form, aren't you?"

"Later Drill, later, I promise," she replied, fluttering downwards. Poking her head around an open door, she returned to her former giggly self.

"Where's the kitchen? I fancy some cake; I've been craving some all morning?" He started to answer but she interrupted him, her tone more serious. "Do they call you Drill because you're always screwing? HAHA!" she teased, pleased with her scintillating wit. "I'M SO FUNNY! ..." He had a hard time keeping up with her. "I really fancy something sweet like cake or ..." she paused dramatically, "Chocolate! I love human chocolate; bet you haven't got any of that Mr smarty pants!" Drillian shouted for a maid to go and fetch the Fairy some chocolate.

"It won't do your teeth one bit of good," he remonstrated sternly, as she sat with the chocolate bar wedged between her thighs, while she greedily chomped off big, thick chunks.

"Never mind the teef, Drill, this is amazing, I tell you, sheer, spaddywhacking heaven. You are so lucky to be able to get this stuff. I hear it takes some serious courage to rob a human child of its chocolate. Poor little spoilt bleeders!"

"You'll want a drink or something to wash that down, won't you?" he said, getting up from the couch and walking over to the drink's cabinet, mustering up a casual air.

The room was bedecked in gorgeous fabrics, the tall arched windows were adorned with luxury cream drapes and on the floor were faux, hugga-hugga bear rugs. The maid was hovering over

Spellbound, collecting the stray pieces of chocolate that had fallen onto the carpet; she secretly pushed them into her pinafore pocket for later. Drillian poured Spellbound a glass of bluebellade and then with only a moment's hesitation, he discreetly emptied the entire contents of Fenella's glass bottle into the liquid and watched it bubble and foam.

Finally, when the potion had settled down to leave a clear, delicious tasting liquid, he walked over and offered the glass to Spellbound, who looked up for a moment from the chocolate bar, which was fast disappearing.

"Oh, Drill, I couldn't possibly drink that!" she groaned, holding her stomach, her face turning a little green. "I think I've overdone it," she let out a little burp. "My innards are aching. Y'know, I think I'm gonna be ..." she heaved twice, "mmmm ... quick Drill, I'm gonna be...!" She hurtled across the room, knocking an antique standard lamp over, smashing the priceless Miffiny shade into a million smithereens. She flew at full speed, out of an open window and yicked up all over the grass. Drillian was motionless and wondered if he should abandon the whole damn seduction scene! This was not working out at all as he had expected. He turned to the maid. "Put Miss Zamforia to bed please. She has clearly over-indulged herself with too much chocolate. See to it now," he snapped impatiently.

When Drillian came into her chamber, Spellbound was lying flat on her stomach in the four-poster bed groaning, her wings pointing northwards and her legs spread wide.

"Feeling better?" he asked, as he placed the glass of potion on the table beside the bed.

"A little," she whimpered. "Mamma's always nagging me about overeating. I've only ever tasted chocolate once before, and even then, it was no more than a slither," she said with a half-hearted smile.

All Drillian could think about was just how much precious time she was wasting. Seeing her spread-eagled on the bed like that, looking all sorry for herself, only made him want to gather her up in his strong arms and smother her with kisses. With a tender gesture, he sat beside her and stroked her copper silken hair away from her eyes.

"Poor little Fairy? You want me to kiss you better?"

"Just fookin' try it!" she said slowly, still looking a little pained. "I know what your game is, trying to sweet talk me. Mamma has given me many lessons in chat up lines, so bogger off, Romeo," she said, swiping his hand away and luckily missing his nose by a cat's whisker.

"You really don't like me, do you, Spell?" he said, standing up, looking hurt. "I'll be downstairs in the library when you feel ready for work." His last-ditch attempt at trying to get close to her had failed miserably. She still hated the idea of him touching her. Maybe all of this was for nothing. He had spent a fortune … but for what!

Spellbound sat up in bed and admired the room. The walls were embellished with rich tapestries and the ceiling was ornately painted with cherubs and fairies from years gone by. In the middle of the ceiling was a huge mirror. She sniffed in disgust. Typical of him to want to look up everybody's arses, she thought. There was a series of buttons on the headboard and she pushed one curiously. Out sprang a pair of fluffy pink handcuffs. She tried another and a little white vibrator with bunny's ears plopped into her lap, making whirring noises. She threw it across the room in disgust and shouted, "Pervy git!" In the corner was a bathtub full of pink, warm bubbling water, surrounded by a beautiful shimmering lace curtain. Spellbound decided that as soon as she got home, she would ask Mamma for one of the same.

From all of the yicking, her mouth felt dry and tasted weird. She pulled her tongue out and made a strange face. Looking around her, she spotted the inviting drink next to the bed and reached out her hand. The first sip tasted like blueberries, the second like fresh oranges, the third was like an exotic passion juice. It was sensational, she thought. Without thinking, she drained the entire contents of the glass and all the sickness and bloaty feelings she had previously felt, left her in an instant.

"Wow, that's luminous stuff," she said aloud. "I must get Drill to give me some more of that." She leapt off the bed to go in search of him when all of a sudden, the sheer mention of his name made her feel all funny and gooey inside. "Oh … Drillian," she said out loud again,

"Where are you?"

Drillian was sitting in the library, a long oblong room, lined with bookcases from floor to ceiling. As he was flicking his way through the Carma Sultry, he heard a commotion from the adjoining hall. Suddenly Spellbound appeared at one end of the library hovering about a foot from the ground. Her wings were perky and bright silver and, in the distance, he could see an intense, cheeky look on her face. Without further ado, she flew as fast as her wings could carry her towards him and then wrapped her long, Fairy legs around his waist, holding onto him tightly.

Drillian was so taken aback that he nearly fell into the fireplace as she planted a thousand kisses all over his eyes and nose.

"Oh Drilly Willy," she gushed excitedly. "Wow, you are such a hottie. I have this funny feeling rushing all through my Fairy veins … muah … muah … muah!" She continued to kiss his face, covering every inch.

Drillian held the Fairy in his arms and even though he had planned this whole event and even fantasised about how she would be after drinking the potion, he was still knocked for six at the result. Fenella had obviously decided that he was going to get his money's worth!

"I think I lurve you, Drilly boy," she cooed. "I do, I do, I luuuurrrrrrve you."

"You do?" he asked, looking shocked, as she continued to shower her with kisses.

"Oh yes, I do, I do, I do. Come on, you gorgeous Elf," she said, throwing her head back and bouncing on his hips, "Show me what all the fuss is about, let's do the rumpy-pumpy thing ... whatever that is! And I wanna see your rodger the todger ... I ain't never seen one up close before ... are your mushrooms twitching, Drilly babe ... Are they? Show me your pork chop, let's have a peek ... don't be shy, hunny!"

"Spellbound ... er ... Spell," he said, overwhelmed by her effusive behaviour. "There's ... er ... plenty of time for that, now settle down, hun ... just try and er ..." In a flash, she leapt out of his arms, whipped out her wand, and zapped his clothes clean off his body. Drillian stood there, butt naked, quickly covering his elfhood with both hands.

"Spell, hun ... what have you done?" he cried. He usually took the lead and he wasn't expecting this! She circled him, taking in every part of his lean, tanned, athletic body.

"Wowwee!" she breathed heavily. "You *are* a cutie, look at that botty! Cor, I never thought you would be the shy type." She took her wand and tickled his bottom with it, causing him to jump and immediately push the staff away. She eyed his Elfhood with wide eyes, inspecting the end with the tip of her wand. "This is all new to me," she said, grinning from ear to ear. "Where *exactly* do you put it, Drilly? Which pee pee hole does it live in? Mamma always refused to talk about the rumpy thing to me."

Drillian was getting more embarrassed by the minute.

"Spell, listen ..." he tried to say, but another zap of magic from her power happy wand saw her stripped off to just a tiny, twinkling, turquoise thong. Drillian gulped at the sight of the naked Fairy and then a second later, Spellbound zapped him again and they were both lying on the four-poster bed covered in shooting Fairy dust and romantic pink stars. She waved her wand one last time over the headboard and out popped the handcuffs, three vibrators and a porno magazine.

He was utterly astounded at the change in her, but still had the presence of mind to press another small button on the side of the nightstand. At once, an array of orange, green and blue Fairy lights whizzed around their heads, obscuring them from view.

"Drilly ... oh Drilly," Spellbound sang lightly in his sleepy ear. There was no response. After a few more minutes of tickling him, nibbling his neck and yanking on his elfhood, she decided to bounce, frantically up and down on his stomach.

"UGH ... HUH ...WHUUUU!"

"Wakey wakey, Elfman," she yelled, "I wanna do it again ... hehe, let's do it again!" she bellowed as she continued to jump up and down on his chest. Drillian, true to form, and with a hearty laugh, gathered her up in his arms.

"I need to eat Drill," Spellbound said, after their sixth marathon session. "Rumpy-pumpy doesn't half make you hungry. I never knew I would like it as much as this. Can we do it every day, Drill?" Her eyes were wide and excitable. "And you'd better not be having none of them other Fairies either, not now that I lurvve you. I'm gonna zap that *Totty* list into another realm where you can't find it. We Zamforian Fairies are very jealous and as you know, we can cast nasty banishment spells at the flick of a wand," she half-joked. He gulped nervously. "Now that I lurve you so much, any funny business and I'll be banishing you, do you hear? Just like Mamma did with Papa." Drillian lay completely naked and depleted on the bed. This was one fookin', energetic Fairy. Sure, he had the stamina, he was renowned for it, but four times on the bed, once in the bathtub, and three times on top of the wardrobe, had left him feeling totally knackered!

"Banishing sounds like a perfect idea right now," he said with a chuckle, rolling her over again.

❧ ❧ ❧

"Something just doesn't feel right, Clifford," Leticia murmured as she paced the room. "Something is definitely amiss. I have this extraordinary feeling in my gut and ..." she paused, scratching her head for a moment.

"I know what it is! It's Spellbound, she's ... she's ..." Swirling her wand three times around her head and chanting something in elvish, she cast a quick spell.

Back at Cumalot Castle, Drillian was seriously enjoying himself, yet again. He was murmuring something romantic in her ear when in a flash, she disappeared into thin air. Spellbound tumbled into the centre of Leticia's parlour, as naked as the day she was born. Her lipstick was smudged across her face and her hair was sticking up like a haystack.

"MAMMA!!! What the fook do you think you're doing?" she screeched, wrapping her wings around her body to cover her modesty.

"More like what the fook have YOU been doing?" Leticia said aghast. "You've been having rumpy-pumpy, haven't you! I can't believe it, Spellbound, you've gone and been rumped!"

"Leticia, now stop interfering," interrupted Clifford. "She has Hester's genes; if she's lain with an Elf, I'm sure that it is all good and proper and that she's in love." He pointed his wand at Spellbound and in a flash a pink velvet cape covered her body.

Leticia ignored him. "Who is the Elf responsible for this?" she demanded.

Spellbound looked down at the floor and giggled. "Clifford's right. I'm in lurrrvve Mamma, I really am."

"WHO, SPELLBOUND?"

"Drilly, of course, oh! He's such a stud, Mamma," she simpered, twisting a lock of her hair coyly.

"That sex-crazed, Elf guy?" Leticia expostulated. "Oh, lordy lord, what have you done you stupid, stupid Fairy?

Clifford could see the highly charged situation was getting out of hand and so tried to introduce some calm and reason.

"If Spellbound says that she is in love with Drillian, then she surely must be. And he's a good catch, one of the richest Elves in the realm. One can't complain about her choice of partner."

"HE'S A SPADDY-WACKING GRUNT FUTTOCK!" Leticia wailed, as she wrung her hands.

"Well, that's a bit steep; more of a young rake, I would say, Clifford, smiled. "But I'm sure he'll settle. I did say that I felt he was sweet on her, so maybe it's not such a bad thing!"

"Yes, but he's still a spaddy-whacker!" she groaned.

"Can I go now?" Spellbound asked impatiently. "It's just that, we were … y' know in the middle of something …"

Clifford waved his hand over Spellbound's face and she vanished as quickly as she had arrived.

Drillian was lying in the ornate four-poster bed. Spellbound's sudden disappearance had left him feeling rather lonely. A puff of purple smoke engulfed the room as she appeared again. She crawled up the bed on her hands and knees and roared like a tigress. His frown suddenly changed into a smile as he reached for her.

"Welcome back, Miss Pussykins!"

As the morning sun peeked through a gap in the curtain, Spellbound felt a tiny, tickling sensation on each of her toes and giggled. Opening her eyes, she stretched her arms above her head and in true-to-form sleepy style, lifted the other leg high in the air and pointed it to the ceiling. Suddenly, she remembered the events of the evening before and sat bolt upright in the bed, covering her face in utter shame. A low throaty chuckle made her look up and there at the bottom of the bed was Drillian Macavity planting tiny kisses on the instep of her left foot. With a kick like a mule, she caught him square on the jaw and he back-flipped off the bed, landing on the floor in an untidy heap.

"I can't believe I let you do those things to me last night!" she shouted. And with a flick of her wand and a puff of smoke, she disappeared into the ether.

CHAPTER 15
MARCO'S RETURN

Leticia scrutinised her reflection in the cheval mirror. She was an absolute vision; not one detail could be criticised. Her red, dazzling ball gown was very slim fitting and the basque bodice, which was covered in clusters of small rubies, showed off her curves to perfection. Her hair was in a Grecian style and she had a tanzanite and emerald tortoiseshell comb holding back the raven-black tresses. She had to look her best as she was going to be interviewed for the Fairyland Live TV show, about the publication of her new Spells and Swoon bestseller.

"Wow Mamma, you look like an absolute Goddess!" exclaimed Spellbound, from the other side of the room. Leticia smiled and went over to her daughter, who was dressed in a long emerald silk sheath, trimmed with a little hood of fake wolverine fur framing her perfect oval features.

"You look magnificent too, Spellbound, and your face is radiant. It's so good to see you happy and vibrant. Have you forgiven naughty, silly Mamma for all that's gone by?" she asked in a strained voice. Spellbound nodded and laughed as she rose two feet in the air and spun around, showering sparks everywhere. Being free of the yearning had improved her magic and her mood, thrice fold.

"I'm sure I'll be completely over it all Mamma, once I can see my Papa again," she said excitedly.

Clifford stood in the doorway, resplendent in damask black silk, a white lace jabot at his throat. Spellbound darted past him, whizzing fairy dust everywhere with her wand.

"See you in a minute or two!" she laughed, and in a flash, she was gone.

Clifford smiled. "She is so joyful, Leticia, and you ... well ..." He came towards her and held both her hands. "I have never seen you look so beautiful."

She looked up into his hazel eyes and touched his cheek fondly. "I don't know what I would have done without you, these last few weeks, Clifford."

He felt a strong urge to kiss her and savour her sweet lips for a moment, but he knew that he must resist, for now anyway.

"Ready?" he asked, offering her his arm.

Fingleberry Manor was alive with cameras and the ever so famous Elf, Jeri Swinger, was swotting up on his notes before the interview. The makeup Fairies were following him around with brushes and powder puffs at the ready. Leticia lifted her skirts and stepped over a huge electrical cable, manoeuvring around the throng of technicians. Clifford's held her elbow reassuringly as he knew how nervous she was. There was less than twenty minutes to go before the broadcast started. She welcomed her guests and thanked them all for coming. Philip and Drillian Macavity gave her a formal bow as she approached them. Spellbound left her group of friends and made her way over to Clifford and Leticia again.

"Mamma, are you okay? Not long to go now, isn't it exciting?" she bubbled, deliberately ignoring Drillian and his father.

Philip feasted his eyes on the alluring swell of Leticia's bodice. "Leticia, you look divine, my dear, truly divine."

She glanced up and nodded.

"And this must be Eyesaurus, your Warlock friend. I bet you are relieved to be out of that dratted ball!"

Clifford pulled Leticia towards him, while looking over at Philip haughtily.

"Madam Zamforia, you are wanted in the library; they are ready for the broadcast," informed the producer's PA, thankfully interrupting the sudden awkward silence.

Leticia followed the PA, hurriedly greeting everyone, as she scurried passed them. She mouthed "See you later" to the Duke, Duchess and Caitlyn, as she waved to them gaily. She hadn't realised how many fae folks she had invited. There must be over a hundred here tonight, she thought.

She had just sat down in her chair, a little flustered by all the lights and cameras pointing in her direction, when Jeri Swinger came over and grabbed her hand, giving it a wet kiss.

"Ah, the famous Leticia Zamforia! What a sight ... what a sight! Loved your new book; stayed up all night reading it and was shattered all the next day," he enthused with a twinkle in his watery blue eyes.

Leticia took a deep breath and did a small spell for composure. The cameras moved in and the interview began.

An hour later and feeling much relieved, she headed towards the refreshment tables where she bumped into Caitlyn. Her old friend was well-read, not to mention highly intelligent, and had painstakingly edited every single book Leticia had written. Being the refined Fairy that she was, every swear word was removed and Leticia's hit and miss grammar was made perfect.

"How did it go, dearest? I hope you didn't fluff your lines?" Leticia took a massive swig of poppy punch and shook her head.

"Went like a dream, Cait, I was so nervous though!"

"Well, it's over now, come on, you have to sign your books. There's a queue a mile long in the lounge."

After an exhausting session of signing copies of her book, Leticia's hand began to hurt, it was time for a short break. There was a cheerful atmosphere in the vast lounge as the poppy punch started to take effect. She stood up and stretched her wings, making her way to the refreshment tables. She could see Spellbound surrounded by half a dozen young Elfmen and Drillian lurking in the background, his face like thunder as he couldn't get near her.

Philip Macavity made another bee-line for her and she frowned. She just wanted a little breather, not all this attention. It had taken her twenty minutes as well to shake off Jeri Swinger after the interview had finished.

"Leticia, you look stunning," Philip said, as he went to take her hand, Clifford caught sight of the situation and was at her side in an instant.

"I see you have the rottweiler in attendance," Philip hissed.

Suddenly, a huge crack of lightning and a purple and scarlet explosion rocked the lounge to its foundation. Twenty of the fifty crystal chandeliers shattered and fell in shards at the guests' feet. Molten balls of fairy dust flew in all directions and some of the guests ducked as great clouds of it billowed towards them.

To everyone's astonishment, Marco Zamforia stepped out of the swirling green mist and the guests gasped. He looked stunning in a silver and black tunic; his emerald green eyes furious yet magnificent. His gaze swept over the room and fell on Leticia, who stood rigidly, her mouth had dropped open in shock. Clifford raised himself up to his full height and firmly brought her closer to him.

"Leticia ... COME HERE THIS INSTANT!" Marco roared.

She tossed her head in the air and spat out coldly, "I see you're back, but you will not get any welcome from me." He strode towards her, his face thunderous. Immediately, a pathway opened before him. He was still several steps away from her when Clifford stood in front of him, barring the way.

"And who, pray, are you, sir?" Marco bit out.

"Clifford Eyesaurus ... sir!"

"The Eyesaurus of the crystal ball?"

"The very same one."

Leticia pushed passed Clifford and Marco's cold gaze scrutinised her from head to toe. Grabbing her arm, he started to march her towards the door, "You have a lot of explaining to do Madam."

"Get your filthy hands off me, Marco. Everything you have endured is your own fault … not mine, now leave me be!" Leticia gasped as she struggled to free herself.

Clifford intervened and forcefully loosened Marco's grip on Leticia's arm, his hand on the dirk at his side.

"Leave her, Marco. Do as she says."

"Let go of my wife, Eyesaurus, or you'll be sorry. Do you think you have some right to her or something?" Clifford laughed softly and the throng watched in total fascination as the Elf and the Warlock squared up to each other.

At that moment, Spellbound ran like the wind across the room and threw her arms around Marco, showering his face in kisses.

"Papa … Papa! Oh, my goodness, It's really you! I've missed you so much and I have so many things to tell you." Spellbound was wrapped around her father, clinging on tightly to him; her eyes filling with tears of joy. Papa, promise me you will never go away again!"

Marco's demeanour changed as he held his daughter slightly away from him. His eyes lit up, and a huge smile graced his lips. He embraced her again, pulling her into his arms, this time kissing her on her cheek. " Spellbound! You're so beautiful, sweetheart, and all grown-up! You have no idea how much I have missed you too. It's been hell not seeing you." Spellbound began to lead her father away from the crowd, wanting desperately to have him all to herself. "Darling wait a moment. I want to know everything, but I need to talk to your mother first," he said. "Would you give us just a little while? Then we can spend the rest of the evening catching up."

Leticia was standing near the door, her head held high. He had got his precious daughter and the quicker she had her own life and got a divorce, the better, she thought.

"Leticia," Marco said, aware that his daughter was watching the scene, he proceeded in a quieter manner. "You have a great deal of explaining to do and I am not going to reveal my private life in front of the whole goddamn Fairy kingdom!" he said.

"Leticia, you must speak with him and get it over and done with," Clifford whispered urgently. "You'll have no peace until it is sorted out and he will not leave it be, that is for sure."

He had barely finished speaking when there was another almighty bang and flash and Tinky Bonk appeared in the middle of the room, bedraggled and worse for wear. She looked confused. Her skin was rather pale and soiled, her hair was mussed, and the ends of her famous wings were a dull grey and bent at the tips. Leticia sniffed and glared at her disdainfully.

"That's all we fookin' need, blewdy Tinky Bonk! Well, at least you won't have to go looking for each other." In a flash, she once again pointed her wand at the bedraggled Fairy and turned her into a fat, slimy slug. Spellbound, watched the commotion and slapped her hand to her mouth in horror as the rest of the guests gasped. An Elf technician edged in from the side-lines, with his TV camera perched on his shoulder. It was clear he was filming the entire event.

"Remove yourself NOW!" she said, pointing her wand at him, "or I'll turn you into her snail companion." Within a nano-second the camera was a pile of dust at his feet. The Elf fled in terror, wailing at the top of his voice.

Marco, not caring about the spectacle, grabbed Leticia's arm and frog-marched her towards the library, her feet nearly leaving the ground. He turned to the throng and announced formally with a stiff smile, "Thank you for your company but the party is over. Spellbound, please do me the honour of showing our guests out."

"Oh, and can you get the butler to remove the slug from the carpet, darling, he can pop it on a cabbage leaf, I expect she'll be hungry?" Leticia shot over her shoulder.

Clifford sprang forward, "I'll be waiting outside the door, should you need me. She nodded and mouthed a silent thank you.

As she and Marco entered the library, Leticia prised her arm from his steely grip and rounded on him furiously.

"How dare you show me up in front of my friends! And take your fookin' hands off me!"

"I see we still have the language of a guttersnipe, that much hasn't changed, has it?" he snarled sarcastically. "Now, start explaining. I want to know WHY you banished me to that desert island for three years and it had better be good."

Leticia rubbed her arm and saw a bruise appearing where he had placed his firm grip.

"Well, I am waiting," he said, folding his arms and looking her over from top to toe.

She squirmed under his intense scrutiny and then bit out coldly.

"You know full well why I banished your sorry ass. Don't pretend that you have no clue!"

"Oh, is that so?" he replied in a clipped manner. "Please do remind me, because I fear I may have FORGOTTEN!"

"If you had wanted an affair with Tinky Bonk, then why did you not say? Why didn't you just come clean and be a real Elf? Why let me discover you both in the Cherub Pagoda, in the hot tub, no least, fornicating like wild rabbits. You disgust me!"

Marco looked astounded. "Are you mad?" he said. "What the HELL are you talking about?"

"Oh, don't give me that. I saw you with my own eyes, Marco, so don't bother lying to me.

"You are one hell of a crazy Fairy Leticia. Fornicating with Tinky? That's bizarre! You banished me for THREE FOOKING YEARS because of something I never even did!"

Leticia was tired, her head was aching with all the stress. She slumped into a nearby chair and placed her hand on her forehead.

"Okay, so I was outraged at the time and perhaps banishing you was a bit harsh but …"

"A BIT?"

"You have to understand, the pain was too hard to bear." Her violet eyes flashed and she looked down at the ground, her voice becoming quieter. "I paid for what I did, and it nearly turned into the biggest nightmare you could imagine. It affected Spellbound terribly. She went into the yearning for you and started to turn into a golden hare. It was truly awful." She gazed up with a venomous look. "I do regret it. I wish more than anything that I could turn the clock back, because you weren't worth the energy, I spent on getting you and your strumpet banished, you weren't worth nearly losing my daughter over."

Marco's nostrils flared, "I was not in any godforsaken hot tub with Tinky Bonk," he snarled. "Your eyes must have deceived you. Can you honestly sit there and say that I was rumping with Tinky Bonk when you know full well that it was you and I who were together that night in the tub, Leticia." He turned his back on her and walked towards the fireplace, rubbing his chin with his hand. "You must have been drunk or hallucinating or something. Maybe you were losing your fookin' mind, I don't know but I tell you this, I don't care what you thought you saw; you are very much mistaken."

"How dare you!" she replied hotly, rising from the chair. "Are you calling me a liar, are you seriously telling me that I don't know what I actually saw or that I might have been inebriated. Oh, well that's rich! Make all the excuses you want Marco ... you are as guilty as sin and you know it!"

Suddenly she was overcome with exhaustion. The recent shock of nearly losing her only child and then his unwelcome appearance in front of her guests, was all too much to bear. She sighed and turned to gaze at him dispassionately.

"What does it matter now? I have said I am sorry for banishing you, I can't do any more. You think you are right and *I know* I am right. I'm sick of arguing with you, I'm sick of hurting and I'm sick of this. Just do us both a favour and leave, Marco. Tinky is waiting outside for you. She'll be back to her usual self in an hour ... just go."

He strode over to her and glared down into her tear-filled, violet eyes.

"You took three years of my life without a thought to how I would feel. If my magic were as powerful as yours, you'd be sitting on that blewdy sand dune right now, do you hear me?"

"I've had three years to get used to not having you around and I want a divorce, Marco. Don't worry, I won't take a brass fettial from you; I have my own wealth and career now, so you can be as free as the day we met. Go and be with your vile Fairy. Our marriage has been a farce for too long. I was a stupid, young, foolish Fairy who got carried away with the romance of it all. I'm fully grown now and I have learned better. Now go and claim the love of your life. I'll get my lawyers to draw up the papers tomorrow!" His eyes were as cold as ice, as he circled her like a wolf does its prey, and then he laughed softly.

"You'll have no divorce from me Leticia. If you have set your sights on another, then you'll have a very long wait!" He spun on his left foot and headed towards the door.

"I'm going to be with my daughter. I bid you goodnight!"

CHAPTER 16
KEEP YOUR DISTANCE

Leticia surveyed the upheaval in her beautiful home. There were broken chandeliers everywhere and crimson and purple dust covered the alabaster furniture. She took her yew wand and with a flourish, she whipped it over her head. In an instant order was restored. Smoothing her dress down, she turned to leave when she saw Clifford leaning in the doorway. He clapped slowly and walked towards her. "Clever little Fairy. No-one would know we had a lightning storm in here last night," he smiled. Leticia was still smarting over Marco's treatment of her the night before, which had made her feel so humiliated. The Fairy phone hadn't stopped ringing, with curious guests calling to express their concern. She would have to think up something very convincing to stop the wagging tongues. They walked into the dining room together and Clifford pulled her chair out before sitting down opposite her. Three butlers placed food, piping hot chocolate and the Fairy gazette on the table. When they had gone Clifford looked quizzically at Leticia,

"Well, are you going to inform me of what happened between you and Marco last night, or do I have to guess?"

She shrugged irritably and bit delicately into a Fairy cake. "He was adamant that he hadn't seduced that loathsome creature and then had the audacity to say that I must have been drunk. According to Marco, it was me he was making love to that night.

Any excuse. Does he think I have old-timer's disease? Oh, and I asked him for a divorce too." Clifford leaned forward and stared straight into her eyes.

"And what did he say about that? He must have agreed straight away."

She shook her head and took a sip of the delicious hot chocolate.

"He refused, Clifford … point-blank refused me and said I would have to wait a long time. I think he wants to punish me for sending him to that island."

"What!" Clifford expostulated. "Refused you?"

"Yes, what a grunt-futtock!" she sniffed disdainfully.

When Marco returned, the family home in Bluebell Forest had been magically transformed to its former splendour, with spectacular turrets and arch-shaped windows, overlooking the rolling lawns. Spellbound had spent the last week with her father and had forgotten how beautiful it was. Her room was located inside of one of the turrets where she could see the pale yellow Elkies, which were very much like tiny deer but they had twinkling crystal antlers. Marco had nearly three hundred in the herd and there was an abundance of babies which played and frolicked.

The only thing which persistently puzzled Spellbound was her father's absolute denial that he had been in the hot tub with Tinky Bonk that fateful night. She had to keep herself from embarrassing him by revealing that she'd seen the shocking scene with her very own eyes, in Clifford's ball.

In the days that followed, Marco paced up and down in the library relentlessly, hands clasped behind his back, still visibly furious with Leticia. How Spellbound wished she could get them back together and be united as a family again but she remembered what her mother had said about how she'd interrupted his Karma with Tinky and so she decided not to press the issue. Deep down inside, she dreaded that Tinky Bonk might one day become her step-mother and wondered how that would pan out! Spellbound sighed and vowed she would never get married. It was all a load of rubbish anyway.

A few days later, Leticia confessed all to the Duchess: what she had seen in the Pagoda and how she'd consequently banished her husband and Tinky Bonk. Esmee nodded and tutted in all the right places.

"I can't believe this of Marco, Leticia. Are you sure that is what you saw?"

Leticia nodded. "I saw the truth, but do you want to know something, Esmee? He's refused point-blank to give me a divorce. I no longer care. I am done with men, the rotten spaddy-whackers."

Esmee gulped. "You asked Marco for a divorce? Surely not, Leticia … not with his pedigree! Could you not overlook his indiscretion, for Spellbound's sake at least?"

"Spellbound knows it all and she accepts my decision. She is free to go where she wants, especially as she's fully grown. I have to cut the apron strings sooner or later, don't I? I'm just going to concentrate on my career from now on," Leticia sighed.

Pavasnotty was performing at the Fairy Opera House and Leticia and Caitlyn had front row seats. She needed a good night out, now that the gossip had finally died down. They were a little late getting to the theatre and had to find their seats in the dark. Pavasnotty was already on stage and in full tenor voice. Trying to be as invisible as possible, they sank down into the deep, velvet, rose upholstery and became immersed in the wonderful performance. As he sang the last cords of *Missing Korma*, Leticia grabbed her little lace hankie and dabbed it delicately at the corner of her eyes. He was genuinely impressive, she thought. Sensing the person next to her was staring; she turned and met the ice green gaze of Marco.

"What the fookin' hell are you doing here?" she whispered aggressively.

"I might ask you the same thing," he bit back.

"Shush, dearest … the whole place can hear you," Caitlyn admonished nervously. She then saw Marco and sighed.

"That's it. I'm leaving," said Leticia, gathering up her bag and stole.

"Be quiet, Leticia, and sit down," Marco said as he pushed her firmly back into her seat. "Would you like another stand-up row in front of a thousand people this time, because I sure as hell can arrange it?" he hissed.

Leticia knew he had an iron will and would do just as he said. She meekly sank back into the chair, inwardly seething.

Caitlyn patted her arm and whispered to her softly, "Just relax, dearest, and watch the opera. Better that, than cause another scene."

The lights went up and it was interval time. Leticia couldn't get out of her seat quickly enough. As she rose, she saw Lord and Lady Wizard waiting for her in the aisle. Marco grabbed her elbow and moved her towards them.

"Marco … Leticia! How nice to see you both, are you enjoying Pavasnotty?"

Marco held onto Leticia's elbow with an iron grip. "Yes, he's excellent, isn't he Leticia?" She was about to pull away when he leant over and whispered in her ear, "Just say one word out of place and we'll have a ring-dinging scene, got it?" She nodded and smiled stiffly, a delicate flush creeping up her neck. Lord Wizard smiled at Caitlyn. "Do join us for drinks and Marco, we can't wait to hear about your visit to the Austrial realm."

"Austrial realm?" Marco cocked his eyebrow at Leticia as they followed Lord and Lady Wizard to the bar.

"I'm just going to powder my wings," she said quickly.

"Don't bother Leticia. You know very well how to do a pee spell." He laughed good-naturedly with Lord and Lady Wizard. Caitlyn looked bemused and quickly engaged Lady Wizard in conversation. When Leticia returned to her seat, she was fuming. She'd had to pretend for thirty minutes to be the adoring wife but what really infuriated her was Marco's enjoyment, he was clearly loving every minute of the charade. She resolutely fixed her gaze on the stage and tried to calm herself.

"Deep breath … deep breath …" Marco smiled cynically, sensing her discomfort.

"You fookin' bladderbart. Do you think this is funny?" she seethed with frustration.

After the fifth encore, Pavasnotty bowed and left the stage, and the audience slowly started to exit the theatre. Leticia was exhausted, but there were at least thirty acquaintances who wanted to stop and greet them. Marco held her hand tightly as he smiled, engaging his friends amicably. He was really prolonging her punishment.

Leticia waved goodbye to Caitlyn and waited for Stanley, her Magpie, to appear. Marco was idly chatting to a few Elves when his Lotus swept up to the entrance causing quite a commotion.

Leticia breathed a sigh of relief. She could finally be rid of him, be able to crawl into her bed and sleep off this nightmare of an evening. She turned and moved a few steps away from him, searching the skies for Stanley, who was unusually late. At this rate, she was thinking of using her own wings to get herself home.

An admiring crowd soon gathered around Marco's flashy car, which changed colour every few seconds. It thrummed and vibrated with the most fantastic chords. How she missed that car, she thought. It was so incredible. It could fly, go underwater and change shape, not to mention turn into the comfiest bed. She spotted Stanley at last and walked towards him, but before she had moved three steps, she found herself magically propelled towards the Lotus and pushed in the front passenger seat. Marco grinned and waved to everyone as he changed the gears expertly and drove off.

"Okay Marco … just what do you think you are doing?" Leticia gasped indignantly.

"You're my wife, Leticia, so try and behave as if you are. I'm taking you home right now."

"You are blewdy well not taking me home, buzzard face. I can't stand the sight of you and I can't wait to be free of you, you two-timing grunt-futtock!"

He stopped the car with a screech of tyres and turned towards her angrily. Pulling her roughly to him, he forced her mouth onto his. After a while, his lips softened as he looked into her incredible violet eyes.

Leticia was so taken aback by his sudden kiss that she momentarily surrendered. It seemed so natural to be in his arms and to be kissed so passionately by her husband, but then all the past events came flooding back and she did something she had never done before, she pushed him away.

Marco pulled her towards him again and once more, he kissed her but this time she froze, as cold as ice. In a magical flash and a sparkle and a lingering smell of her intoxicating perfume, his arms were suddenly empty and Leticia was safely back at home.

She swept into the grand hall and threw her stole and sequinned bag onto the ornate chest, still in a fury with Marco and his arrogant, stubborn attitude. She couldn't bear to be controlled at the best of times, but this really was the last straw. The anger she felt was so intense, she felt like banishing him all over again, back to his coral isle where he belonged!

Clifford was waiting for her, looking resplendent in an olive-green doublet. He seemed to favour the more sombre colours, which were virtually unseen in Fairyland.

"Thank you for teleporting me back home Clifford," she said, while checking her appearance in the cheval mirror. "That's a very handy knack you have of knowing exactly when I need rescuing."

"I sensed there was something wrong," he replied. "Is there? Your face is like a thunderous moon, so I am guessing I was correct?"

She beckoned him into the sumptuous lounge and threw herself onto the sofa with a deep sigh, head in her hands. She then looked up and bitterly declared, "It's him again! He was at the opera tonight and just happened to be sitting next to me. Can you believe that? He proceeded to take over the whole evening, insisting that I co-operate with him and threatening me with another awful scene if I refused. He enjoyed every minute of it too, acting as if we were still married, the ginko!"

Clifford frowned, "But I don't understand this, Leticia. You did reverse the love spell you had over him, did you not?"

She nodded vehemently, "Of course I did. I made sure of that. When has a spell of mine never not worked? No, he is punishing me for banishing him, that's what he's doing. He's always did have a cruel streak and if he wanted his own way, he always got it!"

"Perhaps it might be an idea to cast the spell again and make it more powerful this time. You were very confused and emotional the last time it was performed."

Leticia nodded and sighed. "Perhaps that's what happened. Oh Clifford, will this mess ever get sorted out?"

Clifford walked over and gazed longingly into her eyes.

"Fear not Milady, I will always be at your side. I will guard and watch over you always." He was inches from her, his hazel gaze mesmerising.

Leticia smiled back at him. In his own way, he was as ruthless as Marco.

"But for now, my dear, *you* need a hot tub and a good night's sleep. It will restore your spirits. I'll summon the maid to assist you."

The next morning, Leticia once again went to her table and placed down all the ingredients required to work on Marco and release him from the love spell. She would make sure that it was spot on this time and put in an added dose of everything just to be certain. After a long hour of exacting detail and using three special wands, the undoing spell was complete. She could do no more and that should be the end of it now, she thought.

She sat down, poured herself a shot of poppy juice and smiled to herself before eagerly draining the glass. Now, at last, she could get on with her life. Clifford strode into the kitchen.

"Poppyade before noon, Leticia?"

She responded calmly, her mind on other things.

"Don't worry, Clifford, I don't make a habit of drinking in the day. The spell is complete now."

She had barely finished speaking when she heard the well-known screech of tyres outside on the driveway. It was Marco, and the Lotus was jet black today. She instantly turned to Clifford in alarm.

"What now?" she groaned.

Marco strode straight into the house without an invitation, his green eyes glinting with irritation when he saw Clifford.

"Pack your bags, Leticia. You're coming home and I will not take no for an answer. Now snap to it!"

Leticia threw him a look which would have killed an army of ants.

"Go away, Marco. Who do you think you are, ordering me around?"

"You are my wife and I want you where you belong. I will help you to pack."

Leticia's mind was on overdrive; had she lost the ability to perform magic all of a sudden?

Clifford stepped forward and placed his arm around her shoulder, pulling her towards him a little.

"Sir, Leticia does not wish to go with you, please honour her decision."

"If I were you, I would remove your hand from my wife right now," Marco said slowly, with a steely look.

"Your magic would be wasted on me, Zamforia, so don't bother trying. The lady no longer loves you, just accept that and move on. Give her the divorce that she wants."

"Give her the divorce she wants … so that you can wed her, you mean? I am not a fool, Eyesaurus. It's obvious you're smitten with her, but she will never be yours. She is mine and will always be mine. Now pack your things, Leticia, or I will."

Marco turned his brilliant green gaze on Leticia and he held his hand out. "Now come," he tried to coax.

Leticia turned to Clifford. "I will speak with him, Clifford, just give me a minute," she said gently.

He nodded his head and gave a small bow before retreating. Closing her eyes for a second, she took in a deep breath and turned to face Marco.

"I will not come with you," she said quietly, mustering as much self-control as she could. "Just try and accept that our marriage is over. I have apologised for banishing you and I hope in time you will come to forgive me for that." She watched as his eyes glazed over, and for a moment, guilt swept through her entire Fairy being. "Look, Marco, there is something else you should know. These feelings you have right now are not real. They never were, even in the beginning."

"What are you talking about Leticia, come on, we don't have time for this."

"No wait, I have to tell you. I'm ashamed to say that when you were engaged to Tinky, all those years ago, I cast a powerful love spell on you. I wanted to humiliate her the way she did me, so I deliberately made you mine to punish her. You were programmed to love me for life, you see, and I know it was stupid and I know I shouldn't have done such a thing, but I was young and irresponsible and filled with fury. I have tried twice to release you from the spell, so that you can be free again." She looked down with shame in her eyes. "For some reason, it doesn't seem to have worked. There … I have abased myself. There are no more secrets. You have the truth."

Marco approached her and placed both his hands on her shoulders, looking deeply into her violet eyes.

"Leticia, your magic could never affect me." He said softly. "I fell in love with you from the very first moment I saw you. You didn't need to cast some stupid spell for my love; it was always there. I have never stopped loving you, not for a second and whatever you think you saw in the Cherub Pagoda …you were mistaken." Leticia pulled away from his grasp.

"For god sake Leticia, I did not have rumpy with Tinky Bonk. I had rumpy, yes, but it was with you, can you really not remember?" he asked earnestly. He pulled her back into his arms and his lips gently touched hers. "I forgive you for banishing me. Now kiss me, Leticia … please. Let's be friends, I hate fighting with you." Leticia stood as cold as ice in his arms.

"Marco stop." She said coldly. "Please just stop it." She paused for a moment, releasing herself from his grasp. "I no longer love you; I want you to go. I'm sorry but I can't do this anymore."

With a devasted look, he stared down into her stony face and search as he might, he saw no sign of her softening.

"If that's the way you want it, then I have no choice," he said. The pain in his eyes was evident and Leticia had to look away. "But I will prove to you that I was not with Tinky Bonk in the hot tub if it takes me the rest of my life and then you *will* love me again, Leticia. There will be no divorce and Eyesaurus will NEVER have you." He turned on his heel and with a flourish of green smoke, he was gone.

Later that night, when she was alone in her bed, thoughts of the day raced through her mind. Why was Marco so hell-bent on not giving her a divorce and why did he keep making reference to Clifford wanting to take her for his wife. He really had got the wrong idea. Clifford was her friend, he had protected and looked out for her since she was born. He didn't have any romantic intentions towards her, or did he?

Chapter 17

I Quit!

Drillian looked across the dimly lit dining table at Spellbound as she pushed a Sea Pink aimlessly around her bowl. Mamma had said they tasted more delicious if you ate them alive and this one was wriggling all over the place. She hadn't the heart to gobble it up, especially as it kept making eye contact. She let out a huge sigh.

"Why are you looking so downhearted, Spell? You've barely spoken to me for three days. For goodness sake, if it's about the other night when we were at it like rabbits, I didn't hear you complaining much!"

She glared at him balefully over her bluebellade, then looked away.

"I'm not sure whether I prefer you acting like a hyperactive berry sucker or sulking like a depressed Dodibell. Just face facts that you had a great time and get over it!" he said, shovelling a fork of food into his mouth frustratedly.

Spellbound was listening to every word he was saying but was beginning to feel sick. She had succumbed to his advances, and even enjoyed it! She was supposed to have Aunt Hester's genes and only give herself willingly to the one she loved, instead, she'd leapt under the covers with an Elf who couldn't care a gnat's fart about her! In all of her growing years, she had been told by Leticia how special and unique she was, but she wasn't; she was just like the rest, she realised, she wasn't special at all!

Drillian looked up from his plate. "Will you just stop it with the silent treatment! You're making me feel uncomfortable. Jeez … Anyone would think it was a big deal or something!"

Reality suddenly struck her like a bolt of lightning. She cast her mind back to all the endless hot tub sessions, the floozie Fairy with the camel fags and the endless totty list. She knew deep down that the only reason he needed a PA was for her to coordinate his rumpy schedule and perhaps make herself available for a slot once or twice a week. She may be only ten and eight, but she was nobody's fool!

"Y'know what, Drill?" She said quietly, standing up and casually tossing the napkin down, "I can't do this anymore." She leant over to find her cobweb purse and as she did her wings turned a frosty grey. "I quit, this is not who I am." Drillian nearly choked on his food, his head thrown back in shock. For a moment he thought he'd misheard.

"I'm outta here, have a nice life."

He stared wide-eyed and open-mouthed as Spellbound sauntered gracefully across the beautiful, ornate restaurant towards the door. She then took a deep breath, stretched her arms out and with a little skip, gracefully took flight into the night sky.

Drillian sat at his desk in the library in silence. He was gazing up at the heavy bookshelves, completely preoccupied. Nobbie, his faithful and loyal butler, had brought him in a tumbler of Frisky Whiskey an hour before but it sat untouched on the small oak wood table. It had been four long days since Spellbound had walked out of the restaurant and they had to have been the worst four days of his life. He accepted that she had a tendency to be fickle and even a little outrageous. Still, he never thought for one minute that she would pass up working as his PA and walk away so easily. It was one of the most prestigious jobs in the realm!

He was beginning to regret ever having gone to see the crone Fenella. If only he had waited a while, Spellbound might have come to his bed willingly. Being two years her senior he should have known better. He raked his fingers through his thick, dark hair and hung his head, feeling defeated. If only he were magic or had some kind of power so that he could enchant her back. All he had was heaps of coinage to offer but her family was even more wealthy than his – just his bad luck! He had thought that one night with the beautiful Spellbound would satisfy his passion for her but since that day, and that oh so lovely night, he was feeling ten times, if not twenty times worse! Every single thought that entered his mind was about her; every song he heard playing on the Fairy airwaves related to her; and every time he walked past the big brass four-poster bed in the guest room, memories of that mind-blowing time came flooding back. She was exciting, unpredictable and heady. The rumpy had been dynamic and sent him into an erotic daze. Yes, it was official; he was completely fooked and had to get back to Fenella quick!

"So you're back then?" Fenella said guardedly as he entered the reeking cottage. A worried frown appeared on her face, but she attempted a feeble smile, exposing her stumpy, black teeth.

"If you've come for more of me potion, I'll 'happily sell it to ya, laddy but not if it's for the Zamforian Fairy, mind. No, I took enough of a risk already with that." She motioned for him to sit down on the mushroom stool and he did so gingerly, relieved that there was no sign of her slimy toad hopping about, but he then saw something far more alarming. Warming itself by the hearth was a huge coiled snake which slowly uncurled its massive body. Drillian gulped nervously. He had always had a fear of reptiles, mainly because they were always so much bigger than him. Why anyone wanted to keep one as a pet was a complete mystery! Hissing around Fenella's feet, she stroked its scales affectionally. Spotting Drillian, the creature slithered towards him, menacing eyes full of curiosity. Suddenly, the reptile rose high in the air, its cowled head swaying hypnotically from side to side. It moved in on the trembling Elf. The huge engorged hood flicked out with a snap and its forked tongue flashed quickly in between yellow fangs. Drillian held his breath and screwed up his eyes tightly, as Fenella spoke sharply to the beast.

"Flicka, come to mammy, that's enough now!" The snake stared into Drillian's petrified eyes, about to strike.

"Flicka, I won't tell you again, NOW … AWAY WITH YA!!" The snake turned around and slithered back to the warmth of the hearth.

"He means no 'arm, sir, just a baby really. He's only four-month-old y' see and I'm still training him." She casually picked up a small shrew that sat shaking in the corner of the room and threw it to the snake. Flicka's attention was immediately distracted as he proceeded to devour it greedily.

"Now, where were we, 'andsome chappy?" Fenella cackled. He could hear the phlegm rattling in the back of her throat. "What sort of potion would you like today?"

"It is for the Zamforian Fairy and I'll double the price," he said coldly. "But this time I need it to last for a week. She is still preoccupying my every thought and I think I need to get her out of my system totally; one night was not enough and we had lots of interruptions." Drillian knew that in order to get Fenella to agree to giving him more of the potion, he would have to pay her a handsome fee. He had cleared out his savings account, which should keep the filthy hag in comfort for the rest of her days. Fenella scratched her whiskered chin in agitation.

"Double the price eh? You must be very keen, sir!" she said in a high-pitched voice. Her eyes began darting about the cottage in a shifty manner. When she thought about money or touched it, she would almost have an instant oo'gasm. She was already dreaming up ways to spend the cash and the hopeful Drillian could see that she was giving his request some serious thought.

She suddenly fixed her gaze on the Elf and gave him a sickly grin. "Treble it and you have a deal." Drillian had a feeling she was going to say that and had already counted the exact amount of coins into another brown cloth bag. He tossed it over to her.

"Done!" he said. "Now hurry!"

As Drillian left the cottage and stealthily made his way through the gloomy hollows, he started to feel a sense of self-doubt. He used to be able to control his emotions, so why had he become so obsessed with a Fairy who was clearly out of bounds? He had never ever felt this way about anyone. When he attempted to bed the pretty Jasmine Flower the night before, the image of Spellbound had entered his mind and suddenly his Elfhood had failed to respond, leaving him feeling such a pullock! Seducing one Fairy and thinking of another just wasn't his style! Hopefully, spending one week with his beloved Spelly ... fook! Did he just say beloved? He stopped walking and gave himself a firm slap on the forehead.

"I said beloved," he muttered out loud. "What is wrong with me?"

A grasshopper leapt past him and then spoke in a deep Toncaster accent, "Ehh up, chavvie. I think yer in-love mate!"

The spell phone was yet again darting in front of Spellbound's nose. With a quick flick she tossed it towards her Mamma, who caught it expertly in her right hand.

"Tell him I'm out, Mamma, would you? I am sick to death of him asking me to come back to work."

Leticia tutted and pressed the receive call button.

"Drillian," she said icily, "Spellbound is not here, I'm afraid. She is out at the Mushroom Mall with some friends and forgot to take her phone. I'll make sure she gets the message as soon as she returns." She was becoming a dab hand at lying for her daughter and had done it four times already this week and it was only Wednesday. Surely by now Spellbound should be able to conduct her own affairs, she thought.

"That's funny," said Drillian in a low drawl. "Has Spellbound managed to magically clone herself? I am peering through your kitchen window and I can see her sitting on the chair with her feet on the table, reading the Fairy Mail!"

Leticia's gaze shot towards the kitchen window and she snapped the phone shut with a click. "Spellbound, get your fookin' feet down right now and go and let Drillian in. He's standing outside watching you through the window and he knows that I have been covering for you." She began wagging her index finger vigorously. "This is completely ridiculous, Spellbound, and the last time that you get me to do your dirty work for you, do you hear? If you've had a lovers' spat, then deal with it and do it, pronto! Lordy lord, fae kids, who'd fookin' have them?' Flouncing out of the room she slammed the door behind her making the plates on the dresser rattle noisily.

Spellbound's wings shot northwards as she glanced up from the paper and saw Drillian's dazzling smile through the window. He gave her an enthusiastic wave, as she reluctantly stood up to open the door.

"What the hell do you want; can't you take a hint? You've got a skin as thick as a rhino bug!" she said, clearly showing her irritation, her hands resting on her hips. She was wearing a black crop top and her black, leather hipster jeans revealed a cute sapphire navel jewel.

He pushed passed her and entered the kitchen. "We need to talk," he said in a business-like voice.

"Oh, we do, do we?" she replied haughtily. "Listen, Drill, I have nothing to say other than I don't wanna work for you anymore. It's a stupid job anyway and I'm tired of playing the whore house Madam. I think I can aspire to so much more, given half the chance. In fact," she said, sounding a little more enthused, "I'm thinking of becoming a writer like Mamma or opening a shop, selling potions and wands on the magic web. I haven't decided yet."

Drillian turned to face her. "Well that's nice, Spell, really it is, and I wish you well but you see, I need you to come back to work." He was thinking fast on his feet, "And if I promised that you wouldn't have to play the … er … Madam anymore," he stopped and thought again, "and if I doubled your salary, would you please consider it, just until I can get someone to replace you? It shouldn't take me too long. You have left me a bit in the lurch you know. I can't get into the files on your computer and the system is really clogged up!" He sounded desperate and Spellbound was starting to soften a little as she listened to his pleas. But suddenly she was resolute once again and decided that she would definitely not be persuaded. His eyes became tender and then he gave her a cheeky smile with a doggy-eyed expression, getting down on both knees, he shuffled up to her with his tongue hanging out and his hands placed together as if in prayer.

"Pwease?" he asked sweetly. "Pwetty pwease … I weally need you?"

Spellbound started to giggle at the silly voice he was making and threw her arms in the air. "Get up, Drill. You look ridiculous. Even Eddie isn't this much of a wonker.

"Just a few weeks?" he begged. "Two wickle weeks?"

Spellbound rolled her eyes and chuckled again. "Okay then, two weeks. But I'm warning you. No funny business, you hear? I'm not falling for your charms anymore so this will be strictly work, got it?"

He saluted her, jumping to his feet and smiling.

"Absolutely, Miss Spellbound. Strictly business it is." He stopped and fumbled in his pocket for a second, pulling out a large green glass bottle.

"Oh, I nearly forgot," he said quickly. "I've brought you a present. I know you raved on and on about the flavour changing juice so I bought you a bottle. Drink it all at once though, because it turns sour once it's opened and then tastes like pond water." He placed it on the table and walked towards the door. "See you this afternoon at 1 p.m. sharp or..." he said under his breath, "… maybe sooner!"

Spellbound sat at the table after watching Drillian whizz off on Jock Strap. It might not be that bad working for Drillian again, especially if she didn't have to entertain the entourage of Fairies in the process, she thought. No, she would work for him as usual until a replacement was found and keep him at arm's length, and then in her spare time, continue to work on her entrepreneurial ideas.

Spying the bottle, Spellbound leaned over and poured the flavour-changing juice into a glass. MMMMM ... this was lovely tasting stuff, she thought, as she drank the contents appreciatively. She must find out where he got it from so that she could ... oooooh, she thought suddenly, as a fizzy feeling started to work its way through her veins ... oooooh ... hic! She gave her stomach a gentle pat and let out a little belch.

"Drilly," she shouted as she ran towards the door. "Drilly ... wait for me!!!!"

Leticia watched Spellbound hurtle out of the house in a flurry.

"What is that fae up to now?" she said to Clifford as she walked into the kitchen. "She's always in such a hurry these days."

"Well, thank the heavens that her behaviour has calmed down a little," Clifford replied as he gazed at Leticia adoringly. "I was beginning to wonder if we would have to cast a spell on her permanently to quieten down her mood. And ... erm... while we are on the subject of moods," he said seriously, "There is something I have to tell you."

Leticia was busy tidying up the heap of newspapers on the table that Spellbound had thrown down.

"Yes, dear," she said, without looking up.

"Please be seated Leticia, for I cannot keep this from you for a moment longer." Realising that Clifford had something important to say, she stopped what she was doing and sat down. "I have been imprisoned for so long and now I am free, I have to tell you how I have felt these past years."

"Of course, you do dear. I can't imagine how difficult it must have been for you, encased in that blewdy glass and it's no wonder that you want to talk to someone about…"

"I love you, Leticia," he interrupted quickly. "More than you will ever know. I have always loved you." She felt the blood rush to her head. "You are the only thing that is important in my life, the only thing I think about, night and day!" He strode over to the other side of the table and pulled her out of the chair. Suddenly, he kissed her full on the mouth, taking her completely by surprise. Only Marco had ever kissed her before, she thought in disbelief. Then after a slight hesitation, she pulled away.

"Clifford … I …" He placed a finger gently on her lips, silencing her so that he could continue.

"Leticia … I know a lot is happening to you at the present time and your mind is filled with a thousand problems … but I have to ask you …" He dropped down on one knee, looking up at her longingly. "Marry me, Milady."

"Clifford my dear, I am flattered beyond belief, but this has all come as a bit of shock!"

"You will get over Marco and he will be happy with Tinky and build a new life. You have stolen three years from him. Don't make him any more miserable than he already is, Leticia. You're not a child now."

"It isn't as easy as all that, Clifford," she objected kindly. "I cannot just turn my feelings on and off at the drop of a wand. I have loved Marco for so long. It would not be fair to marry you and still be in love with another."

Clifford quickly interrupted again. "If you would desire it, I can conduct a special ritual that will make you feel nothing for him ever again; your heart will be free to move on and begin anew." Leticia was shocked. This type of magic could only ever be cast by a Warlock.

"Don't you think that there have been enough spells cast? No, Clifford. I would never ask such a thing of you. This is my muddle, I caused it, I created it and therefore I have to live with the consequences. After casting such a powerful love spell on Marco, I have to take my punishment and if that means having a broken heart for eternity, then so be it. I deserve much worse, all this nearly finished off my daughter."

Clifford gently caressed Leticia's cheek, his expression revealing the pain of his longing. "I would gladly do it for you, Leticia. If it means that I may have the chance to live out my years with you by my side, then I would project my power into a thousand realms and face any consequence."

"No, but thank you, dear," Leticia said with a quivering voice.

"Your offer is kind, but I have made up my mind. I will do the right thing this time."

"Then think about my proposal of marriage; we would be a good partnership. You could teach me your gifts and I could teach you mine."

She was quiet for a long time, gazing at the tall, stunningly handsome Warlock. In all of her years she had never had romantic feelings for Clifford, but she did love him in her own way.

He swept her up in his arms and held her against his young, muscular body. "I love you, Leticia. Let me look after you as I have always done, let us raise a new generation of Eyesaurian Fairies. You are young and healthy; we could be happy and have our own family."

She pulled away from him again, her head spinning. What a week it had been. Marco was right about Clifford's intentions and although she had always known that he was fond of her, she would never have imagined that his feelings ran deeper. She walked around the kitchen table, putting a little distance between them both. Good grief, she really needed a drink, she thought and seeing the green glass bottle, she picked it up and inspected the liquid left in the bottom. This must be the stuff Spellbound was raving about, she thought. Without thinking, she flicked the cork out and drained the bottle. Suddenly, she felt a little zip and a fizzle in her nether regions. Clifford looked so handsome. He really was hunky, all muscle and brawn and those sturdy legs and that sexy codpiece … or maybe it wasn't a codpiece after all! Coorrrrrr!

"Leticia, why are you looking at me like that?" he asked in amazement. She sauntered over to him and began to walk her fingers coyly up his big broad chest and then walked them down to the top of his breeches. He gulped and stepped back a few feet.

"Milady!" he breathed huskily.

She crooked her little finger at him and giggled. Pouting her lips and holding her arms out she proceeded to speak in a high-pitched squeaky voice.

"Leticia would like another itsy bitsy kiss, Cliffy."

Clifford shook his head. "You are playing with fire Madam," he grated out passionately, "Are you sure?"

She ran her tongue seductively over her pearly pink lips and blew him an imaginary kiss. Suddenly she stepped forward and pulled his mouth onto hers. His response was instant and he devoured her lips, his hands running over her body hungrily.

"How long is it since you've had rumpy, Cliffy … over three hundred years?" she cooed seductively. "Well now's the time to make up for it, lover boy." She quickly started to undo the buttons of his doublet as his eyes blazed down into hers.

"Are you sure this is what you want, Leticia?" he asked in a tormented whisper.

She responded with another passionate kiss. With that, he scooped her up in his arms and in a flash of purple and silver Fairy dust he magicked them both to her bedchamber.

CHAPTER 18
MOVING IN DAY

Clifford gazed down in amazement at Leticia's face. She was everything he had imagined her to be and more. His happiness was brought to an unexpected end in the early hours of the morning, when an urgent telegram arrived from the Mayor of the Calendonial realm. Two weeks prior, when he'd been freed from the ball, Clifford had telephoned the Mayor informing him of his release, stating that he would be returning within the month to evaluate his estate. The message read that his castle in Trevania and surrounding land, which had been left unprotected for many years, had fallen into rack and ruin. Vampire squatters had taken up residence and were terrifying the neighbourhood. Unless he returned and claimed it back immediately, they were going to knock it down and build a multi-storey Pixie Theme Park. Because of his need to be near Leticia, he had dallied too long, he begged Leticia to join him on the trip to Caledonia but she shook her head sadly and said she couldn't leave Spellbound. He decided that once he had put his affairs in order, he would return to Leticia and after the love and emotion she had shown him last night, she might agree to marry him.

"If you want me at all, sweet Fairy, I will be at your side. Are you sure you won't change your mind?" he said tenderly. "I will be away for only one month. If you think of me as you drift off to sleep and imagine my face, I will come and join you on the astral plane."

Her mind and heart were confused, nothing seemed to make sense. Why had she gone to his bed so willingly… was she mad or perhaps in love?

Spellbound was sitting impatiently at the kitchen table with Leticia. Her mother had decided it was high time for them to sort out their outfits for Edward's nineteenth birthday ball, which was in a week. Leticia had summoned her daughter to her side, much to Spellbound's annoyance as she and Drillian had planned to go on a romantic picnic together. They'd been ready to hop on Jock Strap, their wicker basket saddled to the bird, when Spellbound disappeared in a puff of smoke, only to re-appear in the kitchen, sitting in front of Leticia. She was browsing through last month's Rogue fashion magazine, ticking off the dresses they would consider ordering. Now that coinage was no object, they didn't have to worry about the cost and consequently, their wardrobes were bursting at the seams.

Leticia was enjoying her third cup of hot chocolate and as she flicked through the pages avidly. She stopped as one gown caught her eye. "Why don't we get you this dress?" she asked Spellbound and spun the magazine around to show her the most stunning diamond-encrusted ball gown. The sleeves were long and pointed at the end and the basque bodice was nipped in to show a flurry of cream silk skirts spilling from the hips. "You would look incredible in that darling and make Edward's eye pop clear out of his head," she added.

"Oh, not Eddie again Mamma." Spellbound sniffed, "Thank the goddess I haven't heard from him in a while."

"I still think you should consider him as a potential suitor, dear. He is to be a Duke after all, and they say he has become even more handsome in the last few months. In fact, rumour has it that he has become positively dashing!"

"Well, he can positively dash, right up his Fairy arse. I only have eyes for Drilly," Spellbound said, looking all gooey. "Oh Mamma, he is such a hunky Elf and his rodger todger, Mamma, I tell you, what a whopper!"

"Enough, Spellbound," Leticia said in shock, spraying droplets of hot chocolate all over the magazine. "There are some things even a Mamma doesn't wish to know!" She drew in a deep breath and repositioned her spectacles on her nose.

Suddenly there was a mammoth commotion outside and both Fairies sprang to their feet to see what was happening. Spellbound raced forwards and threw open the patio windows. Instantly her mouth dropped open in surprise as the scene unfolded.

Marco was on his snow-white stallion, resplendent in red and gold, his auburn hair shining in the sun. Behind him were four coaches. His entire entourage of servants were hauling cases and trunks to the front entrance and his secretary, Ella Copter, was barking out orders to the stable boys to get the racehorses and Damselflies into the coral. Three Goblin shepherds were herding the green Elkies and their babies towards the pastureland around the Manor.

Overhead, Marco's Swirleybird was circling the property, just as the famous Lotus car screeched to the gates in a shower of silver gravel.

Leticia joined Spellbound in open-mouthed wonder and gawped in amazement at the spectacle.

Marco jumped off his horse with a flourish and strode towards them purposely.

"Good morning, Leticia, and Spellbound, how are you darling?" He hugged his daughter and urged the entourage to hurry up.

"Just what do you think you are doing" Leticia stuttered.

He stared at her coldly. "Ah, my sweet wife, that's an easy question to answer. As you won't come home where you belong, I have decided to move in here for the time being; until you see sense, that is," he added with authority.

"You are not friggin' well moving in here," she screeched. "Now get your household together and fook off my land!" He sighed patiently, tapping his shiny booted foot on the cobbles. "Now, my dear, you know very well by the laws of Fairyland, wedded couples have total access to each other's properties unless of course you are banished like I was and then it all disappears from view." He turned to face her, an amused glint in his eye. "I can legally take up residence here and that is what I intend to do." Leticia let out a gasp of frustration. "Oh, and don't think of moving elsewhere, for I'll just repeat the process. I'll follow you all around goddam Fairyland if I have to!"

Leticia was red in the face and spluttering uncontrollably, utterly furious and lost for words.

Marco looked at his daughter and winked, "Do you think I should kiss your Mamma better," he said, as he yanked Leticia over to him and planted a long, forceful kiss onto her mouth. Everyone started to laugh, including Spellbound.

After a struggle, Leticia managed to release herself from his arms and slapped him across the face with all the force she could muster. But not one to be phased by a wild cat-like Leticia, he roughly picked her up and threw her over his shoulder, marching her into the house, to a chorus of cheers and more laughter.

"Put me down right this instant, you spaddy- whacking, shit head!" she wailed, as she beat his buttocks with her small clenched fists. "I mean it, Marco, I swear, when I get away from you and find my wand, it's going right up your arse ... you're in deep, do-do."

Spellbound laughed out loud, holding her stomach. She really had the utmost respect for her Papa; he certainly knew how to handle her Mamma, that was for sure!

The hours that followed were chaotic as Marco's household settled in. Leticia sat at the dining room table. She had sobbed so much that her face was unrecognizable. Spellbound kept placing cold compresses on her eyes, but after a whole hour of trying to reduce the swelling, Leticia waved her wand over her face when her daughter wasn't looking and returned herself to her former glory.

Marco disappeared to find a wing inside the Manor that suited him, eventually settling on the East side with the views that overlooked the lake. After three hours, everything went quiet and order was restored.

Marco's servants were squirrelled away to their respective rooms, as the cooks and gardeners frantically began collecting and preparing produce for the evening meal.

Spellbound had gone to her apartments, just as Leticia decided she would go to hers, Marco appeared. She lifted her skirts and brushed past him angrily, but as quick as a flash, his arm shot out and she was pushed down into the armchair. He promptly dragged another chair over to her and sat down, facing her with determination.

"You won't beat me, Leticia. I aim to win this game, even if it takes me forever. If you banish me away once more, you know Spellbound will suffer again and go into the yearning, so it's for the best that you co-operate with me. Do you understand?"

She stared at him, completely lost for words. The unhappiness and desolation in her eyes were plain to see. She quivered on a huge sob.

"Marco, please end this madness and accept that our marriage is over. I really don't love you or want you anymore." Her voice raised an octave. "I had a teenage crush on you, that's all! Why can't you see this and leave me in peace?"

He sat back and his eyes became hooded. This was a Leticia he had not encountered before. He was really becoming confused as to what to do or how to handle her. Her beautiful violet eyes surveyed him impersonally and he could see there was not an ounce of love in her gaze. She was convinced he had been unfaithful with Tinky Bonk and he had to prove that this was untrue. He would do all in his power to make her fall in love with him again.

"And where is your protector, Clifford Eyesaurus? These days he seems to think he owns you," he snapped irritably.

Leticia sighed again, remembering the wonderful time she had spent with Clifford. Her eyes suddenly expressed utter confusion.

"You may as well know, Clifford and I are recent lovers," she said quietly. "So, there you have it, Marco; I have also been disloyal to this sham of a marriage. Maybe that will ease your conscience and lessen your guilt a little!"

She turned her head away from him, thinking about Clifford for a moment. The rush of emotion she had felt previously had somehow subsided, leaving her usual fondness for him but not the intensity she had encountered in the bedroom. How odd, she thought.

"Clifford has returned to his lands in the Caledonial realm for a while, but he will come back and is urging me to marry him. I would like it if you would give me a divorce. At least if I do marry Clifford, I can be sure of his loyalty and know that he truly loves me without any magical intervention." She glanced downwards, looking a little ashamed again. Marco sprang to his feet and started to pace up and down.

"You are lovers? I can't believe it; Leticia, you have actually cuckolded me!"

She shrugged, "So divorce me," she said scowling at him. He walked back towards her; his eyes full of torment as he scrutinized her beautiful features.

"What's happened to you?" he said in a desperate tone. "You are not yourself; I can see that. You have Hester's genes and can only love one man and I am that man. I have always been that man, not Eyesaurus, for fooks sake!"

She placed her hand tight to her chest and interrupted him, "Our marriage is a charade, Marco, it was never real; can't you see that? The only good that came out of all this is Spellbound and she loves you so much. Take comfort from that."

He sat down again, his mind racing with confusion and disbelief. "No … something is amiss, I can sense it," he said determinedly. "You are not getting rid of me that easily, Leticia. Accept the fact that we are a couple once more and when Eyesaurus returns … there will be war, believe me! You, my dear, belong to me and only me!"

CHAPTER 19
DESPERATE DRILLIAN

Spellbound was reclining on the plush cream rug in front of a roaring fire in one of the cosier rooms in Cumalot Castle. Nestled behind her, stroking her wings, was Drillian. To any onlooker, they would have looked like the perfect young couple, with him gazing down and she gently caressing his face with her dainty fingers. He was on cloud nine because Spellbound had been madly in love with him for six whole days and had spent nearly every waking moment by his side. He had organised his staff at Molars Inc. to deal with every eventuality and had given strict instructions that he was not to be disturbed all week. She had lovingly responded to every touch, every smile and had willingly joined him in his sumptuous bed at least four times a day. Who needed a harem of silly Fairies when he had her? He laughed at her jokes with enthusiasm, combed her hair into little ringlets and even let her beat him at billiards. One thing was for sure, he didn't have any control over his emotions anymore and he was definitely in danger of becoming seriously fooked up once the power of the spell diminished.

"Oh Drilly," Spellbound said in a soft dreamy voice, "I just can't imagine my life without you in it." Drillian smiled contentedly before the usual feelings of guilt descended. Just how was he going to cope tomorrow when she no longer gave him a second glance? He tried to dismiss the troubling thoughts with a shrug, but it persisted. He knew that he needed to make the most of the precious time they had left together, so he turned his attention back to Spellbound. He would savour her sweet company until the dreaded moment when she would disappear and leave him utterly heartbroken.

"Shall we have a holiday, Drill? We could go to the Avilonian realm for a month and pretend to be Lords and Ladies. I hear it's great fun." Drillian chuckled and nuzzled his face into her perfumed hair.

"You know you are the loveliest Fairy I have ever had the pleasure of meeting, Spellbound, and if your desire is to go to Avilonia, then we shall make haste, sweet maiden."

She giggled at his mimicking and turned around to face him. She was fiddling with the button on his shirt, her eyes laughing and twinkling as she kissed him gently.

"Drilly darling, I wanted to ask you where you got the flavour changing juice?" she said, nibbling his pointy ear. "It's really tasty stuff. Mamma rang my spell phone yesterday and said that after she tasted it, she went to the market to see if she could get some."

Drillian's heart started pounding. Her Mamma? Leticia Zamforia had sampled the potion?

"She said she scoured every corner of the market, but no one had ever heard of it! I told her you probably got it from Toncaster or somewhere, but I said I'd ask you anyway."

"Yes, Toncaster," he replied cautiously. "I got it from an elf food shop somewhere up there."

This wasn't meant to happen, he thought nervously. Spellbound was supposed to drink the entire bottle, not just some of it. And what had happened to Leticia afterwards? He couldn't bear to think of it, so he pushed the thought to the back of his mind and dragged Spellbound into his arms for another passionate kiss.

"Oh Drill, ya know I really do love you, really I do," she said with a sigh. "You make me the happiest Fairy in the realm. I think I will hold a ball in your honour." With that, she rolled him over onto his back and straddled him. With her wings stiff in the air, she began tickling him. Drillian wasn't paying much attention to Spellbound's face because he was laughing so hard. He failed to notice the gentle, silver mist exiting her body and the confusion appearing slowly in her eyes. Gradually, she stopped tickling him and rose to her feet, nervously smoothing her hands down her pink cobweb dress.

"Oh, goodness me," she said in a small earnest voice, "I feel very confused. It's like I don't seem to know my own thoughts anymore. Oh, dear me, Drill, you must forgive me," she said, flitting towards the door. Drillian jumped to his feet, his face going white.

"Spell, wait...." He called urgently.

"I have to get on home now, Mamma will be wondering where I am and ... and ... I've hardly seen Papa at all. I'll phone you, perhaps sometime next week." Her wings began to flick. "I am so sorry ... I do like you Drill ... I really do but ..." her voice trailed off into an apologetic whisper. Within a nano-second, she spread her wings and flew through the large ornate doors.

Drillian sat on the floor with his head in his hands. The potion had worn off too soon. What was he going to do now? Could he ever live without his beautiful Spellbound?

Drillian approached Fenella's cottage with trepidation. The Widder spiders were in the breeding season and were on every bush, tree and blade of grass. The carcasses of the male spiders littered the webs to be savoured later. Thankfully, he had long riding boots on, and he walked as quickly as he could to the cottage door, which was slightly ajar. With a brief knock, he strode in uninvited and stood rooted to the spot. Fenella was right in the middle of having passionate rumpy-pumpy with Gordon Zola, the ugliest Troll he had ever seen. Flicka the snake, who was now twice the size, spotted him immediately and slithered over.

Suddenly a heavy gust of wind blew the door shut. Drillian raced over and tried hard to open the door to make his escape but the rusty latch was stuck fast and wouldn't budge.

Fenella lifted her head and stared over the Troll's shoulder at the rather confused Elf.

"You'll have to wait a minute, laddy, I'm just having me whiskers parted and I'm nearly there. Make yerself comfortable or better still … come and join us," she leered.

They continued to groan and moan and the bed springs were clanking and cranking in rhythm. Drillian was more preoccupied with Flicka, who by this time had coiled his tail around his left boot and was slowly dragging him to the floor. Its hood was wide and engorged to a deep magenta and the snake swayed backwards and forwards in a sinister manner, its golden eyes fixed on Drillian's terrified face, ready to strike.

Fenella let out an ear screeching wail as she reached her climax. Gordon, the Troll, rolled off in exhaustion. Drillian was dragged to the side of the bed as the snake coiled around his body, squeezing the very life out of him. Suddenly the Troll lifted one buttock and farted. The stench was so incredible it filled the cottage with its poisonous vapours, making Flicka reel and release his grip. Drillian coughed and threw open one of the filthy windows gasping for air, thankful that the reptile had now slithered back to the warmth of the fireplace. When he finally got his breath back, he looked around and saw Fenella shoving a huge wad of banknotes into the Troll's grubby hands.

"See you next week then, Trollie boy," she sang, "And bring the whip, oh … and a pair of Wellington boots!"

Gordon Zola lumbered past Drillian, counting the money carefully. He glanced back at Fenella, sporting a toothless grin. She began pushing her long pendulous breasts into her bodice and with acute precision, she shot a ball of mustard phlegm into the fire before turning to face him.

"And what can I do for you this time, laddy?" she asked, wiping her mouth on her forearm.

"More potions please, Fenella," he said, keeping his eyes on the snake, "and make it quick."

"The potion shouldn't have worn off yet, it's supposed to last another day," she wheezed.

"Umm, yes I know … but it's a long story," he said impatiently. "Spellbound left it lying around and someone else drank the rest of it."

The smell in the cottage was so bad that Drillian wanted to throw up. Was one Fairy worth all this, he wondered as he gazed around the damp, stinking room, now filled with more cobwebs that he had ever seen. The image of Spellbound entered his mind again and he recalled her gazing into his eyes lovingly. He desperately needed to see that look again.

"And who would that someone be?" Fenella enquired suspiciously.

"Er … I would rather not say, Ma'am … bit embarrassing if you know what I mean."

"Tell me now or you are in big trouble," she hissed, "And you'll get no more potions from me and that's a fact. If you try and lie to me, Elfman, I will know, and I just might make YOU drink the potion. I could do with a younger, more reliable model! Or then again, Flicka is waiting to be fed!" She let out a spine-chilling shriek of laughter as she poked the fire.

Drillian shifted nervously and ran his finger around the collar of his doublet. If he told Fenella that it was Spellbound's mother that had drunk the last of the potion, she would surely never give him anymore.

"Well?" she croaked, looking over her shoulder, "out with it!"

"Umm … Madam Zamforia," he ended lamely.

"For fooks sake!" She stopped stoking the fire, her hideous face aghast at the news.

"No … no … I promise you; nothing came from it; all is well there," he said earnestly. Fenella was shaking as she hobbled up and down the cottage, wringing her hands into her filthy dress. She looked at him balefully, shaking her head in terror.

"I'm done for and that's for sure," she yowled. "And YOU … you're nothing but fookin' trouble. I knew I was stupid getting into all of this with those Zamforian Fairies. You need to get out of here straight away d'ya hear and don't you ever come back!"

Drillian went pale and swallowed nervously. "I'll give you whatever you want, Fenella, please reconsider." He scrambled into his pocket and pulled out a cloth bag, this time filled to the brim with more gold coins. He threw it onto the table, but she turned her back on him.

"Take yer rotten, stinking coinage and begone with ya. Get out of my cottage or I'll set me snake on to you," she bellowed.

The door mysteriously opened and she pushed him out with the strength of ten Elves. The cloth bag of money followed him, hitting him soundly on the back of his head.

CHAPTER 20
EDDIE'S BASH

Leticia and Spellbound joined the throng in the Crystal Ballroom at Sparkleshire Hall. The place was heaving with hundreds of guests, all resplendent in their finery. She looked a dream in cream organza and her wings tonight were pale turquoise and rose. Her red hair was hanging in a glossy curtain down to her waist; a dusky dog rose looped behind one ear, making her look positively adorable.

Marco had presented her with his grandmother's ruby and opal necklace, an heirloom that was priceless and centuries old. Leticia had coveted it, all of their married life but the treasure was for Spellbound, and her alone. It glittered, sending prisms of shimmering light all around the ballroom.

It was Edwards's nineteenth birthday party and the whole Fairy kingdom seemed to be assembled. The Duchess rushed up to Leticia, kissing her on both cheeks. "You have all come ... how wonderful ... wonderful! And Marco, so nice to see you again, and Spellbound ... your necklace ... this must be the one that is so famous!" she gushed. "You look divine! Edward has been trying to find you but got waylaid. Come ... come... you must have some refreshments."

Spellbound spotted Pumpkin and Taffeta over the other side of the room and waved excitedly to them.

"Mamma, Papa, I'm going to speak with my gal pals if that's okay." They nodded their approval as she zig-zagged through the revellers. Even though she didn't relish having to come to Eddie's birthday bash, it was nice to meet up with her friends again. These days she would have chosen a Fairy rave over a formal event like this but even she had to admit, a birthday ball was definitely an excellent opportunity to get dressed up and she did look sensational in her gown.

They jostled to the huge oval drinks table and decided on the punch, which was a luminous lime green colour with a purple and orange mist trailing over the edges of an enormous crystal cauldron.

"Hello, you gorgeous, sexy fairy," said a deep voice, from behind her.

Spellbound's gaze travelled up a pristine white satin doublet and then met the gaze of brilliant blue eyes.

"Eddie!" She exclaimed in amazement. Mamma had said he had become incredibly handsome, and he had.

"Hiya Eddie," simpered Taffeta, who was turning slightly pink in the cheeks. He returned Taffeta's greeting with a saucy grin.

"God, you look great, Spelly, is there a more beautiful fairy here? I think not," he complimented her, "apart from the gorgeous Taffeta here that is!" He locked eyes with her friend once more and Spellbound could sense the chemistry between the two of them.

"She's been working around the clock Eddie," Taffeta said with a giggle. "No one has seen hide nor hair of her for three months!" Eddie smiled and turned his attention back to Spellbound.

"Fancy a dance, Spell?" he said, grabbing her hand and spinning her onto the sprung crystal dance floor. "Come on, there is something I wanna talk to you about." Suddenly the music changed to a waltz and the lights overhead dimmed to a romantic, shimmering haze. A look of disappointment fell on Taffeta's face as she saw Eddie and Spellbound gliding around the floor.

Ordinarily, Spellbound would have boxed his ears for grabbing her so urgently but she noticed a change in him, something she had not seen before.

"I'm so glad I've got you on your own Spelly," he said, twirling her under his arm. "Ya see, I need your help with something." Spellbound was all ears. "You know that I have always liked you Spelly, and I still do ... well you see ..."

"Spit it out, Eddie," she cut in. Eddie pulled her closer so he could whisper without anyone hearing.

"Recently, I've been having all these thoughts about Taffy. I really like her, but I'm not sure if she likes me." Spellbound giggled and then spotted Taffeta to the side of the dance floor, looking all forlorn and left out. She waved to her and smiled. Where had slimy Eddie gone, she mused silently? Maybe he wasn't so bad after all; it seemed that he was maturing and turning into quite a nice Elfman. Sensing her relax into his arms, Eddie lowered his head and began whispering again.

"Do ya think that she might be interested in me? I mean, she's never given me even a slight hint that she would be."

"Oh Leticia, just look at them, don't they look wonderful together," the Duchess gushed, "Such a dashing couple!" Leticia nodded contentedly as their children circled the floor together.

"Totally lost in each other and chattering away ... ah, a dream come true!"

"Why don't you just ask her Eddie, you silly thing?" Spellbound whispered back. "What have you got to lose?"

"Yeah well, I've tried that and every time I have the opportunity, my voice cracks. I dunno what's the matter with me!"

As the dance ended, Edward bowed and discreetly led Spellbound to a secluded alcove where they could continue to chat in private.

"I am so pleased that she's ditched that Drillian and come to her senses at last," Leticia confided to the Duchess. "He was far too dodgy in my opinion."

She was just about to say more when Philip Macavity approached, he gave them a formal bow and asked Leticia for a dance. Before she could refuse, he tugged her hand and whizzed her onto the dance floor for a polka. He swept her into the crowd and whirled her around and around until she was dizzy.

"Ah, sweet Leticia, can you remember the last time we danced? What fun we had!"

She stared at him, reprovingly. "Now Philip, we had both had a little too much booze, so you mustn't read too much into it and we are both of us married or had you forgotten?"

"But how could I ever forget you dancing in my arms all night long, sweet Fairy and to have you in my bed would be enchanting, would it not?"

Leticia pulled away from him and marched off the dance floor, straight into Marco, who was visibly fuming, his green eyes flashing with jealousy.

"And pray who is this gentleman that is so familiar with you? Not another lover, surely?"

Leticia shifted from one foot to another and wished for a second that the ground would swallow her up.

"Philip Macavity is my name, sir, and you must be the great Marco Zamforia, the one who everyone has heard of." He gave a slight bow, glancing at Leticia's bright scarlet dress and alluring cleavage.

"Sir, are you ogling my wife?" Marco bit out. Philip's eyes twinkled down at Leticia knowingly as she rolled her eyes to the heavens, fanning herself in exasperation.

"One cannot help but ogle her, sir, such a vision. Perhaps we will dance later, Leticia," he said quietly in her ear, before spinning on his heel and heading straight for the refreshment tables.

Marco glared down at her losing his patience, "Just what have you been up to since I have been away?"

"Oh fook off, Marco. You don't own me. And for your information, that Elf is the head of Molars Inc. and has employed your daughter for the past few months. Just take your hands off me and go and visit your solicitor. I want a divorce and the quicker, the better!"

When Drillian arrived, the ball was already in full swing. His eyes scanned the room for Spellbound but he couldn't see her anywhere. He had missed her so much this last week that he had drunk himself into a stupor every night. She had refused to come into work on Monday saying she had a headache and hadn't returned any of his calls since!

Usually, he wouldn't have bothered attending this sort of event but because he was so desperate to see her and because he had to try and convince her they belonged together, a swarm of wild hornets wouldn't have kept him away tonight. Having made an extra effort with his appearance, he looked incredibly dashing and debonair in his dark green velvet doublet slashed with black satin. His ebony hair was tied in a prince's plait and entwined with real gold thread.

As he entered the ballroom, five Fairies gathered around him, laughing, joking and all vying for his attention, desperate to be the chosen one for the evening. He noted dryly that he had bedded each and every one of them at some point. Lily Lavia, a silver-haired Fairy in a bright magenta gown, pulled him towards her and gave him a long smoochy kiss, running her hands all over his torso. Maybelle then grabbed his shoulder and twisted him around so that she could have her turn. Spellbound and Eddie watched Drillian's entrance from across the room and Spellbound hung her head in shame. She was no better than any of them, she thought; if only she could turn the clock back. To think she had been to bed with that male whore bag. She shuddered a sense of disgust sweeping over her once again.

"You okay, Spell?" Eddie asked, a little concerned. He took his doublet off and draped it around her shoulders tenderly, being careful not to squash her wings.

Drillian noted Eddie's show of affection from across the room. She sighed deeply as Eddie looped a stray tendril of hair behind her ear.

A flame of wild jealousy rocketed through Drillian, something he had never felt before in his life. He stood agape, his heart beating wildly, and then, before he could catch his breath, Sally Slapper had claimed his mouth for a blistering French kiss.

Spellbound and Eddie strolled towards their beaming parents and Eddie was at last formally introduced to Marco. They were chatting amiably when Philip Macavity approached the group again and bowed. He looked over at Leticia warmly and in his most formal voice, he said, "Madam, can I claim this dance?"

Leticia felt uneasy as he offered his arm and took her to the dance floor, making Marco frown deeply as he clenched his fists in an effort to control his anger.

"And Spellbound," Drillian said, stepping up to them and holding out his hand, "Could I claim the next dance with you?" He had shaken off the Fairy gang and decided to take action at last.

Spellbound was on the point of refusal and Eddie stiffened at her side. With a quick flick of her wrist, she was tugged abruptly onto the crystal surface, as Eddie's jacket fell to the floor in a crumpled heap. Drillian's dark brown eyes blazed down at her.

"What the hell are you doing cavorting around with him, letting him wrap his doublet around your shoulders?"

"Ha!" she laughed. "You are a fine one to talk, rocking up here with your totty entourage in tow, making a real spectacle of yourself. You are nothing but a spaddy-wacking, perv! You really are disgusting!" She tried to break away from him but he held her fast.

Eddie had finally drummed up the courage to talk to Taffeta and they were dancing within earshot.

"You having trouble there, Spelly? Just say the word and I'll clock him one for ya."

Drillian gave him a steely glance and steered her into the middle of the throng.

"Spellbound," he said in a strained voice, "I have really missed you this last week. I don't know how much longer I can go on like this. One minute we are lovers, the next you don't even return my calls!"

Spellbound had felt slightly guilty about her behaviour, which had been very out of character. Leticia had said that her hormones must be to blame and all the drama of turning into a hare, hadn't helped, so she could be forgiven for making a mistake.

"Look Drill, I am sorry about all that, really I am. It's not that I don't like you or anything, I do! You're really not that bad as far as Elves go and you were very supportive when I was going through the yearning. But let's face it, you can have any Fairy you want and you *do* have them, most of the time. No, when I settle down, I wanna be with someone who I know will be true to me, and with the best will in the world Drill, you couldn't keep your todger in your breeches if your life depended on it!" The music ended and Drillian led her into the same alcove that she and Eddie had chatted in earlier. He looked down at her sugar pink lips longingly and lowered his head. Spellbound turned her face away and although she would have loved to have boxed his ears, she sensed that he was unhappy and managed to refrain from doing so.

"I said I didn't want any more of that lovey-dovey crap, Drillian," she said coldly. "You are really quite spoilt; do you know that? The only reason you want me is because I am not interested and you can't have me. You need to leave me alone, Drill. Go someplace to pamper your ego and go and service the rest of the Fairy kingdom while you are at it!" With a no-nonsense stare, she half walked and half flitted to the other end of the ballroom.

Drillian ran his fingers through his hair in agitation. He really must try and persuade Fenella to part with some more of the love potion or he'd go insane. He sauntered over to the refreshments table and took a schooner of punch and drained it in one huge gulp. Then he filled it again and did the same. His mind was going into overdrive. This obsession was far more than just mere lust or a simple crush, he mused. Suddenly the potent punch took effect and he felt a red-hot ball of heat hit his stomach. He hadn't eaten much at all for two days and the drink was working in double-quick time. He emptied another glass and finally the sharp edges of his anguish started to blur into numbness. He had to have her and not just for one night or for one week; he needed her by his side for always and forever or he just wouldn't be able to live a normal life again!

He suddenly felt very squiffy.

Leticia was trying hard to dodge Philip, who insisted on keeping her in conversation, even though the music had stopped five minutes ago. He was trying to pin her down for a supper date and she could feel the noose tightening. She tried to explain that Marco was back now and it would cause all sorts of difficulties but he persisted. And then, just when she thought things couldn't get any worse, Marco was at her side, looking more than annoyed.

"Leticia, we were wondering where you had got to. The Duchess wishes to speak to you ... come," he said, holding his hand out and glaring at Philip Macavity as he led Leticia away.

"Does every Elf in the goddamn place have to ogle you? What is it with you, Leticia? You're no better than an alley cat," he bit out in a jealous rage.

Instantly she yanked her hand out of his grasp and hissed under her breath "Me an alley cat? Question your own morals before mine!"

They both fell silent as the Duchess approached them.

"Ah, there you are, Leticia, we are all going to make our way out to the gardens for the dragon display. Eddie is so excited as he has never seen a dragon before, so this is our gift to him," she said happily.

The gardens were beautiful, with marble pagodas and shimmering lakes dotted around the grounds. Romantic hologram statues that looked life-like were lit up for the occasion and there was even a love seat for two.

A fanfare of trumpets blared out across the grass to signal the start of the show, and with a gasp, everyone looked up into the night sky. Twelve gargantuan dragons with their wings outstretched were looping and diving in synchronicity, as they breathed out orange and crimson flames.

Spellbound watched enraptured as the creatures performed their amazing feats. Two of them swooped over the crowd so low that she could count their purple scales. Everyone ducked as the other ten followed. The air smelt of brimstone and fire and voluminous plumes of greens and blues made magical patterns in the air. They flew off to one side, leaving the words 'Happy Birthday Edward' in sparkly fifty-foot letters. To end the spectacle, a thousand fireworks exploded in the starlit sky above them. The crowd went mad, clapping and cheering as the dragons disappeared over the horizon. Spellbound walked towards a small lake nearby, pushing her way through the dense crowd. Before she knew it, Eddie was at her side hopping about excitedly.

"Did you enjoy the display, Spelly?"

"It was amazing, Eddie, truly amazing. Your Ma and Pa really know how to put on a show, that's for sure."

"I took your advice," he said chuckling. "I asked Taffy out on a special date, will you help me choose a gift for her?"

Spellbound giggled. "Of course, I'd only be too happy. I think you two will make a lovely couple."

"Do you really think that we could be ready to have a long term grown-up relationship, what do you think Spelly?"

Suddenly there was a sarcastic laugh. "Spellbound's already had a very grown-up relationship ... with me. Haven't you babe?"

Spellbound spun around to see Drillian leaning nonchalantly against a nearby tree. He straightened up and walked towards them purposefully.

Eddie looked down at Spellbound in amazement, "Hold on a sec ... you have Hester's genes, which means ..." His voice trailed off as he scratched his head, looking perplexed.

"I am NOT in love with him!" she snapped vehemently. "I must have some of my Papa's genes as well! Mamma said turning into a hare could have confused my brain and my hormones too. Everyone knows hares bonk all the time and I, unfortunately, did just that for a while with this slimeball."

Drillian draped his arm casually around her shoulders and gave Eddie a 'get lost' look. In an instant, she moved away and turned her back on him. "You're drunk ... get off me buzzard face!"

"Come on, Eddie, let's get out of here and leave this sorry specimen to sober up."

"Take one step towards her and you'll be dead meat, Elfman." Drillian slurred.

Eddie leaned towards her and held out his hand. "He's raddled Spelly. Come on, it's my birthday, we've got some more dancing to do."

As Eddie put his arm around Spellbound's waist, he was suddenly smacked in the jaw by Drillian's fist of iron. He staggered backwards, seeing more stars than the firework display, a few moments before.

"Get your filthy hands off her," Drillian grated, desperately, rubbing his fist which had begun to burn with pain.

Spellbound was so outraged that she zipped into the air and grabbed Drillian's prince's plait and spun him around and around. Swooping down and with a left hook, she sent him flying across the grass. By now, a crowd had started to gather as Spellbound, screamed for help.

Drillian was up in an instant, knocking Eddie clean off his feet. Seconds later, the two were slugging it out like prize-fighters.

"Stop it, stop it!" she bellowed as she hovered in the air.

Leticia rushed up and shouted to her daughter, "Come down, Spellbound, get away from these crazed Elves for goodness sake. Lordy lord, what is all of this about?"

Philip Macavity saw Drillian collapsed on the grass and Edward diving onto him, fists flying. With no more ado, he waded in to prise them apart, only to be thumped hard on the nose by Eddie. The

Duke saw the kafuffle and tried to pull Eddie away by the scruff of his neck, but this made Eddie's punch miss Drillian and ended up smacking Philip Macavity again. Eddie turned and looked sheepishly at him as he mouthed the words "Sorry."

Leticia screamed at Marco, "Do something, for goodness sake, before they all kill each other!"

Marco grinned and like a swallow, he nose-dived into the melee, his fists pounding at Leticia's annoying admirer relentlessly.

"I didn't mean for you to fight too, Marco. For fooks sake, you're as bad as they are!"

The Duchess was crying and dabbing her eyes with her lace hanky; her beautiful party was ruined. Glancing at her downcast face, Leticia tutted and took her wand from the pocket of her gown. She waved it over the Elfmen, who all froze like statues.

"That will have to do for the minute," she thought, "until I can think of something better."

A few moments later, she started to chant in Gaelic and a huge white cloud engulfed the frozen fighters. When it cleared, the space was empty.

"The show's over folks," she declared. "They've all been returned to their homes and will be tucked up in bed by now, fast asleep. The spaddy-whacking, bladderbarts!"

CHAPTER 21
TINKY BONK

Spellbound slept very late the morning after Edward's party. The Duchess's spirits had been revived as the merrymakers had decided to stay well into the small hours and congratulated her on the most fantastic party ever when finally leaving.

Leticia was still sleeping, when Spellbound emerged from her bedchamber, so she thought she would venture to the west wing to check up on her father. She was sure that he'd be surprised to find himself tucked up in bed after the rumpus with Eddie, Drillian and the Duke, and Papa really shouldn't have fought with Philip Macavity just because he was enraged with jealousy. It was such a sorry mess. She pushed open the door to her father's study and found him with his head in his hands, looking depressed. Spellbound immediately ran over to him and gave him a huge hug.

"Papa, what on earth is the matter with you?" she asked with deep concern.

He looked up at her with strain in his eyes, shrugging his shoulders despondently. "I really don't know what to do, Spellbound. Your mother doesn't love me anymore; she's so cold and unfeeling. She has admirers everywhere I look. At least Eyesaurus is out of the frame for the moment because I know for a fact that she is seriously fond of him."

Spellbound noted the torment in her father's eyes and stroked his back with her little hand.

"Your mother is convinced that I was unfaithful to her with Tinky Bonk and no matter how much I try to defend myself; she just won't believe me. I swear to you, Spellbound, I was not with Tinky Bonk that night in the Pagoda!"

Spellbound looked down at her silver slippers and sighed. "Papa, I hate to go against you in any way, you know that and you know I love you and all, but," she paused for a moment and then looked him directly in the eye. "I know the truth Papa. I saw it with my own eyes when Clifford was trapped in the ball. Mamma didn't get it wrong. I saw it all and I mean everything ... all the gory details ... the lot!" His head shot up and his brilliant green eyes blazed into hers angrily.

"I DID NOT HAVE ANY RELATIONS WITH TINKY BONK WHATSOEVER!" he shouted, "Why the hell won't anyone believe me?" She coughed in embarrassment. "Please say you believe me, Spellbound. I don't care what you saw, it was a pack of lies, I tell you. I was banished by your mother for three years and now our marriage is a sham. Even you think I'm a philandering liar!"

"I still love you, Papa, whatever you've done," she told him. "I missed you so much; it was awful but it doesn't matter to me what you did. I am just so pleased you are back and we can be together again."

Marco's eyes were filled with anguish and for a moment she thought he was going to cry with frustration. "Go to your room, Spellbound," he clipped dismissively.

This was just awful, thought Spellbound, as she sat on her bed contemplating what to do next. Her Papa wouldn't even talk to her. He had ordered her out of his sight and that had never happened before. Spellbound started to try and think of a solution and after a half an hour of coming up with nothing, decided to go against all the rules and try to contact Moonflower. She would know what to do; her Godmother was wise and told her she was always watching over her. Now she was out of yearning her powers had increased thrice fold and although she wasn't allowed to visit the astral planes until she was much older, she could do it easily … it was an emergency after all!

She retrieved the Moon Orb from her top drawer and held it tightly in her hand. No sooner had she laid flat on her bed and begun to concentrate, Moonflower appeared in a flash of brilliance and smiled down at her charge.

"Spellbound … how lovely to see you, although you shouldn't really be venturing onto the astral, dear, well not yet anyway!"

Spellbound gazed around at the familiar pink clouds and the beautiful wheat-haired vision of her Fairy Godmother.

"I need you," Spellbound said sadly. "I don't know what else to do and I figured that you might help me."

"Well my dear, I will try my best but you know that there are only certain things I can help with, don't you? I may be your guardian and can intervene in life or death situations, but my assistance is limited to a certain extent."

Spellbound wasted no time in relating the entire tale of woe about her parents and Tinky Bonk.

"I know Papa is lying because I saw them in Clifford's ball as plain as day, but he still keeps insisting he didn't do it with Tinky Bonk," she lamented. "Mamma doesn't love him anymore and he is so depressed, it's just a crock of shit, I tell you!" A secret smile flicked over Moonflower's face. As much as she had evolved into the perfect guardian, pure of mind and pure of soul, she did love Spellbound's raw energy and found her quite hilarious at times.

"Do you think that you would be able to find out the truth for me? You know, tell me exactly what happened that night. Can you?" Spellbound pleaded with Moonflower.

Moonflower beckoned her over to a small pool and motioned for her to sit beside her.

"Well, dear, I suppose we could try," she said hesitantly. "I am not really supposed to interfere with these kinds of matters; it may affect your Karma, but I can't see the harm in having a sneaky peek, just this once."

Spellbound's face immediately broke into a smile as she positioned herself to take a more in-depth look into the pool.

"Now, be patient, dear. I have not done this for many years, so I may be a little rusty."

Moonflower removed the crystal pendulum from her neck and waved it over the pool. Small bubbles started frothing on the surface and a thin mist trailed over the edges and then deepened in the centre until the water was completely obscured. Suddenly it cleared into a crystal-clear screen and the pictures of her father and Tinky were brought to life on the surface. Spellbound quickly turned away in embarrassment and started fiddling with the pearl ring on her finger.

"I hate this bit," she said, screwing up her face. "It makes me feel sick, it does. It's really not natural to see one of your parents doing the humpy rump ... ooooh ... makes all the hairs on the back of my neck stand up ... yuk!"

"It's all right, dear," Moonflower said, "you can look up now." The images had disappeared and the water in the pool continued to lap against the bright turquoise reeds. Moonflower spoke apprehensively, with a slight frown puckering her forehead.

"Spellbound, it seems we have somewhat of a problem. Have you ever heard of Fairy Glamour?" Spellbound frowned and shook her head. "No, perhaps you haven't; it was banned hundreds of years ago by the Feathered Ones because it caused so much mayhem. I need to explain this to you, dear, so it will finally end all of this confusion."

Spellbound looked worriedly into Moonflower's eyes and signalled with her hands, urging her to speak.

"Fairy Glamour was used for many generations to captivate humans and also entrap unwilling Fairies into love matches. If you like, it's a form of shapeshifting. A Fairy could change how they looked at the drop of a hat, just like the human Witches were supposed to do in medieval times. They could be whoever they wanted to be. A regular Fairy could change shape and become a Goblin, a Troll, a beautiful Queen, a Dodibell or a Swannikin, whoever and whatever. Many fae folk used this power to spy on a loved one or find out information that was secret to them. Spellbound, I think your father had this spell cast upon him. Now, I want you to try to be brave and look into the pool again."

Reluctantly, Spellbound let her eyes drift over the crystal surface and gasped in surprise as she now saw her father passionately kissing her mother.

"You see, your father believed that he was, in fact, making love to your mother. It seems he is innocent in all of this and has been telling the truth all along, although what the Feathered Ones will say when they hear that someone has resurrected Fairy Glamour is another thing!" Moonflower was seriously concerned and began repositioning her diamond crown.

"Oh, poor Papa, he really thought he was with Mamma," she exclaimed, "He kept saying it over and over again and no one believed him. Tinky Bonk used Fairy Glamour to look like my Mamma! I tell you; I am gonna find that slime ball and zap her right up the arse with my wand and give her serious haemorrhoids, I am. Just you see, she's gonna be dead meat after this ... dead meat ... nasty fookin' Fairy ... nasty, nasty ..."

"Language, Spellbound!" Moonflower remonstrated with her gently. "You really must try and act more Fairy-like, dear. Your tongue does not reflect your inner beauty."

"But I just don't get it," Spellbound went on frantically. "Why couldn't Mamma see what Papa saw? Why couldn't she see that Tinky was impersonating her? My Mamma is the most powerful Fairy in all the realms, why didn't she clock the truth?"

Moonflower held her hand and smiled down at her tenderly.

"Fairy Glamour is the most disruptive of all spells, dear. It plays havoc with the mind and will only bewitch the one that has the spell put upon them. Your mother saw the truth; she saw Tinky making love with your father, but your dear father was affected by the spell and truly believed that he was making love to his wife. You must tell him what has happened," she explained. "He will know how to deal with Tinky Bonk after that, and he must do it as soon as possible. It would be best not to tell your mother for the moment, not until he has sorted it all out. Now, you must return dear," she added, and quicker than a cat's whisker could twitch, Spellbound was back in her room with her fairy duvet neatly tucked up to her chin.

Her eyes flew open. She must speak with her Papa and right this minute, she thought. She flew down the stairs and crashed into his study, frightening the life out of him. Throwing herself into his arms, she showered him with a hundred kisses.

"Papa, I have some wonderful news to cheer you up. I know it's wrong and I'm not supposed to do it, but I've just whizzed up to the astral plane and visited Moonflower. She's my Godmother by the way, and oh, Papa ... you'll never believe this; she just showed me something that's gonna change everything and I mean EVERYTHING."

He prised her fingers from around his neck and laughed into her earnest little face. Without pausing for breath, she related the story. His eyes lit up with fury and his lips stiffened.

"So Tinky Bonk used Fairy Glamour? No one this side of the human realm dare use that kind of magic and go against the will of the Feathered Ones. The consequences are too great." Marco raked his hand through his hair, a look of consternation washing over his handsome features.

"Come to mention it, how on earth could Tinky cast such a spell? Her magic was never that superior. Her spell-casting was only ever considered average."

Spellbound shrugged and waited for her father to speak. He thought for a few seconds then stood up, placing his hands on her shoulders and looking down into her green eyes reassuringly. "Don't worry, Spellbound, I think I know what to do about Tinky Bonk now, and you can be as sure as hell I will be beating a path to her door. This mess needs clearing up once and for all so that I can have my wife back in my arms where she belongs!"

Marco summoned the Lotus and went North of the forest in search of Tinky. The beautiful contraption got him there in three minutes flat and as it glided down into a clearing, he could see her humble cottage set back in a small copse of trees.

He marched to the door and rapped on it loudly. Eventually, it opened and Tinky Bonk stood staring at him, open-mouthed. He pushed straight past her into her small parlour and then turned around to face her, his green eyes boring into her in rage. She reeled backwards in shock and then desperately clasped her throat.

"Marco, what do you want?" she croaked.

He pushed his face close up to hers. "I want an explanation from you and it had better be good or I'll snap your wings straight off your back, do you hear?" He knew by the look on her face that she was already guilty.

"Start talking NOW!" he yelled. She shrank away from him and put a chair between them for safety. "Do the words Fairy Glamour mean anything to you, Tinky?" he asked, slowly sidling towards her. She went a deathly white and her eyes darted around the room like a trapped animal seeking an escape. "You have broken a hundred-year rule that was set in place by the Feathered Ones. You made me think I was making love with my wife when all along it was you! You had better tell me the whole sordid tale, Tinky because I am not leaving here until you do!" She sank weakly into a tulip chair, her mouth moving, but no sound coming out. Marco dragged another chair over and sat down, his eyes fixed furiously on her face. Eventually, she found her voice.

"We were to be married … or had you forgotten?" she sobbed. "She stole you from me, took you straight out from under my nose. I figured that all is fair in love and war, and I fought fire with fire, especially after she turned me into a slug. TWICE! I will never forgive her for that!" Tears pricked her eyes as she recalled the memory with a shudder of repulsion.

"How did you get such a powerful spell put on me, especially one that has been forbidden in these realms for so long?" he said, eyeing her venomously.

"I was left a large inheritance from my Grandpapa in the Nether Realm," Tinky continued desperately. "As much as I hate the place, I had to go there to receive it and it was there at one of the underworld balls, I met an old fae Witch."

"Who is this hag?" he spat angrily. Leaping out of his chair, he approached the quivering Fairy. Tinky jumped up out of her seat and ran behind it in the hope that it might give her some protection.

"I don't know who she was. She … she had a stall outside the great hall and was selling all kinds of potions at bargain prices. As I was browsing, she sensed that I was filled with vengeance and said for a large fee, she could sell me a potion that would put an end to my suffering and punish those who had wronged me." Marco was seething.

"Tell me her name Goddammit, I am going to tear her limb from limb."

"I don't know," she wailed. "She was a wizened old thing that kept spitting green gunk on the ground every few minutes. We struck a deal and then I slipped the potion into your drink that night of your party and the rest is history. It cost me the whole of my inheritance, a small fortune. I stayed down by the lake and watched you go into the Cherub Pagoda. I thought that once she had thrown you out, you would come back to me and we could begin again." Her eyes pleaded with him for understanding but his gaze was as cold as ice.

"I was banished for three years because of you and missed my daughter growing up, and she went into the yearning! " he hissed.

"I was banished too," she screamed back at him. "You weren't the only victim, Marco!" She watched the pained expression on his face and immediately fell quiet. "Look, forget Leticia," she said, moving cautiously towards him. "I hear she wants Eyesaurus now anyway. We can be together like it was originally planned. I will somehow try to accept your daughter and make her part of my life. Let's forget the past and try again."

He reached out abruptly and grabbed her by both arms, his eyes glaring at her coldly.

"I will never forgive you, Tinky. And you are lucky that I haven't sought my own revenge and turned you into a slug myself. I will let the Feathered Ones decide what they want to do with you and may the gods help you!"

He spun on his heel and left her in a crumpled heap on the floor.

"Yes, she admitted it all, Spellbound, she never tried to hide it," said Marco, as he paced up and down the room.

"What I don't understand is why this fae Witch agreed to even be a part of something that would affect my Mamma. I mean, everyone knows that she is the most powerful Fairy in the realm. Why would she be so stupid as to sell Tinky a Fairy Glamour potion?"

"She probably didn't know who the potion was for dear. No Fairy in their right mind would cross your mother." Marco was incensed and if he ever found out who this Witch was, he would see to it that she never made another potion again!

"But at least we know the truth now, Papa, and you can tell Mamma and she will have to believe you ... won't she?" asked Spellbound. Marco still looked perturbed and scratched his chin uneasily.

"What are you two plotting?" Leticia said from the doorway.

Both looked at her guiltily and then Spellbound turned and faced her mother with determination.

"Papa has something to tell you."

"He's leaving? Oh, good and about time too," she spat out bitterly.

"Won't you just hear him out and stop being so spiteful all of the time? Honestly Mamma, sometimes you can be a real pain in the arse."

"Oh, thank you, daughter. And we certainly know where your loyalties lie, don't we?"

"Just listen, Mamma, will you?" She relented and a few moments later they were all sitting in front of the log fire, watching the flames snap and crackle. Leticia sat in complete silence as first Spellbound told her about Moonflower and then Marco related the story of his visit to Tinky Bonk.

"But this is unbelievable. Fairy Glamour has been banned for a hundred years; how could she have got someone to resurrect it? Even Clifford and I do not have that power! Who is this Witch anyway? I must meet with her and turn her into a gnat on the arse of an Elkie, the fookin' harridan!"

"Mamma, do you know what this means?" Spellbound said excitedly. "This means that you and Papa can finally be reunited and we can all be happy again. Oh, I am so, so bleedin' happy at last, I really am! This is just the greatest day and I love you both so much ..."

Leticia lowered her head. "Marco, I am truly sorry that I caused such trouble when you were innocent all along. Really, I must apologise from the bottom of my heart."

"You are forgiven," he replied with a smile, "I have never stopped loving you, not from the first moment I met you on the dance floor."

"Awww! Ain't it all so romantic?" Spellbound gushed, as she rose into the air, her wings flapping wildly with joy.

Leticia looked at them absently and then said in a matter of fact voice. "But this doesn't change anything. There's too much water under the bridge for that! Maybe this all happened for a reason. Our marriage cannot come back from this, Marco. Too many spells, too much time apart, too many painful memories, my infidelity. No, I'm sorry. We need to face the fact once and for all that it's over."

"Your infidelity?" Spellbound said aghast. *"Who with?"*

CHAPTER 22
DECISIONS, DECISIONS, DECISIONS

Drillian woke up with the sunlight streaming through the curtains and a throbbing pain in his chin. Rubbing it lightly, he began to recall the events of the previous evening. Deep longings washed over him at the thought of Spellbound. Slowly rising from the bed, he found that it was not only his chin that was aching. His back and left knee, not to mention his heart, were extremely sore as well. As he went to look in the mirror, he let out a disgruntled moan. His top lip was the size of an acorn and his right eye was virtually closed. That must have been some fight, he thought. But he would have slain the darkest demons just to have Spellbound by his side again. Without any more ado he threw on his clothes and headed out of the door, with a very clear sense of purpose.

Spellbound was seated at the kitchen table, surrounded by fifty bunches of bluebells and twelve bottles of bluebellade.

"What's with the long face darling?" Leticia said as she entered the room and flicked her wand at the kettle, it boiled instantly and poured the hot water into two assembled coffee cups. Two cubes of sugar plopped into the liquid and a silver spoon efficiently stirred the ingredients together. Spellbound took the coffee cup which was suspended in front of her and sipped the piping hot liquid. Leticia glided across the room, to join her. She looked beautiful today, her iridescent wings were soft pink and turquoise and matched her lilac day dress perfectly. "All of these flowers I tell you. You'll be drinking bluebell juice until the Dodibells come home, now come on dear, tell Mamma what's troubling you."

"Oh, I dunno," she said despondently. "I'm all confused with myself."

"Confused with what?" Leticia replied, sitting opposite her daughter at the table.

"Oh, this business with Drillian. I actually thought I loved him and then I didn't and now well, I'm not sure! Mamma, I did things with him that I am so ashamed of. I have Aunt Hester's genes for gawd sake! I am not supposed to get all hot and bothered until I fall in love. And I did fall in love Mamma, I really did!" Leticia nodded sympathetically.

"Yes, I admit it is all very strange dear, but don't worry about that right now and just enjoy being carefree." Leticia reached across the table to touch her daughter's hand.

"You are so young and there is plenty of time. Besides, you have to face facts; not every Fairy in these lands is destined to fall in love, Spellbound. The things I write about in my Spells and Swoon books very rarely happen. Some folks never find happiness; they just spend their entire lives looking for the right Pixie or Elf, wasting time and valuable energy. No one is ever guaranteed to find their soul mate, dear, so maybe, for now, it's best to get these romantic notions out of your head and just do what needs to be done to secure an affluent life. You could always marry Drillian darling or Eddie, they're both rich!" she tittered. "Marriage isn't always about love, for many, it's about coinage and security."

Marco glared at his wife from the doorway.

"Is that what you did, Leticia?" he spat out. "Was that why you wanted me? Money, position ... my lands ...? Yes, it all makes sense now. Well, you certainly made sure you got the whole package, didn't you? Got me to fall in love with you, casting your spells and messing around with my emotions and then you got bored and coldly detached yourself. Do you ever think about anything or anyone but yourself Leticia, do you?"

"Oh, shut up, Marco, this isn't about us. This is about Spellbound and safeguarding her future."

"Like you safeguarded yours, you mean?" he sneered, "You must have been pig sick when you banished me and all the wealth disappeared."

"Spellbound and I managed very well without you thank you and besides, I am rich in my own right after receiving that legacy."

"The only reason I am back from your banishment is that OUR daughter went into the yearning, heaven forbid, if she hadn't, I would still be a thousand miles away living in solitude! You really can be a dark, wicked Fairy at times. You don't think about the consequences and worst of all, you don't care. And now I am back and you know the truth, you still don't love me, so what am I to do now, Leticia eh? What next, or don't you care about that either? Even after it has been revealed that Tinky Bonk duped us both by using Fairy Glamour, you will still not see reason and mend this marriage."

"OH, FOOKIN' BLEWDY SHUT UP, THE PAIR OF YOU," Spellbound shouted at the top of her lungs.

Both parents' heads shot up and they echoed the words simultaneously, "STOP SWEARING, Spellbound!"

"Well, he's got a point, Mamma. You did cast a love spell on him to make him yours. It's no wonder he's pissed off now."

"Yes, but I undid the spell, TWICE actually, and you know very well I did. If your father is still in love with me then it's not my fault. Hell's teeth, why are the pair of you always ganging up on me?"

"Are you dense? Have you already forgotten what I told you, Leticia? I was in love with you long before you cast any spell on me.

Your magical meddling would have had no effect on me whatsoever. And as much as it pains you to hear this, I will never go away and if you think that I will stand back and allow another Elf, or Warlock for that matter, to step into my shoes, you can think again because it will never happen!"

Spellbound looked towards Leticia and nodded knowingly at her father's comment.

"He won't either, Mamma, you know he won't!"

"Oh, Spellbound, you always did take your father's side and after everything, I have given up over the years. Honestly child!" Leticia felt a pang of guilt rise in her heart. After all, Marco was innocent all along; he never did make love with Tinky Bonk intentionally. It must be an agony for him ... loving her and not having it reciprocated. She sighed. Even now that the whole truth about what had happened was out in the open, their problems still hadn't gone away. If anything, things had become even worse. What was the matter with her?

Drillian approached the main doors to Fingleberry Manor and was greeted by Biff the butler who formally took his coat. He was shown into the library where he paced the floor anxiously waiting for Spellbound's arrival. There were raised voices in the distance and after what seemed like an age, he decided to take one of Leticia's books off the shelf and sit down in one of the chairs placed in the corners of the room. He was casually flicking through the pages when his attention was immediately distracted. He whistled through his teeth and laughed out loud at the sexy portrayal of the heroine's antics. Spellbound's Mamma could certainly teach him a thing or too he mused. Suddenly he heard tiny footsteps approaching and he placed the book hastily back on the shelf. Spellbound was muttering some obscenity at having been disturbed. She threw open the doors with a flourish and with her hands planted firmly on her hips, she glared at him, her eyes blazing.

"What do you want? And just look at the bleedin' state of your face!" she said, shaking her head, obviously irritated by his presence.

Drillian sprang to his feet and in three short strides, he was standing in front of her. Regaining her composure for a moment she took her wand out of the back pocket of her denim jeans and waved the staff under his nose. His handsome features were restored immediately.

"Well, what do you want?" she snapped irritably.

"Spell, this isn't easy," he said with sheer determination and adoration in his eyes. "I never imagined that I would be here saying this but ... but ..."

"Oh Drill, spit it out will you, I'm having a massive bitch fight with Mamma and I was winning for once. You've got three seconds."

"Forget that," he said. "I need to speak to you urgently and I need you to listen to me."

She was just about to argue with him when he clasped her hand in his and fell to his knees. Spellbound stood open-mouthed and gawped at him.

"There's no other way of saying this, Spell," he said softly, "but I have fallen in love with you. Massively even. You are in my thoughts from morning to night and I know I can't function if I don't have you with me. I go to sleep dreaming about you and I wake up longing for you. Marry me, Spell," he said with tears in his eyes. "Make me the happiest of all Elves and agree to be my wife."

Spellbound was fixed in a trance, open-mouthed and wide-eyed. She attempted to speak but couldn't make a sound.

"Don't answer me now," he said, taking a beautiful Tanzanite ring from a silver jewelled box. He quickly placed it on her outstretched, pointed finger. "Just take this betrothal ring and promise me you will consider it."

He stood up and swiftly headed for the entrance before she could answer him.

Spellbound was sitting on her bed, drinking a glass of bluebellaide, examining the ring Drillian had given her the day before. She held it up to the light and stared at its beauty. It had to be the most enchanting thing she had ever seen. The deep royal blue crystal shimmered in the centre of a cluster of diamonds and the sparks of magic could be seen dancing inside the stone like sprites on a still pond. It must have cost him a small fortune.

When Drillian asked her to marry him, her first instinct was to laugh in his face, but over the last twenty-four hours, she had actually began warming to the idea. Her parents wanted her security and were keen for an engagement. He did love her after all, and he had sent her five huge bunches of bluebells every hour, on the hour, since their meeting the day before, knowing they were her favourite flowers.

Leticia was sneezing so much that every time another bunch arrived, she zapped it away into the greenhouse before Spellbound could read the note.

Marco had received a visit from Drillian that morning and was quite impressed at the Elf's determination.

"I'll say one thing to you, my lad," Marco said with his hands tucked stylishly behind his back. "It's obvious that you hold Spellbound in high regard and I have no doubt that you would lavish your worldly goods on her. But if my daughter does accept you, and you so much as step one foot out of line, I will use every ounce of my magic to see to it that you never see the light of fairyland again!"

Drillian stood his ground and bowed like the true Elf he was. "I would expect nothing less, sir," he said with sincerity.

Leticia was pacing the kitchen surrounded by endless bunches of bluebells, a delicate muslin mask tied over her nose and mouth. "Spellbound darling, this is getting silly now. There are so many flowers that I've had to start magicking up vases; we have the whole of fookin' Bluebell Forest in here, not to mention in four green-houses and the orangery. You know Mamma is really allergic to Bluebells, they give me hay fever and make me sneeze. I'll get cook to take them away to the kitchen and make a few more vats of blue-bellade. With this lot, we'll be set up for life, pity I can't stand the taste of it!"

Spellbound giggled. "Oh Mamma, you look so funny in your mask," she said with a twinkle in her eye. "I totally agree with you though, no more bouquets; it's gone beyond a joke."

"This Drillian fellow, he's certainly not one to be ignored," Leticia remarked. And Clifford said I wasn't to interfere with your Karma, so whatever you decide to do is fine with Papa and me."

Spellbound's thoughts drifted to Drillian; his handsome face, his beautiful dark brown eyes. His passion for her was infinite and unbelievable and whether he knew it or not, he certainly had made her wings flap on more than one occasion! Shocking her mother, she sprang to her feet and in a shower of silver sparkles, she zipped out of the kitchen through the large ornate doors, into the garden. She whizzed in and out of the trees, her sylph-like body gliding with perfect precision, not even knocking one leaf off a branch.

Cumalot Castle was really magnificent, not perhaps as grand as the family home or Fingleberry Manor but its stunning light mar-blestone work screamed of wealth and nobility, and the four large phallic-shaped turrets stood proud and superior. She raced towards the main entrance and before she could even greet the guardsmen, they threw open the door, letting her fly straight inside.

Drillian was waiting in the 'blue room'. It had been recently redecorated and had now become his favourite of all the places in the castle. Heavy ornate tapestries hung on the walls, each one embroi-dered with full-length images of Spellbound in flight; Spellbound laughing; Spellbound waving; Spellbound winking; Spellbound cuddled up in bed surrounded by Dodibells and Spellbound hop-ping on one foot, balancing her wand on her nose. He immediately rose to his feet as she approached him.

"I hoped you would come," he said in a strained voice, and she noticed he looked pale and a bit on the skinny side. With a laugh, she hurtled towards him, leaping into his arms and wrapping her legs around his waist.

"The answer's YES," she declared, her green eyes staring into his intently.

CHAPTER 23
TEARS AND TANTRUMS

Leticia sat back in her chair and closed her eyes. She had not slept well the night before and felt shattered. It was still quite early in the morning, but the house was unusually quiet for a Friday, so much so that she stood for a while near the window to see if there was any activity outside. With a resigned air, she went back to her chair, her thoughts turning to Marco and intense feelings of guilt washed over her with him being incarcerated on the island for three long years. He had been innocent all along. She shook her head in despair. Poor Marco, he didn't deserve that and after all she had done to him, he still loved her and had forgiven her so readily. In the last few days her heart had softened towards him and her eyes had started to light up when he entered a room. Maybe she had been too harsh, she thought. Her mind then drifted to Spellbound and the upcoming nuptials. It was to be a huge event and money was being lavished on the best of everything for the couple. Their golden carriage was to be drawn by four snowy white unicorns which were rumoured to be the only four in all the realms. Leticia had a strong bond with animals and had visited the outer astral to confer with them. She was over the moon that they had agreed to draw Spellbound's crystal coach on her wedding day.

Leticia was still unsure about the match with Drillian but Spellbound seemed to be happy and madly in love and Marco approved wholeheartedly. She was worried about her daughter being so young and not really knowing her mind yet but then reminded herself that she was roughly the same age when she and Marco had wed. Why did she feel so uneasy about it all? She sighed as she gently tapped between her eyebrows to soothe herself; the last thing she wanted was a headache. She closed her eyes wearily. Perhaps she would just have a little nap and try and catch up with some sleep.

Sometime later she awoke with a jolt. The unusually quiet house was now a hive of activity. She stretched her arms above her head, flapped her wings a couple of times to remove the creases and glanced over at the clock. It was well past noon.

"What is all that racket about?" she muttered to herself, going out into the corridor. Looking down into the hall, she saw two maids and three Elves carrying boxes and cases out of the front door and there, with his back to her, was Marco. He signalled to one of his gardeners, beckoning him over. Next, Spellbound appeared from one of the rooms downstairs. What a vision, she thought to herself, but she failed to notice the sad expression on her face. The once little Fairy was now blossoming into an exotic beauty. Her sweet tiny figure was changing shape and curves were appearing in all the right places. Very soon she would be married and … her thoughts were interrupted by shouting.

"But Papa, why are you leaving? This is so stupid. I've never seen you walk away from a fight in your life, so why are you running away now? I just don't get it!"

"Spellbound, my sweet child," he said softly. "Try to understand that sometimes there are things in life that are no longer worth pursuing and I have to accept the situation is beyond repair."

Leticia sped down the stairs and into the commotion, her eyes full of concern.

"What is all this?" she asked in alarm. Marco turned wearily to face her and as she searched his features for the usual love and adoration, he showed her, she was shocked to find it had been replaced with a blank expression of coldness and indifference.

"You have your wish, Leticia," he clipped dismissively, whilst directing one of the valets to a chest in the corner of the grand hall. "I am going to relieve you of your wifely duties and leave you in peace to marry whoever it is you wish to be with. I have spoken with my lawyer and the divorce documents you so desperately want will be drawn up and on your mail mat as soon as possible. Please do not tarry with them. The sooner you sign them, the quicker we can go our separate ways."

Her lips tightened and her posture stiffened.

"This is your entire fault, Mamma," shouted Spellbound, "See what you went and did?" Tears sprang into her eyes as she looked at her mother with disdain.

"Now stop it, Spellbound," Marco said. "All is fair in love and war, just like your mother said. If her feelings have changed then who am I to stand in her way? She knows that I am innocent of any infidelity, yet still she regards me with scant care. No, it is best this way. Spellbound turned towards each of her parents desperately and let out an ear-piercing wail of utter grief. Leticia shuddered in her shoes, as her only daughter fled from the house, crying heart-rending sobs.

"Marco," Leticia said softly, but he was already walking away, barking out orders for the rest of his entourage to vacate the Manor at once.

There was a deathly stillness and all that could be heard in the deserted hall was the ticking of the ancient grandfather clock. Leticia felt totally dejected as she wandered from room to room, not knowing what to do next. Now that Marco had gone and Spellbound had left, a great feeling of loneliness engulfed her; maybe she should go to Clifford on the astral, he would know what to do, she consoled herself.

"There, there, sweets," Drillian crooned whilst cradling Spellbound. She had somehow managed to wrap her legs and her arms around him so tightly that he was having severe difficulty in breathing.

"I just can't stand it," she sobbed into his neck. "Mamma can be such a stubborn frog at times. You don't think I'm gonna go into the yearning again, Drilly, do you? Oh, blewdy hell, what if I yearn again ... oh no!"

"You're not gonna go into the yearning again, sweetness," Drillian reassured her as if she was a child. "I'll make sure that nothing bad will ever happen to you again, I promise." Drillian's shirt was drenched in tears as she looked up at her future husband, imploringly.

"Prr ... promise?" she gulped gently.

"I promise, now come and tell me the story from beginning to end."

It was no good, thought Leticia, I will have to go and speak with Marco. He had been gone from the house for two hours and the more she thought about it the worse she felt. Who was she kidding? It wasn't Clifford she should turn to, although he was the sweetest of Warlocks and a life-long friend. No, she had loved Marco for over half her life and even though he had bonked the wicked Tinky, it wasn't his fault, he was under a spell. Despite everything that had happened, deep in her heart, she would always love him.

Pulling herself together, she left the Manor on her silver broom stick, speeding through Bluebell Forest, towards his house. She felt a sense of urgency as she flew, her heart beating as fast as bat wings. As she approached, she stopped, smoothed down her dress, making sure she looked perfect. Marco was seated in the library, hunched over with his head planted firmly between his hands. When he heard Leticia enter the room, he lifted his head slightly and looked at her with raw pain in his eyes.

" Leticia why the hell are you here?" he asked bitterly. "Leave me be so I can heal myself."

"We need to talk, dear," she said softly. "This just won't do; we need to discuss our marriage and the best way to move forward."

He glared at her in disbelief. "Have you not played enough games with me already?" Dark smudges were under his eyes and he laughed bitterly. "You have some brass neck, I'll say that. You banish my sorry ass to some forsaken place for years, then you find out I was innocent the whole time but that still doesn't make the slightest bit of difference to you. You caused our daughter to go into yearning and nearly lose her magic. You then take your Warlock for a lover! ALL THIS SHIT, I was prepared to overlook, because I am so fookin' stupid and you still saunter over here wanting to call the shots! Is this some kind of sick joke or something? What's the matter with you, can you not bear to lose your infantile game? Is that what all this is about?"

The venom in his voice shocked Leticia and as she approached, he instantly raised his hand as a warning for her not to come any closer.

"Now get out of my house and don't you ever come here again; do you hear me!"

"But Marco!"

"I said, go! There will be no more negotiations except with our lawyers. I can't bear the sight of you."

He quickly stood up and left the room, leaving Leticia alone again.

As sure as daisies were daisies, and just like he had promised, the next morning, the dreaded divorce papers fell with a resounding thud on her mail mat. Feeling wretched her eyes scanned the document. Marco had offered her half of his fortune on the condition that she never make contact with him again. He really meant it. She panicked and then chastised herself for pushing him away these past weeks.

In desperation, she reached for her spell phone, which was lying on the kitchen table, and called her cousin, Larissa.

"The trouble is that you have always been so wilful and contrary," she scolded Leticia. "What did you expect? First you cast your spells to make him love you, then you magically banish the poor Elf, then you cast a spell on him to make him not love you, then you cast another to bring him back. It makes my head spin my dear, it really does! No, no, darling fae. In my opinion, it's about time you realised that using magic to solve your problems often makes things worse. You have got yourself into this sorry old mess and I'm afraid I have a hot date with a fairy horny Pixie in half an hour so you will have to figure this one out by yourself. What you sow is what you reap and all that. Gotta fly darling, bye-bye for now."

Larissa put the phone down and Leticia sat motionless at the kitchen table. Of course, Larissa was right. She did use magic all of the time and in this instance, it had backfired dramatically. She reached for the phone again and tapped in Caitlyn's number.

"Oh dearest, you do sound so very sad," Caitlyn said gently. "But it was bound to happen sooner or later. You do have this habit of making sure you get exactly what you want. Dearest, I am your best friend, so I know that you won't take this personally, but you have always avoided the real issues in your life. As soon as something emotional or dramatic starts to surface, you whip out your wand and magic it away. I guess you have to face the fact that weaving this magic can have a negative reaction. Maybe just for once you should try and sort things out the right and proper way." Then Caitlyn, whispered her usual "I love you, dearest" and hung up.

Spellbound walked into the kitchen and gave her mother a steely stare.

"Mamma, I'm off to stay with Pa for a while. He needs me. I don't know when I'll be back."

"Huh! But I need you too, Spellbound. This isn't easy for me either, you know!"

"Mamma, I love you so much, but he is unhappy right now and I need to try and sort him out before my wedding. In less than six weeks I'm marrying Drill and Papa has sunk into a deep depression and we all know why, don't we? Leticia saw a young, responsible, grown-up Fairy, instead of the childish sprite she was before. "When I think of what you have put him through, you should be quite ashamed of yourself and should be thinking more about him and less of yourself. You cast love spells on him, you twice turned his fiancé into a slug, then you banished the pair of them for three years. You really have rubbed his nose in the fox shit Mamma. You know, all your meddling made me go into yearning and I can't even begin to explain how crappy that felt. No, he really needs me right now, so I am going." Spellbound whizzed out of the front door and into Drillian's Roller Royce. In no time, they had driven away, leaving Leticia all alone again.

In the days that followed, Spellbound divided most of her days between visiting her father and being with Drillian, leaving Leticia to make a difficult decision to leave Bluebell Forest behind for a while and revert to her previous plan to spend some time with Clifford at Trevania. Larissa, Caitlyn and Spellbound were told of her imminent departure and she promised Spellbound faithfully she would return in time for her wedding. Deep in her heart, she knew Clifford would know what to say and do and as he had always been there to advise her, it was only right she seek his wisdom now at this desperate time. She also needed to tell him that although she cared for him, she could never return the devotion he had declared for her. He deserved to have his answer and now she felt she must give him her response.

That night, she connected with him on the astral plane and in less than two minutes, she was transported to his huge, medieval castle in the deepest part of the Caledonial realm. He looked charming in deep magenta silk and was grinning delightedly from ear to ear. The handsome Warlock took two strides and swept her up in his strong arms; closing his eyes, as he breathed in the familiar aroma of her perfumed hair.

"Oh, Clifford, it is so good to see you. I have missed you so, so much, dear friend," She placed her arms around his shoulders and embraced him for a few moments.

"Come, Leticia, what is all this about?" he asked, a little confused. "I gather things are not looking so good back at the homestead?"

"They are not dearest," she said choking back a little sob. Clifford led her to the East Wing of the Castle, which was the only part of the ancient building that was still intact. When he had arrived, Fairy vampires had completely taken over the place and it took him several days of magical intervention to remove them. Many of the rooms had fallen into wrack and ruin so he was planning on a complete refurbishment to return it to its original splendour.

Leticia was seated on a baronial chaise lounge, sipping sweet, nettle tea; her long black hair, cascading to one side, over her shoulder.

"Pray tell me Milady," he said fervently. "Have you thought any more about my proposal of marriage?" Leticia placed her cup down on the small wooden table at her side and looked kindly into his eyes.

"Clifford," she said hesitantly, "I don't know what came over me that day we went to my bedchamber. I love you dearly, you have been my friend and advisor my whole life but what I did was completely out of character dear and I came to realise afterwards that I have been so very unfair to you." She saw the hurt in his eyes and began to feel even more ashamed. "I've been unfair to everyone!" she expressed immediately. "My meddling and messing have caused so much harm; I can't marry you; it just wouldn't be right. It breaks my heart to hurt you. Can you ever forgive me?" Clifford's head dropped down and when he looked up, a pained expression crossed over his handsome features. He walked over to her seat and sat beside her, holding her dainty little hands in his own. Her journey to Trevania had been late at night, and he could see how exhausted she was from all the stress. Gently he kissed the palm of her hand and clicked his fingers once. Instantly she was in a deep sleep, and he lifted her effortlessly to the bedchamber which had been so lovingly prepared for her arrival.

"Something is not right," he said under his breath while he gazed down at the sleeping Fairy. Some piece of this puzzle did not quite fit, but he couldn't pin down the cause of his uneasiness. He began to think back to the day of their union. She had given herself to him quite freely, instigating the event without any hesitation. Of course, he knew that Leticia was at times reckless but having given it more thought, she was right, it wasn't at all like her. Taking his crystal ball from under his cloak, he tossed it into the air and it slowly hovered over Leticia's sleeping form, crackling and sending out electrical sparks which showered all over her. He summoned the ball back to him and with a slight frown, looked deep within its depths. Staring for what seemed like an age, he finally had the answers he needed. A spell of enchantment had been cast upon her. She had ingested something in liquid form. Who would dare do this to her, he frowned again, as he lovingly pushed back a stray lock of her raven black hair? For the next hour, Clifford worked tirelessly, magically restoring her energy patterns and lifting any negative vibrations that Leticia had encountered in the past few months. When she awoke, she would be cleansed, refreshed and positive once more.

For a whole week, Leticia spent every waking moment with Clifford. After never being away from him for more than a few days in her entire life, she realised just how much she had come to miss her dear and trusted friend. Her heart ached deeply for Marco, so much so that at one point she feared that she had connected with the yearning and felt what Spellbound had experienced. The situation was hopeless.

Clifford, yet again, offered to cast a "love removing" spell on her, but she had remembered Caitlyn's words and sadly declined again. She must face her pain head-on even though it did hurt like hell, and for probably the first time in her life she wasn't going to resort to spellcraft to solve her emotional problems.

On the last evening, she looked fondly at him and placed her small hands in his. His sorrow was apparent yet his beautiful hazel eyes held dignity. As he spoke, he gave her a wistful smile.

"You know that I will always love you, Milady," he said sincerely. Leticia smiled shyly and nodded in agreement.

He sighed and suddenly got to his feet standing like an Adonis in front of the huge baronial fireplace.

"I also have something else to relate," he said, looking down at his feet. "After our magical time in the bedchamber together, one which I will carry close to my heart forever," he said with intensity, "and also on the first night you came to stay here, I sensed something that I could not identify. You must not blame yourself Leticia for enticing me to your bed. I fear it was not your fault. A few days ago, while you were sleeping, I looked into the crystal globe and was shocked to see that you had been enchanted in some way. Regrettably, you did not come to my bed with free will, something supernatural had intervened. I must find out what happened, but so far, I haven't managed to make any real headway."

Leticia was mortified and gasped, her hand clasping her throat as she reeled in shock.

"I will get to the bottom of this, I promise you that, and when I find out the person that has done this to you ... then woe betide them," he said with a vengeance.

"I can't believe it!" she said, in horror. "Who would do such a thing to me and why?" She searched her mind for a few moments, but no answer came.

She joined him in front of the fire and placed her arms around his waist, laying her head on his chest. "Clifford, if I did have some kind of spell cast upon me, I don't regret it," she told him. "You have a very important place in my heart and you always will. You are my best friend and I love you, so dearly." For a moment, both Fairy and Warlock stood locked in a silent embrace.

"I still have essential business to attend to here regarding my estate, and your daughter's wedding is fast approaching. You should go now Leticia, I'm sure you will be needed."

She looked up at him, her sadness visible in her beautiful violet eyes. He couldn't bear to have her so close to him anymore. The longing he felt was just too much, too painful.

"As hard as it is for me to say this," he said, with his voice suddenly cracking, "you belong to Marco. You must try and rekindle this marriage." Leticia saw a tear prick his eyes. "I have decided to spend my time getting the Castle renovated. I plan on opening a school for sorcery in the coming months. There will be much to do." Leticia nodded and pulled away from him.

"You are right dear," she said in a deflated manner. "I must be there for Spellbound; she will need me to help with the preparations. I'll make the arrangements immediately," she said.

The castle was eerily quiet; only the sound of the old grand-fairy clock in the hall could be heard ticking. Clifford stood in front of a long wooden table in the drawing-room, scrutinising all the ingredients he had assembled to cast his spell. A bubbling cauldron was placed in the adjacent fireplace in preparation. He gathered up a handful of dried hyssops mixed with a blend of rag-weed and ginger root and tossed it into the pot. A spark erupted, followed by a green and purple flash. He then submerged a large, glass phial into the cauldron and filled it with the hot liquid, which he took back to the table. He breathed it in as the plumes of magical smoke drifted into his nostrils. Suddenly a holographic image of Leticia appeared before him. She was busying herself in her bedchamber, gazing at her reflection in a large silver mirror, she patted her powder puff over her nose.

Taking a large, Malacca wooden cane, which was embellished with a roughly hewn quartz crystal, Clifford banged it on the ground three times. In a loud commanding voice, he spoke the spell aloud.

"I summon the magic of Warlocks beyond,
I call on the power of the staff and the wand,
Cast out the love that I carry in me,
I detach from Leticia, prey set me free."

He gulped down the potion and within an instant, the longings he had once felt for Leticia were finally gone.

"Mamma … Mamma ... you are back! and I have missed you sooooo much!"

Spellbound flew into the hall scattering Fairy dust everywhere. Leticia waved her wand over the door and her luggage immediately appeared and ascended the giant staircase. Spellbound spun her around and around until she was dizzy.

"Now Mamma, I want you to come and look at my dress, oh and tell me the names of the four Unicorns so I can have their bridles engraved in gold and could you do a special spell so that they will stay for at least a week before they have to go back? And do you think I could actually hitch a ride on one of them?" Spellbound was babbling on as usual but this time it was clear that she was giddy with happiness.

It was less than a week before her wedding, the preparations were in full swing, and Leticia's Manor was in a flurry. Over sixty guests would be staying with her and at least fifty with Marco. The rest would be occupying every Fairy motel in the realm, and the seamstresses, caterers and maids had been summoned to attend to their every need.

The whole Manor was undergoing an extensive spring clean and extra food was being brought in for the uninvited guests as well. Goblins were high up on ladders, hanging golden sun-spheres from the ceiling and a band stand was being erected for a hundred musicians. Spellbound was still chattering on to Leticia when she was tapped cheekily on the bottom.

"Drilly, oh, Drilly!" She spun around and hugged him with as much strength as she could muster.

"Hello gorgeous bride to be," he replied, winking at Leticia over her shoulder.

Leticia gave him a frosty smile, still worried about the uneasiness she felt about him. And she kept reminding herself that Spellbound did have Aunt Hester's genes, so if the coupling wasn't meant to be, then her darling daughter wouldn't be giving him a second look!

Drillian pulled Spellbound towards him and kissed her passionately. Leticia's left eyebrow shot up and she turned her head discreetly away to give them some privacy. The kiss seemed to go on much longer than she had anticipated and as she quickly glanced back at the couple, they were still locked in a firm embrace.

Spellbound was letting out little giggles of pleasure and Drillian's hands were sliding up and down her bottom. Leticia sighed irritably and zapped her wand at them; they sprung apart in surprise.

"That's quite enough of that, Spellbound. There is a time and a place for such things, dear, and the hall isn't that place. And you, laddie," she said, giving Drillian a withering look, "stop showing my daughter up in public. Surely your parents have taught you some decorum?"

She motioned to Spellbound to come closer and when she was in front of her, she took a snowy white hankie from her gown. She spat on it and rubbed furiously at her daughter's smudged lipstick. "If you are to continue with the kissing thing, daughter, it might be an idea for you to whiz up some of that magic lip gloss, dear. You know ... the stuff that doesn't smudge?"

Drillian gazed lovingly at Spellbound and reached out his hand, linking his finger in hers. Leticia took a silver comb out of her pocket and brushed Spellbound's hair back into place. "And Drillian, please don't mess her hair up again, we can't have her anything but perfect! Now you two, run along and let Mamma get her breath back. We will catch up later when I've bathed and rested, though goodness knows how one can rest with such a commotion going on in the Manor!"

She flitted up the spiral staircase leaving Drillian and Spellbound staring after her. As she disappeared out of sight, they threw their arms passionately around each other and locked lips once more.

Marco stared into the fire moodily and angrily drained another glass of Randy Brandy. Leticia had run straight into Clifford's arms, he mused bitterly as he poured himself another shot of the liquor. It was going to be very hard for him to act normally around her at the wedding tomorrow. News of their divorce proceedings was being held back until after the nuptials. This was Spellbound's time and he must not distract any attention away from her. The gossiping would be rife soon enough; he must let her have her day. Besides, Leticia had not even signed or returned the papers yet. What was she playing at? Suddenly there was a huge flash and a spray of electrical sparks cascaded in the corner of his study. The smoke was a hazy pale green and Marco coughed and waved his hand from side to side to see who had intruded in such a way.

Clifford emerged from the magical fog and bowed formally before walking towards Marco, who rose to his feet in anger.

"I come in peace Sir and all I ask of you is that you hear me out."

Marco shrugged apathetically and stared out of the window to the lakelet beyond. "What do you want, Eyesaurus? Don't you think you have ruined enough of my life already? It's you she wants, not me so just take her and be done with it."

"You are mistaken, Marco. It is not I she loves."

"Oh, give me a break!" he spat out. "She couldn't get to you quick enough, could she?"

"You must understand that I have protected her from birth. It was only natural that she sought me out, everyone had turned against her; she had nowhere to turn, except to me."

"You've slept with my wife. She told me that herself, and you've probably been enjoying her every night since," He sighed, a tone of resignation in his voice. "You cannot deny that, Eyesaurus."

"I will not lie to you. Yes, I did share her bed once but whether you care to believe it or not, we did not make love when she visited me in the week past."

"Spare me the lies."

"You need to stop pitying yourself and listen, Zamforia. I have since found out that the reason she gave herself to me so willingly was that she was under a form of enchantment spell. You have to help me get to the bottom of this and find out who did this to her."

Marco's eyes suddenly lit up incredulously. "Enchantment? But who would have the power to do this to Leticia? Who would even dare?"

"I will find a way soon to clear up the mystery," Clifford promised. She would never have gone to the bedchamber with me under normal conditions, just as you would never have lain with Tinky Bonk in the Cherub Pagoda." The light appeared once more in Marco's eyes. Eyesaurus was right. Everything was back to front.

"Leticia has always been besotted by you even when she was a teenager. I should know, I had to sit in the ball and listen to her drone on and on about you till I fear, I nearly fell asleep with boredom. Even when she banished you, she talked incessantly about you and made me seek you in the ball, so that she could look at you on your desert island. It all got rather tedious for me; I must say. And remember … last but not least, she does have Hester's genes."

Clifford smiled kindly. "Marco put an end to this nonsense and reunite with her. She truly does love you. And alas, I will always adore the very ground she walks upon, but sadly, it is not I that she wants. Come, let us not be enemies."

Marco's heart soared. She really did love him and not Eyesaurus! They could be happy again. They WOULD be happy again! He crossed the room to where Clifford was standing and grasped his hand. "Clifford, would you do me the honour of being my guest tonight and attending my daughter's wedding tomorrow?"

Clifford bowed slightly. "I would be more than delighted, Sir."

CHAPTER 24
DO YOU TAKE THIS ELF?

"I'M GETTING MARRIED, I'M GETTING MARRIED," bellowed Spellbound from the top of the stairs. "Mamma! Where are you? Come here and hug me right now! … HA HA HA!!!! MAMMA … MAMMA … YOU NEED TO GET UP HERE. IT'S MY BIG DAY!"

Leticia slowly opened her left eye and sighed. She shook her head. "Why does she always have to be so blewdy loud and excitable?" she said to herself.

She grabbed a pillow and held it firmly over her head to drown out the racket.

"MAMMA!" Spellbound shouted, bursting into the bedchamber like a hurricane. She flopped down onto the rose petal bed and began chatting incessantly about her upcoming nuptials. Leticia dragged herself upright, trying to listen patiently.

"I never thought this day would come. Drilly is so handsome, Mamma, he really is. You know, I think I picked the most perfect husband. He is gallant and kind and rich and … sexy." She winked at Leticia. "And he has a SUPER … DUPER big …"

"Erm … it's a little early in the day to be discussing the Elfin anatomy, dear" Leticia said, yawning. Spellbound giggled and jumped into bed snuggling up to Leticia, pulling the covers tightly around them both.

"Oh, I do love him, Mamma," she said. "I wonder if he is as excited as me right now!"

Leticia turned to face her daughter and propped herself up on one elbow.

"Are you really sure about this, darling," she said kindly. "It bothers me, especially as you have not known him that long. You're still so young. You know, if you did want to change your mind and postpone it for a decade or two, your Papa and I can stand the shame, I'm sure!"

"Oh, Mamma, how can you say such a thing, especially today of all days. No, I am very sure that he's the one for me, stop being so negative." She prattled on enthusiastically.

"Yes, well … that may be so. But seriously, Spellbound, I worry that you haven't thought it through." Leticia eased herself out of bed and walked over to the ornate dressing table and started to brush the tangles out of her hair. "Then again, I suppose you can always divorce him if it doesn't work out. I know it would cause an outrage, but what the heck, we've created far worse scandals in this family."

"Mamma, why would you say such a thing!" Spellbound butted in irritably.

"Oh well then, if you are so firmly set on it, just enjoy it and know that whatever happens, I love you very much. Just as long as you don't go having any faebies straight away."

"Didn't I tell you not to eat all that bleedin' human chocolate your future husband keeps stuffing down your throat? I knew it! I just knew it when I saw you eating that big bar of Toad-la-Roam the other day that we'd have trouble fitting you into your gown." Leticia was trying frantically to cram Spellbound into her wedding dress but as hard as she tried, the seams were just not meeting.

"Just how many of those bars did you shove into your greedy mush anyway?" she fretted, getting all red-faced and flustered.

"Erm … not sure, Mamma, one, maybe two … a day even?"

"Oh, good grief, Spellbound! I really didn't want to use magic, today of all days. I wanted everything to be perfect without any kind of wand intervention and now you leave me no fookin' choice, you greedy little maggot! The dress has thousands of crystals and diamonds and there's no way I can let it out. Typical fookin,' Taurean Fairy... always thinking about the next meal, you all scoff like Tommy Trotters!"

"Excuse me, Mamma," Spellbound exclaimed. "Just who did a blewdy body transformation spell recently? Have you forgotten that already, Mrs Perfect?"

"I am going to have to go downstairs and get out the figure reducing potion and try and resize you for this gown!" She marched out of the room, cursing at the top of her voice.

When she returned with the magic elixir, Spellbound had the most peculiar expression on her face.

"What's with the sour face?" Leticia snapped, tapping her little booted foot on the floor in annoyance. "Why do you look like you've just licked fly piss off a stinging nettle?"

Spellbound gave her mother a worried look.

"What ... what will that potion do to me, Mamma. It won't turn me into a hare again or anything sinister?" she asked anxiously.

"Of course, not dear ... please trust your Mamma. It will make you a size smaller that's all, so stop fretting. Tomorrow you can go back to being a lardy bum again. You know that I drink it all the time. How am I supposed to stay looking this good and still eat all those fookin' cream buns, eh? Answer me that! Now come along, it stings a bit on the way down but after a couple of seconds you'll feel fine!" Leticia pushed the pink glass flume towards her, encouraging her to drink it.

"No Mamma, I really can't drink it, I'm afraid to!"

"Afraid? What of, dear? Come now, you silly Fairy, hold your nose if it makes you feel better but for fook's sake, drink it up, we can't stand here arguing all day. You're supposed to be getting married in less than an hour so get a wiggle on!" Spellbound held her nose and threw the potion to the back of her throat. She experienced a tingly, fizzy feeling racing through her body and suddenly the glorious dress fitted like a dream.

The Manor and grounds were buzzing with activity and guests were starting to arrive. Cascading rainbows fell from the sky and landed on the lawns in unison. The trees were dripping with glitter dust and a spell had been cast to make the brickwork of the Manor change colour every six seconds. Marco hadn't had a chance yet to speak to Leticia about salvaging their marriage. He decided that he would discreetly try and get her on her own after the wedding ceremony so that Spellbound's special day would not be disturbed in any way.

Spellbound was a vision. Her dress was a shimmering blush and ivory concoction, embellished with thousands of sparkling diamonds and pink pearls. The strapless gown was laced with gold thread and tiny fragments of blue tit feathers, which was their wedding gift to her. The back of the dress plunged down leaving her pale pink and gold, iridescent wings resplendent. The train of the gown draped behind her for what seemed like a mile, but under the circumstances, Leticia had made sure it was as light as air.

Spellbound's fae friends were in attendance as hand-maidens and each one of them looked adorable.

Leticia inspected her daughter in the bedroom, arranging the gossamer veil around her diamond crown. A tear pricked her eyes.

"Oh darling, you look just perfect," she said. "Your eyes are sparkling and your hair is as glossy as satin and this dress, even though I say so myself, is the most stunning thing I have ever created ... even better than your birthday gown!"

Marco waited silently at the door, observing the two most important Fairies in his life. He loved them both so much and no words could ever explain the feelings he was experiencing right at this moment. The last three miserable years were forgotten and his heart was singing with happiness.

"You two look truly beautiful," he said quietly. Both turned to look at him. He walked up to his daughter and let out a sigh. "Oh, Spellbound, what can I say!" He met Leticia's eyes for a moment and smiled at her kindly. She returned his look but said nothing.

"The carriage is outside darling," he said, turning back to Spellbound, offering her his arm.

Drillian was standing in front of the stone altar inside the hand-fasting chapel. He was dressed in a spectacular red satin doublet, encrusted with tiny diamantes and emerald crystals, a snowy white cravat at his throat. His black leather breeches were skin-tight, and on his feet, were full length black boots, with silver flashing buckles. His hair had grown a little longer and was tied behind in a prince's plait, making him look breathtakingly dashing.

Every female Fairy held her breath as they caught sight of him. They were truly sad that he would no longer be available. He was so engrossed in Spellbound and the forthcoming nuptials that he hadn't noticed any of them. This was his day, the day he had dreamed about. Finally, he would have Spellbound by his side, wearing his ring, to be united for life.

His heart started to beat very fast, as his eyes scanned the hundreds of guests all seated in the pink marble pews. Many were quietly chatting and others glanced in his direction and gave him a respectful nod. His father stood up and bowed to him and all the staff from Molars Inc. smiled and waved. Glancing to the right, he could see Spellbound's family and friends already seated and he espied the famous Aunt Hester, whose gaze travelled over him frostily. She was a beauty and must have captivated many admirers in her youth. What good it did them, he thought smugly, with her being fookin' frigid and all!

Just as he began to see who else was present, Leticia swept down the aisle and the crowd gasped. Even he had to admit that she was a vision of loveliness. She was dressed in a lavender ball gown with silver tips to her deep purple wings. Her raven black hair was swept up into a chignon, with the magnificent, Zamforian emerald tiara, placed perfectly in the curls. With elegance, she arranged her skirts and took her seat, waiting patiently as she fanned herself slowly with a huge turquoise Swannikin feather. Daughters were supposed to take after their mothers, he thought and if Spellbound looked as stunning as that in a few years from now, he would be one happy Elf.

The Duchess let out a little sigh as Leticia sidled up next to her. "I did so have my heart set on a coupling between Edward and Spellbound and although I am very happy for the bride and groom today, it really does sadden me."

Leticia looked around her and took Esme's hand and whispered, "Between you and me dear, I think this entire affair is a crock of fox shit!"

Esmee gasped in surprise. "We'll speak later about it," Leticia sighed irritably.

Caitlin, who was sat on the pew behind her, tapped her gently on the shoulder and as she turned around, she caught sight of the Duke and Duchess sitting further back with Eddie.

"I've never seen you look more beautiful dearest," she said kindly. Leticia smiled at her friend and whispered under her breath, "thank you!"

The chapel suddenly became hushed, as twelve Elfin musicians took their golden trumpets and blasted out the fanfare announcing the beginning of the service. Drillian's heart started to beat even faster as everyone turned their heads to see Spellbound standing at the far end of the aisle. Marco, dressed in a shimmering silver doublet, stood proudly with his daughter, her hand lightly placed on his arm. A ripple of astonishment filled the grand hall as she proceeded like an angel down the walkway, carrying a perfect bouquet of pink and blue Jonnikin flowers, which had never been seen in the realm before. Moonflower had left the blooms on Spellbound's pillow that morning. Her train was carried by the airborne Fairies, Pumpkin, Taffeta and Daffodil. They all looked stunning, in cob-webbed pink, tulip dresses with crystal pointed stilettos on their little feet and fresh freesia garlands entwined in their long hair. As they reached the foot of the Altar, the Fairies dramatically released the train, which billowed like a silken cloud around the bride.

Drillian gazed into Spellbound's veil and saw her sweet smile through the gossamer lace. The assembly were enraptured as the High Priest, Degar, stepped forward to begin the ceremony. For a moment, not a single sound could be heard, until Mike Hunt broke the silence, shouting, "Blinding, hey hey!"

Spellbound passed her bouquet to Pumpkin and Drillian slowly lifted the veil from around her face. She was glorious, he thought, and all his ... forever and ever. How was it possible to be this happy?

Clifford had been anxious and uneasy and was not looking forward to the ceremony at all. Since his return to the Brittanic realm the day before, his Warlock senses had been warning him that something was definitely amiss. He decided to make himself invisible and move around the congregation to eavesdrop for any information.

Sitting right at the back of the throng, in a secluded corner of the chapel, were the uninvited guests, Fenella Phlegm and Carmella Cacklejuice. Fenella's old battered tiara was askew on her matted hair, which she had tried to comb into some semblance of order. Her dark purple ball gown looked quite presentable but when she smiled tipsily, the sight of her black stumpy teeth spoilt the whole effect.

"I can't quite understand how you did it, let alone why," Carmella whispered furtively behind her hand.

"The Elf is a fool, but a rich fool," crowed Fenella, "and when he offered me Prince Fitzwilliam's baby tooth, how could I refuse? Do you know how much that thing fetched on the Elfbay auction site before he bought it last year? Two million zigagons, can you believe it?" Carmella's eyebrows shot upwards, as she mouthed the amount in astonishment.

"I may be an old crone, my dear, but I'm a fookin' wealthy one now!" Fenella cleared her throat and swallowed a huge ball of mustard phlegm with relish. She was an elite Fairy now and wouldn't spit it out at such an excellent function.

"So, let me get this right," Carmella said with a wicked chuckle.

"Drillian Macavity gave you Prince Fitzwilliam's baby tooth for a love spell that would make the Zamforian Fairy his for eternity? That's just brilliant! But how on this earth did you manage to whizz up that kind of magic?" Carmella asked in amazement.

Fenella looked around shiftily, making sure she wasn't overheard.

"I laced a hundred and fifty bunches of bluebells with a love potion. I cleared the forest of every flower," she cackled. "The Elf boy sent them to Spellbound, who of course, smelt every bunch. I heard on the grapevine that Leticia Zamforia had her cook turn them all into bluebellade ... ha ha! That just enhanced their power even more! It'd take a hell of a fookin' spell to reverse *that* magic I tell ya!"

Fenella leant backwards and took a small hip flask of liquor from under her wing and glugged it down greedily. She then wiped her mouth with the sleeve of her gown and belched with satisfaction. She leaned in towards Carmella and whispered again, "I'll let you into another little secret. Leticia Zamforia accidentally took a sip of one of my earlier love potions for Spellbound and rumour has it that she bedded her Warlock as a result! I didn't believe it when Macavity told me about it, but I scanned the crystal ball after he had left and had a good look. Watching her stroking her sugary pink nails all over the naked, Eyesaurus was just hilarious, and what a fookin' body he's got too! Who knows, if she had drunk some of the last batches of bluebellade, it could have been her standing up there at the altar today!"

Both Fairies chortled with smothered laughter.

Clifford Eyesaurus stood silently behind the pair of crones; his invisible body stiffened; his Warlock blood turning to ice.

"Should there be any Fairy, Elf or Gnome present who objects to this wedding, speak now or forever hold your codpieces!" Dregar said with gusto. In an instant, Clifford materialised in a shower of black and silver electrical shards. The congregation gasped as he emerged from the plumes of acrid smoke. With his hand on his dirk, he stormed down the aisle. His cloak billowing around him. Pulling Spellbound away, he towered over Drillian and glared into his eyes.

"I OBJECT!" he bellowed. "THIS MARRIAGE IS NOTHING BUT A FARCE." Taking his staff, he turned and pointed it menacingly at Fenella. "Maybe the old crone, who is sitting at the back of this chapel would like to tell you all what she has been up to!" All heads immediately turned to focus on Fenella. Clifford's voice was pure ice. "Fear not, I shall save her the bother and inform you all myself! This excuse for an Elf here, has paid the filthy witch a small fortune to make a succession of endless love potions in exchange for his father's prize possession; Prince Fitzwilliam's baby tooth!" The crowd let out cries of disbelief. "This bride is under enchantment and would never have agreed to a wedding under normal circumstances."

Philip Macavity stood up and glared in astonishment at his son, whose face had turned scarlet. Spellbound reached over and held Drillian's hand gently.

"Aww, that's okay, Drilly. We can still get married, take no notice of crappy Clifford, nothing is going to spoil our big day."

Leticia was by their side in an instant and Marco sped down the aisle to Fenella. She saw his approach and quickly collected up her skirts to speed off.

"Fookin' ' ell … gotta fly!" she croaked to Carmella. "Might be gone for a while!" With that, she disappeared on the spot.

Leticia grabbed Drillian by his cravat and stared sinisterly into his face. "YOU … YOU JUST WAIT, YOU GRIMEY ASS WIPE!" After what seemed like a lifetime, she roughly thrust him to one side and stood before her daughter. She took her wand out of her lavender chiffon gown.

"Marco, Clifford, guard him while I fix this fookin' mess. I haven't finished with him yet." Immediately Marco sped back down the aisle, gripping Drillian's left arm, while Clifford took his right.

"Mamma, stop making a scene please!" Spellbound looked around in embarrassment.

"Quiet, Spellbound," she snapped, closing her eyes in deep concentration. She circled her wand three times over her daughter's head, chanting a secret rhyme in Elvish.

As Leticia vocalised her spell, every candle in the place went out and the whole chapel started to shake. A huge swirling neon light raced over the guests and the four Unicorns charged into the hall, fire shooting from their nostrils. They had been duped and were all filled with fury, an emotion the peaceful creatures very rarely felt. Zarius, the head of the herd raced towards Drillian, his glowing horn lifting the Elf clean off his feet before landing him in an untidy heap on the floor. The unicorn glared down at him, steam snorting from his nostrils, as he pounded the floor angrily with his golden hooves. Drillian was in fear for his life and covered his face with his hands.

In an instant, all four unicorns let out an ear-piercing whinny and disappeared in a puff of scarlet smoke.

An eerie mist started to swirl around Spellbound, as she pirouetted in circles in the air. With every spin, she caught her mother's stare, her expression looking more bewildered by the second. Suddenly her feet hit the ground and she put a trembling hand to her forehead.

"Mamma!" she said disbelievingly as she let out a heartbroken sob … "Why am I in this dress ... why am I getting married ...? I don't want to get married, I don't even like him! Aunt Hester, why am I here?" She looked over at her beloved Aunt imploringly. Hester sped to her side and put her arms tightly around Spellbound. "Shush, shush, sweet fae, I am here, all will be well now," she soothed. Glaring at Drillian in disgust, Spellbound whispered, "Get me out of this chapel and out of this dress! Papa … oh, Papa, where are you?" She started to cry, long heart-rendering sobs, her tiny body shaking like an aspen leaf.

Hester stepped aside and Marco was there in an instant, folding his daughter into his strong arms, gently stroking her hair, whilst piercing Drillian with his eyes. "Hush darling … I am here …. you're free of the spell, and free of *him* forever."

"Marco, will you take our daughter out of here please!" Leticia said, in a low and controlled voice. "There is some unfinished business I need to attend to." He looked at Leticia apprehensively and placed a hand on her shoulder.

"Don't be rash Leticia ... promise me, think of your Karma?" Her eyes flashed purple fire, an expression he had never seen before.

"Just take Spellbound away from here, please. I do not want her to witness this. Take her now!"

Marco nodded, "Come Spellbound." He saw his daughter's lower lip start to tremble and quickly put his hand around her waist and led her away.

In a nano-second, Clifford waved his staff and both father and daughter disappeared.

Not taking her eyes away from Drillian, Leticia pointed her wand at the huge chapel doors and they slammed shut so that no one could leave. The congregation cried out in fear. In the next moment, her wand was directed at him, as he slowly began levitating from the ground. Suddenly, he was whizzed thirty feet into the air and she dangled him there for all to see.

"Leticia ... I beg of you, please don't harm him." Philip Macavity knelt before her; his hands clasped as if in prayer. Irritably, she pointed her finger and zapped him straight back into his pew. Drillian started to slowly rotate and then he began to spin faster and faster like a Catherine Wheel. Leticia's wand shot out an electric current and he ricocheted like a tennis ball off every surface. Everyone started to wail, while Philip let out shrieks of fear for his son. Clifford was by her side. "Your Karma Milady ... remember your Karma," he remonstrated sternly. She glanced at him briefly and then with one last powerful movement, she swished her wand and the unfortunate bridegroom clattered to the floor. In an instant, he was transformed into the ugliest, evil-smelling Troll. The doors flew open and he ran screaming towards the woods with his father following him in hot pursuit. Seeing Philip fleeing from the scene, Leticia zapped him with her wand and he yowled in terror, as a bolt of electricity hit his backside, lifting him clean off his feet.

Five hundred Dodibells stormed into the chapel. They had broken free from the woods and were being chased by a herd of eight magnificent, equine Trotalongs, who were supposed to be guarding them. The whole scene was one of bedlam and most of the guests took the opportunity to escape to safety.

Aunt Hester stood up and waved her crystal staff high in the air, sending the errant Dodibells and Trotalongs back to the wood. Leticia collapsed into one of the pink marble pews utterly exhausted. Hester and Larissa were by her side in an instant, making soothing noises to calm her down and waving smelling salts under her nose.

"I will take her home now," Clifford said, as he took Leticia's hand and pulled her to her feet. He flicked his fingers once. "Sleep," he said firmly, and she was in his arms, his velvet cloak wrapped tightly around her. In a shower of starlight, they were gone.

Chapter 25
Leticia's Fury

It had been at least two hours since Clifford had overheard the conversation between Fenella Phlegm and Carmella Cacklejuice. He paced up and down Leticia's library in agitation, his anger simmering beneath the surface.

"I really wish you would stop doing that, Clifford!" Leticia said as she entered the room.

"You can't keep zapping me asleep as and when you feel like it." She walked over to him, her temper still seething. "How the fook do you have the power to do that to me, anyway? I will never understand!"

"Milady, I was only concerned about your energy levels. You used so much power when you sent Macavity careering around the walls and ceiling of the chapel, not to mention hanging him in the air and turning him into a Troll. I feared, with your massive hissy fit, you may have collapsed from exhaustion! You really need to show some restraint!" he expostulated.

"Yes, yes, stop fookin' nagging me and tell me, how in heaven's name did you find out about all of this?"

"I had a bad feeling," he replied, "so I chose to make myself invisible. Whilst I was concealed from the crowd, the old hag, Fenella, was boasting to local shrink about how she had laced the bluebells with magic and how you had turned them all into bluebellaide."

Marco suddenly walked through the large golden doors, looking ashen faced.

"Spellbound is resting in her room," he interrupted. Walking over to the drinks cabinet he poured himself a double shot of Randy Brandy.

"The entire wedding was a mockery," Leticia spat furiously, "and this Fenella creature was behind the whole thing," she rasped. "I knew it, I knew something was wrong. I had a feeling within my very being that something sinister all along."

"As far as I could gather, her motives seem to be entirely related to coinage and nothing more," Clifford chipped in. "But alas, I think you both should sit down," he frowned, "I have more disturbing news to convey."

"How could anything else you say to me be worse than this?" said Leticia, plopping down on to the cream sofa, indicating for Marco to do the same. Clifford stood near the fireplace, his legs astride and his hands clasped behind his back.

"An hour ago, I gazed into my crystal globe again and this time I saw exactly who was behind the Fairy Glamour spell." They both looked earnestly at Clifford.

"I saw Tinky Bonk liaising with no other than the same old witch, Fenella, and handing over a hefty sum of money to her in exchange for an elixir."

"Now it all makes sense!" said Marco, leaping out of his chair. "Tinky said that she had got the potion from some old witch in a market. So, it was Fenella the whole time!"

Leticia's blood started to boil, her temper spiralling out of control once more and she began pacing the floor.

"I'm going to kill her!"

"Wait!" said Clifford worriedly. "You need to stop and calm down. Killing her will only get you exiled for certain."

"I agree," Marco interjected. "Do not be rash because your temper has the better of you." Leticia was staring into space, her voice monotone and icy.

"First, she goes against the Feathered Ones and resurrects the Fairy Glamour spell, which makes my husband think he is making love with me, when all along it's that trollop Tinky Bonk! I then banish him for three years, which just happens to result in my daughter going into the yearning and nearly turning her into a fookin' golden hare. Then, she sells Macavity a love spell so he can seduce my daughter and low and behold, I drink the remains of the spell and end up in bed with Clifford! Next, she sells Drillian yet another potion, enabling him to marry Spellbound." Leticia's wings were flicking and electrical sparks were making them change in series of strange murky shades, her small frame shook with fury from top to toe. "I AM going to kill her!" she hissed. And in the blink of a cat's eye, she conjured her silver broomstick, which automatically positioned itself for flight. Clifford and Marco watched in horror as Leticia waved her hand across the Manor door and it crashed open. Within a nano-second she disappeared in a blast of purple smoke into the night.

"Oh, crap!" Marco shouted, "now what are we supposed to do?"

Leticia's faithful broom, which she only brought out on hay-days and holidays, was programmed so precisely that she only had to think of a destination and it would take her there at the speed of light. Seconds later she was at the edge of the dank forest, hovering over the putrid hollows. Her explosive arrival caused many of the sinister creatures and insects to scatter into their homes. They huddled together for fear of straying into her path.

Her beautiful hair had become loosened from the chignon and locks of it were whipping across her face in the wind. Her skirts rippled behind her as she paused for a second to push her hair out of her eyes and get her bearings.

"We need to think this through," said a voice to her left. She turned and looked in amazement at Marco, then turned around and saw Clifford to her right. Both were hovering in the air next to her.

"Oh, typical, the fookin posse has arrived! How did you two get here so quickly?" she gasped in amazement.

"Your Warlock has this knack of knowing exactly where you are!" Marco told her. "And although I hate to say it, this time, I am ... well ... grateful for his second vision!"

Clifford pulled out his crystal globe from a secret pouch.

"My faithful friend never fails me," he said confidently and then promptly waved his hand over the ball so that it disappeared. "Now come. Before you go charging in there, we need to discuss our next move." Leticia was in no mood for discussions. She had been wronged and she would take her revenge. If nothing else, it would make her feel better and help her to rectify the injustice.

"There is nothing to discuss, Clifford," she snapped. "I know exactly what I'm going to do!" Both Warlock and Elf watched as the distraught Fairy suddenly propelled forward and sped deeper into the dank forest.

"Let's hope for Fenella's sake she only does the slug spell," Marco said, as he raced to keep up with her. "She always does that when she is seriously pissed off."

Clifford raised his eyebrows. "No Marco, this time I fear she'll have blood on her hands. Make speed, we need to stop her!"

Leticia stood a few feet away from Fenella's cottage, her eyes wild with fury and her heart beating like a drum. She paused for a moment, catching her breath at the stench of the forest and then fumbled inside her skirts for her abalone wand. Slowly, she pointed the staff at the door and it flew open with a bang. A wizened old Fairy emerged, holding her hand slightly over her eyes to shade them from the blinding light. She was gripping an old battered suitcase in front of her, ready to make her escape. With a terrified wail, she recognised Leticia immediately and scuttled back inside, closing and bolting the door frantically behind her. Leticia aimed her wand at the door again, this time taking it clean off its hinges with an astounding crash.

"Face me, you filthy, wretched hag ... let's see how powerful your magic is now!" Leticia yelled. "Show yourself to me so that I can scatter your flesh and bones all over the forest and send your sorry ass into an eternity of hell!"

Fenella huddled in the corner of her decomposing cottage, shaking uncontrollably. With purple fire in her eyes, Leticia strode into the room, followed by her two guardians. Her wings were deep red and twitching in a sinister fashion and the air suddenly turned icily cold as she viewed the pathetic Witch. Fenella was still wearing her crown and was a little worse for wear with the copious amounts of poppy punch she had consumed earlier that evening. Her eyes darted around the room, looking for an escape.

"Flicka" she screeched at the curled-up snake snoozing by the fire.

"FLICKA, KILL HER!" she howled frantically at the top of her lungs. The snake began to stir and opened an amber eye menacingly. Leticia had never seen such a large monster before; it took her breath away.

The reptile began to slither threateningly towards the three of them and then, realising his mistress was in danger he reared upwards towards the roof of the cottage and bared his fangs, moving his head back slightly, ready to strike. Leticia was fearless and pointed her wand at the venomous creature, and screamed the words, *"shrink this beast and leave it deceased."* In another blast of smoke, the snake shrank down to the size of a worm.

With the spiked heel of her shoe, she ground him deep into the dusty grooves of the cobbled floor, killing him instantly. She turned her attention back to the shaking crone.

Fenella cried out in anguish as she stared at the remains of her pet on the floor. "You have killed my Flicka," she groaned, wringing her hands together pitifully.

Leticia laughed quietly, "And now my dear, it is your turn. Do not fear, you will be joining him in a minute."

"Don't kill me, oh, please don't kill me," Fenella begged. Marco and Clifford stood back and watched cautiously; both knew not to interfere.

"Oh, but I am going to kill you, make no mistake about that," Leticia's voice dripped venom, "and I am going to relish every moment of it, that's for sure! You will never interfere with a Zamforian Fairy again, do you hear me? NEVER AGAIN CRONE!" She raised her wand and began to chant slowly, as she recited the spell over and over again.

Suddenly a silver pulsating light flew round the cottage scattering showers of starlight into the room.

"You'll be killing no-one, Madam Zamforia," a deep male voice cut in. "Not tonight or any night." Three glorious Angel beings hovered directly in front of her. Their shimmering white gowns cascading around their celestial forms. The dramatic wings were feathered and luminous.

"Oh, great, the Feathered Ones!" Leticia declared. "How can this be?" The male in the center, a blonde vision in oscillating light, stepped forward and smiled at her kindly. He waved his hand over her face and instantly, some of her rage subsided.

"Come now my dear Leticia," he spoke sympathetically. "This is not the way we want you to behave. We gifted you these mighty powers because as Spellbound's mother, you have been chosen for the task to guide her and teach her about her future abilities. She is going to be twice as powerful as any Fairy in these lands one day and will be given high status throughout her life."

"But …" He raised his hand to silence her.

"We understand that you are aggrieved and upset but we *will* intervene if you attempt to kill this Witch."

"But …" Leticia repeated, keeping a beady eye on Fenella. The females in the trio immediately teleported to each side of Fenella, guarding her. "If you continue with this nonsense Leticia, I shall strip you of your magic and take your wings away. Whatever this Witch has done, no Fairy is permitted to kill another. So, enough!"

All three Feathered Ones turned to face Fenella and held their hands over their heads. The brightest of lights emanated down from the tips of their fingers and seconds later, Fenella vanished into thin air.

"Spellbound is to be all-powerful?" Marco said, looking astonished.

"We have plans for her," one of the females said, turning back around to face him. "She has the purest of hearts and a genuine kindness that is deep-seeded within her very soul. As a reward for this, with each year she grows, so will her magic. Your daughter is destined to teach her craft to the generations of the future but for her to reach her goal, you Leticia, must assist by teaching her everything that you know. You are probably the most knowledgeable fairy in all of the Realms."

"What the fook does that have to do with me killing the old Witch!" Leticia protested petulantly.

"I repeat," the male being replied sternly, "Fairy law insists that one must not take the life of another and Leticia, you have to set a good example."

"Ha! Leticia boldly butted in. "You are a fine one to talk. You're supposed to be the ever so important ones, the wise ones of the skies, the highest of the high, the mightiest of the mighty, and you're all *so* fookin' powerful that you completely missed the fact that the Tinky, floozie tart acquired a Fairy Glamour potion, and you had no idea that MY daughter was under some kind of enchantment. Call yourselves the Feathered Ones! I'm sorry, I don't know who you are or what you are supposed to represent, but I do know this ..."

"SILENCE!" the male being stated firmly. "I am your Godfather and you shall show some restraint!" Leticia's mouth dropped open. "My name is Angelo and you will heed me, Leticia. I have been assigned to you throughout your life and have given you the inspiration to many of your magical accomplishments. You have always been wild and wilful and I have despaired of your antics and tantrums over and over again, yet despite all of that, I have always loved you. I have never interfered, until now, that is." She stepped back in amazement, a new respect showing in her eyes.

"Of course, Godfather," she said, dropping him a small curtsy and bowing her head in shame. "I'm sorry, I …I … didn't realise."

"Come," he said kindly and cupped her face in his hands so that she had no choice but to look directly into his beautiful bright blue eyes. "You are incredibly talented but you're also impulsive. I cannot have you ruining your Karma and losing your power, by reacting to this fiasco in such an unruly manner. I will, however, consider and grant any punishment that you want to deliver to the Witch, as long as it doesn't result in death. You, my dear, are free to choose her fate, so think carefully before you decide, show me at last you have wisdom in your soul. Let me be proud of you."

Instantly, the angelic group vanished. Clifford, Marco and Leticia stared at the vacated space and wondered if it had all been a dream.

CHAPTER 26
DO OR DIE

"I can't believe that fookin' snot bag witch, enchanted me!" Spellbound said sulkily over breakfast. "And Drillian, the pervy ginko git, he knew I didn't care a fig about him." Leticia, who was still outraged at the recent shenanigans, looked over sympathetically.

"I know darling," she said, reaching over the table and touching her daughter's hand. "You must be hopping mad at the entire affair and I feel like I've let you down. I should have persisted when I knew something was amiss."

"It's not your fault Mamma, you tried to warn me so many times, even on my wedding day." Spellbound dabbed away a tear from under her eye.

"I did turn him into a foul-smelling Troll for the day," Leticia replied reassuringly. "And you know, it's completely up to me to administer his final punishment. How about I devise a spell to keep him like that forever?"

"I just can't believe that he did such a thing. Elves are devious bladder-barting bastards, they're all complete grunt-futtocks," Spellbound snivelled.

"Darling, we do have to be a little more refined from now on," Leticia whispered cautiously, her eyes darting around the room. "We're being observed all of the time by the FOs, they have eyes and ears up their arses!"

"FOs?"

"Yes, you know, the Feathered Ones. Spellbound my darling, you are destined for such important work. I admit, I was filled with fury concerning that Drillian creature, but when my Godfather Angelo informed me that your future pathway has been planned to such a high degree, and as mother and daughter we have to work together, I nearly burst with pride, I tell you! My daughter," she said, smiling, gripping Spellbound's hand tightly, "my beautiful daughter is to be the most esteemed Fairy in all of the realms." She settled back into her seat and sipped her tea delicately, looking very pleased with herself. Of course, it was obvious, she thought. Leticia Elva Zamforia had produced the most perfect fae child in the four realms and why wouldn't she? She suddenly came down from her daydreams with a bump. She still hadn't decided what to do about Fenella either, but she would think about that later. For now, her mind was focused on fulfilling her destiny and giving her child as much guidance as she needed.

Spellbound bit delicately into her celandine toastie and dabbed her lips with her gossamer napkin.

Suddenly, there was a loud banging on the door, which could be heard throughout the Manor. Both mother and daughter turned to watch Biff the butler speedily answer it.

"I want to see her now! I need to see her RIGHT now," the familiar voice bellowed, as he forced his way inside.

"What is all this commotion about?" Leticia said as she flitted into the hall with Spellbound chasing quickly behind her. Philip Macavity stood in the centre of the gallery, crouched down and shaking uncontrollably.

"Please, Leticia don't zap me with that dreaded wand of yours. I need your help. You must come now," he said in desperation, panting for breath. "I am begging you. You are the only one who can fix this mess." Taking two strides towards her, he grabbed her arm forcefully and began dragging her out of the door.

"Just what is this all about and why are you handling me this way? Get your fookin' hands off me!" she screeched.

"Mamma, what's going on?"

Clifford miraculously appeared in his usual blast of purple air and wrenched Philip's grip from Leticia's arm. He glowered down at him menacingly.

"Unhand her Sir, or you will regret what is coming to you!"

Philip started sobbing, his head in his hands as he crumpled in a heap to the floor. "I am begging for your help ... please come with me, this instant, I implore you!"

"Not until you spit out whatever it is you want to say," Leticia said coldly.

"I cannot even find the words to describe the terrible monstrosity that has befallen us," he cried. "It's Drillian, I fear he's dying!"

"Dying?" everyone said in unison.

"Dying my arse!" Leticia sniped. "... of all the dramatic things to say!"

Marco was driving his new Bug Beetle 700 and pulled up outside of Fingleberry Manor. If Clifford was right and Leticia did, in fact, love him, he would talk to her and win her over and ask her if they could make a fresh start. He climbed out of the vehicle, closed the door and patted his Bug on the bright red and black hood.

"Stay here and wait," he commanded kindly. "I'll be as long as it takes." The Bug trilled in agreement and settled down for a little snooze. Suddenly Marco heard raised voices. Clifford, Spellbound, Philip and Leticia burst out of the large front doors and on to the driveway.

"Where exactly is he?" Leticia shouted.

"He's in the depths of the dark forest," Philip wailed.

"We can get there much faster if we fly," Spellbound said encouragingly.

"What in heaven's name is going on?" Marco said, approaching the group.

"Drillian is supposedly dying," Leticia said, rolling her eyes. "Although I am sure Macavity here is overreacting."

261

"Please make haste," Philip cried, "we don't have a moment to lose." Clifford clicked his fingers and a large wooden staff appeared in his right hand. He twisted the sparkling amethyst crystal on the top and banged it on to the ground three times. Immediately, the entire party were transported to the edge of the dark forest.

As they descended into the heart of the wood, the dense canopy of trees hid the sun and the temperature dropped rapidly. Instantly, Leticia produced her wand and magicked warm cloaks for Spellbound and herself.

"This place is fookin' creepy," Spellbound said shuddering.

"You should have stayed behind dear, but Clifford didn't ask before he whizzed us all here in a flash, DID HE!" She sniped at Clifford.

The smell of decay drifted through the air as they ventured deeper into the forest, strange noises could be heard in the distance. Suddenly, there was the sound of loud squawking and the flapping of wings. Leticia looked up and encircling them were five tetradactyl-like creatures.

"For fook's sake! That's all we need!" she said impatiently. "The Wallopers are here. Spellbound, stay close to me, if they come too near, I shall try and see them off."

"What the hell are Wallopers?" Spellbound gasped, following her mother's gaze.

"They're large, ugly birds that are from centuries ago and only dwell in the remotest part of the forest. They were totally banned from Fairyland, the blighters. You have to have eyes up your arse dearest because these spaddy-whacker's certainly live up to their name."

"Can't you just cast a spell and turn them into something smaller, like you usually do?" she responded.

"No, she can't!" Marco chipped in. "They have the advantage of being protected from any kind of spellcraft. Their one aim in life is to wallop any Fairy, Elf or Troll they can find with their wings, and the harder, the better! Then they eat their unfortunate victim alive!"

"Oh, great!" Spellbound said sarcastically. "This is all we need. Drillian better be fookin' dying because if he isn't, *I'm* gonna kill him!"

In the distance, a huge dark green and orange bird espied Spellbound and began swooping towards her. She flew swiftly into the air and turned sharp right to avoid it, but it dived down, smacking her right across the back of her legs. She shot head-first into a mossy bank, kicking and screaming. The Walloper hovered above her screeching and squawking, sending a signal to the others that prey was near. After a struggle, she managed to lift her head from the bank and turned to face the approaching bird. It looked Jurassic, with a huge dark grey beak and tattered feathers running from the top of its head to the base of its tail. As Marco raced over to his daughter, another one swooped down and cracked him on the backside, knocking him sideways.

"Dratted birds!" he bellowed as he pulled his cloak over his head. A deep purple and navy blue one hung over Clifford, its sinister talons glowing red, as it cackled in anticipation, but he kept it at bay with his Rowan staff. Leticia floated over in a white fizzy bubble and in an instant, she swished her wand and everyone joined her safely inside.

"What in hell's teeth!" Spellbound gave a relieved sigh as she settled into its protection. "Thank the fook we don't have them where we live!"

"Yes dear," Leticia said steadily. "I've only encountered them once before when I had a fight with my mother as a child and ran away into this forest. I managed to get down a badger hole and stayed there until they got fed up and left. They won't get through this bubble though, so relax," she reassured her. The enchanted bubble drifted through the trees for a few minutes, travelling further into the dense forest. The Wallopers screeched in ear-piercing annoyance and reluctantly gave up and flew away.

"Look ... over there!" Philip said, pointing. "There he is! How do we get out of this thing?" he cried. Leticia looked around to make sure the birds were completely gone and then pierced the bubble with her wand. They all floated down into the under-growth. Philip ran over to the base of a tree and fell to his knees. Leticia let out a horrified gasp and Spellbound clasped a hand to her throat in shock, no one could quite believe their eyes. Drillian, was in a trance, propped up by the trunk of an old oak tree. His body from the waist down had transformed itself into the bark and it was plain to see that it was only a matter of time before the tree would ultimately claim him. A beautiful, mysterious Dryad who was keeping watch over him darted into a huge bush when she saw the party.

Philip eventually managed to speak. "I sent out a search party when I realised, he was missing and as soon as I found him, I fetched the doctor, but he said it was the yearning and that nothing could be done. My only son, my only child and I am going to lose him forever." He knelt before Leticia and grabbed her skirts as he began to plead.

"Help him, please, I implore you, fine lady." He spoke pitifully. "Your magic is so powerful, there is none like yours; please say you can save him. I know he has been a cad and behaved dreadfully. It was a stupid and wicked thing to do, really it was but will you please try and forgive him, find it in your heart to be merciful?"

For once, Leticia didn't know what to do. She had never encountered an Elf's yearning before but she did know how Philip was feeling; the desperation of knowing that your child might die at any moment was an all too familiar emotion.

"I don't understand it, Marco," Leticia said, as she scrutinised the bark of the tree. "Why didn't he turn into a hare-like Spellbound nearly did?"

"Elves are different, they are closely related to the Dryad spirits. I thought you would have known that! Hence his Dryad guardian we have just seen."

"Why would I know that? I'm not a friggin' Elf" she said irritably. "For fook's, sake, am I supposed to know EVERYTHING! Clifford, what do you suggest dear?" Clifford was scratching his chin as he peered into Drillian's face.

"Mmm … it seems his infatuation for Spellbound has created a problem. We will need to get him to bed, bark and all, and see if the Moon Orb Spellbound has can work its magic like it did before."

"Of course, yes, we have the Orb don't we!" Leticia said confidently. "Although, how we prise him out of this tree, I'll never know!"

Whilst everyone was discussing how they were going to remove Drillian from the trunk, Spellbound quietly walked over to the oak tree and wrapped her arms around it tightly.

"Mighty Oak, lift up your roots, plant your feet in safer ground,
Feel my hands upon your trunk, and in our Manor-Land be found."

A gust of icy wind blew through Spellbound's red hair and suddenly the ground began to shake violently. Leticia and the others stopped talking and looked over at her in astonishment. In the moments that followed, the tree started to vibrate and uproot and in a second, magical sparks flew out of every branch and the tree with Drillian attached to it; disappeared clean out of sight.

"DRILLIAN!" cried Philip, looking frantically around him.

"It's okay," replied Spellbound. "I've just sent him back to our place."

Leticia was speechless. "Darling, what do you mean, you sent him back to our place, just how did you manage that?"

"I dunno Mamma, I just thought about it, visualised our front lawn and a little poem popped into my head, so I said it and whoosh, off he went!"

"It seems your daughter's powers are fast becoming extreme," Clifford said, smiling proudly. "Now let's get back and see where he's landed."

When Leticia and the others arrived back at the Manor, the large oak tree was standing proudly in the centre of the rolling lawns.

They all hurried over to it, all apart from Spellbound who went directly inside to retrieve the Orb. When she returned, she couldn't help but notice the look of worry on everyone's faces.

"We need to be quick!" Clifford said urgently. "We don't have much time. The branches are creeping around his throat now. Place the Orb on the ground and everyone hold hands. We'll form a circle around the tree."

Spellbound placed the Orb in front of Drillian and joined hands with the others. It thrummed musically as it lifted from the grass, dipping and whizzing in and around Drillian's body. A deep trembling sensation was felt by everyone and at the exact same time, all heads flew back as a bolt of lightning connected them all. They fell to the ground and Leticia let out a little cough. When the mist had cleared, Drillian had been released and lay limp at their feet.

"We need to get him to a bed," Marco announced. "Let's make haste."

Spellbound sat on the bed next to Drillian and stared into his sleeping face. His skin had now turned the colour of dust and his lips were cracking. She submerged a little sea sponge into a bowl of cooled witch hazel water and dabbed his forehead repeatedly. Why wasn't he improving, she thought? He was dying in front of her very eyes and there was nothing she could do. A tear trickled along his cheek causing a twig to protrude from his ear; a small leaf sprouted rapidly and entwined itself over his nose. Taking some little silver scissors, she snipped it off, frightened it would interfere with his air supply. After a while she felt utterly hopeless and tossed the sodden sponge into the bowl. Falling on to her knees she placed her head on Drillian's chest, and sobbed wretchedly.

"After searching every manuscript, I could find, there was only one book which mentioned an Elf's yearning," Clifford said in a deflated manner. "It's the same procedure as with a Fairy in yearning, if their hearts become too heavy, they shapeshift into something else, in Drillian's case, … a tree!"

"There must be something we can do," said Leticia urgently. He's been in that bed for four days now and there's no change. When Spellbound had it, she was cured by now and driving everyone insane with her stupid happiness! I mean, if he carries on like this Clifford, he'll turn into a fookin' conker, we'll be roasting him on a fire come Yuletide! Oh, what are we to do!"

Spellbound felt sick with worry. She hated Drillian for what he had done but she would never in a million years want him to die. Philip Macavity had sat by his bed day and night for three days before her father had suggested he go home and get some rest. She had to do something, anything, to end this. Her eyes caught sight of the magical Moon Orb, sitting by the bed on the nightstand. She carefully held it over Drillian's dying body and began to make a wish.

"I command all of the power in every realm to heal this Elf and make him sound!" She opened one eye to see if anything had happened but there was no change. Drillian remained lifeless.

"I DEMAND all of the power in every realm to flow through me and heal this Elf!" she said again, this time with more vigour. It was no use, she thought. The Orb wasn't working. It was probably burnt out.

"Oh Moonflower, where are you when I need you most!" she cried in desperation. "Can't you just whizz down here and fix this!"

Moonflower suddenly descended into the room on a pink lotus flower, filling the space with an exotic perfume.

"Hello little fae," she said gently. "I see we are in a bit of bother, are we not?" Spellbound leapt from the chair and ran over to her, throwing her arms around Moonflower's neck. She began to sob.

"He's in the yearning and dying, all because of me. The Orb hasn't worked, it just released him from the oak tree but he's still unconscious and there's bleedin' twigs sprouting from every fookin' orifice, please help me Moonflower!" Spellbound's Godmother smoothed her hair with her hand and spoke very gently.

"Drillian's fate is in your hands' Spellbound; it is not the Orb this time that holds the power, it is you! The solution is very simple. All you have to do is forgive him. Not just say it, but mean it, with all of your heart. If you can do that, then he will recover. It's really that easy!" As Spellbound opened her eyes, Moonflower had disappeared as quickly as she arrived. She wandered over to the bed and sat down in the chair, feeling defeated.

"Ya know, I really do think you are a spaddy-wacking crock of shit Drill," she sniffed, "but I do forgive you. You're a git, that's for sure, enchanting me like that. What the hell did you hope to achieve? Just snap out of this and we'll say no more about it." Another twig protruded from Drillian's nose and started to weave itself across his closed eyes.

"No, no, I didn't mean it!" she said frantically. "I forgive you; I really do. I forgive you, I said!" More leaves sprouted from the stalk and started to entwine around his face. "Oh, my gawd, Drillian, now listen here will you? I forgive you, you stupid bladder-bart!" More and more stems sprouted their way across his head, his skin now turning as brown and gnarled as a trunk. She gasped in horror and then began to sob in desperation while she desperately snapped off the offending stems. As the foliage started to claim him, she saw another crystal tear run from his eye and roll on to a newly formed ivy leaf; this just made her feel worse. She dropped her head on to his chest, her little arms spread across his body and began to weep inconsolably.

"Please don't die Drillian. How can I live knowing that your feelings for me eventually killed you? I forgive you, so please wake up, please open your eyes, just don't die Drill."

Spellbound didn't notice the tiny sparkles of magic escalating from his body until the room was filled with an intense light, so bright that as she lifted her head, she had to cover her eyes for fear of being blinded. There lying in front of her was Drillian, free of the yearning and fast asleep.

CHAPTER 27
THE ENCHANTED LAKE

Leticia was in the library, sitting at her moonstone crystal desk, her little diamante spectacles balanced neatly on her retroussé nose. Glancing down at the divorce papers she was consumed with a sickening feeling. With all the drama over the past few days, she had no time to give Marco the signed papers he had wanted. Taking a deep breath, she waved her hand over the scroll and her signature magically appeared. She placed the documents inside a large vellum envelope and then taking her tanzanite handfasting ring from a small jewelled box, she dropped it inside. Gesturing her hand in a swift motion, she sealed it.

"Madam, you have a visitor." Biff Wellington bowed as he entered the room. Leticia blinked away threatening tears and quickly composed herself.

"Philip Macavity is here to see you," said Biff, and he ushered the Elf in.

"SIT." She ordered, signalling to the chair opposite. Philip obeyed Leticia's command and sat down without question. Dark rings circled his eyes and he looked tired and weary.

"So, you got my message that we have freed Drillian of the yearning?" she said stiffly.

"I did … yes, I came straight over. Oh, Leticia, what can I say, thank you so much," he said humbly. "I am so relieved that he is alright."

"He is approaching the end of his healing sleep right now so once he is awake, he can return to you. You can save your thanks because it wasn't me who magicked him out of this sorry mess, you need to thank my daughter. It was because of her tender heart and forgiveness that he is cured." Her tone was clipped and abrupt. "If it were me, I would have happily used him as firewood!" Philip shuddered, lowering his eyes in shame.

"My wife and I are forever in your debt Leticia," he said earnestly. "I need to repay you in some way, name your price. I'll pay anything, I'll do anything. Just let me do something to make amends!"

Leticia raised herself imposingly from the chair and placed both hands on the desk, staring down at him menacingly.

"There *is* something I want," she said firmly. "I am not as forgiving as my daughter and I warn you if I ever encounter that shit-bucket son of yours again, I will not be responsible for my actions. As soon as Drillian is awake, I want you and your toe rag Elf boy to leave this forest and I forbid you to ever return, is that clear?" Philip gulped but realised she meant every word that she was saying.

"I can take him to Toncaster," he replied sheepishly. "We have a second home there and we can run the corporation from the Northern office. Am I permitted to come back to see my wife?" he asked in desperation. Leticia raised her eyebrows mockingly at him.

"You have obviously not listened to a damn word I have said to you Macavity?" she said, raising her voice.

"Okay, okay, I'll move us *all* up there. I promise Leticia, you will never have to see Drillian again, or any of us for that matter."

"Well, that's settled then," she said curtly, relaxing a little she walked away from the desk. She glanced down at her crystal watch. "You can go, and we will deliver Drillian to you when he is conscious, the quicker the scum bag leaves my abode, the better."

"I just can't get her out of my head!" Eddie said excitedly. Spellbound was sitting by the lake sipping a delicious gooseberry-fizzle dip and watching a group of Fairies laughing and diving into the crystal blue waters.

"I'm really happy for you and Taffeta," she said absently, not paying much attention to him.

"Not me and Taffeta!" he laughed. "You ain't listening to anything I'm saying Spelly? No, it's Daffy. I really fancy her. She makes my heart flutter every time I see her. Do you think she likes me? Can you ask her for me, huh?" Spellbound put down her drink with a thud and gave him a withering look.

"What the hell, Eddie! Last month you were fawning all over Taffy and this week you're in lust with Daffy. I can't keep up!"

"I know, I like em all," he said, his eyes filled with laughter. "But Daffy is so hot. I really wanna spoil her, buy her something nice. What kind of thing floats her boat?"

"Floats her boat? Eddie, she's not a barge and what about Taffeta? Have you told her that you're now hankering after her bestie?"

"Oh, me and Taff had a fun time but she binned me off for some hunky Elf waiter after two days, told me over text, which I thought was a bit crap but hey ho, plenty more tadpoles in the pond I say!" He chuckled, leaning back on the bank to soak up the sun. Spellbound shook her head in disbelief and took another sip of the ice-cold drink. These blewdy stupid numpty males, they're all a crock of shit she thought to herself.

Leticia had arrived at her marital home with a large brown envelope in her hand. She would deliver the papers to Marco personally and be done with it once and for all. She was exhausted and so tired of all the drama. Clifford had returned to Trevania that morning to continue with the building for his forthcoming school of sorcery. She always felt safer when he was around but sadly, she understood that he had to go and make his new life. Drillian had finally woken up from the yearning and was returned to his father. He left the house very subdued around noon and once he had gone, Spellbound had rushed off for a well-needed catch up with her gal pals. Leticia sighed. It was time to make a new life for herself too and spend lots of time teaching Spellbound everything she knew about magic. She would dedicate the coming months to spells, potions and wand practice, in between writing a new book. She had it all figured out.

Walking into the house, she spied Marco in his office standing by the window, gazing out over the adjacent woodland.

"I believe this is what you want!" she said tersely, throwing the envelope on to the desk. Marco turned around and caught sight of Leticia. She was dressed casually in a pink and white dress which touched just above the ankles; her dark hair was tied neatly in a loose bun on the top of her head. Feathery tendrils fell around her face romantically. She took his breath away every time he saw her.

"Leticia!" he said gently. "I'm pleased you have come. I tried to speak to you the other day but what with everything that happened and …"

"Save it, Marco," she interrupted abruptly. "I'm not in the mood for this. I think we've done enough talking don't you?" She turned her back on him and proceeded to head for the door.

"But Leticia wait," he called out. With her back to him and clipping her high heels over the polished parquet floor, she raised her hand dismissively in the air and she was gone.

It was early evening and Leticia was sitting on her oversized, plush cream sofa, making notes for her new book, when Spellbound flitted into the room, wrapped in a large yellow, fluffy blanket. She snuggled in next to her mother and placed her head on Leticia's arm.

"Mamma, before Clifford left today, he asked me if I would like to stay with him for a month in Trevania and study Wizardry with him. It would be after he has done the renovations of course so it wouldn't be immediately. I've been having a think about it and I really feel it'd be good for me!"

"Why that's an excellent idea darling," Leticia replied, placing an arm around her daughter's shoulders. "Clifford is a very powerful Warlock and has great knowledge of all things magical. I'm sure he'll be able to pass on some wonderful insight, if I wasn't so busy, I'd join you."

"Are you sure you'll be alright with me gone?" Spellbound said cautiously. "What with all this fuss going on with you and Papa and all. I do worry about you both." Leticia smiled down at her daughter and let out a little sigh.

"Darling, you mustn't fret about us. Just because your Pa and I are not together, it doesn't mean that we don't love you. We are both still here for you and we always will be. No, you must go and learn these new skills and when you return, we can commence your tuition for advanced spellcraft." Spellbound got up from the sofa and leant in to kiss Leticia on the cheek.

"Okay Mamma, I love you. You're the best! I'm off to get ready now as I'm going to a gothic rave. I've concocted the most fabulous costume."

Leticia cocked her eyebrow and smiled. "Have a wonderful time darling. " She watched as Spellbound left the room and settled back down to her notes.

After a few minutes of uninterrupted peace, tiny silver sparks began dancing around the room. She stood up quickly and reached for her wand, ready to zap anything that might pose as a threat. What was this? In a dazzling flash, her Godfather Angelo, was in her lounge, emerging from a golden mist. His large, white, feathered wings unfolded from behind him and flapped a little as he adjusted to his new surroundings.

"That journey always did make me a little lightheaded," he said cheerily. Leticia immediately put down her wand and made a small curtsey. "You really don't have to keep doing that you know my dear."

"To what do I owe this honour?" she said respectfully. She still couldn't quite believe that she was able to converse with her Godfather. It was just unheard of and extremely rare.

"I need you to come with me." He said flatly. "And no arguments do you hear? Personal issues are not something we tend to get involved with but in your case, we have made an exception and have decided to intervene." She looked confused as he reached out to her. She tentatively placed her small hand in his. Instantly, Angelo's glorious wings wrapped around them both and they disappeared in a puff of angelic sparkles. Seconds later, they were by the most magnificent lake she had ever seen. In the centre was an island that housed a beautiful silver and golden folly, the large expanse of turquoise water shimmered under the sunset. She saw movement in the reeds and heard tiny chirps of joy emanating from the undergrowth. At least a hundred Dodibells began singing in sweet harmony, whilst Swannikins and graceful coral Leggiducks glided silently across the lake.

"Where are we?" she asked in wonder.

"This is the Lake of Enchantment my dear," he said in a matter of fact way. The waters here contain powerful properties and can remove any hurt or pain that magic has created. When a Fairy has been under the influence of dark magic like you have, these crystal waters will bathe away the negative emotions left behind, but without you forgetting what has happened. Now you must submerge the whole of your body under the water at the edge of the lake and when you surface bathe your wings in the waters for at least ten minutes. The water is not wet so your beautiful attire will not be ruined," he said kindly.

"That's very nice and all Angelo but I think Spellbound should be here. She is the one needing to be cleansed!"

"All in good time, my dear," Angelo replied. "Moonflower will bring her along soon enough." Leticia took his instruction and kicked off her pink, pointy shoes. She walked towards the water, and delicately dipped a toe into the crystal liquid. Turning around, she lowered her body slowly, the tip of each wing disappearing into the lake and finally her head. A shower of golden rays engulfed her, racing through every atom in her body as she surfaced. Angelo waited patiently until the cleansing was complete, then signalled for her to come out.

"Now my dear," he said, pointing towards the folly. Leticia glanced over to the center of the lake and saw Marco standing inside the structure, resplendent in a white suit with a deep purple cravat at his throat.

"Your husband has already been cleansed and now it is time for you to repair your relationship."

"But ..." Leticia turned to face her Godfather, about to speak. He held his hand up to silence her and put a finger to her lips.

"You shall both remain here until you mend this marriage," he said sternly. "And only when it is fixed will you be allowed to return home." With that, he slowly disappeared in a shimmering golden mist.

Leticia stared at Marco in the distance and he returned her look, giving her a tentative wave. The cleansing had made her feel optimistic and less irritated and for the first time in a long while, she yearned to be with him. Silently her tiny form lifted from the ground and with her wings outstretched, she glided gracefully across the lake to him. The Dodibells let out trills of excitement and their voices blended in wonderful harmony. A spotted yellow and purple one began swinging from the railings of the folly. It dropped into her arms, sucking its little thumb as it cuddled into her. She smiled and placed it back on a tree branch and turned to face her husband nervously.

In three strides, he was in front of her and then he sank to one knee and lifted her hand to his lips. She gazed down at him in astonishment and he laughed outright.

"Leticia, oh my darling Leticia. I love you so much and try as I might, I can't live without you," he said sincerely. The Dodibells were thrumming even louder and she could hear the faint sounds of romantic music drifting through the trees. She smiled down at him enchantingly.

"Marco, can you ever truly forgive me?" she said with guilt. "I was so wrong to banish you away like that. It was reckless and stupid!"

"The past is the past," he said warmly. "You weren't to know my love. " Seeing her handsome husband knelt at her feet sent a ripple of joy into her soul. "This family have been caught up in so much dark magic my darling. Let's banish it all and put it behind us." Rising, he gathered her into his arms and whispered ardently, "I love you; I always have and I always will." He took the Handfasting band from his pocket and placed it back on her finger where it belonged.

She gazed at her beloved ring and then into his incredible green eyes before caressing his cheek gently with her trembling little hand.

"And I love you," she said tearfully. He gathered her to him again, lifting her in the air and as he brought her down, he kissed her passionately. The Dodibells were running around the lake squeaking loudly in delight and others were swinging off the branches, singing, "Jiggy! Jiggy Jiggy!" They were making so much noise that Leticia and Marco had to stop kissing and cover their ears, as the racket became unbearable. Holding on to each other they started to laugh until the tears ran down their cheeks.

"Leticia can I interest you in an afternoon of red hot Jiggy… jiggy…jiggy and I promise you, no dratted Dodibells?" She nodded her head still in a daze, then in a flash of pale lavender smoke and a sparkle of dust, they were transported back to the Manor and Leticia's giant bed.

"MAMMA… MAMMA, HAVE YOU SEEN MY HAZELWOOD WAND ANYWHERE?" Spellbound shrieked from the bottom of the stairs.

"I KNOW I PUT IT SOMEWHERE. HAVE YOU GOT IT UP THERE MAMMA, HAVE YOU BORROWED IT AGAIN? … MAMMA!"

Marco grinned and rolled over to kiss his wife. "Still as loud as ever, isn't she, do you think she was a Dodibell in another life?" he said, pulling the covers up over their heads.

"Well she doesn't get it from our side of the family, it's surely got to be yours!" Leticia replied, tickling him.

"Lies, all lies, Leticia, I seem to remember you being that noisy as a teenager!" he replied, lying back into the pillows. He had to be the happiest of Elves. Here he was, in the most luxurious of all beds, snuggled in tight with the most beautiful Fairy. His Fairy, his wife. "You know, we could just try and ignore her for half an hour or you could take her wand you have hidden under your pillow and zap her lips shut!" He nestled in closer, in the hope that she would respond to the gentle kisses he was feathering on the side of her neck. Leticia shivered and wrapped her arms around him.

"BLEWDY HELL...SO THERE YOU BOTH ARE! WOULD YOU FRIGGIN' LOOK AT THE PAIR OF YOU!" Spellbound bellowed like a fog horn and then lapsed into a fit of hysterical giggles. "And about time too! My parents sharing the same bed at last. So, I gather you two are back together? Have you just had rumpy-pumpy, huh … yeah … huh?"

"Spellbound … don't be so personal!" Marco laughed. "She might be nearly fully-grown Leticia, but her vocabulary and manners are still way down in the gutter!"

"I tell you, Marco, I don't know where she fookin' gets it from!" Leticia tittered. Spellbound leapt on the bed and sandwiched herself in between her parents.

She bellowed at the top of her voice. "YIPPEE! I'M SO APPY! APPY! APPY!"

CHAPTER 28
THE FINALE

"Ya know, I think I'm gonna call you Uncle Cliffy from now on," Spellbound said, as she polished Clifford's large crystal ball on the oak table. "You are kind of like an uncle, I mean you have been there my whole life!" He walked over to her, looking slightly amused. "You watched me grow up from a faebe in hankies into the Fairy nightmare I am today, and as much as I disliked you over the years, mainly for always ratting me out to Mamma," she said grinning and wagging her index finger at him, "you have always looked out for me." Clifford smiled. She was so much like her mother and it was true, he did regard her as part of his family, especially now that he was back in his Warlock form and free from the emotions he had felt for Leticia. Spellbound had been in Trevania with him for nearly a month and he was going to miss her very much when she returned home. She brought young, fresh life back into the Castle and took her studies extremely seriously, absorbing everything he was teaching her. Yes, it would be very quiet without her but once she had matured properly and was fully trained in the art of Fairy-craft, he hoped that he might encourage her to teach in his school of sorcery someday.

"Spellbound my dear," he said, walking over to where she was seated, "I have served your mother and the generations before her for countless years and nothing gives me greater pleasure than to

278

look out for you. I consider you one of my own and I will always be at your service."

"Aww, you are sweet, Uncle Cliffy." She said sitting down in front of the ball and peering into the glass. "Before I go home, can you teach me how to get this thing to work then?" She lifted the glass globe from its stand and gave it a little shake.

"Ahhh! Spellbound, my dear, do be careful with that. It is not to be shaken." He rushed over to the table and took it out of her hands.

"This is identical to the ball I was imprisoned in and is a window into everyone's world. It's very precious and has to be respected, much like your Moon Orb."

"I understand," she whispered contritely, "but how does it actually work?"

"To access the power, you simply have to concentrate very hard on who it is you want to see, and the ball will show you the rest."

"May I have a go then, please?" she said enthusiastically. "There's so much I want to see."

Clifford smiled, raising an eyebrow.

"Of course," he said, placing it back on its ornate stand. "Now carefully rest your hands on the globe and focus hard on who or what you want to connect with. I'll have to leave you to it for now though as I have a pressing appointment with the carpenters but if you have any trouble, just give me a shout." Clifford turned away from the table and left the room hurriedly. Spellbound placed her small hands on to the glass and immediately thought about her parents. Moments later, a hazy white mist appeared.

Leticia and Marco

"When are you going to stop staring into that computer machine darling?" Marco said to Leticia as he stood behind her, his arms embracing her.

"When I've finished this love scene and not a moment before." She replied, engrossed in her typing.

"I can think of a love scene of our own," he said, spinning her chair around so that she was facing him. "I'm sure I could give you lots of tips for your book!" She chuckled and removed her spectacles and they began kissing passionately.

"Okay…erm … eww," Spellbound said. "That's enough of that malarkey!" She shook her head in embarrassment and settled down to await her next vision.

Eddie

"Ma, Pa, I'd like you to meet Mike Hunt!"

The Duke and Duchess were taking afternoon tea in the Orangery when Eddie strolled in with his companion at his side. Mike nodded to them both then caught sight of a long mirror to his right and primped himself discretely, smoothing his hair which was caked in slugga slug gel. Puckering his full lips, he arched his eyebrows. "Without a doubt … I'm sex on legs," he smirked.

"Okay so here it is," Eddie said bravely. "I know neither of you are expecting this BUT, I've decided to come out."

"Come out, dear?" The Duchess said smiling. "Have you been somewhere? Coming out from where dear?"

"Ya know Ma, COMING OUT, like erm… oh, how do I put this?"

"He's batting for the other side dear," the Duke said in a monotone fashion, without looking up from his newspaper.

"I beg your pardon dear. I thought you said he was…"

"GAY my dear," he repeated, this time peering over the top of his glasses. "I think our son is trying to tell us that for this week at least, he is gay." He shook the paper irritably and carried on reading.

"Yeah, I am Ma, well at least I think I am. Gay, yeah, that's the word. See, when I spend time with Mike Hunt here, I get all these fluttery feelings in my stomach. I think he's the real deal." Mike smiled a smarmy grin and nodded.

"We started a womantic welationship last week and so we wan all the way here to tell you that we weally like each other, don't we Ed. Ha-ha, it's blinding, hey hey!"

Spellbound swung back on her chair, laughing so loud she had to stop to catch her breath. Silly Eddie, she sighed. One of these days he'll make his mind up and find himself.

Her attention returned to the ball as she started to think about Tinky. Leticia had been granted the free will to punish anyone who had wronged her family in any way that she saw fit and so she decided that as Tinky Bonk had already spent three years banished to a cave in some far off land, she would strip her of her magic and make her feel useful by putting her to work for a whole twelve months. When the year was up, she would be allowed to go about her business as usual, just so long as she never showed up within a hundred miles of Leticia and her family.

Tinky Bonk

As the mist cleared in the ball, Tinky was dressed from head to toe in a blue nurse's uniform and was walking around a ward full of patients. She looked forlorn and thoroughly miserable, as she lifted back the bedsheet of an ancient Pixie. Looking the other way and screwing up her nose, with cloth in hand and a bowl of hot water at her side, she proceeded to give the Pixie a bed bath. He began letting out little groans of pleasure.

"You're fookin' enjoying this, aren't you? You filthy old perv!" she sniped under her breath.

The Pixie leered and sniggered and then replied, "Down a bit lovie... up a bit ... rub it harder, there's a good lil Fairy! And wipe me thighs, nice and dry nursie." Taking the cloth, she had been using, she rolled it up and shoved it hard into his mouth.

"Er.... Nurse!" A deep, Scottish voice reprimanded from behind her. She turned around to face a handsome Elf with jet black hair and the largest, pointiest ears she had ever seen. He was tall and muscular and wearing a very official suit. She glanced at his name badge, which read 'Paul Macok, Head of Elf and Safety'. She quickly composed herself and smiled sweetly.

"Now we doon't waant any shenanigans nurse," he said, giving her a sexy look. She tittered, and her eyes sparkled. "Nay more trying tae choke him, dae ye hear?" She nodded demurely and removed the cloth from the

suffocating Pixie's mouth. Just as he was walking away, he turned around and slipped his card into her hand.

"Ah think ah might have ta take ye oot fer a wee dram. Are ye free tonight?" Tinky nodded excitedly and tucked the business card into her cleavage.

"Oh, and nice knickerbockers there lassie," he said, pointing to her bottom. "They're absolutely cracking, they are!" Tinky turned to look over her shoulder at her back and noticed that after visiting the tootlehole earlier, she had inadvertently tucked her skirt into the back of her knickers. Her face went bright crimson with embarrassment.

Spellbound rocked back and forth on her chair. "Oh, that's brilliant, that is!" she gasped, wiping the tears from her eyes.

After a few minutes of composure, her mind drifted to the old Witch, Fenella. Leticia wasn't going to risk going into exile by killing the hag, even though she was seriously tempted, so had chosen a fate that she felt more fitting. Fenella was banished to the same island that Marco had occupied but had the added punishment of being stripped of her wings and all her magical powers.

Fenella

Fenella was walking along a stretch of beach. She looked more bedraggled than usual and even more grimy, with her matted grey hair, rotting teeth and sweaty brow. Spellbound imagined that her stench was acrid, in the blistering heat of the sun. She was forlornly tossing pebbles into the sea when in the distance she saw a native Elf spying on her curiously. His tanned body was naked, all apart from one undersized leaf, which was barely covering his quite large Elfhood. His hair was black and tied into a braid down his back and his thin little body was covered in tribal tattoos. When he spotted her, he quickly began to run in panic as fast as his legs would take him, heading off in the opposite direction. Fenella, with a strange lascivious look in her eyes, started racing towards him. Despite her age, she was quite athletic and as she caught up with him, she tackled him to the ground, breathing her fetid breath into his face. The Elf gagged and nearly fainted at the stench.

"Hello there, my sweet little coo- ca-choo," she cackled excitedly, as she tried to grope his Elfhood. "OOH, now then...yer a fine healthy specimen!

Fancy parting me whiskers, my little lovely?" She snorted loudly and turned to spit a big blob of grey phlegm into the sand. The Elf, seeing an opportunity to escape, twisted around and leaping to his feet he sped away. Fenella, not to be out done, picked up her tattered old skirts and chased after him.

"You will be mine, me little boy toy … he! he! … I like a bit of kiss chase!"

"Oh, this is classic!" Spellbound gulped hysterically. "I must ask Uncle Cliffy if I can borrow this thing. Who needs PouTube when you have this!"

Spellbound skimmed her hand over the ball again, this time thinking about the Macavity's. She wasn't as angry with Drillian as she should have been, under the circumstances. He did a stupid thing and wasted so much of her time, but aside from all of that, she didn't wish him any ill will. The mist in the glass cleared once more and showed Philip Macavity and Drillian seated in one of the Molars Inc. offices in Toncaster.

Drillian

"Here are the forecasts for the next six months, son," Philip said as he handed him a silver high pad. "Look them over and then pass them to Anna Prentice, the new temp. She started today and … just a minute, let me call her in so you know who I am talking about!" Philip left the room and summoned the young female Elf, who sauntered in, dressed in a skimpy red mini skirt, long stripy socks and a white crop top. She was sucking a lollypop with the stick poking out of her mouth. Catching sight of Drillian, she began gazing at him dreamily. His eyes inspected every inch of her body clinically and then he gave her a cheeky grin and a wink.

"Hi, I'm your boss Drillian, no doubt we will get to know each other a little more intimately in the future!" he said, standing up from his seat. After the brief introduction, she giggled and left the room, still sucking on her lollipop.

Spellbound gazed into the glass in horror. "He's still a fookin' bladderbart! Even after everything that's happened! Fookin' spaddy-wacking, pervy headed git!"

"Did you shout for me?" Clifford said as he entered the room swiftly.

"No, no," Spellbound replied, looking up from the globe. "Just talking to myself and all."

"Alright my dear, well listen, I've just had an astral message from your mother and she is expecting you back very soon. She said to tell you that she has made your favourite meal for this evening; earwig stew and woodlice dumplings!"

"Lovely!" she replied through gritted teeth, screwing up her face and looking a little horrified.

"I said I would escort you home, so we really ought to make haste."

Spellbound abandoned the crystal ball and got up from the chair. As they both left the room, she thanked Clifford again for allowing her to stay. He replied by giving her an open invitation.

"My Castle is your Castle, my dear, whenever you want to come, you are always most welcome."

" I've really enjoyed myself this past month uncle Cliffy," she replied, placing her hand on his arm. "I can't wait to show Mamma all of the things I've learned. You really are the best teacher!" He smiled as he positioned his staff on the ground, once again twisting the amethyst crystal at the tip. In an array of purple smoke, Spellbound and Clifford were gone.

Back in the empty library, the lone crystal ball was still active; the images and pictures playing away to themselves, without being witnessed.

"Nice to see you have recovered your Elfy appetite for the female species, especially after everything that happened last month." Philip pulled up a chair and sat opposite his son. Drillian was bored and was drumming his fingers on the desk. "I know I have said it before boy but that was very irresponsible of you, what a commotion you caused. You frightened me half to death when you nearly turned into a tree! Anyway, it's so good that you are well again and have finally put the Spellbound Fairy out of your head!"

"Oh, but that's where, you are mistaken Father," Drillian said in a low drawl. "I haven't put her out of my head at all. On the contrary," he said,

swivelling his chair around and glancing out of the window. "No, I am not over her and I doubt I ever will be. But I can be patient and she WILL be mine again. I'll win her back one way or another, you mark my words!

THE END

Beleta Greenaway

Beleta Greenaway is a well-known palmist and clairvoyant in the UK with a vast knowledge on all subjects relating to the esoteric. She is the founder of The Psychic Study Center, where she and her daughter Leanna, tutor students in Tarot, Palmistry and Wicca in the Southwest of England. Over her forty-year career, her accuracy and precision have earned her a large following of people and because of this, she has gone on to become a prolific writer and has spoken on BBC Radio in the UK. She is author of Palmistry Out of your Hands, Orion – Angels, Plain and Simple *(Red Wheel Wieser)* and the Catalog of the Unexplained, co-written with Leanna *(Llewellyn)* which will be released in 2021.

Leanna Greenaway

Over her 16-year history of writing for Take a Break's Fate and Fortune magazine, Leanna has acquired a large following. She has spent many years co-writing with Shawn Robbins in the US and is co-author of Wiccapedia, Wiccapedia Journal: Book Of Shadows, The Witch's Way, The Crystal Witch Practical Spellcraft, *(Sterling)* Wicca Plain and Simple, Tarot Plain and Simple, *(Red Wheel Weiser)* and her most recent book written with her mother, The Catalog of the Unexplained *(Llewellyn)*.